LIE OF THE LAND

Helen JR Bruce

First published in Great Britain

in 2021 by Blue Cedar Printworks Publishing, Glastonbury

Copyright Helen JR Bruce 2021

Helen JR Bruce has asserted her right under the Copyright, Designs
and Patents Act 1988 to be identified as the author of this work.

ISBN 978-1-913325-02-2

Typeset in calibri and copperplate gothic bold
Printed and bound in Great Britain by Blue Cedar Printworks

For Joanne Hayes

LIE OF THE LAND

1. Remedy

2. Burial

3. Promise

4. Return

5. Newgrange

6. Justice

7. Fire

8. Thief

9. Descendants

10. Sanctuary

11. Defiance

12. Debt

13. Heat

14. Destiny

15. Reunion

16. Duty

17. Ritual

18. Allegiance

19. Dewerstone

20. Divide

1.
REMEDY

Hoofbeats thundered through the forest, iron shod hooves slicing the brown skin of the earth. Chasing the last light of the day, the rider spurred on his steed and speckled the brambles with blood.

"Cabell!" cried a voice. But the rider paid no heed. "Squire Cabell!" the servant pressed, "we are losing the light!"

"Have a spine, man!" retorted the horseman, cracking his long leather whip. White and tan hounds surged past him, noses to the ground, tongues lolling over their teeth.

"But- but-" stuttered the servant, batting low branches of beech and oak from his face. "Do you not fear the fae?"

Squire Cabell tipped up his head and roared a laugh, his eyes glassy in the greying light.

"Let them come. This hunt is not over."

He urged the horse on, heedless of treacherous roots or stones, cursing every time the beast stumbled. Then he caught sight of it ahead. His prize. Triumphantly, he called the hounds. Wild yips and hollers filled the air; the mingled voices of animal and man.

Trees and bracken became a blur, racing past as a green smear that stretched out to the thud, thud, thud of hooves, changing rhythm now and then as Cabell tore at the reins to weave through the forest. Ahead of him, a black shape darted between the brambles, fleet and lithe and always just out of reach. Horse and rider plunged recklessly through the low canopy of leaves, Cabell shielding his eyes as twigs scratched at his face. The horse skidded to a halt, snorting and blowing, the whites of its eyes displayed in terror. Dense woodland gave way to a hidden clearing.

The hounds paced the perimeter uneasily, panting from the chase. Their eyes were fixed on the huge yew tree which stood in the centre of the clearing, multiple gnarled trunks twisted around a rotten, hollow core. Beneath its branches the earth was bare; poisoned by years of leaf-fall from the ancient tree. It was here that Cabell's prey stood at bay, amber eyes glinting defiantly in the halflight; black fur blending in with the shadows.

"Have at it then," Cabell hissed to the hounds. They whined and cowered, noses twitching at the faint scent of carrion and honey. He cracked his whip impatiently, catching one of the pack over the rump. It yelped, but moved no nearer the tree. "Very well then," said Cabell quietly, a cruel smile curling his lips. He dismounted, unsheathed a sharp knife and stepped forward.

The black fox met his gaze. Rich amber and stone grey eyes blazed with a wordless challenge. *If you dare*. Cabell fingered the knife. Why was he hesitating? What was one more beast, in a long line of deaths at his hands? He took another step. The air thickened. It caught in his lungs and sent his heart thudding wildly in his chest. But this was the thrill of it. He pressed on, knife hand raised. Shadows flowed, thickening and congealing ahead of him, lapping against the trunk of the yew. Almost lazily, the fox blinked, and the amber eyes disappeared. When they opened again, they were in a completely different place. And they belonged to a woman.

Cabell gripped the blade until his knuckles turned white. He had heard stories of skin turners who could clothe themselves in feathers and fur. But he was not a man to show fear, and he had been keeping out the evening chill with gin. The smile still hovered on his lips.

"Tell me," he said, drawing the knife slowly down through the air, "would I have to skin you in layers?"

The woman laughed. Her voice was rich and silky, liquid as the amber of her eyes. She stepped forward into the twilight, the fading glow illuminating her pale skin and waist length black hair. There was no fear in her.

"You would turn that knife on yourself before you were three paces from me," she said.

Cabell was immediately aware that it was true. He felt the muscles in his arm tense against his will, and watched as he spun the knife towards himself. His ferocious will ebbed away, and for the first time in his life he felt the terror of his prey; a sharp, brief horror.

"But you need not try," the woman said.

At once, Cabell's arm went limp, and he dropped the knife. She stepped closer, her movements sinuous and predatory. She was the amber and Cabell was an insect with all of that slow eternity closing in. Every instinct within him begged to run, but he was fixed to the spot by her gaze.

The woman stopped and, without any hurry, bent to pick up the knife. She offered it back, handle first. Cabell didn't move.

"Where's your heat now huntsman?" she purred, "where's your hunger?"

"S-sorry," the squire stuttered.

A sharp sound rang through the clearing, as the woman struck him suddenly across the cheek.

"Don't demean yourself," she spat. Then her hand was on his chest, the long fingers resting spidersoft on his jacket. "I've seen you."

Cabell shivered in the gathering dusk. He knew

3

tales of the fae; of young folk who had walked in these woods and not returned. Or worse, returned changed. The gin had worn off and the blood ran cold in his veins. A muffled shout caught his attention.

The woman swung her head to one side, releasing him from her gaze. The unsettling smile appeared on her lips again.

"Your servant is out there. Looking for you no doubt...." she turned back slowly, shrugging her long hair back over her shoulders. "But he will not find you."

"Let me go woman!" Cabell cried.

Her eyes widened in genuine surprise. "Why?"

Night came greedily, shadows thick as treacle clogging up the woods. The servant cursed under his breath. All of the trees looked the same. He turned his horse down yet another path which petered out all too fast into an impassable animal track.

"Cabell!" he cried, and then added 'curse you to Hell!' inside his head.

In the clearing, Cabell stood face to face with the wytch, the impatient night filling the last little space between them. She kissed him. It was long and lingering, but there was no love in it. It left him on his knees.

As she drew back, he called after her.

"Woman, your name!"

She laughed again, cold and beautiful.

"I will tell you it," she said, "and in all of your days, in your waking and sleeping, your living and dying, it shall be on your tongue."

Immediately, Cabell knew her name. It rose in his mind like a body in water.

4

"We will meet again," she told him.

"Yes m'lady."

The road was quiet. It had been quiet for so long that a line of grass grew down the middle. Either side the briars and brambles spread with tangled enthusiasm, only occasionally disturbed by the passing of the more intrepid type of driver. Or someone who was lost.

"Is this enough yet?" Adrian asked Gemma, waving his bowl of blackberries in her direction.

Gemma leaned backwards to look. The bowl was perhaps a third full.

"How many have you eaten?" She offered her own almost full bowl in comparison. Adrian grinned, revealing a set of purple teeth.

"One or two," he admitted, "I had to check them."

"Of course you did." Gemma carefully unhooked a thorny tendril of bramble from her jumper and moved along the hedgerow. She began picking in a new patch, glancing over her shoulder at Adrian once in a while. She could see him popping every other blackberry he picked in his mouth. She smiled to herself.

The air was heavy with the busy drone of insects, feeding on the overripe fruit, and the oily autumn sunlight fell slow and thick as honey. Adrian almost looked like his old self again. There was a flush of colour in his cheeks and it was rare now that his eyes took on the blank, faraway look that had so often haunted him when he first woke up. But dying, being brought back to life and then spending three days asleep can do strange things to a person. Especially if they were a little bit strange to begin with.

A cloud crawled across the sun. Gemma watched

its progress on the mossy tarmac, catching the ground inch by inch in shadow. She remembered the cloying darkness of Grimspound, the suffocating smell of death and Adrian's cold body on the dewdamp grass. She remembered Gabriel, cruel and graceful as he dealt death to the necromancer and his servants. But all of that had been too late. So a bargain was made. Owain's words haunted her; *to drag life back is an abomination*.

"Is this enough now?" Adrian pressed.

Gemma jumped, nearly knocking the bowl out of his hands. She blinked, struggling to focus on the full bowl of berries.

"I think so," she managed to say.

"Good, because I'm getting hungry." Adrian tucked his bowl into the crook of one arm and began to walk slowly backwards, waiting for Gemma to follow. She unhooked yet another bramble stem, and then did.

They crossed the carpark, which contained only a few cars this late in the day, and passed the white pillars of the Princetown Visitor Centre. Gemma hurried by without looking. A few months ago the displays had been mildly intriguing, but now they were an unpleasant reminder that she had experienced more mythology than she could handle.

"Does Mike have flour?" Adrian asked, glancing in the direction of the village shop.

"Yes, and butter," Gemma replied. Owain, the Huntmaster's Apprentice, had arranged something that meant Mike never paid for food.

The front garden of Mike's cottage was neatly mown, with a row of freshly planted lavender lining the path. Above his front door, an iron horseshoe hung upside down. It was a replacement for the original, which Gemma had used to deter the fae. Owain had pointed out afterwards that an iron horseshoe, applied directly to the face, can effectively deter almost anything.

Mike greeted them with a tea towel in his hand and put the kettle on. Adrian waved his bowl of blackberries excitedly.

"Good pickings then?" Mike asked. His sleeves were still rolled up from doing the washing up, revealing the tattoos of keys that covered his skin.

"Loads of berries," answered Adrian.

"Double that amount if you count what he ate," Gemma added.

"Hey, I was doing you a service by testing these!"

"I bet you were." Gemma put her own bowl down on the side and began lining up the rest of the ingredients on the worktop. Mike hummed to himself as he finished making the tea, taking a seat at the kitchen table with his mug when he was done. A laptop was open in front of him.

"How's the article going?" Gemma asked him.

"Oh, it's coming on slowly," Mike replied, "I just want to check a few more things."

She nodded, taking a small sip of tea. Writing the article about the Beast for *Legendary Dartmoor* had been a good thing for Mike. It helped him to focus and hold onto himself between bouts of forgetfulness.

"Well, there's no hurry." Gemma glanced over to see if Adrian was ready. He stood by the sink, with his back to her, his gaze seemingly fixed on something out of the window. "Adrian?" she said. He didn't move. She walked over, leaving her steaming cup of tea on the side. One hand reached out, but she stopped a few inches from his back. The memory of Grimspoud hit her again, harder this time, and it made her stagger. She felt the cold of his skin before she touched him.

Then Mike was there, sending a chair toppling backwards in his hurry. He caught Adrian as he crumpled, eyes rolling upwards into his head. Gemma's hand flew to her mouth.

"It's happening again!" she cried.

"Put the cushions down," Mike said, supporting Adrian with both arms. Gemma rushed to the adjacent living area and threw the mismatched cushions from the sofa onto the carpet. Mike gently manoeuvred Adrian over and lay him down. "And a blanket please."

Gemma nodded, turning and taking the stairs two at a time as she ran up to fetch the quilt. It was made of old, ugly fabrics, but there was a comforting weight to it that made it part of the go-to kit for this situation. Mike arranged the edges of the quilt and looked up at Gemma. Their eyes shared the same concern. Adrian had been blacking out like this ever since Gabriel brought him back.

"It's getting worse," Gemma blurted out.

Mike pressed his lips into a thin line. Who knew what damage dragging someone back from the dead could do? There were strict rules about such things; the Huntmaster may travel between the apparent world and the Otherworld, *but he must never bring souls back*. Mike shook his head, the thought catching him like a deeper than expected puddle. But, quick as the knowledge had surfaced, it sank away again.

"Do you have the cutting?" he asked.

Gemma rummaged in her pocket and pulled out a much folded and faded square of newspaper. She had cut it out the same day Gabriel carried Adrian back to the cottage.

"Listen to me," she said, trying to keep her voice

from cracking, "listen to me Adrian. We're waiting for you here. Everything has been done. The necromancer is gone. The walkers and their son were found." She pressed the cutting flat on her thigh and then held it close so Adrian could smell the ink. It was a link to a strong memory. It had worked once before. "There's no trapped spirit. There is nothing for you to do anywhere else. We need you here." Silent tears tracked wet lines down her cheeks.

Fian padded over and rested his muzzle on her shoulder. Gemma reached up to touch the hound, one hand resting on his warm, white fur. Fian, too, had died and been reborn. Owain had thought it impossible, but Gemma had seen the fae child dragged down into the strange earth of the Hound Grave, and then the white dog emerge. She was getting used to impossible things. But this, right now, was beyond her. She needed someone who-

"Elaine!" she said suddenly, snapping to her feet. Fian circled away, and then lay down next to Adrian. Gemma was already stabbing at the buttons of her phone, willing the temperamental reception to hold out just long enough. "Elaine, hello?"

'-*will call you back. Please leave a message,*' the answerphone suggested.

Gemma threw the phone down on the sofa, glancing frantically from side to side. Mike was muttering quietly to Adrian, but it was making no difference. The blackouts didn't normally last this long. She watched Adrian's chest. Was it rising and falling? Barely. His skin was pale against the clashing colours of the quilt. There had to be something else she could do, before it was too late. She considered, for a heartbeat, getting help from Gabriel. But the Huntmaster hardly had a mobile phone. Would she have to set up a circle of candles and summon him? She

9

might have laughed at how ridiculous it was, if it wasn't so terribly serious. But the thought of white candles wasn't entirely useless...

She sprinted upstairs again, pulling open the drawer by Adrian's bed. What had he been going on about in the car on the way to Dartmoor? Something about using a black candle to open up the portal to the world of the dead, and then a white candle to guide the spirit back? She grabbed the rolled-up sheet of instructions from the drawer and ripped off the tape. Unrolling it on the bed, her eyes scanned the words.

Chant three times:
By hoof and horn, by blood and bone
By ancient wood and standing stone
On moonlit path and starlit track
Let what is lost be carried back
Let what is lost be carried back

There were more instructions about circles and directions, but none of them made sense, and there wasn't enough time. Gemma snatched up the paper, repeating the words in her head. She ran back down to the kitchen, throwing open cupboards and turning over drawers as she searched for a candle. Her efforts yielded one dusty green stub, which she gripped fiercely. She needed this portal opened, she reasoned, so that Adrian could come back. Remembering his explanation, she wrapped the black sleeve of her jumper around the candle before lighting it.

Fian and Mike stared up at her as she approached, one arm tucked against her body to leave enough spare sleeve to cover the candle.

"Here goes nothing," she murmured. Folding

awkwardly to her knees, she raised the candle and looked down at the words on the paper. "By hoof and horn-" she began. The flame flickered, and around it the room seemed to grow darker. Mike lay a hand on Adrian's chest. "-by blood and bone, by ancient wood and standing stone," Gemma continued. Adrian took a sudden gasp of air, his chest heaving, and when he exhaled his breath rose in a swirl of mist. Gemma shivered. Next to her, Fian was backing away, his hackles raised, a low growl rumbling in his throat. "On moonlit path and starlit track, let what is lost be carried back. Let what is lost be carried back."

The air was cold and sharp, laced with the scent of earth. Adrian's eyelids flickered fitfully, but he still didn't wake. Gemma took a deep breath and began again. She was halfway through the second repetition when there was a heavy thud on the door. She ignored it. The knocking became more frantic, and then it was accompanied by a voice. But it seemed a long way away. Gemma finished her second repetition. The candle flared, caught in a sudden draught. "By hoof and horn-" Gemma said again. The front door flew open. It banged against the wall, drumming out an urgent rhythm. Then a hand closed over Gemma's own hand, and the candle went out.

It took a few moments for the room to return to normal. The light slunk in slowly, as if it was still nervous. Then Mike was dealing with a confused taxi driver, Fian was sniffing the bag which had been dumped in the kitchen, and Elaine was cradling a blinking Adrian. Gemma opened her mouth to say something, but Elaine spoke before her.

"First, coffee."

Mike did the work with the kettle, and in a few minutes served up four quite passable beverages. Adrian had been helped up onto the sofa and Elaine was holding a bowl of sugar while he ladled spoons of it into his cup. Gemma sat cross legged on the floor and Mike dragged over the chair he had upturned earlier. There was an expectant silence.

"Mike, this is Elaine," Gemma said finally.

"I've heard a lot about you," Mike said.

Elaine smiled. "Likewise." She sipped her coffee, curled up on the end of the sofa not occupied by Adrian. Her brown hair was tied up in a high bun, and Gemma couldn't help noticing there was more grey in it.

"That was good timing," Gemma added lamely, "thank you."

Elaine leaned forward, both hands clasped around her mug. Even though Gemma knew that Elaine couldn't physically see her, as the woman was completely blind, she felt nonetheless that she was being gazed at intently.

"I must applaud you on your bravery," Elaine said at last. "Opening a portal to the land of the dead is no small trick. You were very lucky."

Gemma fidgeted awkwardly with the edge of the ugly quilt. "What would have happened?"

"If I hadn't stopped you? Well, you must have felt the shift already. The veil was growing thin; in this room the apparent world and the Otherworld would have merged."

"And Adrian?" Gemma asked.

"He may have come back. But, more likely, you would have wandered off after him," Elaine said.

Gemma shivered, remembering the way the room had turned cold and how the shadows had grown thick and crowded. She felt her cheeks beginning to burn. Hot tears pricking at the corners of her eyes. How could she have been so stupid? Although, and this thought still scared her, what else could she have done?

Adrian held his sweet coffee in front of his face, halted mid sip by his thoughts. He remembered darkness and, further back, the scent of carrion and honey.

"I think it's time," he said levelly, "for me to hear the whole story."

Gemma began instinctively to shake her head. "There's nothing more to hear," she said, glancing at Mike for support.

Adrian stood shakily and reached for the discarded candle stub and roll of paper on the ground. He handed them to Gemma. "I think there is."

Gemma opened and closed her mouth a few times, her eyes flitting from face to face. Mike gave her a small smile.

"It's beyond us now," he said gently.

"I think I can guess what you haven't mentioned to me. But I'd rather hear it from you, all the same," Elaine said.

Gemma took a deep steadying breath. Then she took two large gulps of coffee. And then she told the whole story.

She included the bloody sacrifice made at Houndain to bind the pack anew. She recounted her impatience and horror as she waited for Gabriel and his hounds to clear Grimspound of the necromancer and his servants. She choked over recalling how she had found Adrian's body, slumped over the body of a woman, as if he had been protecting her to the end. And last of all, with her eyes fixed on the carpet, the explained the unnatural bargain she had made with Gabriel to bring Adrian back from the dead.

There was a heavy silence.

"So I didn't hit my head?" Adrian asked.

"Well, you probably did, at some point," Mike volunteered, "either before or during your death."

"Thanks for clarifying," Adrian said.

Gemma turned to Elaine, a pleading look in her eyes. "The blackouts, they're related to all this?"

Elaine nodded slowly.

"There's the other thing too. The bones," Gemma said.

"They're a pain," Mike added.

Adrian looked between him and Gemma with raised eyebrows.

"Well, they are," Mike shrugged.

"It doesn't happen every night anymore. It's only sometimes that you sleepwalk and summon animals back from the dead," said Gemma.

Adrian raked a hand through his blonde hair, revealing the darker roots. "Is that supposed to comfort me?"

"What happens when he sleepwalks?" Elaine asked.

"Just normal getting up and walking, except he goes out into town or onto the moor. Then he stops and a set of bones sort of just, climb up out of the ground and follow him home."

Adrian's face was moving through a kaleidoscopic display of emotions. He was travelling the bumpy track from horror to delight via such destinations as 'can I really have insane superpowers?' and 'I've become a total freak!' It was exhausting. He leaned back on the sofa and clamped a hand over his eyes.

"Can you fix me?" he asked Elaine.

The blind artist shook her head. "Your soul is loose. There's a part of it still in the Otherworld, calling you back. If there is a remedy for this Adrian, then I don't know it.

2.
BURIAL

The parish church of St. Andrew sat a little way back from the road that wound from North Weald airfield towards Epping. It had stood for nine hundred years and survived two world wars, remaining miraculously untouched even when the nearby airfield was heavily bombed.

But the wood and stone which had survived the ravages of time were nonetheless falling prey to a different decay; indifference crept over the graves, curling as tendrils of ivy and spreading like moss. The lychgate swung open in the breeze and slammed shut again. Gold paint peeled forlornly from the noticeboard, which stated that the position of Priest-in-Charge was currently vacant.

As the first shades of dusk greyed the air the resident rooks began to gather, circling and screeching in the sky before settling down to roost for the night. The only other sound in the graveyard was the rhythmic scrape and spatter of somebody digging.

The figure stopped to rest for a moment, wiping their brow with a shirt sleeve and leaning on the shovel to survey their work. Behind them, neat rows of white gravestones marked out the RAF graves, presided over by a towering white cross with a sword fixed to it. If the digger had stopped to read the inscriptions, he would have learned that the ground beneath him held the very first British casualty of the second world war. But he hadn't. He was only thinking about how the earth would soon hold the very last casualty of the war. Or part of him, at least.

Franz leaned down to inspect the pit he had dug. Night was falling, and the gathering shadows seemed to pool inside it. It was where he ought to be; rotting in the ground alongside the wreckage of his downed plane. But he wasn't. Strange magic had clothed his bones with flesh and filled his lungs with breath. Although the world was changed, and the gift of life hung heavy on his shoulders.

Kneeling, he unwrapped a bundle of material. The familiar feel of the woollen tunic set him shivering, sweat turning icy on his skin. With a sudden movement, he rewrapped the package and dropped it into the hole. Then he reached into his pocket and pulled out a small model plane. It was dull metal, rubbed smooth by handling. Franz remembered gripping it like a lucky charm while he waited in the Messerschmitt for his pilot to board. It hadn't brought him much luck. He lifted his arm, ready to toss the toy plane on top of his uniform.

A sound disturbed him and he spun around, one hand reaching into his other pocket for his pistol. His shoulders and grip relaxed when he saw who it was.

"Do you feel better?" asked Evangeline.

Franz could hear her car engine still running out on the road. She was eager to be gone.

"For what?" Franz asked.

Evangeline shrugged. "For this," she gestured towards the hole in the ground, "for this burial. For joining the glorious dead, or whatever else they like to say."

Franz looked down at the model in his hand. It was a crude likeness of a plane; nothing more than a child's toy. But he remembered it being flown between the banisters, out into the garden, round the apple tree and back. He remembered his younger brother holding it up high, so that the sky stretched wide and inviting behind it, and he could just imagine it was real if he squinted. He also remembered the goodbyes, the tears on his uniform jacket, and the model plane being pushed into his hand.

Just borrow it, his little brother had said, *just borrow it and bring it back*.

Franz blinked, looking out across the graveyard. Next to him, in an overgrown corner, were more white gravestones. They were similar to the RAF ones, except some of these lacked any names. Enemy casualties, buried in foreign soil, too burnt to recognise.

"There are no glorious dead," said Franz. He closed his hand over the plane and put it back in his pocket. With his other hand, he pulled out the luger, and examined it in the last of the light. After a moment, he threw the gun into the hole.

Evangeline watched him shovel earth back in. Perched on the edge of the memorial cross, she tapped her fingernails against the marble, one eye on the moon as it rose into the sky. Night came early this time of year, but they would need all the time they could get.

Finally, the hole was filled. Franz placed the neat square of turf he had cut back over the soil and stamped it down with his foot. Eva was already striding back towards the gate, reaching for the latch as she neared it. But something stilled her hand. A silhouette loomed in the glow of her headlights, blurred at the edges by the rising mist.

"Is someone there?" called a voice.

Eva released the breath she was holding. The voice was female, old and not unkind. "We're just leaving," she replied.

The old lady pulled the gate open and held it, her features growing clearer as Eva got close.

"Good timing," the woman replied, "I forgot to lock the gate. It gets dark so much earlier now, doesn't it?"

Eva nodded, glancing back to check that Franz had caught up. He emerged from the darkness, carrying the shovel. She scrabbled for an explanation.

"Is this your friend?" asked the woman.

"Yes," said Eva, "we were just... doing some gardening-"

"Saying goodbye-" Franz added at the same time.

The woman glanced between them, and then nodded good naturedly. "I do a bit of gardening here. It's just voluntary; keeping back the weeds and clearing the graves. And I lock up two days a week," she added.

"Yes, well done," replied Eva, attempting to sidle past.

"It keeps me busy, since losing my husband."

Franz walked through the gate, the shovel clamped to his side. The woman pulled it shut behind him, groping around in her pocket for the keys.

"You know," she said, addressing Eva's back, "gardening can help. But if you're finding things really hard, you could always speak to the reverend."

Eva turned round slowly, her fixed smile beginning to falter. "Thank you," she said coldly, "but I think we're a long way beyond that."

A thin mist entangled the stunted oaks of Wistman's Wood. Gabriel sat on the treeline, looking down at the restless water of the Dart. It ran fast and deep, well fed by the autumn rains, crooks in its course snaring the bodies of unwary livestock. Fen lay by his feet, her sleek black head resting on one of the many scattered boulders that thrust up from the earth. Her breathing was shallow, barely keeping up the illusion of life.

Had he not been fae, he wouldn't have heard the velvet soft footfall that stalked through the trees behind him. But he did hear, even though he made no show of it.

"Lady." He greeted the figure that approached, without turning around.

"Huntsman," replied the woman mockingly, "you should use my name." She stood behind Gabriel, her clinging grey dress the same shade as the mist. Gently, she rested her fingertips on his shoulders.

Gabriel didn't stir. His eyes were on the Dart, tracking the suck and swirl of the water as it raced onwards and away, dragging the last memories of summer with it. Fen raised her head and stretched, a low growl rumbling in her throat.

"You know I hate her like that," said the woman.

"I know that Morgana." Gabriel rose to face his visitor, breaking away from her hands. Fen stood between them, black fur bristling down her spine.

"You prefer her like this, I suppose?" Gabriel asking, keeping his gaze on Morgana. Between them, Fen stretched again, her bones clicking sickeningly beneath her skin. Her shiny fur turned slick, peeling back at the ribs to reveal rancid flesh and rotten muscle. Her gums shrank back from yellow teeth and her amber eyes shrivelled and hollowed to smouldering coals. She stopped bothering with breathing.

"I prefer the truth," said Morgana, lowering her hand to touch the hound. Fen growled a warning and Morgana recoiled, scowling.

"Your truth," said Gabriel.

"It is our truth!" she cried, sidestepping the Wisht Hound to stand closer to Gabriel, her long fingers gripping his forearm. "Who else could understand? Who else here has been through death and back again? Who else has hundreds of years of blood on their hands, but still dares use them for love?" Her other hand had followed the line of Gabriel's arm up, tracing the curve of his neck to his cheek. It hovered there defiantly.

"Too many of us," said Gabriel, catching hold of her hand. She leaned into him, but he pushed her back. Fen forced herself protectively between them.

Morgana snatched her hand away with a shriek, her rage sending a pair of disgruntled crows squawking and screaming from a nearby tree. "What have I done to deserve this coldness?" she snarled.

"Nothing," said Gabriel, softening slightly and resting his hand on his forehead.

"When you came to me for the magic that your beloved demanded, I obliged. When you came to me for the dreamwork that would call her back here, I obliged. These were deep works and dark crafts; old magic of blood and bone, bound into being by a thousand years of sacrifice."

"I know it." Gabriel half reached out, spreading his fingers as if he would take her hands. But he faltered.

"You repulse her. You saw it yourself," Morgana said.

Gabriel's lips tightened, his blue eyes turning stormy with the pain behind them. His fingers curled into his palms.

Morgana leaned closer. Her pale hands wrapped around his, pushing them down as she tilted her head to whisper in his ear. "But I know you."

She breathed in deeply; woodsmoke and carrion, old blood and honey. The familiar smell of his skin; his hunger that night in Houndain when she had first come to him. She pressed her lips to his, suddenly ravenous.

He gave in to her embrace. The glamour that he wore withdrew, receding to reveal winterwhite skin drawn tight to the bone. His pale hair shone like spidersilk and a row of wicked spines raised along each of his forearms. Fen shook free a little more loose flesh, and then raised her head to the sky and howled.

Gabriel pulled sharply away. His eyes were an inky black and wide with horror. "What did you do?"

"Why do you fear it?" spat Morgana, shaking her head. "Why are you ashamed of what you are?"

"Of what I am?"

"What. Who. It is unimportant. These are mortal concerns." She reached out to him, but he caught her wrist. "I want your truth, Huntmaster," she said.

Gabriel narrowed his eyes. They were turning blue again, but the iciness lingered. "You forced the change. How did you do that?" he pressed.

Morgana laughed mirthlessly. "I can do anything I choose," she said.

"No. Not that. This is my curse and I am master of it!" The hand that gripped her wrist was shaking. "I am in control." He let go and she pulled back, massaging the skin where his fingers had dug in.

"Of course. Like the river in spate, overfull with rainfall and pressing at the banks." She glanced down at the Dart, which was dragging a fallen sapling along in the flow. "Do you think the water wastes time wishing for humanity?"

Her question lingered on the air, hanging like the mist. Gabriel diminished, wrapping his glamour around himself like a cloak. He couldn't have looked more human, standing there in a waxed jacket and hat. Fen sat beside him, sleek and glossy like an obedient gundog. Morgana bared her teeth in disgust.

"I must go. The clan in Meath expect me," Gabriel said.

Morgana laughed, sharp and mirthless. "The dedication!"

"It is my duty. And she is blood."

"Such love for the sister who tried to kill you," said Morgana, "but none spare for anyone else!"

"You know well that-" Gabriel snapped, but Morgana cut across him, her hand scything the air for emphasis.

"Mortals do not count. It is a cursed match when we stray from our own. You ought to be better, Huntmaster. Our Clan deserves better."

Gabriel looked at the ground, his lips thinning to a pale line. The air around him stilled and a chill crept over the woods, cruel and clinging, heavy and cold as the grave. Morgana's breath froze on the air.

"And what do I deserve, Morgana?" He met her gaze defiantly.

She scowled, hoarfrost prickling across her shoulders, lacing the grey of her dress with the shimmer of ice. She watched fern fronds of frost uncurl from her cuff, blossoming at her wrist and spreading over the skin of her palm. The same pattern spread up from Gabriel's collar, unfurling across his neck and creeping over his cheek. It crept further, freezing the grass beneath his feet, growing over the boulders and tracking down through the damp earth towards the water below. The Dart grew sluggish, scraping against the banks as it heaved shards of ice.

"Let me show you," said Morgana. Her voice turned coaxing. Her skin glowed radiant and her eyes shone emerald green. Glamour blazed around her as she spread her fingers in front of her heart, burning away the frost and flushing her cheeks. Gabriel wavered against the full force of her will. She pitched everything at him; all of her power, all of her desire and longing. "Come," she commanded, the word dripping with promise.

Gabriel turned away.

This time there was no sound; no shriek of anguish to betray the pain. It smouldered deeper, in silence, like a wildfire creeping through the dry peat. Morgana watched Gabriel leave. She listened as the Dart broke free from the ice, and a grim smile curved the corners of her mouth.

"Very well," she told no one in particular. She turned sharply, dropping to the ground, her hands becoming paws before they touched the earth. She shook out her sable fur, pointed ears twitching at faint sounds on the breeze. One last time, she turned amber eyes back towards the woods. Then she ran.

Woody heather and damp, tufty grass rushed past her as she raced along, agile fox feet carrying her safely over sinkholes and stones. Grazing ponies watched her warily and an old ewe stamped her foot in warning, shielding her lamb behind her. But this fox wasn't hunting. It bounded on, a speeding shadow, pausing only for a moment now and then to sniff the air, before plunging ahead. Here and there it scattered birds, or startled a roe deer, cutting a midnight silhouette out of the dull grey sky as it crossed the higher tors. But it never stopped for long, and it only slowed when it got to the road. Here it was more careful, sticking to the hedgerows and slipping from shadow to shadow as it skirted the edge of town. But a fox stirred little interest in Buckfastleigh, and very soon it came to the wooden gates of the church.

On either side, a narrow country lane wound away into the darkness, barely wide enough for a car. The lights of the town twinkled nearby, but somehow didn't reach the sky here, as if they believed the idea that this place was best avoided.

Morgana sprung up to rest her paws on the gate. It was latched closed but not locked. Between breaths, there was a shift, and the weight of a woman leaned against the wood. Pale fingers found the latch and the hem of a long grey dress dragged across the gravel, catching up fallen leaves which littered the path.

She stalked through the dark churchyard, eyes still shimmering from the shift. Gravestones cluttered the ground on either side, some so old that the carved lettering was illegible. To her left, the ruins of the church reared up towards the sky, roofless and gaping. Only the stone has survived the fire, although well-meaning locals had petitioned to have the stricken bell tower half shielded with glass so it could still be used. The effect was unsettling; like looking through a clear dressing to the innards of the building.

The fire had been blamed on Satanists. But Morgana knew better.

She paused at a crossroads in the path. To the left was the church, ahead were the ruins of another, older chapel, and to her right was a second gate and then large agricultural fields. It was no accident that the tomb had been built here. Not only had a heavy stone sepulchre been built on top of the grave, but also a stone building had been raised around it, accessible only via a heavy oak door. The grave could be viewed through a long opening on the churchward side, which was fitted with thick iron bars.

The villagers had really tried. But they hadn't known what they were dealing with. Demons at least obeyed some sort of rules; dislike of holy water, lack of appreciation for religious texts and suchlike. But before angels and demons there were far older things, and the fae were among them. There were other things as well of course. Arguably, they were worse, but it was best not to think about them at all.

Morgana peered through the bars. Inside the tomb was dark, and a few dead leaves had blown in to pile up in the corners. The air was still and stale, laced with the dampness of old stone and sodden earth. She trailed her fingers along the bars, drawing a low hum from the metal. Then she touched the door. Of course, it was locked, the keyhole rusty from disuse.

She smiled, spreading her fingers and pressing her palms against the wood. The old oak creaked and cracked, swelling suddenly with sap and recalling the deep soil, and the sky, and the spring. It groaned, constrained by the stone around it, living wood heaving with the desire to grow. A thin branch pierced through an old knot mark and the keyhole and lock were forced out like a foreign body. The hinges hit the grass with a dull thud and the door fell aside. Morgana stepped through the opening.

Inside, she touched the stone of the sepulchre. Under her hand, it remembered the deep, warm seas and the comforting crush of the earth. The stone crumbled and slid aside. Only the coffin was left. It had been fully lead lined, and although the wood had rotted the soft, grey metal remained. With an unwholesome eagerness, Morgana gripped the lid and tore it off.

She regarded the skeleton inside with glinting eyes. She could already feel it; the lingering curse that bound spirit to bone and compelled both to serve her.

"Cabell," she whispered. Three hundred years had passed, but she remembered his cruelty and his love of the hunt. She knelt, almost reverently, her grey dress spilling in tattered folds around her. One hand traced a bare cheekbone and the other rested on gaping ribs as she leaned over the coffin. The bones remembered. The air was dense with anticipation. Morgana gripped the grinning skull and kissed it.

Beneath her lips, muscle spread like ivy. Skin blossomed like lichen spreading over a rock. Flesh bubbled, filling the hollows and clothing the bones. She drew back and the man gasped, filling his newmade lungs with the first painful taste of air. Morgana crossed her arms, perching by the coffin as Cabell scrambled to sit up. His eyes darted wildly between her, his own hands and the doorway.

"Shh," she soothed, "this is a great night. You have returned to me, just as I said."

Memory trickled back. Cabell recalled the hunt, the black fox and the woman. It had stayed with him, that night, but it hadn't made him any kinder. The wickedness ran too deep. His breathing slowed and he began to catalogue his surroundings with a cold interest.

"See how they feared you, even in death," Morgana explained, her hand making a sweeping gesture round the sepulchre. "Buried at a crossroads, on consecrated ground, behind iron and stone in a lead lined coffin." She stood, offering him her hand. He stood with her help, still easing into his body. "But they are no match for us."

She led him outside, where he eyed the extensive damage to the church. Morgana held onto his arm.

"They tell a story where running anti-clockwise seven times round your tomb will summon you. They say that, at midnight, the shadows of your hounds are cast in hellfire on the wall." She laughed, cold and shrill. "But that is child's play."

Morgana turned to face Cabell, one hand gripping each of his upper arms. Her expression was triumphant and earnest. "I have a gift for you," she said. Her eyes blazed amber and then dulled, her hands shaking as the magic passed between them. Cabell blinked, then stared back with amber irises. "You will do a small thing in return," she told him.

Cabell nodded, the power burning through his veins like a strange elixir. He raised his hands, his fingers curling into claws as he dragged at the darkness, calling it to himself. And it came. Flakes began to fall, soft as snow and black as ash. They congregated, cloying together, fusing along quick, searing lines. The darkness made the shapes of hounds; too many to count, charred skin cracking with each movement to reveal the magma beneath. He reached out and a horse formed in the same way. The strange shadow settled and faded to a convincing grey as he swung up onto it. Around him, the hounds sniffed the air and shook themselves, impatient for the chase. The horse pranced, metal hooves leaving steaming scars on the grass.

"See how they caged you. See how they cursed you. You must make them suffer in return!" cried Morgana.

3.
PROMISE

The cottage smelt of sweet fruit and pastry. Gemma was washing up after dinner and Elaine was drying. In the oven, the blackberry pie was bubbling and browning in the heat.

"This bargain," asked Elaine, "what is it?"

Gemma glanced over her shoulder. The living area was empty, and snatches of sound told her that Mike and Adrian were watching TV in another room. She looked back at the sink and shrugged, for her own benefit, as Elaine wouldn't see it. Gemma was glad that her embarrassment could go unobserved.

"A sort of, open IOU, I suppose. Gabriel brought Adrian back from the dead and I will have to do... something."

"Something?" Elaine echoed, arching an eyebrow.

"I know, I know. Stupid life decision, right?" Gemma scrubbed a clean plate with nervous vigour. She could feel her cheeks blazing, and was once again glad Elaine couldn't see her.

"What will you do?" Elaine asked.

"What can I do? Other than do it, whatever it is, and hope it's nothing too bad."

Elaine let the silence stretch out, until Gemma felt compelled to fill it.

"You think it'll be bad? You think I could get out of it?" she guessed.

Elaine felt for the counter and gently placed down the cup she had been drying. "A promise is a promise," she said, "especially when it comes to the fae."

Gemma looked down at the dishwater. A delicate,

oily rainbow stretched across the surface. What had she been hoping for, some kind of miracle get out clause? Her thoughts trekked back to Grimspound, and to before; to the Plume of Feathers and the Fox Tor Cafe.

"Your message," she said, recalling the garbled voicemail, "you said to stay away. You said to run."

"I did. You know what he is."

"I do now," Gemma replied.

"Yes, and I only regret that I didn't in the beginning. I was caught up in what he wanted me to think, and I ought to have known better." Elaine rubbed a dry plate until it squeaked.

"He has a way of doing that; making you think how he wants you to."

"They all do," said Elaine.

Gemma cocked her head to one side, suddenly curious. Elaine hadn't mentioned that she was familiar with the fae, and if she was, well, some advice earlier on might have been helpful. Her mouth began to form the question, but Elaine started to talk in a hurry.

"I'm sorry about that message though. I should have waited to word it better. I didn't mean to frighten you; not any more than was needed anyway." She reached out expectantly. Gemma passed her a fresh plate and Elaine began to dry it very attentively.

"Do you know much about the fae?" Gemma asked. There was a long pause.

"No," Elaine said eventually. She turned to Gemma and smiled. It was the sort of stiff smile that leaves the eyes dark and fails to spread to the edges of the face. "Shall we check the crumble?" she asked.

Gemma glanced at the oven and back again. It took a few moments for the suggestion to sink in.

"Yes," she agreed. Walking to the oven, she looked back. Elaine had both palms on the worktop, her thumbs hooked under the edge as if she was bracing herself against some invisible onslaught.

The room filled with the hot, sugary scent of baking. Gemma leaned back from the blast of burning air, waving the checked oven glove in front of her face. "This is done," she said.

There was a magic to the smell that brought Adrian and Mike back into the room. Elaine held one hand out, sensing her way, and with the other she placed four freshly washed plates on the kitchen table. Mike sat down, his eyes moving meaningfully between his empty plate and the oven.

"Go on, you're forcing me," he said.

Elaine laughed, freeing her face from the tension it had held. She took a seat next to Mike, resting her hand lightly for a moment on his shoulder.

"It's a hard life, is it?" she mocked.

"The hardest," he replied, almost seriously.

They were all working on second portions when Mike stood up, striding over to the other corner of the room. He returned armed with glasses and a bottle of whisky.

"Nightcap?" he suggested.

Gemma raised an eyebrow. Mike had been teetotal since Gabriel had brought Adrian back to the cottage.

"Maybe one," said Elaine, "it feels late."

"The night is young!" Mike assured her, squinting to examine the label on the dusty bottle. "This is the finest single malt, all the way from-"

"The local shop?" Adrian teased.

31

"No! Well, yes, but Scotland before that. It says so on the bottle. Will you have a wee dram?" Mike asked.

"Go on then," laughed Adrian.

"Why not," seconded Elaine.

"I'm good," said Gemma.

"Wait, wait, I know what you'll have," Mike told her, waggling one finger in her direction while he overfilled two glasses on the table. "You'll share a ginger beer with me, am I right?" he produced a second bottle from the cupboard.

Gemma relaxed. "Yes please," she smiled.

Mike touched Elaine's hand lightly and placed a glass between her expectant fingers. Then he poured two ginger beers and raised his up.

"To friends," he said.

"To friends," everyone chorused in answer. There was a short silence while they drank, and then Adrian caught Mike's eye.

"How about a story," he suggested.

Mike smoothed his hair back, and then took a sudden deep interest in his hands. "You've heard too many of my stories already." His cheeks were tinged with a faint pink.

"I haven't heard any," protested Elaine. She smiled encouragingly and sipped her whiskey. The pink tinge to Mike's cheeks intensified and he eyed the bottle of alcohol wistfully.

"Maybe just one," he agreed.

"A new one," added Adrian, "one we haven't heard."

Mike took a long draught of his ginger beer, nodding to himself. "A new one, well. Have you heard the tale of Kitty Jay?"

They all leaned closer, bound by the spell of his

voice as he caught his stride, words forming slow and melodic on his tongue.

"Kitty was a poor farm girl. Poor, but pretty. She caught the eye of a local lad and he did all in his power to woo her. He was rich, and he promised she would be a lady and have fine clothes and ride in a carriage across the moor. Kitty thought him very handsome and grand. She thought she would look rather fine in beautiful dresses, with a maidservant and a spaniel in a polished black coach with white horses.

"So, after many pretty words and promises, Kitty at last made up her mind. It was full summer; the moor blazed with yellow gorse and purple heather. The sky was endless blue, and the bright sun cast long shadows in wild secret places where two young lovers could hide. They bathed in cool stony streams and followed the sheep tracks that wound their way through ruined dwellings. They danced round the nine maidens and rested their backs against the cool stones of the circle.

"But summer stretched thin. Autumn came creeping through the hedgerows, fierce and golden, swelling the hawthorn berries and the sloes. With the change of the season, Kitty's belly began to swell also. The long, carefree days on the moor were suddenly long ago and the young man became distant. Chatter spread through the village; the silly farm girl and the young Lord who could never marry her. Kitty's mood grew dark. In the cruel winter, cold and barren, the darkness wrapped her loneliness. But the noose held her last.

"Now taking your own life was a deadly sin in those days. They cut Kitty's body down, and they buried her on the crossroads, so that her spirit might not return to rebuke them. After that, you might think poor Kitty Jay was

33

forgotten.'"

Mike paused for emphasis, catching the gaze of his rapt audience. A smile flickered on the edge of Elaine's lips; expectant but patient.

"But that isn't the end of our story. To this very day, Jay's grave is a mystical place, and each day fresh flowers appear adorning the unmarked stones. Some say that it is the ghost of Kitty's young man, returning in his regret to make amends for abandoning her. Perhaps one day she will forgive him, and they will pass into the Otherworld together. Or, maybe, he is cursed to visit her grave and lay flowers for the rest of time."

A hush lay thick on the room. Fian had stirred from his bed and padded over, laying his sleek white head against Gemma's thigh. It was as if the moor had grown closer and the chill of dusk had crept in through the keyhole. Mike's eyes held a glassy gleam and his attention was far away, following his words to somewhere darker.

Gemma glanced from side to side. "Mike," she said, "do you know any, you know, cheery stories?"

Mike stared at her blankly, then shook his head as if trying to dislodge something. The room grew warmer and the electric light beat back the shadows. His eyes refocused and he began to laugh. "You're asking me for a cheery folktale, are you?"

Gemma shrugged, aware that Adrian was eyeing her as if she'd just announced that faeries weren't real. Or that coffee wasn't important. "Is that weird to ask?" she added, already aware of the answer.

"Well, let me think," replied Mike, rubbing the very beginnings of stubble on his chin, "I suppose there is the legend of the hairy hands!"

Adrian snorted into his whiskey. Mike wiggled his

own fingers in the air theatrically.

"The hairy hands appear unexpectedly out on the moor-" he began.

"Doesn't everything?" Gemma joked.

"I suppose it does," countered Mike good naturedly, taking her mocking in his stride. "They appear unexpectedly out on the moor when you are travelling alone. Not even your car will protect you. One minute you're going along nicely and next minute there's these great, hairy hands gripping the steering wheel and sending you veering off, SPLASH, into the bog!" He accompanied the statement with such an enthusiastic impression that his chair wobbled precariously on two legs and his glass of ginger beer slid some way down the table.

"How dreadful," laughed Elaine, savouring her last sip of whiskey.

"Hands up if you thought that was cheery," said Gemma.

"Hands up if you have been affected by the hairy hands," countered Mike.

Adrian half raised a hand. "I think I'm a victim."

Gemma arched her eyebrows at him and he burst into body shaking laughter. Mike reopened the bottle of whiskey and refilled Adrian and Elaine's glasses.

"I'm not sure about another," she said, "I still need to get a taxi home."

Mike spun his glass with his fingers, staring into the half-drunk ginger beer. "I suppose I thought you might stay here, what with it being late-" he stumbled over the words, examining the liquid in his glass intently.

"I'd hate to impose," Elaine replied.

Mike was trying to catch Adrian's eye, but with no success. The storyteller was fine with wild beasts and supernatural monsters, but right now he was out of his depth. The table wobbled slightly, almost as if Gemma had trodden on Adrian's toe underneath it.

"It's no problem, we have plenty of room, don't we?" Mike prompted.

"Loads of room," Adrian echoed, scrambling to catch up with the conversation, "and Mike stays up late reading and falls asleep on the sofa half the time anyway."

"Well," smiled Elaine, "if you're sure, I'd be very grateful."

"Good. That's settled then." Mike picked up his glass and drained it out of habit.

Adrian's concentration had wandered again. He tapped his fingers restlessly against his glass. "Jays grave," he said, returning to the subject that still occupied his thoughts, "is it still there?"

"Yes, mysterious fresh flowers and all," said Mike.

"Well I was wondering-"

"-if we could go and see it?" Mike finished Adrian's sentence with a grin. "Certainly we can. How about tomorrow? We could take the birds out as well. Have you ever flown a buzzard?" He addressed this question to Elaine.

Gemma rubbed her forehead. Someone who didn't know Adrian might have been foolish enough to think that perhaps being sacrificed to the undead by a necromancer and then dragged back from the Otherworld by the master of the Wild Hunt might have put him off anything vaguely supernatural. But no, true to form, here he was getting excited over the slightest sniff of a mystery. Give him a haunted grave to explore and wave goodbye to him having attention for anything else.

"Why are you so interested? You haven't had any

more dreams, I hope?" Gemma's tone was light but her eyes were serious. Seeing your best friend dead once was enough.

"Nothing in particular," Adrian shrugged, looking down at the table, "I'm just interested. You know, curse buddies." He gave Gemma a watery smile. She smiled back, suddenly realising that she had been so caught up in thinking about herself that she hadn't considered how scared Adrian must be. Being told your soul was loose was no small thing.

"We're going to fix that, somehow. I promise," she said.

Mike and Elaine were happily making plans for the next day. Gemma thought of Pandora the buzzard, who seemed more than happy to simply sleep and eat in her large aviary at the end of the garden, and wondered whether exercising the bird was Mike's main concern.

A lone car climbed the narrow road that wound up onto the high moor. Headlights beat back the darkness, bright but small in the wide, sleeping landscape. The night was still and cold. A thin mist gathered in the hollows, rising as the car sped past but swirling softly back behind it.

"You remember the place?" Franz asked Eva.

"Of course." She kept her eyes on the road, waiting to see the pull-in she would recognise. There was little chance of her forgetting. In a life that had held many horrors, the sight of the Huntmaster torturing her father was sharp and clear in her mind.

She slowed, peering through the mist. She knew that beyond the narrow pull-in the ground dropped away as a steep slope. If she misjudged it, they'd never get the

37

car back. If they survived the descent.

"After this, I'm going to kill him. I'm going to feed him to his own hounds and leave what's left on the moor for the crows." She turned suddenly, swerving to the left and slamming on the brakes. The car skidded to a halt and she threw open the door, gulping in lungfuls of crisp night air. It tasted of distant decay and the deep, damp earth.

"The Huntmaster is not mortal," said Franz, climbing out from the passenger side and opening the boot.

"That doesn't matter. Anything can die."

"Perhaps." Franz lifted out the shovel and hefted it across his shoulder. "But is it down to you to decide?"

Eva stood on the grassy bank, the twin tors that flanked Grimspound rising dark and brooding behind her. She wrapped her tweed jacket tighter against the chill and crossed her arms.

"He killed my father. He tortured him for sport. That kind of monster has no place being alive."

Franz looked back at the car. Many things in the world had changed since 1945; but human nature, he suspected, was the same. He gripped the shovel tighter, his knuckles turning pale with the effort. Eva noticed his silence.

"Don't think I include you in that," she added.

Franz shook his head. Perhaps he wasn't a monster in the same sense as the Huntmaster, but he was monstrous enough all the same. It was Eva's will that animated his bones and wrapped his body in flesh. Beneath that, he was still a corpse in a bog with a downed plane.

He looked up and Eva was gone. Slamming the boot, he strode after her, glad that his jackboots were the one thing he hadn't buried at St. Andrews. The moor was wet, and each footstep drew a squelch from the earth. Beneath

38

the grass, the water table was high and, off to his right, Franz heard a small stream running fast and full.

The path up to the ruined Bronze Age settlement had been picked out with large stones. They stopped erosion of the thin layer of soil and they marked the safest way to ascend. Halfway up, the track forded the stream with a large slab, and the water gurgled greedily under it. Franz strained his eyes and thought he could just make out the figure of Eva ahead. He quickened his pace.

She was waiting for him by the outer edge of the settlement. The tumbledown wall enclosed multiple ruined hut circles, which Franz could just about pick out in the darkness.

"Is this it?" he asked.

"Almost," Eva replied. Her tone was less angry now, as if the climb had drained some of her defiance. Franz took his chance to rest for a moment and stood, leaning on the shovel. He could feel the sharp metal edge biting through the skin of the earth.

"Are you ready?" he asked.

Above them, the stars glinted bright and indifferent. A barn owl drifted across the heather, silent as a ghost, unseen to the last by the mouse clutched in its claws.

"No," said Eva. She looked younger, huddled in her mother's jacket that was a little too big. The moor spread wild and dark around her, as if it rolled on forever and she and Franz were the last people left alive.

"You can wait," he suggested.

She shook her head. "No I can't." She held out a trembling hand. Franz stepped forward and took it, taking the weight of the shovel once again on his shoulder. She led him on through the ruins and out between two standing stones. The earth swelled ahead, rising as a smooth mound.

It betrayed almost nothing of the previous excavations which had allowed the burial chamber beneath to be used. The undead minions of the necromancer required life force from the living as sustenance, and these donors required storage away from prying eyes during daylight.

Eva knelt, feeling around the edges of a patch of ground that looked no different to that around it. Gripping a tuft of grass, she tugged sharply, and a square of turf separated neatly from the earth. She dragged it aside and then peeled back three more squares, leaving a large bare patch of soil.

"Did you father need to do this for each body that he raised?" Franz asked.

"No. They sort of, clawed their way out."

Franz nodded, realising that he had no recollection of how he had got out of the bog and onto solid ground. All he remembered was a burning pain in his lungs, and the sudden, overwhelming need to breathe.

"So is that what will happen now?" he asked.

Eva eyed the shadowy patch of earth. The moon was a thin curve, and she daren't use a torch or the light on her phone to illuminate it any further.

"I suppose so." Her voice was small and quiet, and the earth was deep and cold, brimming with bones and memories. Her knees were already sodden and the chill was creeping into her core. She clenched her jaw to stop her teeth chattering. She had made a promise, and she intended to keep it.

Closing her eyes, she thrust her hands down into the damp soil. It was loose after being dug out and replaced over and over. It accepted her palms hungrily, yielding to her touch like it had found a taste for flesh. Eva didn't flinch.

She forced her shoulders to drop and her breathing to slow. She found the fury within her, burning low but hot. She embraced her fear, huge and frantic, fluttering in her chest like a caged bird. Then she gathered them both in a blazing tangle of power. Raw energy coursed through her, drawing a scream from her lips and driving her fingertips deeper into the earth. Like before, the power was reckless. Since raising Franz and the plane, Eva had done no work to tame her talent, and the call ran wild and unwieldy. It sparked from stone to stone, exploring the hollow of the burial mound like a thousand thirsty roots.

The call spread further, seeking out the dead. Eva tensed, closing in on herself as her consciousness stretched thin. She dragged her focus back, achingly slowly, until she sensed that her energy was mainly focused on the tomb below. It seemed like forever. She began to tremble. Her teeth chattered and she shivered uncontrollably, slumping slowly towards the earth.

Suddenly someone was dragging her back, away from the comforting dark. She tried to beat them off, but she was too weak and cold. Franz wrapped his jacket around her, holding her close and rubbing her arms in an effort to warm her.

"What are you doing?" Eva stuttered, trying to twist back to the ground.

"Stopping you." He felt her will turn against him, but it was barely enough to loosen his hands.

"But I was doing it. I need to. Franz I need to-" her words dissolved into sobs that shook her whole body. The fight left her and she went limp; a dead weight in his arms. Hot tears rolled down her cheeks and chilled quickly in the night air.

Beneath them, the earth lay still and silent.

Nothing shifted or stirred in the underground tomb. Franz stared up at the bright, distant stars and held Eva as she cried.

4.
RETURN

It was still dark when Mike rose. He opened the back door and stood on the threshold, one shoulder resting on the wooden frame. He watched the first hint of blue bleed into the sky, subtle as watercolour while it spread from the East. In the old, gnarled holly tree in the corner of the garden a blackbird began to sing. Its voice rose, shrill and clear, coaxing the coming dawn to stoop and kiss the earth. As the skyline began to separate into ragged hills and open sky, the bird fell suddenly silent. Mike glanced around and saw Elaine behind him. Her bare feet made no sound as she trailed one hand gently along the wall to orientate herself.

"You wake early too, then?" Mike asked.

A smile blossomed across Elaine's face. She reached out, and Mike guided her to the doorway. The air was crisp and refreshing, laying soft and still in the secret time before the world has woken.

"I always loved to watch the sunrise," Elaine said, her unseeing eyes turned towards the garden and the moor that rolled away into the distance behind it.

"Shall I describe it to you?" Mike asked.

Elaine tilted her head towards him, her hand finding his and closing gently over it. "That would be wonderful."

"Well," said Mike, "the first indigo has already chased back the night. Now comes the violet, lending a pink blush to the clouds. The valleys are still dark, but the higher hills are gently waking in shades of green and grey, as if they've never been so glad to see the sun."

Right on cue, the blackbird started up his song

again, and accompanied Mike's words as he narrated the rising of the sun. When the sky was light, he and Elaine stood and listened as the lone songbird was joined by a thrush and, somewhere further away, a pheasant.

"Thank you," said Elaine, "if I miss one thing, it's the colours."

"So you weren't always blind?"

"No, not always."

The last of the stillness seemed suddenly precious, as if an answer that had been eluding Mike for years was just the width of a word away. If only he could find it, before the world woke and frightened it back out of reach. Behind him, the floorboards creaked. He closed his eyes, trying to protect the fragile memory as it formed, but it was already fading.

"Do you want tea?" Adrian called.

Like the darkness, whatever it was, was gone. Mike's shoulders dropped slightly. He patted Elaine's hand and turned towards the house.

"We're coming now," he said.

Gemma would have slept later, but the bustle of noise, and the smell of toast and fresh coffee lured her downstairs. It seemed a long time ago when she had been rising to an alarm and rushing to work. It was a month, but she felt sure her meagre savings wouldn't withstand another. With skill gained from practice, she pushed that thought to the back of her mind.

In the kitchen, Mike and Elaine were sitting at the table while Adrian raided the cupboards for preserves. There was a plate piled with brown toast and a large teapot complete with tea cosy. Gemma couldn't help smiling.

"Morning," said Mike, pulling out the empty chair

next to him. Gemma sat and helped herself to a piece of toast.

"I thought we should have a big breakfast before going out exploring," Adrian said happily. It was definitely him who had dug out the tea cosy, Gemma thought.

She had forgotten about their plan to visit Jay's grave today, but even this reminder couldn't dampen her mood. Mike wasn't likely to be drawn into anything dangerous with Elaine in tow, and his precious birds weren't to be put at risk either. It was just a walk, with good friends, on a sunny autumn day.

There was a firm knock on the door. Mike glanced at the clock, and then stood up, his eyebrows drawing together. It was very early for visitors. Not that they ever had any. The knock sounded again; polite but with an underlying urgency. Mike took a step closer, and Gemma noticed that Elaine was gripping the edge of the table again, just like she had when they were discussing the fae last night. Her head turned slowly towards the door.

"There is no stopping it," Elaine said.

Mike put his hand on the latch. Gemma held her breath. The door swung outwards. A lanky young man with red hair was standing outside, shifting his weight from foot to foot nervously.

"Owain!" cried Gemma. She braced one elbow on the table and breathed normally again. It wasn't the Huntmaster. Owain may be his Apprentice but he was also, sort of, a friend. The clumsiness of his youth stole much of the deadly grace which made the fae seem unsettling.

"Hello," said Owain, "can I come in?"

Mike hesitated, but then stepped aside, moving to stand protectively next to Elaine.

"I see you have plenty of food. That's good," Owain

observed.

"What is there no stopping?" pressed Adrian.

Owain hovered near the door, his knee-high boots and wax jacket out of place in the warm kitchen. There was a wildness to him, even in the way that his body never quite settled into stillness.

"Many things," he replied, "the flow of the Dart. The change of the seasons."

"Talk sense, boy!" Mike snapped.

Owain looked over at Mike, his eyes narrowing almost imperceptibly. For a few long seconds he stared, and the storyteller held his gaze defiantly. Eventually, Owain dropped his gaze, with a stiff nod.

"Gemma, you must come with me," the Apprentice said. A chilly realisation crept through her. How could she have presumed that only Gabriel would come to call in her debt? She thought she might have had years, before he thought up something fitting.

"What the hell is this?" asked Mike.

"It's alright," Gemma reassured him, rising from her seat. "This is my own doing."

"What do you mean?"

"She offered a trade, for Adrian's life," Elaine explained.

"You did what?" Adrian demanded. He was still holding the butter knife in one hand, and he gripped it resolutely.

"Look," said Gemma, "it's nothing much. I'm just going somewhere for a bit. I think." She looked pleadingly at Owain. *Don't frighten them anymore*, she begged wordlessly, *Adrian is already fragile*. She knew that the fae had some ability to influence the human mind, but this was the first time she wished Owain could read hers.

"You're not going anywhere without us," said Mike. His hands were in fists by his sides. Adrian raised the bread knife in agreement.

"Take it from me, going off on your own is a bad idea," he said.

Gemma smiled at him. It was the kind of smile that runs so deep that it tests the border of tears. His life was small and precious in this huge, terrifying world. Even though he was an idiot, and undeniably ridiculous, she knew that she would face a hundred Huntmasters if it meant that he was alright.

"I've only got two tickets," said Owain.

"See?" said Gemma, "you hear that? Tickets. They're hardly going to offer tickets to some demented fairyland on the National Express are they?"

She glanced at Elaine, wishing inwardly that she had never coined the phrase 'demented fairyland'. The blind woman smiled, and Gemma knew that, even without her eyesight, Elaine could see right through the bravado. She could see into Gemma's core, where a knot of fear writhed unpleasantly.

"What do I need to bring, Owain?" Gemma asked.

"Listen," said Mike, stepping forward, "this doesn't have to happen." He lay a hand gently on Gemma's arm. His eyes were wide and frightened.

"I think it does," she said quietly.

"Tell me what you did."

"I told Gabriel that I would do anything if he brought Adrian back to life." Gemma felt her cheeks burning. It sounded worse when she admitted it out loud.

"It's a standard faerie bargain," suggested Owain helpfully.

"I know how it works," growled Mike dismissively.

He didn't take his eyes off Gemma. "Why didn't you tell me?"

"Or me?" added Adrian.

"How could I have told you? How could I have just, you know, brought that up over dinner?" she countered.

"In a house where your two companions are plagued by monstrous black dogs and can animate bones, I would say pretty damn easily." Mike's expression was grave.

Gemma had never seen him like this before; it was as if a fire within him had been lit and it burned behind his eyes. She recognised it as the same fierce flame that flared through her when she imagined Adrian being in danger, and she understood that Mike would face all the hounds of Hell if he had to. Friends fight for each other. Suddenly Gemma's eyes were stinging and she pressed her palms against them to halt the tears.

"I'm sorry Mike," she said, "and I'm sorry Adrian. I should have told you. I told myself I was being brave by keeping it to myself. But really I was frightened of what you'd say, which would have all been right. I'm very stupid, and in a list of bad life decisions this one is ranking very high."

"Well, join the club," replied Adrian consolingly.

"I just, wish I had known," said Mike quietly.

"There's nothing you could have done. There's little any of us can do now, except wish Gemma the best," Elaine said. Her tone was practical. "What does she need to bring, Owain?"

"Nothing," Owain replied.

"How long will she be away?"

"Three days."

Elaine nodded to herself, only the tight set of her lips betraying any turbulent internal thoughts. "Get a jumper, a thick coat and a good pair of boots," she advised Gemma.

While Gemma ran upstairs for the clothes, Elaine began to untie the intricate knots that held a length of leather thonging around her neck.

"Can I trust you, Owain?" she asked.

The Apprentice shuffled his hands into his pockets, diminishing to an awkward teen under her gaze. "Yes," he answered eventually.

"Good. I will hold you personally responsible if Gemma comes to any harm. Do you understand?"

Owain nodded, slowly raising his head until he met the blind woman's gaze. He knew that she saw him, in all of his truth, without a scrap of glamour to hide behind. "I understand," he replied.

Gemma stomped back downstairs with a thick jumper on. She began to pull on the walking boots which sat on the mat by the door. The trick here was to keep moving, she thought. If she stopped she would freeze, and then the fear would get in. If she didn't let her mind think any further ahead than getting out the door, then there was nothing to worry about. Yet.

She stood, facing her friends. Adrian was still in his dressing gown and the toast had gone cold on the table.

"Well, I'll see you in a few days," she said.

"Don't do anything I wouldn't do," said Adrian. Then he pulled a thoughtful face. "Actually, scrap that. Think what I would do and then do the opposite!"

Gemma smiled. It was so forced that it almost hurt. How could she leave Adrian when he needed her more than ever? The sleep walking was frightening enough, but now there were the blackouts. She would never say, but there was no doubt they were getting worse. Adrian was on borrowed time. Was three days too long?

"I'll be here when you get back," said Elaine.

Gemma felt relief tingle through her. Elaine would look after Adrian.

"But for now, I'd like you to take this." Elaine held out her hand. Sat on her palm was a smooth grey stone with a hole through the middle. A loop of leather was tied through the hole so that it could be worn as a necklace. "I was given it many years ago, but I think you'll have far more use for it now. Look through it to see the truth."

Gemma took the stone and put it on, tucking it safely under her jumper.

"I have something too," said Mike. He was rummaging around in a cupboard. "Here we are!" He produced a dented metal drinks bottle. "Always bring your own water," he said seriously.

Gemma filled the bottle from the sink and then turned to Adrian. "No strange spiritual missions or late-night adventures while I'm away, please," she said.

Adrian put his hands in his dressing gown pockets. "I promise," he said.

Gemma caught him up in a firm hug, closing her eyes and imagining for half a second that the stories were still just stories and that none of the myths were real. But they were, and one was waiting for her by the door.

"I'm ready Owain," she said, turning back towards him with her best business as usual smile.

"Good," he said.

The same sun that had spilled dawnlight gently across Mike's garden also gradually illuminated the wider moor. At Grimspound, it was slowed by the shadows cast by twin

50

tors, flanking the ruined settlement like granite guards. But still, eventually, the light trickled in. It lit the rough, grassy slopes that dipped down towards the tumbledown stone wall enclosing the ruined hut circles. It softly touched the low, lone hawthorn trees that clung to life in defiance of the wild winds and poor soil. It also shone on a single figure, who replaced a final square of turf and then rested gratefully on his spade.

Franz wiped his forehead with his shirt sleeve. Despite the chill autumn morning, he was sweating from the exertion of digging. The whole process of excavating and infilling a barrow mound each night was much easier if you had your undead servants to do it, he was sure. But he had kept his promise to Eva, and he had checked if her father's body was still inside. Which it was.

He began a slow walk down the winding path that led from Grimspound back towards the road. The stone slabs which marked out the route made the descent easy, and his eyes wandered gently over the rolling green and brown landscape that spread like a patchwork quilt around him. This was a place where you could lose yourself, he thought, and part of him would give anything for that chance. But was it even possible? Could he fade into a world which had outpaced him and hide the truth of who, or what, he was?

He stopped beside a small, fast stream. A short way ahead it crossed the path and was forded by a large slab of granite. The water ran crystal clear, racing impatiently between rocks as it sped on down the hill. Franz cupped his palms and caught some, savouring the feeling of the cold spring water on his blistered hands. He drank a few mouthfuls and considered how best to explain what he had seen in the barrow to Eva. It wasn't complicated; he just needed to be gentle. *Your father is dead Eva, and I presume he wishes to stay that way.* As to why her ability to raise the dead had worked on him but not the man in the barrow, he had no idea. There were older corpses in there too, only bones really, and they had shown no sign of stirring.

In his previous life, this would have been heralded as a breakthrough. One of the things which the Department of Mysteries had been researching was methods of making men invincible. An army of corpses would be just that, and only one necromancer was required to raise them. It was almost beyond thinking about. The earth was bulging with the dead, and at the word of one woman every one of them could return. All of them, except the one she wanted to.

Franz continued his walk, hefting the shovel back over one shoulder. Somewhere nearby, a blackbird was singing, and further out on the moor a pheasant croaked raucously. The black Range Rover was parked where they'd left it, although the pull-in was now also occupied by a small red car.

Franz looked in through the tinted window at Eva. She was just as he'd left her; curled in on herself on the passenger seat, a spare jumper tucked under her head as a pillow. She looked small and fragile in the large 4x4 parked in the middle of the even larger moor. Franz felt bad to wake her, but standing around with a shovel might draw the wrong kind of attention. She stirred sleepily when he knocked on the glass. A second later, the locks clicked open, and Franz was able to stow the spade in the boot. He climbed into the driver's seat.

"Did you find him?" Eva asked.

Franz paused. He had rehearsed his reply, but that hadn't made it any easier. "Yes," he said.

Eva pulled herself up in her seat, scrambling for the door handle. "Then I need to try again."

Franz lay a gentle hand on her shoulder. "It's daylight now," he said softly.

"It doesn't matter. I don't care," she said. The door was half open and cold air invaded the car.

"Listen," said Franz, "you need to rest. There are people nearby, and if we rouse their attention they might call the police. Then your father will be taken away, and laid out in a morgue, and be put through all manner of tests. And we will go to prison, quite possibly."

Eva sniffed. Her body went limp, as if her last reserves of energy had suddenly run out.

"Keep the warmth in, would you?" Franz asked.

Eva closed the door weakly and leaned her head against the misty window. For a few seconds, there was just the sound of her breath, and the throaty whistle of the wind outside.

"What did you see in there?" Eva asked quietly.

Franz looked at her. She didn't meet his gaze. Her eyes were fixed on something outside the window.

"Well, there's more room in there than you might think. After the narrow entrance tunnel it widens out into a chamber you can just about stand in. There are two huge stone slabs with flat tops. From the looks of it, the tomb would have held a high status burial once; before it was looted some time in the past. Your father is laid out on one of the stones, like a pagan king, with his servants entombed alongside him."

Eva turned her head slowly. Her eyes were shining with tears. "But why can't I get him back?" She held up her hands and spread her fingers, staring at them like some broken piece of machinery.

"Maybe," said Franz carefully, "he doesn't want to come back. If life was, in many ways, a burden, it might be a blessing not to return."

Eva finally met his gaze. Her eyes were fierce and weary. They were almost the same blue as his, meaning they passed easily as brother and sister. But hers were colder, and in their depths was an icy sharpness that no amount of reason could heal.

"Then at least the Huntmaster will join him," she vowed.

5.
NEWGRANGE

Gemma clutched the water bottle with both hands. It felt cold and real in the middle of the strangeness that surrounded her. Owain drove, just as at home behind the steering wheel as on an undead horse. Gemma blinked, as if it might clear her vision and return her to the sparse bedroom in Mike's house where she had begun to feel at home. The brass rubbing of the Beast which she had made in the Visitor Centre was stuck to the wall by her mirror. Adrian had made her do it. At the time it seemed childish, but now it was a reminder of simpler times.

"It's nice to see you," ventured Owain.

Gemma turned to him and forced a smile. None of this was his fault, after all. "And you," she said truthfully.

"I'm sorry that you're frightened."

"Me too. I should be braver."

Owain took his eyes from the road to glance over at her. "I think you are brave, Gemma," he said.

"Really?"

"You made a pact to save your friend. That's quite brave, given the fact you didn't know what task would be required in return."

Gemma leaned back into her seat, pressing her head against the padded headrest. "I think it was very stupid," she said.

"Do you wish you hadn't?"

"No."

For a while they drove in silence. The moor rolled past, wild and mostly empty. A few of the small parking areas contained lone cars owned by the more intrepid dog walkers. A wind was getting up, and it scoured uninterrupted across the boggy valleys and sharp granite hills. The sky was low and grey; even the sun wrapping itself in clouds against the cold.

"Where are we going?" Gemma asked Owain.

"Wales," he replied.

"What are the tickets for?"

"The ferry to Ireland."

Gemma relaxed a tiny bit. There had been no mention of any weird alternate land so far, and the ferry might not quite be the National Express but it was almost as mundane.

"Have you been on a ferry before?" she asked Owain.

It was the Apprentice's turn to look nervous. "No," he said.

Six hours later Owain was having his first experience of travelling by ferry. So far he had discovered three different complimentary sickness bags.

"What is this?" he moaned, clutching a wipe clean seat on the communal viewing deck. Wraparound windows provided a panoramic view of the restless sea, which could be enjoyed with a selection of quite expensive coffees. Food was not included in the ticket, and with a captive audience for two hours the onboard cafe and restaurant were busy. Luckily, Owain didn't look like he needed to eat.

"You're seasick," Gemma told him, tentatively rubbing his back. She wasn't sure what else to do.

"But why? And why aren't you seasick?" his face had taken on a light green tinge and his knuckles were white from gripping the seat.

"I think it's something to do with the liquid in your

56

ears. Your body doesn't like the way the waves move. I bet lots of other people on the ferry feel ill."

Owain nodded mutely, his mouth clamped closed against another wave of sickness.

"Let me get you some water," Gemma said.

She joined the queue for the drinks kiosk, checking on Owain over her shoulder while she waited. Fian was locked in the car with a blanket, and she hoped he wasn't feeling seasick as well. Owain had been adamant that only Gemma had been invited to wherever-the-hell-they-were-going, but after more than a few failed attempts to peel the dog away from her side, he had finally given in. Gabriel might be annoyed, but he would be more annoyed if none of them arrived at all. So Fian had boarded the ferry, assisted by an old receipt charmed with glamour to look like a pet passport. Gemma smiled to herself. She could have sworn that the white hound looked smug as their car was waved onboard.

"Can I help you?" asked a tired voice. Gemma looked up, and realised she had reached the front of the queue.

"One water and a refill please."

She carried the bottles back, wondering light-heartedly if any horror of the task ahead could match the unnatural price of refreshments on the ferry. After travelling all day everything felt a little surreal, as if their destination was never really getting any closer. Perhaps this was actually Purgatory, and the ferry was filled with people who had made poor life decisions and been cursed with seasickness and overpriced beverages forever.

Owain accepted the bottle weakly and leaned back on his seat. The worst of this bout seemed to have passed, and his skin looked a little less green.

"I meant to ask," said Gemma, "where did you get the car?"

They were travelling in a posh Range Rover, and it was a few steps up from the pickup truck which Owain had stolen previously. The young Apprentice couldn't keep a grin from appearing on his face.

"I checked the necromancer's pockets before we buried him," Owain explained proudly, "and there was a set of keys in one of them. From there, it was just a case of finding the car."

Gemma's mouth dropped open. "So you stole the dead necromancer's ride?" she asked incredulously.

"What?" countered Owain, "He wasn't going to need it!"

By the time the ferry had disgorged its passengers at the Irish port, the first gloom of evening was touching the edges of everything. The sky had turned a darker grey and the water of the channel looked deep and cold. Gemma turned up the heating in the car and reached behind her seat to stroke Fian.

"How long is the drive now?" she asked Owain.

"About an hour to Meath."

"And what happens in Meath?"

"Newgrange is there," Owain replied, as if this explained everything.

"Owain," said Gemma, "all these names mean nothing to me. Has Gabriel actually told you what I need to do when we get to New-whatever?" Nothing bad had happened so far, and after the boredom of travelling she was feeling a little bit braver.

"Newgrange is an ancient passage tomb, older than Stonehenge, and the main dwelling place of the

Meath faerie Clan," replied Owain.

"Sounds cosy." From all of Adrian and Mike's talk of tombs she knew that even the larger ones wouldn't hold more than maybe twenty people, and that would be a squeeze. She wondered briefly if taking photos to show them would be possible, but remembered with disappointment that she had never seen Gabriel or Owain use a phone. Owain laughed.

"There is a little more than meets the eye," he told her.

After half an hour of driving Owain pulled into a lay-by on a quiet country road. Gemma peered out of the car window into the gloaming.

"Why are we stopping?" she asked.

"I need to cast your disguise."

"How?"

"With glamour, of course."

Gemma raised her hands in front of her. She had suspected that something along those lines would be needed, as just rocking up to some other faerie Clan as a random human would probably cause a bit of a stir, but she had presumed that Gabriel would be doing it. Owain was still learning, and after he had charmed the leather hound mask to grow into her face at the Visitor Centre, she wasn't keen on being the victim of his practicing again.

"I didn't think you were, you know, at that stage yet," she said, attempting to be tactful.

"I've been practicing," he assured her.

"Look Owain, I'm really not sure-"

"How long you'll survive as a mortal in Newgrange?" Owain put on a mock thinking face, "Oh yes. Minutes."

Gemma shivered, despite the warmth of the car. It

was all beginning to feel rather real again. Owain was asking her to put her life in his hands. It would only be his glamour stopping this other Clan discovering the truth, and her ensuing certain death.

"Can you do it?" she asked quietly.

"Gabriel thinks I can. And I promised Elaine I would keep you safe, didn't I?"

Gemma nodded and slowly dropped her hands.

She had been expecting something grand, but as Owain pulled a look of concentration she felt almost nothing. There was the lightest of tingling, like a strand of spiderweb touching her skin, and then everything seemed to be over. She smiled kindly. The Apprentice was still learning and charming a human to pass as a faerie couldn't be the easiest of tasks.

"Don't worry about it Owain, I'm sure Gabriel will do it."

"Do what?"

"The glamour stuff."

Owain looked confused, but then his face broke into a slow smile. "You didn't feel it? That means I'm getting good!"

Gemma dragged down the sun visor and peered into the small interior mirror. She did look different. Not unrecognisable, but her skin seemed to have a slight pearlescent glow, and her features were very symmetrical and was there, perhaps, a brighter glint to her eyes? It was subtle. She hoped it was enough.

"This is great," she said, "But won't it stand out that I'm plastered with glamour?"

Owain shook his head. "It's normal for fae to alter their appearance. You have seen how Gabriel can shift."

Gemma tried to make her muscles relax. She felt

tense, as if her body was primed to flee even though her mind knew she couldn't. Perhaps it was a good time to bring up the task ahead again. "Alright, well I'm all glammed up now. Can you please tell me what I need to do when I get there?"

"Oh," said Owain, as if it was the smallest detail that he'd forgotten to mention, "you just need to pass as Gabriel's consort for the gathering."

"His consort?"

"Yes. It's a term for two folk who share-"

"Yes alright. You don't have to explain the birds and the bees."

Owain frowned blankly.

"Never mind," said Gemma.

Clara Merryweather was feeling very pleased with herself. She paused to take a quick photo of her crystal layout, which she would post up on her blog later, and spread open the pages of *Practical Spells for Teenage Witches*. It was, it must be said, many years since Clara had been a teenager, but since going part time at work she had rekindled many of the passions of her youth. Witchcraft was one of them. She had read online that witches could be either white, black or grey, and so far she was leaning towards black because wearing black was meant to be slimming. If this were true, then Clara might have passed as the grim reaper. In reality, she looked like a woman wearing lots of layers. But they were all black. Plus, she had accessorised with a scarf covered in silver moons, as many gemstone rings as she could fit on her fingers and a velvet cloak she found in a charity shop. The overall effect was memorable.

She licked her finger and flicked ahead a few pages.

The spell she was trying out tonight was one to discover the initials of a future lover. The crystals were her own addition, but she thought they added to the overall ambience, and the circle of candles had the right feel as well. All she actually needed was a red apple.

She peeled the skin in one continuous piece and threw it over her left shoulder, as instructed. Then she crouched to examine it for answers. Tilting her head to the side it could maybe be an S, or even a swirly C if she looked the other way. It would be easier to see if there wasn't a hoof in the way. The grass began to steam gently. Clara looked up. Into the eyes of a tall, dark stranger.

He was tall because he was on a horse. Concerningly, parts of the horse seemed to be on fire. Beneath its hooves, the grass had curled and blackened and the occasional flame flickered from its nostrils. Clara thumbed through the spell book to see if there was any mention of demons. There wasn't, which she supposed was because that sort of thing was more advanced magic.

"Did I summon you?" she asked the man hesitantly.

"No," replied Cabell. He regarded her with a predatory interest. He had been planning to simply kill her, but the woman was clearly a witch, and witches understood fear. All it took was for one person to start talking, and then hysteria could spread like wildfire. "But I do have a message for you," he added.

"Oh," said Clara, "is it about the name of my future lover?"

"It is not." Cabell glanced behind him, and hounds began to gather at his wordless command. They slunk from the twilight shadows, lean and lithe. Their fur was dappled white, black and tan, but as they moved their thin skin cracked along fault lines to show the magma beneath.

62

Clara stepped back into the centre of her circle. The ring of guttering candles stood between her and the demon huntsman, and she wondered if her earlier cleansing of the area with sage would offer any protection. Cabell paused to pick a fleck of mud from his lapel, and then spurred his horse forward. The sage had no effect.

One candle toppled aside. The front half of the horse was within the circle and the man astride it seemed undeterred by Clara's earlier protective incantations. Admittedly, she may have pronounced some of them wrong.

"I'm a witch, you know!" she warned in her best no nonsense voice. It was the voice she used at work when little Kayden refused to stop eating the crayons.

"I know it, hag," Cabell purred, "and that singular fact is why your flesh remains upon your bones. Now listen."

The fallen candle had bled a pool of wax, and now the grass around it was alight. The flames licked hungrily from candle to candle, turning the flickering circle into a solid ring of fire. Clara listened like she had never listened before.

Gemma took a last look at her altered self in the car wing mirror, and then ran after Owain. He was walking fast across the grass towards a large domed hill.

"Our clothes," she said breathlessly, as she fell in beside him, "you haven't changed them."

"No need. We both travelled in disguise. We can change for the evening once we're inside."

Gemma stopped. Owain halted a pace ahead and turned back to face her. He looked agitated, as if they might be late.

"Remind me of everything. Please," she asked. Her voice was shaking. Above them, the moon climbed into the sky, cold and indifferent. The same stars shone now as back in Dartmoor, but the safety of Mike's cottage seemed more than a world away. Owain's expression softened.

"Tonight is the opening of the gathering. The Meath Clan will be celebrating this visit from the Huntmaster of the Dartmoor Clan. There is great ceremony attached to everything, which would take years for you to learn, so just follow my lead. We are on familiar terms, as you are my master's consort, so you may still address me as Owain. I will address you as Elyn."

Gemma rolled her eyes, the familiar feeling of frustration elbowing the fear aside. That name. Whoever Elyn was, she was the real reason why Gabriel had saved Adrian. It was Elyn that he cared about. She was the fae woman who he had loved, a hundred years ago, and who had promised to return after living one life as a mortal. Except she hadn't. And Gemma wasn't her, however much Gabriel wanted her to be.

Although she needed to be tonight.

Owain strode on, and the structure that dominated the skyline crept closer. It was a huge, circular mound of earth. The sides had been clad in white marble, and the pale stone glowed with the reflected light of the moon. They passed between two standing stones, and Gemma felt the increasingly familiar tingle of glamour washing over her. There was no going back now.

Ahead of them was a narrow entrance. Shadows gathered thick in the doorway to the hollow hill, and a huge oval stone lay in front of it like a guardian. There was also a wooden fence. Owain reached it first, stopping half a pace away with his arm out to halt Gemma as well. He turned and smiled at her reassuringly. She took a deep breath, nodded, and they climbed over the flimsy wooden barrier.

Gemma stood shoulder to shoulder with Owain, gazing down at the large grey boulder. It was covered in carvings. Intricate swirls crept across its surface, entwining and flowing into each other. Access for tourists had been re-routed via two sets of steps, which avoided approaching the guardian stone. Even without Adrian here to point it out, Gemma could immediately understand why. The stone was alive. The more she stared at it, the more complex the pattern of swirls became, until the whole surface was seething and breathing in serpentine lines.

The Apprentice pressed both palms to the stone. He did it reverently; a request rather than a command. There were times to display his growing power to compel the earth and lead the hounds, but this not one of them. The carvings responded to his touch, gathering around his hands like a flock of restless grey birds. Gemma gripped his arm. His muscles were tense, as if braced against an invisible onslaught. But all there was were the shifting carvings and the strange tingle of glamour on the air. At last, Owain dropped his hands. Gemma felt him relax, as if some unspoken test had been passed. Then her mouth dropped open, as the stone sunk slowly into the earth.

The entrance to the tomb loomed ahead of them. Except now the shadows had lifted, and the narrow entrance flickered with light from within. Owain extended a hand to Gemma. She hesitated for a moment, worried that his palms might now be printed with the same living swirls, but they remained pale and unadorned. Shaking the thought from her head, she allowed him to lead her inside. Fian sniffed the air, and then followed.

Beneath their feet, the stone passageway sloped

gently downwards. There were thick candles burning in regularly spaced hollows carved into the walls, and the yellow light felt welcoming rather than eerie. Nevertheless, Gemma stayed close to Owain, trusting her safety to his confident stride as she allowed her eyes to wander. He seemed at ease now, so she needed to appear the same.

Ahead of them, the tunnel opened out abruptly into a circular chamber. Gemma just about had time to take in the sight of a shallow central pool and four diverging tunnels, before Owain pressed a steering palm to her back. She spun round to face a small man dressed in grey. He was waist high to her, meticulously neat and grinning broadly.

"Welcome, welcome," he said, "you must be the houndmarked from Dartmoor."

"Yes," replied Owain, "I am Gabriel's Apprentice."

"Good, very good." The small man bowed elegantly and extended a hand to Gemma. Her eyes darted to Owain in panic, who subtly mimed giving her hand in return. She did so, and the man kissed it. "You are most welcome to Newgrange, our humble abode. I am Amergein, and it is my duty and honour to ensure that you want for nothing. So come, you must be eager to change out of those strange clothes. The hound is welcome also."

They followed their guide down the leftmost of the four corridors. As they delved deeper into the earth, Gemma noticed the stone walls becoming more ornate. At intersections along the way, where other tunnels meandered off into unknown warrens, the ceiling was supported by carved pillars decorated with curling fern fronds and vines. Their pace was fast, and Owain kept Amergein talking about details of the planned festivities this evening, so that Gemma was left alone. After a short while, they stopped outside a grand wooden door set into the wall. Like the pillars, it was intricately carved with fern fronds, and it was lit on either side by braziers cast as ivy clad branches.

"Everything you may need is inside," said Amergein, bowing extravagantly to Gemma.

"Thank you," she said.

"Your room is a little way further, if you will follow me," he told Owain. He had taken a few steps before he noticed the Apprentice hesitating. A gleeful smile spread across his face. "You would woo the Huntmaster's mistress, houndmarked?"

"Of course not!" Owain had turned a shade of red that would put the hordes of Hell to shame.

"Of course not," Amergein chuckled, his black eyes twinkling. He led the mortified Owain on down the corridor.

Gemma pushed open her door. The room inside was large and elaborately decorated with more of the popular fern frond designs. A large four poster bed stood against one wall and a table was laid out with bread and wine. She clutched her metal water bottle and leaned for a moment against the inside of the door. She was here, in some demented fairyland, exactly where fear suggested she might be. But nothing bad had happened. Yet.

All she needed to do was survive tonight and tomorrow, convincing a whole gathering of fae that she was Gabriel's consort. *Elyn*. She rolled her borrowed name around on her tongue. It tasted of a longing that she wasn't sure if she shared or not.

She remembered that she was meant to be getting changed, and cast her eyes about the room for what she needed to put on. *Everything you need is inside*. She opened one side of a large wooden wardrobe and discovered a choice of two floor-length gowns. Hesitantly, she opened the other door of the wardrobe. It contained a black shirt, jacket and pair of trousers, alongside another empty hanger. As she had suspected, the room was not hers alone.

There was a frantic knocking on the door.

"Elyn," hissed a hurried voice. It took her by surprise, even though she had just been thinking about her temporary identity. The voice belonged to Owain.

"Wait a second," she replied, grabbing the green dress that was hanging up. She pulled off her jumper and jeans and bundled them into the bottom of the wardrobe. Then she slid the silky gown over her head and examined the effect in an ornate mirror.

"This does not look good," Owain informed her from outside.

"Well come in then." Gemma moved to view herself from a different angle. The dress was beautiful, and the gossamer thin green cloth fell around her like summer haze. The glamour that lingered lightly on her skin made her lips glossy, and her hair hung long down her back like she had always dreamed of as a little girl.

Owain stopped and stared at her. He was dressed in brown, with delicate embroidery of autumn leaves adorning the shoulders and cuffs of his jacket. His red hair was swept black neatly, gathering in small curls at his neck.

"We scrub up alright, don't we?" Gemma smiled.

Owain nodded.

There was another sharp tap on the door. The Apprentice visibly sagged, his cheeks regaining a pink tinge.

"I will announce you at the gathering now, if you permit me." Amergein's voice rang from outside.

Owain darted nearer, hovering with his hands clasped close to Gemma. "Just so you know, I'm not wooing you," he whispered awkwardly, "I just need to stay near you to maintain the glamour."

She clamped her hand over her mouth to stop herself laughing. If anyone could make going to a faerie ball feel like an outing to the school disco, it was Owain. Gemma felt a rush of warm gratitude for having a kind and familiar face by her side, whatever it was that lay ahead.

"I know that," she replied, patting his arm.

Amergein raised an eyebrow as the two of them spilled out of one room, but he didn't make any further comment. They followed him back to the round chamber with the pool and then turned down another of the tunnels. This one grew gradually wider, and there were no doors or paths leading off from it, although there were regular alcoves in the wall holding squat, white candles. Gemma had to push herself to keep pace with the two men. She had lost all concept of time, but she had a feeling that Amergein was working to a schedule.

The alcoves with candles in were replaced by ornate brackets, decorated in the same swirling fern fronds and vines. Ahead of them were a pair of wooden doors, intricately carved, and flanked on either side by man-high metal birds. The wings were outstretched, cluttered with many more candles and dripping wax like white feathers. At last, Amergein slowed. He turned and took in their appearance for a moment, nodded, as if they would do, and then pushed open the doors.

Gemma tensed her jaw to stop her mouth dropping open. They stepped into an enormous room, lit by a thousand candles and the lustrous glow of gold.

"I give you Owain, houndmarked of the Dartmoor Clan," said Amergein, his voice rich and earthy.

Owain bowed lightly to a smattering of curious

chatter.

"I give you Elyn, consort of Gabriel, Huntmaster of the Dartmoor Clan," Amergein said.

The curious chatter increased, and Gemma dipped a quick bow before glancing at Owain for guidance. He was being led down the steps and up to a table on a raised dais that surveyed the room. She followed, taking the offered seat to his right. Looking around, as casually as she could manage, she counted two long wooden tables on either side, with a clear area directly ahead of her. The tables were full of people. *Not people*, she corrected herself, *faeries*. The kind of creatures that considered human lives of little consequence.

A drumbeat rolled across the room. The chatter died. A sudden breeze stirred the air, swirling as the rhythm swelled, catching the candles so they flickered and spluttered. The golden light grew dull. Flames guttered and failed as the high ceiling grew dark, gathering shadow like the night had bled in from outside. The drumbeat sped up. Gemma saw that it was Amergein who played it, keeping rhythm as he paced slowly down the steps into the centre of the room.

He raised the instrument, the low glow of the surviving candles illuminating the drum skin like a brown moon. Tracing a slow arc above his head, he quickened the beat again, both ends of the beater tapping against the bodhrán in a hypnotic blur. The rhythm became a racing heartbeat, which Gemma could feel in her own chest. It rattled against her ribs, pulsing through her flesh with an ancient beat that her bones remembered.

Then the air grew thick; filled with the frantic fluttering of countless birds, their wings pressing against her eyes and forcing their way between her lips. She tried to brush them off, but the drumbeat held her, helpless against a tide of restless wings. Then, as quickly as they had appeared, the birds were gone. The rhythm began to slow. The air tightened; still and expectant.

A lone cry pierced the silence. Gemma opened her eyes. She didn't recall shutting them, but she saw now that Amergein had moved aside. In the centre of the room stood a swan, great white wings outstretched and beating a challenge to the receding darkness. It hissed, curving the elegant length of its neck to take in all of the room. Then it cried out again; a haunting, undulating note that spoke of icy water and deep memory and an ageless, bottomless yearning.

A hand fell lightly on Gemma's shoulder.

"Welcome," said Gabriel.

6.
MEMORY

Simon Holloway was a wealthy man. He lived on a sprawling farm near the edge of Ashburton and he spent his days trading stocks and shares online. His manicured lawn stretched down to the banks of the river Ashburn, and the stone stables behind the farmhouse had stood empty ever since he moved in. With this fact in mind, the sound of hooves on the cobblestones outside was troubling him.

"Margaret!" he called, without moving.

A woman stopped slicing celery for the green smoothie she was making and leaned into the living room. "What is it? You know I have my online yoga class in a minute," she said.

"There's a horse outside, can you get rid of it?" His eyes remained on the TV screen.

"Do I look like I'm dressed to deal with horses?" she countered petulantly, gesturing to her matching activewear.

"Just do it will you?"

"I'm not going outside dressed like this! Plus, the last time there was a pony outside I tried to shoo it away and it bit me. And the time before that, when the horrible hunt churned up all of the lawn, I thought you told those nasty old toffs exactly where to stick it."

"I did," replied Simon, finally dragging his eyes away from the screen.

"Well get out there and say it again."

Simon rose reluctantly from the sofa. "What is this town coming to?" he muttered under his breath, eyes falling wistfully on the single malt whiskey and Cuban cigar he had lined up for the start of the game. If he went out and dealt with this now, then at least he could be back inside in time for kick-off.

He pulled on the jacket and wellington boots which he kept in the hallway. The noise was louder now, without the drone of the television to drown it out. There was no mistaking it; the distinctive clatter of iron shod hooves on cobblestones. Pulling a torch from the hook on the wall, he threw open the back door. "This is private property!" he bellowed, "I have CCTV and a direct line to the police!"

It was very dark in the courtyard. High up, under the eaves of the stable block, a security light flickered fitfully and went out. Simon raised the torch and peered down the beam of light. "I know you're here." He swept the torch across the front of the abandoned building, sagging half doors framing dusty darkness within. A sharp clang caught his attention and he jerked the torch in the direction of the noise. Illuminated by the beam, a rusty old horseshoe settled clumsily on the ground.

Simon felt his shoulders drop. He relaxed as he traced the torch along the line of old stable doors. An iron horseshoe hung above each one, fixed there by goodness-knows-who, and thick with red rust after years in the weather. The noise had simply been the old nails giving up at last. Lowering the torch, he turned his thoughts back to whiskey and cigars.

Then another horseshoe fell off. He watched it until it lay still on the ground. It was strangely unsettling, all those old nails giving up at the same time.

He shone the beam of the torch onto the final horseshoe. It was hung pointing upwards, so that the luck remained held inside. As he watched, it began to tremble. It rattled against the wood, fighting the nail that held it, swinging from side to side as if in some unseen wind.

Simon's eyes widened. One point of the horseshoe pinged loose and it lurched drunkenly to one side. Behind him, hooves rang out on the cobblestones.

Simon turned slowly, the torch trembling in his hand. From the darkness came a huntsman astride a great grey horse. "I've told you before," said Simon weakly, "this is private land."

Squire Cabell glanced languidly from side to side. "So it is," he remarked.

"What- what do you want?" Simon stuttered.

"What I want, is for you to know how long the centuries stretch out trapped inside a coffin. I want you to know how it feels to have insects eat your flesh, while your skin slips slowly from your bones and pools as putrid liquid around you. I want you to know how it feels to have your soul denied either Heaven or Hell, while the village folk build a stone prison around your grave."

Cabell smiled savagely. Simon backed away, the torchlight dancing a frightened jig.

"But, in reality, all of that would take too long," the huntsman added. Behind Simon, the final horseshoe fell to the ground with a metallic clang. "So I will settle for just watching you die."

Hounds slunk from the shadows, pouring from the tumbledown stables and padding across the courtyard. Their claws clicked sharply against the cobbles, and amidst them the horse pawed restlessly at the ground. A spark flew from its hoof, searing a quick line through the night. Cabell flicked his whip, urging the hounds towards their prey.

"Have at it," he commanded, putting spurs to his horse. It started forward, steam pouring from flared nostrils and wildfire dancing in its eyes. The hounds wailed and hollered, their black and tan skin breaking open along lines of licking flame.

Simon screamed, his back pressed against the stable wall. One hand trembled towards the phone in his trouser pocket, but the first hound knocked it out of his hand. The world went dark. Around him, the hounds snapped and bickered as they squabbled over shares of the meat. Cabell watched until the scraps of clothing and bone weren't recognisable any more, and then he turned his horse lazily away. One hoof struck up another spark. It fell on an old hay bale which had been left in the stable.

The huntsman rode off. One by one, his hounds joined him, licking the last taste of blood from their teeth. Behind them, the sky blazed with red light, flickering fitfully between black and yellow.

Gemma glanced up at Gabriel. He was wearing grey and gold. It suited him, with the lustrous light of the room lending his pale hair a metallic shine. She managed a mute nod of thanks, and then turned back to the scene in front of her. The swan was almost gone. She caught the last few seconds of the transformation, as the bird stretched and spilled a ruffle of feathers, which settled as the shoulder adornment of a long white cloak. It was a woman, now, who wore it. But Gemma could still see the swan in her proud, defiant stance and the darting movement of her amber eyes.

The swan woman surveyed the silent room.

"This is sacred time," she said, her voice strong and melodic, "this is sacred space." Her amber eyes flowed from face to face, wordlessly acknowledging their presence.

Gemma wondered if the gaze lingered slightly

longer on her, or if she had just imagined it. She could feel Gabriel sat a few inches away, his glamour laying soft against hers. On the table, tall candles glowed gently as all the world seemed to wait. All at once, it became apparent what for. The grand wooden doors were once more heaved aside. The swan woman dipped her head gracefully, and everyone in the room arched their necks towards the newcomers.

The couple in the doorway required no introduction. They were tall and lithe, their bodies clad in resplendent brocaded fabrics. The man wore only gold; from the fall of his glistening cloak to the clasps of his leather boots. Beside him, the woman was dressed in deep green, verdant as water meadows and vibrant as the sun on spring leaves. Both of them bore ornate crowns.

Amergein bowed low and led them to their seats on the top table. The Queen was next to Gabriel, and it was all Gemma could do not to stare. Long red hair fell in loose waves to the faerie woman's waist, and the jewels in her crown were eclipsed by the gleam of her eyes. Gabriel caught Gemma's gaze, and an amused grin played across the corners of his lips. She quickly looked away.

"Tonight we gather in fellowship with our brothers of the Dartmoor Clan," the King announced. His voice carried effortlessly to every corner of the room. "In these waning years, we are less than we were. But we are still here. We are still the first born of the earth; blood as the water, bones as the stone." He glanced at the Queen, who smiled radiantly, and reached her pale arms out towards everyone assembled.

"Make merry tonight. Cast aside your cares for tomorrow. Let our visitors want for nothing, and leave telling tales of our hospitality." She gifted Gabriel a welcoming nod, and Gemma was surprised by a sharp twang of jealousy.

A swell of chatter rose in response, and gentle music began in the background. Amergein appeared again in front of the table, bowing extravagantly, bodhrán back in his hand. Then he departed in the direction of the other musicians, and the swan woman took his place. She flowed into an elegant acknowledgement of her Queen. Her white hair was shorn short and her dress beneath the feathered cloak was striking but simple.

"The omens are strong," she said softly, "a shift is on the wind and in the water. Friendship is our ally now, more than it ever was."

Owain dipped his head in respect, and the swan wytch looked at him with grey eyes still flecked with amber. "For you, Apprentice, most of all." Then she was gone, flowing away on silent, graceful feet. Owain watched her go, his face set in a frown of concern.

"What do you think that means?" he whispered to Gemma.

She shrugged back at him. "No idea. What is it with talking in riddles all the time?" She said it very quietly, but immediately worried it wasn't in keeping with her character. Then she noticed Amergein on the other side of the room, his eyes taking in everything while he drummed, and she shuffled her chair a little further from Owain. This had the effect of moving her closer to Gabriel, who turned round in response to the noise. His eyes widened slightly, as he wondered what had brought on her sudden desire to be closer.

"You look wonderful," he said, taking in the fitted fall of her dress.

"Thank you." She spoke slowly, mentally scanning

her words for anything that might give her humanity away. "Did you choose it?"

"I described something that I liked, and Amergein picked out the garment." Gabriel leaned closer, his voice silky and sweet. "I described a spring day, on the threshold of summer, when the late morning light catches the young leaves of the silver birch. I thought that would look good on you."

Gemma felt her blush spreading, even through the glamour. She was rescued by waiters arriving with food. They presented a platter to the King and Queen first, before serving their guests, and then the other folk seated at the high table. On the other side of the Queen, the King was flanked by a dark haired man and his younger companion. Gemma used the excuse of the food arriving to glance down the table and get a better look. She guessed that the older man was this Clan's Huntmaster, and the silver scars just visible on his hands backed up her assumption. The young man, who sat with one elbow on the table, was probably his Apprentice.

A blonde woman, dressed in the trademark green and gold, offered Gemma a drink from a glass jug. Instinctively, Gemma raised a hand to refuse, but immediately felt Owain nudge her foot under the table. Her shoulders sagging slightly, she accepted a cup of the pale liquid.

The long ferry journey had given her plenty of time for online research, and the top tip for avoiding eternal entrapment in the faerie realm was to avoid all food and drink. But Owain was right, she could hardly sit at this grand feast and not touch a thing. She raised the cup to her lips and sniffed it. It smelt sweet and floral, in a way she recognised.

"Elderflower wine," Owain told her, sipping from his own cup.

Gemma nodded. She knew the scent from the hedgerow, when she had gone out on long walks with Adrian. They were the kind of outings that involved Adrian insisting that he absolutely knew where they were going, and then admitting they were lost an hour later. Sometimes there had also been haunted ruins, or almost unnoticeable bumps in the ground with a small plaque explaining what they were. Adrian would have given anything to be here, beneath a faerie hill. It felt wrong, somehow, that it was her rather than him. Adrian would have called this an adventure, but Gemma was mostly finding it awkward.

"Try it," Owain suggested.

Gemma obliged with a small sip. As a rule, she didn't drink. Occasionally she might have something, but generally there was no appeal to it. Although, this wine was delicious. She took another mouthful, and then tried tasting something wrapped in leaves on the platter. It was equally enjoyable.

"Tell me," she heard the Queen saying to Gabriel, "do you have much trouble with secrecy in Dartmoor?"

"Our home is well guarded, if not as grand as yours," Gabriel replied.

"We do well enough," she agreed, "but we are always troubled with the risk of discovery. Our Huntmaster is often dealing with foolish mortals."

"Our remoteness has that advantage. Walkers who stray too close are easily turned away."

The Queen raised her perfect auburn eyebrows in surprise. "You let them live?"

Gemma paused with her fourth leaf-wrapped-something halfway to her mouth. The Queen noticed.

"Is something not to your taste?" she asked.

Gemma froze. Thoughts raced through her mind at a frantic pace, and not one of them was a helpful explanation for her discomfort. Gabriel laid a hand on top of hers.

"The travesty is mine," he apologised, "I have allowed you to run out of wine." He stood and gestured to one of the servers, who came over with the ornate jug they were carrying. Gabriel took it, attentively refilling Gemma's glass. "Forgive my lack of attention tonight, I have a number of matters on my mind. I trust that you will find the company and entertainment diverting enough to satisfy you."

"Yes. Thank you," Gemma managed to say, with barely a stammer. Gabriel had just given her the perfect excuse for keeping her distance. But his elegant movement, and the glint in his eyes as he poured out the liquid, suggested she may prefer not to.

Around them, the candles burnt a little lower in their holders, and the servers began to hand round platters of sweet cakes and crystallised fruits. Gemma tasted each one, and every mouthful was more delicious than the last. The elderflower wine seemed to be unending, and Owain chattered happily beside her, laughing as he recounted escapades of his out on the moor.

"-of course, the feral stood no chance against me," he explained emphatically, glancing at Gemma to check she was impressed.

Then there was a sudden hush. Gemma followed the gaze of Gabriel, and everyone else, to the centre of the room. Amergein had left his accompanying musicians behind, and he was walking slowly towards the high table with a gold harp in his hand. He bowed very low, and then began to play.

The music was alive. That was the only way that Gemma could have described it, and she listened with tears lacing the corner of her eyes. Although Amergein sung in another language, ancient and melodic, she could still see what he described unfurl as images in her mind.

She saw the earth when it was young; wild and benevolent, and she watched the fae wander it freely without needing to hide. Then came the grey smoke of battle, and the flickering flames of fire on the hills. The newcomers were hostile; they had weapons of iron and a will to conquer all that lay before them. The surviving fae were forced underground; seeking the shelter of barrow mounds and cairns, and gathering gold to remind them of the sun.

When the last verse ended, there was a feeling of loss that lingered like the last vestiges of a dream. Some folk on the long tables were crying softly, but others gripped their glasses with a barely contained rage.

"We should take back the land, in honour of our fathers!" cried one.

"This island was ours. Why are we too scared to defend it?"

"I would spill my blood gladly, if it rid us of this human plague," another added, swilling red wine as he gestured.

The King rose slowly to his feet. There was a weariness to the otherwise graceful movement as he surveyed his subjects seated before him. The brocaded jacket that he wore was intricately embroidered with gold thread, depicting the familiar swirls and vines. Gemma noticed he wore a belt, and on it was the empty scabbard of a sword.

"If, like me, you do not mistake our quietness for cowardice," the King began, "and if, like me, you do not mistake our secrecy for surrender, then you will understand why it is that we remain here. Yes, the world was ours once, but we remain now as relics of a brighter time. It is our duty to abide, and remember, until the day comes when we can walk in the sunlight again."

There was a smatter of grumbling, which was quickly silenced when the Huntmaster stood up in support of his King. The leader of the Meath Clan's Wild Hunt was tall and muscular, with a few days of stubble and dark, darting eyes. No one in the room seemed inclined to question him.

The Queen clapped her hands and music started up again. This time it was fast paced and cheerful, with the sound of whistles and drums begging tapping feet to dance. A young woman approached the high table and asked Owain to join her. He stiffened with nerves, but Gemma pushed him forward, and soon she could see him enthusiastically attempting to learn from his giggling partner.

Gabriel leaned close, amused eyes following his young Apprentice. "I want to show you something," he said to Gemma. She looked round and he turned towards her, suddenly very close. His gaze noted her fear, and dared her to give in.

"Last time you said that, I watched your dog die," she said. The air between them was electric, warm like the wicks of the dripping candles.

"And be reborn," he countered. "You came to no harm."

Gemma could have questioned Gabriel's definition of no harm. She could have said that, right now, the only thing keeping her from serious harm was a light dusting of magic. She could have put forward the theory that Adrian might not have a loose soul currently if they had never crossed paths with Gabriel on the moor. But all these thoughts were flowing away from her, dissolving in the elderflower wine and floating off with the music.

"Alright," she agreed.

Gabriel took her hand. He rose and whispered something to the Queen, who smiled indulgently in Gemma's direction. Then they were leaving the top table behind, weaving though the dancers, and heading towards the door. It shut smoothly behind them, dulling the chatter and music to a low drone. The candles in the swan sculptures burnt bright and yellow, long flames licking at the dripping wax.

Corridors snaked past as Gabriel guided her deeper into the labyrinth. Arriving at the circular chamber, he chose another of the tunnels. It was lit more sporadically than the two leading to the guest chambers and the feasting hall, suggesting it was less often used. It seemed there had once been passages branching off of it, although these were now blocked with large stones. Gemma's hand remained wrapped in Gabriel's. Occasionally he would glance back and smile, his eyes glinting in the low light. He moved like a predator; silent and lithe, sure of himself in this strange world beneath the earth.

The tunnel ended abruptly. But what seemed like a dead end dissolved into tendrils of ivy as Gabriel pushed them aside.

Outside lay a hollow. Sheer rock reared up on two sides, old fault lines spilling out moss and the arrow shaped leaves of lords and ladies. At the far side was a pool. It reflected the light of the moon, glistening like mercury and glinting like the distant stars.

"This place is Tobar na Gcuimhní, and the well holds the Waters of Memory," Gabriel said. He strode on, while Gemma hesitated outside the tunnel.

The air was cool and fresh, scented with the deep musk of decaying wood and night blooming flowers. Gemma touched a fern frond to check it was real. The shiny leaf felt wet and waxy in her fingers. Then she reached for the holed stone hung beneath her dress. Squinting through it, the hollow looked no different. But Gabriel was transformed.

He had taken off his boots and shirt to step into the pool. Waist deep in water, he basked in the night like some heathen god, black eyes and bone pale skin revealed through the magic of the hag stone.

"Come to me," he said.

Gemma dropped the stone.

He raised his hands, cupping the cool water and letting it drip slowly back into the pool.

"Once you taste this water, you will remember everything. It has the power to recall the past, and return lost fragments of memory," he said.

Gemma took off her borrowed shoes and crouched by the edge of the pool. She dipped her fingers into the silver water.

"But you must drink from the source," Gabriel added. He gestured towards a smooth stone in the centre of the pool, just breaking the surface of the water. Fresh water bubbled endlessly out of it.

Gemma measured the distance between her and the stone in her mind, and watched as a wicked smile spread across Gabriel's lips.

"Do not ruin the dress," he told her.

She took a deep, steadying breath, and pulled the dress off over her head. The night air was cold on her skin, but the water was even colder, raising gooseflesh as soon as her toes touched the surface. Three steps led down into the pool, and she shivered with each one, the shock of the water jolting up through her body. When she reached the centre, Gabriel guided her hands. She felt his body behind her, skin against skin, and the slow strength of his hands beneath hers as she raised the water to her lips. It tasted metallic; like minerals and the earth.

Once she had drunk, Gabriel gently turned her to face him. His expression was searching, blue eyes boring into hers as he searched for the first signs of memory returning. He trailed two fingers in the water, traced them across his lips, and then gave Gemma the same blessing.

His first kiss was soft; a request for permission. Gemma gave it to him. Her fingers found the smooth arc of his spine, tracing the patterns of old scars up to his shoulders. The weight of his body fell against her, his lips turning ravenous, as if all he could taste would not be enough.

Death had never set foot in this hollow. There was no blood and no monsters, no hellhounds or horses, and all the hounds of the Wild Hunt lay asleep in the earth. There was only Gabriel, and the moonlight and that memorable scent of wood smoke and honey. Gemma caught one hand in his hair. The other rode the curve of his hip. His hands worked to remember the wants of her body, fingertips trembling with the depth of his hunger.

A polite cough ended their solitude. Gabriel tensed, his teeth bared like a wild beast robbed of its kill.

"The King will speak with you," said Amergein, "It

concerns the matter of your sister."

7.
FIRE

"Have you seen this?" Adrian waved his phone in the air, almost knocking over his cold cup of tea. Mike looked up from his laptop.

"What is it?" he asked.

"Hellhounds on the prowl," Adrian quoted, scrolling down through the article on his phone. "Local witch, Clara Merryweather, has told reporters about her recent encounter with what she is calling the Wild Hunt. She spoke with a man on horseback, surrounded by black and tan hounds, after her wiccan ritual was interrupted out on the moor."

"Sounds like the human hunt to me," replied Mike.

"Wait, there's more:

'the hounds looked similar to foxhounds, except for that fact that their eyes were on fire. The horse was demonic as well, with nostrils pouring out smoke and hooves that left burn marks on the ground.'"

Mike put his laptop to one side. "Does she describe the rider?"

"I think she does. Hang on." Adrian skimmed through the text. "Here we are. She says he was wearing a red coat and black boots. His eyes were a strange amber and his hair was brown."

"Not our blonde friend then?"

Adrian scowled. "Gabriel is somewhere with Gemma and Owain. They were talking about tickets, so I guess they're not near Buckfastleigh."

"Then what the hell is out on the moor?"

"That question has been troubling me for some time." Elaine leaned on the doorframe, one hand massaging her forehead.

Mike stood up and put the kettle on. "Bad night?" he asked.

Elaine paced towards the table. She knew the house well enough to move freely now, but her body was agitated. She gripped the back of one of the wooden chairs, as if for support. "There is something not right," she said.

"You're not wrong," Mike agreed.

Adrian read out the entire article. Mike made everyone a fresh cup of tea. Elaine steepled her fingers and tapped them against each other as she listened.

"I don't think it's the Wild Hunt," she said.

"Are you sure?" Adrian asked.

"The description is off. The hounds are described as aflame from within, and the horse is pouring out smoke. When I warned Gemma that Gabriel was a demon, I think it might have been this that I was sensing. I'm not saying that he's good news, but this thing is far worse, whatever it is."

"Should a witch know the difference?" Adrian asked.

Elaine shrugged. "Probably. But even the folklore round here gets confused. If you listen to some of the stories then the master of the Wild Hunt is the Devil.

"That's it," said Mike, pausing with his mug halfway to his mouth, "there's a story. There's a story about all this!" He abandoned his tea and ran upstairs. There was the sound of drawers being hastily emptied, the odd muffled swearword, and then he bounded back down brandishing his prize.

Licking his fingers, he thumbed through the well-worn pages of a thin book. "There you are," he said at last. Adrian leaned over the flattened page and Mike read the relevant passage out loud for Elaine.

'*To this day, locals believe that the body of Richard Cabell does not lie at rest. During the Second World War, when iron was being collected for the war effort, the bars of his impressive tomb were left firmly in place. It is said that running around his grave seven times at midnight will summon Squire Cabell and his demonic hounds, whose fiery shadows will appear on the church wall opposite.*'

"So he's a ghost?" Adrian asked.

"Not quite," said Elaine, "a person can be cursed to return from the grave in some altered form."

"It says here that he was a monstrously evil man. His greatest passion was for hunting, which he would partake in even on a Sunday," Mike added.

"Quiet time for the Devil, if that was enough to get cursed," Adrian said.

"He murdered his wife as well," said Mike.

"That'll do it."

Elaine finally sat down, leaning both elbows on the table. She felt heavy, as if her limbs were weighted with lead. "My dreams have been filled with fire. There is worse to come of this. I just wish I knew exactly what." She raked a hand through her long hair in frustration, turning up the streaks of grey that ran through the brown. "Where is Cabell buried?" she asked Mike.

"Holy Trinity, Buckfastleigh," he replied.

"That's near where the witch was! She said she was just outside Buckfastleigh!" Adrian exclaimed. He stood up with so much enthusiasm that his chair was left rocking behind him. Elaine folded her arms. Mike looked up at him levelly. "What's that look for?" Adrian asked.

"I seem to recall a promise," said Elaine.

"No strange spiritual missions or late-night adventures," added Mike.

Adrian's shoulders dropped. He straightened his chair and meticulously lined it up with the table. "It's definitely the morning," he said half hopefully.

Elaine reached over the table and Mike took her hand. Her lips were pressed together and her forehead was creased with worry. For a moment she seemed frail and, for the first time, Adrian wondered about her actual age.

"You're expecting me to advise against this, and perhaps that's what I ought to do. But this thing frightens me. The less we know about it, the less prepared we'll be when we cross paths with it. And we will. We will cross paths with it," she said.

"We can be back by the afternoon," said Mike.

Elaine nodded, releasing his hand. "I'm going to set up my easel, if you don't mind. I need time to think."

"Of course, I'll get it now," Mike said.

"So, we're going to Buckfastleigh?" asked Adrian incredulously.

Elaine smiled a little. "You're going to Buckfastleigh," she said.

The clouds hung low and grey over the churchyard. There was a small layby, just large enough for two cars, and Mike's Land Rover took up most of it. The threat of rain in the air had kept most people indoors, and the only noises near the church ruins were grumbling wind and muted birdsong.

There had been activity here recently though. Adrian pushed open the gate and headed for the tomb cordoned off with plastic stakes. Tattered police tape fluttered in the breeze, and half the temporary fencing was scattered over the ground. The sepulchre itself was open.

Mike caught up, stopping Adrian with a hand on the shoulder. "This is it. This is Squire Cabell's tomb," Mike said.

"Or it was," Adrian replied. He pulled away, peering into the damaged structure. The wooden door had been ripped open and a strange network of branches and roots were tangled around it.

"For three hundred years that door stood between Cabell and the superstitious townsfolk," said Mike.

Adrian stepped over the fallen barrier and dropped to a crouch. "Whatever opened it forced the lock straight out of the wood." He passed Mike the discarded mechanism. "What can do that?"

"Something we don't want to meet," said Mike darkly.

"Worse than Gabriel?" Adrian asked, ducking into the gloom of the sepulchre.

"Yes. Worse." Mike followed Adrian, his mouth falling open at the destruction inside.

The grave itself had been torn apart. The heavy stone lid lay discarded to one side, cracked down the middle. There was no sign of a coffin, although a shape in the earth spoke of where it had been. Dry leaves piled against the walls, blown in over the years, and the air held the putrid scent of old flesh disturbed.

"They've taken the body then," observed Adrian.

"Who?"

"The police, I suppose."

"I rather doubt that," Mike replied. He pulled a handkerchief from his pocket and held it over his mouth.

"You mean, the body that was here is really running rampage on the moor?" Adrian struggled to hide his fascination.

"You listen to me," said Mike, "this is no scary story for the fireside. This is no tale to tell in the pub over drinks. The Dark Huntsman has rules. The Beast is wary of humans. This thing, if it's half what we fear, has nothing to stop it."

Adrian scuffed at the dirt with his shoe. There were moments when he was so paralysed by the horror of what had happened to him that he lay awake and just breathed. It was all he could do; count one breath, move onto the next, and push down the memories of the woman who had died in the dark by his side. He would forget to exhale, feel his heart thudding through his ribs, then cough out the air far too fast. His lungs ached from the effort, but he would shudder and imagine them empty.

"I do understand," he said to Mike. He wondered if he should prefer all the scary stories when they stayed as just stories. But part of him didn't.

"I know you do." Mike's tone softened. He looked out at the ruined church through the iron bars. "It looks like they're treating this as a simple case of vandalism."

The wind was strong enough now to sway the limbs of the trees in the churchyard. A few leaves worked loose and whipped across the moss covered path.

"Can you hear that?" asked Adrian.

Mike strained his ears. Then he caught something, just audible over the whistling wind. "Get out!" he said. He half dragged Adrian out of the sepulchre, darting towards the yew hedge at the edge of the graveyard.

"What are you-" Adrian managed, before Mike

clamped a hand over his mouth. The branches were sharp, but they parted just enough for Mike to force himself into the heart of the hedge and pull Adrian with him. Next to the thicker trunks was a small gap where the leaves had died off from lack of light. Both of them gulped in shallow, sap scented breaths.

The noise outside grew louder. It was clearly recognisable now; iron shod horseshoes on the tarmac road. Adrian peered through the dense, evergreen leaves. A grey horse cleared the stone wall of the churchyard, countless black and tan hounds pouring over behind it. The man astride the horse wore a red jacket and an expression of disdain. He pulled the creature round at a canter and approached the damaged sepulchre, one hand trailing a bone handled hunting whip.

"There will be meat enough later," he said to the hounds. They gathered close, eager eyes glinting with a fiery malice. Adrian felt his stomach turn. Their eyes were actually on fire. It was just how the witch had described.

Mike had a hand on Adrian's shoulder. His grip was firm, and although the older man didn't make a sound, Adrian understood the message loud and clear. *Make a noise and both of us will die*. He pressed one hand across his own mouth and willed his drumming heart to slow.

The strange hounds formed a ring round the sepulchre. They paced impatiently, circling and snapping at each other as they awaited word from their master.

"Do not fear," he told them, "we have not returned here to rest. We have rested enough, these last three hundred and thirty three years."

One hound turned on its companion, vicious teeth bared, rancid saliva dripping from its tongue. The other creature countered, viper fast, and bit off a chunk of flesh in retaliation. No blood spilled from the wound. Instead, the ragged edges of flesh turned up, greying and crumpling like ash. Where there should have been flesh there was oozing magma. It crusted over in the chilly air, turning black as coal.

"They thought they could cage us with iron and stone," Cabell continued, "they thought they could bind us in dark dreams of earth. But deeper than memory lies longing, and that heat does not fade." His horse pranced on the spot, wild eyes rolling and spitting out steam. The hounds crouched and snarled, their hackles raised in unrelenting hatred.

Cabell dismounted and walked towards the sepulchre. His pale breeches were flecked with soil and dried blood. A smile spread slowly, like smouldering peat, across his face. "They were wrong."

He reached out for the iron bars and gripped them in both hands. His face tensed with concentration and the hounds whimpered and whined. "Where there is smoke," he said through gritted teeth, "there is undoubtedly fire." Beneath his fingers, the metal grew red hot. It glowed like a furnace, paling to almost white, and then eventually gave in. The bars dripped, as liquid iron, down the wall.

The metal hissed and spluttered where it touched the grass. The earth was damp, and had once been consecrated. But Cabell stepped back, raised his hands, and unleashed three hundred years of fury. Liquid iron dripped from his palms. Where it fell, the grass caught light, hungry flames licking upwards with unholy hunger. The ground around the sepulchre was aflame. The old leaves inside caught immediately, crackling as the flames consumed them.

Adrian had always believed that stone was not

flammable. But, in front of his eyes, the sepulchre was burning. Cabell watched it for a short while. Then he turned heel, as if suddenly bored. He climbed nimbly back onto the horse, and gathered round his rabid hounds. With a flick of the whip, they were racing away, leaping the churchyard wall and gathering pace down the lane.

Mike loosened his grip on Adrian's shoulder.

"He really likes fire," Adrian said. Then Mike was pushing him out of the hedge, and the burning tomb loomed even closer. "Should we do something?"

Mike stood beside him, surveying the damage. "What could we do?"

Adrian shrugged. He didn't have any ideas and felt suddenly unsteady on his feet. Nausea washed over him, his eyes sliding in and out of focus.

Mike shook him hard. "Don't go now! Not here!" he cried. There was a note of panic in his voice.

Adrian tried to listen. But the world was overlaid with black. Everything was shadowy and slow. Only the fire remained; a flaming beacon in the landscape of darkness. He wanted to reassure Mike that everything was alright; that this was where he belonged. But his mouth wouldn't form the words.

"Not here!" Mike repeated, his tone verging on frantic, "not after all that!"

Cabell was a demon of this world and the other. He dragged with him the darkness of the Divide, which the souls in this churchyard might refer to as Purgatory. He could cross into that no-mans-land, but was blocked from travelling any further. But Adrian could continue; all the way to the Otherworld.

"Gemma needs you! I need you!" Mike yelled. He looked deranged, standing in a graveyard with a limp body leaning against him, while the grass around them burned.

Adrian was watching the fire. Mike's voice was a distant distraction, like a wasp on a summers day. He half raised his hand, trying to bat the noise away. The shadows around him were comforting, although he felt a growing unease about the fire. It wasn't meant to be there. Slowly, as if moving through water, he walked nearer to the blaze. On closer inspection, the flames looked strangely like hounds, each of them writhing and snapping as they sought to devour one another. But, however they tried, they couldn't catch hold of their companions. Adrian felt their frustration. He stretched his fingers towards them.

Mike had his heels dug into the soft earth, pulling Adrian back with all his might. But all the strength he could muster was not enough. Adrian's face was set in a serene rictus, his hand inches from touching the fire. "Stop! For God's sake!" Mike cried.

The churchyard was filled with the sound of screaming. It sounded like lots of voices at once, but slowly they mingled until Mike realised that it was only him. Adrian was slumped in his arms, blinking as if he'd just woken up, and cradling one blackened hand. In the ruined church, the ancient bell was tolling. It rang on and on, devoid of any melody, sounding an eerie klaxon over the neglected churchyard. Mike shivered as the sound rolled raucously across the steaming earth.

"My hand hurts," said Adrian.

Mike glanced around for something to cool the burn. Dragging a stumbling Adrian beside him, he raced for the ruins, sighing with gratitude as he saw the stone altar base still in place. It had been worn down by the elements, and was half full with reflective rainwater. Mike plunged Adrian's hand into the pool. The water seemed to steam, although surely skin couldn't be close to that hot. Adrian writhed in his grip, but Mike held him, knowing deeply that the wound must be cooled.

Eventually, Adrian ceased to struggle. His head rested on Mike's shoulder and the water stilled, returning to mirroring the grey skies above.

"What happened?" Adrian asked. His voice was weak, but normal.

"I'm not sure," Mike replied.

The Land Rover struggled to do seventy; but Mike pushed it all the same. They made it back to Princetown in record time, and they found Elaine in the kitchen waiting for them. She stood up. Her hands were shaking.

"You wouldn't believe-" Mike began.

"Trust me, I would," Elaine cut across him.

Mike helped Adrian to a seat and examined his hand. Elaine gently flattened the fingers that were curled into a fist. A black scab, with the texture of coal dust, spread across the tips of two fingers. "Tell me exactly what happened," Elaine said.

Adrian did, as best he could. But his mind was blank when it came to the moments before plunging his hand into the fire.

"I couldn't stop him," Mike explained, "all of my strength made no difference at all. He was, more than himself, somehow. No offence." Mike gave Adrian a half smile of apology.

"None taken. I'm aware that I'm a total weakling."

"But you were so keen to get to the fire that you fought Mike off without difficulty. Why?" Elaine looked at Adrian. He knew that she was blind, but somehow he still felt her looking at him. Or into him.

"I don't know," he said, pressing his brain for some sort of explanation. After Cabell had left everything was a blur. There was only the darkness and the strange presence of the fire. "The fire shouldn't have been there." He floundered for the thought, clutching hopelessly at it as if flowed from his memory. "That's all I've got."

Elaine was perched on the edge of her chair. "What time is it?" she asked Mike.

"Almost two," he replied, immediately remembering his promise to hurry back. "We better go," he added. Elaine already had her bag to hand, and Mike helped her out to his waiting car.

"Please," she said to Adrian, pausing by the front door, "don't move from this room until we get back."

"I promise," he replied. He had absolutely no desire to, and he would have preferred to not be on his own. The front door shut, and immediately he was confronted with just how much he missed Gemma. She might have some kind of rational explanation for all this. Or if not, she'd at least have a hug and a mug of hot coffee. Adrian put the kettle on himself and waited for it to boil. It wasn't the same, but at least it was something.

He presumed that phones weren't allowed on faerie adventures. It was only three days, but this second day was already stretching into eternity. Was Gemma alright, he wondered. Was it a terrible ordeal? Or, was she in Gabriel's arms right now, distracted from all thoughts of her human friends? Adrian's fingers flexed back into a fist.

The town of Ashburton was usually a slow, sleepy place. But today, Eva was watching police cars whizz back and forth outside the coffee shop window. Franz sat opposite her, sipping from a bone china mug as he stared out through the glass.

"What do you think happened?" Eva asked.

"No idea," Franz replied. Then he leaned closer, dropping his voice to a whisper. "But it's nothing to do with us." Eva seemed to relax a little. There was no reason for the police to go snooping around on the moor. Even if they had heard anything, there was nothing to link a little turned up earth at Grimspound to here.

"May I join you?" asked a vaguely familiar voice. Eva stiffened involuntarily, looking up for the speaker. Her eyes widened in recognition. It was Blake, the antique enthusiast who they had met at North Weald airfield. He had arranged the sale of their plane to the mysterious Maximillian Early. His presence still made her uncomfortable.

Franz gestured to a spare seat at the table, and Blake seated himself gratefully.

"What are you doing here?" Eva asked.

"Oh, this and that," Blake replied smoothly, fussing over the placement of his silk neckerchief. "I come here to visit acquaintances sometimes. They run the local antique shops, and they know to keep any items of special interest aside for my inspection." He leaned forward and gave Eva a conspiratorial wink.

"Have you found anything special?" Franz asked Blake.

"Perhaps," he replied, rocking back on his chair. The waitress passed and Blake raised a hand for her attention. "A pot of Earl Grey for me, and my friends-" he left the offer hanging.

"We've had drinks," said Eva.

"Just the Earl Grey then," Blake smiled.

"It's nice to bump into you, but we were actually just about to get going," explained Eva, standing and pulling on her coat. Franz followed suit.

"My apologies on holding you up," replied Blake, "and I hope that our next meeting will allow us more time to talk." His tone was sickly and somehow unsettling. It left no room for the hope that they wouldn't cross paths again.

"Until then," said Franz. Blake was using a pair of small, bird footed tongs to pick up and examine the lumps of white sugar on the table. He chose one he liked and popped it into his mouth.

"Before you go," Blake said, seemingly as an afterthought, "I ought to give you this." he reached into his waistcoat pocket and pulled out a small black business card.

"Thank you," said Eva, almost snatching it in her impatience to leave. She stuffed it into her pocket without looking at it.

"Until our next meeting," said Blake. Eva didn't turn around, but she could imagine the self-satisfied smile sitting smugly across his face. She gulped down the cold autumn air outside. Franz closed the coffee shop door firmly behind them.

"Time to disappear," she said.

8.
THIEF

Gemma woke to the sound of knocking. Whether it was late or early, she couldn't tell in the artificial light. Wrapping the silk sheet around herself, she quickly sat up.

"Come in," she said.

Amergein pushed open the door, a silver tray balanced in one hand. He placed a cup of something hot on the dressing table and then lay down a dish of fresh meat for Fian. The white hound stirred from his spot at the end of the bed, enticed to wakefulness by the scent of food.

"Gabriel sends his deepest apologies that he could not join you last night," Amergein said, "and he instructed me to tell you that he will make up for his neglect tenfold this evening."

Gemma felt the blush spread across her cheeks. At least Amergein might give up on accusing her of flirting with Owain. "Thank you for the message," she said, suddenly remembering that she was meant to be an elegant fae woman, instead of a sleep deprived human.

"Did you sleep well?" Amergein asked.

"Yes," Gemma replied. Half-forgotten dreams rose to the surface of her mind, and the blush deepened as she recalled Gabriel's teasing hands. "I was very comfortable."

Amergein bowed low in gratitude. "If you require anything else, do not hesitate to ask."

"Yes, thank you."

"A light meal will be brought to you just after midday," the small man said. He was dressed all in green today, with a bronze brocade waistcoat. He couldn't have been more friendly, but Gemma felt vulnerable keeping up appearances alone. She had a building urge to check if her glamour held in the mirror.

Another knock on the door came as a welcome distraction, and it opened before she had a chance to call out. Owain almost ran in, slowing when he caught sight of Amergein.

"I won't disturb you two any further." Amergein bowed out, a knowing smirk spreading across his face.

Gemma threw a hand to her forehead as he left. Any positives of being caught in a compromising position with Gabriel had been quickly undone.

"Sorry. Bad timing," said Owain.

"Don't worry about it. Did you enjoy last night?" Gemma had last seen Owain dancing energetically with his new friend in the candlelight.

It was Owain's turn to look a little abashed. "I did," he replied. "I wanted to check on you earlier, to make sure the glamour was intact. But I overslept."

"You can sit," said Gemma. She was leaning against the headboard, legs drawn up against her body. Owain perched on the far end of the four-poster bed. "Gabriel showed me the Well of Memory last night. And that's not a euphemism."

Owain's eyes widened. "I've heard of it," he said, "the water is meant to heal the mind. It allows the recollection of memories that were otherwise lost."

"That's pretty much what Gabriel said."

"And," pressed Owain, "did you remember?"

Gemma looked at the young man opposite her. It was almost unsettling how easily she could forget that he was Huntmaster in training, and that he would one day lead the Wild Hunt himself. Sitting there on the end of the bed, asking her about something that had happened yesterday, he reminded her strongly of Adrian. But with better self-preservation. "No," she said.

Owain dropped his gaze and began to fiddle with the embroidered blanket. "It might take a bit longer," he suggested.

Gemma took a deep breath, glancing around the ornate room as she did so. She didn't belong here. Amergein must sense that something was off. Perhaps they were lucky that he thought she and the Apprentice were up to something; it was keeping his attention from the truth. "Elyn isn't in there," she said.

Owain shook his head, as if it was a silly suggestion. He opened his mouth to disagree, but Gemma cut across him. "Look, do you really think I'm so dense that I've been carrying a whole load of memories of another life round with me, and never even had an inkling they were there?"

Owain examined the pattern on the blanket with redoubled fascination.

"You've seen Mike," Gemma continued, "there's no doubt he has something going on. There are memories shut away in his mind that keep almost coming up, and then he gets that weird expression and forgets what he was talking about. If anyone could do with a dip in the Well of Memory, it's him."

"That might not be wise," said Owain.

Gemma barely heard him. A ridiculous idea was dawning on her. It was so stupid that she felt sure Adrian would approve. And it might work. It just might work. "Do you know what time it is?" she asked Owain.

He shrugged. "Late morning?"

"So I have a bit of time before lunch?"

"Yes, I think so."

"Good. Well, in that case, I think I might sit and shut

my eyes and see if I can remember anything if I really concentrate," Gemma said.

Owain dropped his shoulders, the muscles loosening with relief. "Good idea," he agreed.

"Is my glamour still working?"

Owain narrowed his eyes in concentration for a moment. Gemma felt the, now familiar, light tingling of enchantment across her skin. "Working perfectly," he confirmed.

"Well then," said Gemma, feigning an impressive yawn, "I'll see you after lunch."

"Good. Yes." Owain jumped up, as if the bed had sprouted thorns.

Gemma threw off the covers as soon as the door shut. The green dress was hung over a chair, left where she had thrown it. Nothing else in the room had been disturbed. Gabriel had been out all night, and clearly not returned.

She lifted the thin garment and examined it in the candlelight. A flecking of mud graced the hem, and it was creased from being worn over wet skin, but it was all she had to wear. The wardrobe still contained the grey gown, clearly intended for this evening, and her everyday clothes rolled up in a ball. In the centre of the bundle was the metal flask.

Gemma unwrapped it, thinking longingly about the comfort of her jeans. The metal was smooth and startlingly modern in the sumptuous room. She glanced round for another layer to put on. Her hosts had not, for some reason, thought to add pockets to the delicate green dress. Her eyes fell on a wool cloak, hung next to the door, and she swung it over her shoulders. There was enough grey material to wrap round herself and conceal the tell-tale container. It was an unremarkable outfit, within the faerie hill. She hoped.

Fian looked up from his empty bowl and trotted over. Gemma stroked the soft, smooth fur of his forehead. His curious eyes were upturned, tracking the indecision which flickered across her face. His lean frame had filled out in the time since dragging himself out of the earth in Houndain. There was a little flesh over his ribs now, and muscles moved smoothly beneath supple skin. The white hound was hardly out of the ordinary, given the circumstances, and she felt braver at the thought of company.

"Alright," she said to the dog, scratching gently behind his ears, "you can come."

Fian wagged his tail excitedly, and they slipped out of the guest quarters together.

The tunnel was quiet. Perhaps the inhabitants were still sleeping off last nights celebrations. Gemma wondered if faeries got hangovers, and the thought amused her as she strode along, trying to look like she belonged. Only twice, she caught the eye of a servant hurrying past, but their errand was too pressing to pay her much attention. She was beginning to relax by the time she came to the circular chamber with the pool. It was just how she remembered it, and mercifully deserted. She paused for a moment, looking up at the dark, slick rock of the ceiling. Every so often a drop of water would fall and shatter the stillness of the pool with spreading ripples, like the growth rings of an ancient tree.

It was hypnotic, how the black water stirred and then slowly returned to glassy stillness. Fian nosed at her elbow, and she realised she was kneeling, her face bowed low to the pool. How long had she paused there? She shook her head, attempting to wake her sluggish thoughts.

The dark water reflected the ceiling, mirroring perfectly the wet rock and spreading moss that survived only by candlelight. Gemma was suddenly glad that she hadn't touched it, as if breaking the surface of that black skin was the ultimate profanity. She straightened up, wrapping the cloak tighter about herself. The hard lump of the flask was a timely reminder.

"Thanks Fian," she said, bending to stroke the white hound. She had been too confident. Letting your guard down might be your last mistake in this strange world. She swore to be more vigilant and took the righthand tunnel at a purposeful pace. The air was very still here; not stale exactly, but with a thickness brought on by being rarely disturbed.

Blocked off passageways passed either side of her, and she wondered why these tunnels were no longer used. Fian trotted along at her heel, occasionally darting off to sniff at subtle scents on the rocky walls. The ivy-clad opening appeared suddenly, clinging tight to the shadows until it was startlingly close. The hound raised his nose at the hint of fresh air, and Gemma gently pushed the tendrils aside.

The soft moon had been replaced by pale daylight, filtering slowly through the trees. The first breath of autumn lay on the forest. Green leaves were tinged with creeping brown and sickly yellow. Oak and alder slowed their steady heartbeats, sap sinking from branch down to root. The leaves were left to die.

Gemma shivered in the crisp air, despite the warmth of the cloak. There was a hush to the place that unnerved her. Not a leaf trembled or a branch stirred. The only sound was the endless bubbling of the spring, which spilled up over the smooth rock and into the cold waters of the pool. Her footfalls made no sound on the mossy ground, and even the slight noise of her breath was dulled on the air.

Fian was tense. He paced the edge of the hollow, inspecting the curling fern fronds and sniffing the leaves of lords and ladies with disdain. His red tinged ears pricked at the ghosts of sounds, straining to decipher the strange stillness. It felt wrong; as if the air was a touch too heavy in his lungs.

The well was less than ten paces away, and there was no one there to witness her trespass, but Gemma tiptoed over to the water. A glance behind her confirmed she was alone, though her shoulders still knotted with worry. She pulled the metal flask from beneath her cloak and dipped it into the water in one jerky movement. It seemed to take an eternity to fill. Her fingers felt icy cold where they touched the water, but her brow was dappled with sweat.

Fian barked. It was the sharp sound of warning. Every muscle tightened. She slowly raised the flask and screwed on the lid. Along the back of her neck, the fine hairs were raised, prickling like needles on her skin. Fian barked again, the sound falling away to a guttural growl. Gemma turned her head slowly, concealing the guilty flask in her cloak. She saw the hound first, his ears flattened and the short fur standing straight down the length of his spine. He stood his ground, paws placed firmly in the damp earth, showing his rows of sharp teeth. Beyond him was something else. Something that raised the hackles on a creature that was born from the blood of sacrifice.

Gemma took a deep breath. There was a new scent on the air, overpowering the sweet musk of rotting wood. It tasted of stagnant water and the brown mould that

109

blossomed over half rotten bones. She forced herself to look. Turning her whole body, she stood, one arm clamped against her side with the precious flask. The other reached towards Fian, who stood to her right. There were three skeletons between them and the tunnel.

Moss clung to skulls, giving them a green pallor, and tiny mushrooms sprouted from sodden tatters of cloth. Unsettlingly perfect, gold torques gleamed around the necks of the ghouls.

"I should have known," Gemma hissed through gritted teeth, "everything was far too easy." She wasn't an expert in animated skeletons, and she found herself wishing again for Adrian's expertise. But she had seen the undead raised by the necromancer at Grimspound, which taught her enough to know they weren't friendly.

Fian's movement caught her eye again, and she followed his gaze. One of the stones edging the well was moving next to her. It trembled, shedding a little loose earth, and began to rise up from the ground. A moss filled eye socket revealed that it wasn't a stone after all. Gemma recoiled, leaping a pace closer to Fian. He curled his body protectively in front of her, splitting his growls between the new threat and the previous ones. The emerging skeleton freed an arm bone, tearing upwards through the earth like a pulled root. Fian lunged towards it, snapping at the hand and catching it between his teeth. He shook it sharply, ripping bone from socket, and flung the limp fragment towards the edge of the hollow.

Gemma watched the other three skeletons. They had been still, but Fian's attack spurred them on. They stalked towards her, strangely smoothly, rotten garments stirred by some unseen breeze. There were gold cuffs on their wrists, and circular cloak clasps hung from scraps of thin cloth. One wore a glistening crown. Around them, the whole hollow seemed to writhe. From the corners of her eyes Gemma glimpsed slow movement, realising that what she had taken for stones were, for the most part, remains. The well itself was ringed in grisly brickwork.

She braced herself. Fian barked another warning, his teeth having already dealt some damage. *I'm sorry Adrian*, Gemma mouthed to the hollow. But the trees were indifferent, and the earth was uncaring, and the water would flow just as brightly over her bones.

The skeletons were close now. The white hound paced a circle, snapping and snarling. But bony fingers caught hold of his legs, gripping like the teeth of a trap, threatening to drag him back down to the womb of the earth. Gemma felt the same grip on her ankles. Her blood ran as cold as the water in the well. If this was the end, then she told herself she would try to be brave. But a scream gathered in her throat all the same.

A piercing cry rung through the air, rattling the bones like an icy gust. It rose and fell, haunting and hypnotic, sorrowful as the keening of a mother. Then there was silence. The bones were still. Gemma watched a figure weave through the hollow; light on her feet and moving without fear. Her white hair was cut short on her head and the dress she wore was plain linen. But her bearing was more noble than the faerie Queen. Gemma recognised the swan woman.

The wytch drew close to a moss speckled skeleton, laying a hand on its back. The touch was light; almost loving, and the soft smile on her face showed a reverence that seemed out of place.

"Wights," she said, withdrawing her touch. The skeleton sank serenely back into the earth. The seething soil lay still. One by one, she lay the roused remains back to rest. "They are the guardians of this place. The water seeps up, filtering through layers of bones, dreaming in the dark of the ancestors. This is how it gains its power."

Gemma realised that her mouth was open, and closed it. Fian had sat down; she could feel his warm body against her leg.

"What were they protecting the water from?" the wytch asked Gemma. She felt her hand moving, and before she had thought of an excuse, the flask was already held out in front of her. The swan woman raised an eye at the modern container.

"Why would you take it?" the wytch asked.

It didn't even occur to Gemma to lie. She told the woman about Mike, and the black tattoos of keys that jostled for space on his body. She recounted the times that he would half speak a story, and then stop, as if something in his mind had failed. She described the longing in his eyes, which was then replaced by an unsettling blankness.

"And this man is mortal, like you?" the woman asked. Gemma felt her hands begin to tremble. The flask was suddenly heavy in her grip, and her skin was laced with a cold sweat. She was expecting guards, or the stern Huntmaster and his languid Apprentice. But no one else appeared. A few long moments stretched lazily across the hollow. "Put your fear aside," said the wytch, "I knew your nature from the moment you set foot in the hall."

Gemma wanted to ask if the glamour had failed, or if the King knew, but what she said was, "Yes."

The wytch nodded. "Very well. But tell no one; your life depends on it."

"I'm getting used to that." Gemma had said it before thinking to censor herself.

The swan woman laughed; the sound as sweet and clear as a flowing brook. "I dare say you are." Her tone was knowing, and the smile on her face was warm and genuine. Despite all her instincts, Gemma couldn't help but to feel at ease.

They fell into pace together, Fian trotting behind them. The wytch led Gemma back along the deserted corridor with the sealed off tunnels on either side.

"These are burial chambers," she explained. "In the winter, the water flows high here, and it washes over the bones on its way down to the river. The river Boyne itself is sacred, and deadly, in equal measure."

Gemma walked in a daze. She had seen this woman transform from a swan to greet the gathered faerie Court. Why was she not raising the alarm, if she knew a mortal was among them? They paused by the circular pool, and the wytch took a glass bottle from a pouch on her belt. She dipped it into the dark water, disturbing the smooth surface as little as possible, before quickly corking the container.

They arrived back at the wooden door of Gemma's quarters. The candles outside burnt low in their ornate metal holders. The wytch turned, and Gemma found herself facing the woman. Her bright eyes were blue, and there were lines on her face that did nothing to detract from her beauty.

"Why?" asked Gemma, wondering how to articulate the complexity of her fears.

"Because this world is filled with division. I have feared your ancestors, and you have feared mine. But, as you saw today, our kin have the same bones beneath differing flesh. Fear is the true enemy. Not each other." She smiled and touched Gemma lightly on the shoulder. "Tonight will be different to last night," she said, "eat well

113

now and rest." Then she was flowing off, moving down the corridor with a swanlike grace. Amergein appeared, as if on cue, with a platter.

His greeting reassured Gemma that no one else saw through her glamour. Amergein followed her through the door and lay her food down on the table.

"You were speaking with Segain?" he asked, eyes narrowed with curiosity.

"Yes," said Gemma, linking this new name to the swan woman. "She was telling me about tonight."

"Well, what did she tell you?" Amergein asked.

"That I should eat well now." Gemma reached for the plate.

A half smile curled up Amergein's lip. "Sage advice," he agreed.

Gabriel stood overlooking the Boyne. It ran fast and full, pressing high against the wide arc of its banks. Behind him stretched the wider complex of Brú na Bóinne, with Newgrange on the highest ridge, rising from the emerald grass of the valley. The raised earth beneath him was known as Dagda's Mound, named for the lover of Boann, who gave her life to the river.

Afternoon sunlight caught the smooth surface of the water and fractured into a fine dusting of gold. Beneath the swell, the current ran cold and deep, caressing smooth stones and forgotten treasures.

Gabriel watched the water without seeing. His thoughts were back with Asterra, in her small sparse chamber, with blood beneath her nails. Fen paced restlessly, missing the company of the rest of her pack. He comforted her half-heartedly. He felt her distress, thrumming through his veins like a lacing of poison. But his attention was elsewhere.

His sister had been distant with him for years. She had attempted to kill him by raising his own hounds. But was it his failure for abandoning her when she needed a brother? Was it his crime that had left her condemned?

He clenched his fists, turning his face to the greying sky. Asterra's fierce eyes haunted him, deep as the river, and preparing to drown.

9.
LEGACY

Dusk crept over Princetown. It came earlier each day, touching the leaves and making them shiver. In the narrow lanes the briars turned brown, bearing thorns but no fruit. The gathering gloaming whispered of winter, and long nights, and promised a cold that would chill to the bone.

Adrian pulled the duvet tighter around his shoulders. It seemed Mike and Elaine had been gone for a long time. It was just a routine hospital appointment, the blind woman had explained, but Adrian couldn't shake an unsettling concern. Elaine's recent frailty had not gone unnoticed.

A laptop was balanced on the arm of the sofa and Adrian's phone was next to him, still open on a page about Holy Trinity church in Buckfastleigh. He had been trying to learn more about Squire Cabell, and the folklore was easy to find; the man even had his own entry on Wikipedia. There was also a wealth of articles about the strange ruins of the church. He had been skim reading them all, hoping to find something useful, and now his head was swimming with Satanists and devilish deals. A shiver shook his shoulders, despite the weight of the duvet.

Run seven times round the sepulchre, and Squire Cabell will bite your fingers through the bars. Squire Cabell rides out in a midnight black coach, pulled by a team of black, headless horses. On the night the Squire was buried, a pack of phantom hounds came in from the moor to howl at his tomb. Adrian closed his eyes and snapped shut the cover of his phone. All the stories were blending into one, and not a single account had any suggestion of what to do when confronted by the demon huntsman. The tales spoke of supernatural hounds, but none of them described how that black and tan skin cracked, spilling out a line of hot lava and the scent of sulphur. They noted that Cabell was wicked, but they failed to convey how that humourless smile curved up the corners of his pale, thin lips.

The sharp ping of a notification caught Adrian's attention. He dragged the laptop onto his leg and clicked through to Devon Live. Leaning close to the screen, he felt the hairs prickling along the soft skin of his neck.

DARTMOOR DEATH CONNECTED WITH THE MURDEROUS WILD HUNT

He read the headline again, hoping his eyes had deceived him. But this wasn't the result of reading too many ghost stories. The words remained stubbornly same, and the article was dated as written today. His lips moved silently as he scrolled down through the paragraphs. One described again how the witch had met a figure on horseback while doing a ritual. Another recounted the strange and unpleasant circumstances surrounding the death of local man, Simon Holloway. His wife stated that she heard horses outside, and that Simon went out to send them away. Then there was the sound of screaming, and howling dogs, and the old stable block was set alight. Simon Holloway has been presumed dead, by the blood and bone scraps left on the ground, but no body had been found.

Adrian grimaced. It was all too believable, given the hunger he'd seen in those unholy hounds. The next paragraph was almost entirely made up of quotes from Clara Merryweather, the witch. She explained how the Wild Hunt gathered souls, and suggested that the Dark

Huntsman was back on the prowl. On the next line she mentioned that she was working on protective amulets, which would be available in her Etsy shop.

The writer of the article called on all locals to be vigilant, and to report any strange occurrences immediately to the police. Adrian failed to suppress a dark laugh. How would the police react if he told them that he had seen Squire Cabell return to set light to his hated sepulchre? He read through the details of Simon Holloway's death again. The information was sparse, perhaps due to the reporter trying not to put off his readers. More focus was put on the legends mentioned by Clara, and there were hundreds of comments with further conspiracy theories already.

"Great," said Adrian out loud. It was bad enough having to worry about Gemma keeping company with inhuman monsters. It was inconvenient to have to hide from Squire Cabell with Mike in a bush. But now the newspapers were getting involved. And normal people were dying.

He folded his laptop and stood up, shaking the pins and needles out of his feet. What did Squire Cabell want? The stories repeated his curse to lead hellhounds across the moor, but no mention was made of any motives for murdering. Other than he just enjoyed it, perhaps. Adrian filled the old kettle and placed it on the hob. He poured a generous spoonful of coffee into a mug, followed by an even more generous serving of sugar. Then he tapped his fingers on the worktop as he waited for the water to boil.

The locals had added a heavy slab to the Cabell family grave after Richard Cabell's death. The iron barred building was a further precaution. The heavy wooden door was designed to keep Devil worshippers out. All of this seemed to have contained Cabell, up until now.

Adrian poured boiling water over his granules of coffee. Someone had set the squire loose, and he was pissed about being stuck in his grave for so long. He was angry enough to come back and burn the building to the ground, iron bars and all. But how else might he play out his revenge?

"A stone grave, iron bars and a wooden door," said Adrian, addressing the milk as he grabbed it out of the fridge. "Stone, iron and wood," he repeated, pouring milk into his coffee. A chill tracked through his veins. His eyes widened and milky liquid overflowed from his cup. "Of course!" He dumped the milk to one side and made a grab for the laptop, almost throwing it open on the kitchen table. A quick search brought up a basic website and hundreds of pages of photographed documents. He got to within ten years of Cabell's death and scanned through the entries in the parish register. And there it was; *Samuel Holloway, stonemason.*

There was the sound of a key in the lock. Adrian glanced up, face flushed with his discovery. Mike looked strangely pale, and Elaine even more so.

"Is everything alright?" Adrian asked.

"Would you put the kettle on? It feels cold in here," Mike said, by way of reply. Adrian refilled the kettle and placed out some cups. He saw Elaine leaning on Mike as she stepped through the door.

"Are you having tea?" Adrian asked her. She looked at him and smiled weakly. The skin across her cheeks was drawn tight, and there were dark circles he had never noticed before ringing her eyes.

"I'll just have a little lie down," she said, "would you bring the tea up?"

120

Adrian nodded. He half watched as Mike helped Elaine up the stairs. Usually she moved confidently, despite her lack of vision, but her pace now was slow and laborious. The kettle whistled again and he filled up two more cups. The excitement of his research was wearing off. Squire Cabell may be terrifying, but his fear for Elaine was far more immediate. Mike came back downstairs, and the two men locked eyes.

"Can we go to the pub?" Mike asked.

Adrian nodded. He picked up Elaine's cup and slowly climbed the stairs. The bedroom door was a little ajar, but she didn't answer when he called. Feeling a sudden panic, he pushed the door open wider and peered into the room.

Elaine was tucked under the covers, one arm resting on top of the duvet. Her eyes were closed, but Adrian was reassured by the subtle rise and fall of her chest. The embroidered frills of the pillow fell around her, bright against her dark hair, forming a kind of floral halo. He tiptoed in and placed the tea by her bedside.

Downstairs, Mike was hovering by the door. He had his boots and coat on, and the look of a man in need of a drink.

"The Plume?" asked Adrian, already knowing the answer. Mike nodded and hurried out the door. He set a quick pace, striding along the path without looking back. Adrian had to jog occasionally to keep up, and by the time they reached the Plume of Feathers he was out of breath. Mike ploughed on, only slowing at the bar. He bent his head low to the barman.

"Shandy please. Extra lemonade."

The barman raised an eyebrow, but poured the drink without comment. "And for your friend?"

"White wine please," said Adrian, one hand on his aching chest.

In the corner of the pub, surrounded by vintage horse brasses and bedwarmers, sat a small knot of people. They were speaking low and fast, faces bowed over their drinks. Every so often one of them would look up furtively and glance around.

The barman caught Mike's gaze. "The Wild Hunt Investigation Committee," he explained, handing over the shandy. "Newly formed, I believe."

It was Mike's turn to raise an eyebrow. "What are they doing?" he asked.

"Mostly talking. And drinking. But once night falls, and they've had their fill, who knows?"

"What do you mean?" Adrian asked, handing over the money for the drinks.

"I mean what I say. I know those folk. All it takes is one bright idea and they'll be racing out with air rifles on the moor. Gods know what good they think that will do." The barman gripped something that hung round his neck through his shirt. "But I'm watching them. If I can keep the drinks flowing, then, with any luck, the only thing they'll be ready to take on is their beds."

Mike nodded in approval. He walked over to a table and sat down, half draining his weak shandy out of habit. Adrian recognised the table. He remembered the dark brown cup rings stained into the wood. They had sat here the night he and Gemma argued, and he retaliated by running out onto the moor.

"Are you alright?" asked Mike.

Adrian shook his head, realising he was staring at his glass. "Not really. How about you?"

"Not really," Mike replied.

They sat for a few moments in companionable silence. Adrian allowed the quiet to stretch out, hoping Mike might volunteer some information about the hospital visit and Elaine.

"She won't tell me," Mike said eventually. He picked up his shandy, and looked surprised that the glass was empty.

"Another?" Adrian offered.

"Yes. Extra lemonade."

Adrian went back to the bar. He waited at the left-hand end, straining an ear to catch the conversation of the shifty committee. Feigning an interest in the skull of the Beast hung on the wall, he wandered a little closer.

"We all know the stories," hissed one voice, "the Dark Huntsman murders children."

"I heard that anyone who lays eyes on him dies within a month," said another.

"No, it's as soon as you catch sight of him and his hounds. You're frozen to the spot with fear, and then he has you!"

"The hounds! They're what drags your soul back to Hell," explained a woman, with obvious delight.

The shabby skull looked on with an expression of disdain. There was a mayonnaise packet stuffed inside one of the eye sockets. Adrian wandered back to the bar and ordered Mike's shandy. The discussion in the corner grew suddenly more heated.

"That's the headless horseman, you idiot!" cried someone in exasperation.

"Oh horseman, huntsman, what's the difference?" another retorted, even louder. Then there was the sound of exaggerated shushing, and the conspirators were forced to air their opinions more quietly.

123

"I don't think they'll do much," Adrian told Mike, placing a fresh pint down, and twitching his head towards the loud table.

"Thanks," Mike said. "I meant to ask you, about earlier. Are you hurt?"

Adrian uncurled his hand, revealing the blackened middle and index finger. There was a thin scab, like a smear of ash, but not any pain. "I've survived worse."

"That you have," agreed Mike.

"Listen though," said Adrian, "I did some research while you were out. I think I know what Squire Cabell wants."

"You do?" Mike leaned closer, a little of the old light back in his eyes.

"Yes. I looked through the parish register, and guess what name came up?"

"Go on."

"Holloway. It's the same name as the man who was killed. His ancestor would have built the stone bits of the Cabell family tomb."

Mike's eyes widened with understanding. "And we know how he felt about being stuck in there."

"Exactly. He's going after the people who helped trap him."

"So that means," said Mike thoughtfully, "there will be more."

Adrian took a generous sip of wine from his glass. He hadn't thought too much about that part. But Mike was right. "Yes. That's stone, but there's still iron and wood."

"I wonder what part our witch played?" Mike mused.

"And more importantly, why she survived," Adrian added.

124

There was the sudden screech of a chair being flung back. Mike tensed, gripping his empty glass for comfort. The Wild Hunt Investigation Committee had hit another contentious topic. One of the men climbed onto his chair, flinging both arms out towards his companions.

"Listen!" he cried, "we all know what to do. We know that the Wild Hunt rides out from Wistman's Wood. What is there to stop us going there, and putting the fear of God back in this monster?" He shook his fist for emphasis, and the wooden chair rocked beneath him.

There was a mixed grumble of response. "Yes!" cried one voice, sloshing their beer in conviction.

"You heard the witch," said another, "we can't face this thing."

"I heard she sells reasonably priced protective amulets," someone else volunteered.

"What are you?" spat the man on the chair in exasperation, "afraid of a bit of old folklore?"

"Wise men are," said the barman. His voice was firm and soft. "We all remember the stories, told on dark nights round flickering fires. Do you think our ancestors would have told them, if they were a load of old rubbish?"

The grumbling turned muted, and there were a few nods of agreement.

"You know all about it, do you?" the speaker on the chair sneered.

"I know enough," the barman retorted, "like I know how you like a flutter on the horses Steven. I might be inclined to think you started this whole committee as an excuse for people to buy you drinks, as you're too broke to finance a pint. That's just my inkling though." His words were silky smooth, as he made a show of wiping over a few tables nearby. Steven climbed down from his chair, a definite red tinge spilling from his collar up onto his face.

"I think it's your round," suggested the woman nearest to him.

"Well, the thing is-" Steven stuttered, backing away as if the huntsman himself had appeared in the pub.

"Tell you what," said the barman graciously, "what about a round on me, and no more talk of burning brands and pitchforks?" His tone was light, but there was a tension still lacing the air.

"Cheers to that!" replied the man who had already sloshed beer on himself. The air cleared. Adrian emptied his lungs in relief. The barman dropped a nod at him and Mike as he walked past.

Mike was tapping his fingertips against the table in thought. He was delivered a shandy on the house as well, and he began to drink without looking at it. "I wonder if we need to talk to this witch," he said to Adrian.

"Maybe we do. What was her second name again? I wonder if she's on the register too."

"Merryweather. Maybe she isn't, as she's still alive."

Adrian swallowed his last mouthful of wine and stood up to put on his coat. The barman appeared beside him, giving Adrian the feeling he had been watching their conversation the whole time.

"You ought to pass on word to your friend," the man advised.

Adrian pulled a puzzled expression, wondering how to get word to Gemma, wherever she was.

"He means Gabriel," Mike clarified.

Realisation dawned on Adrian. He nearly retaliated with a haughty reassurance that *he's not my friend,* but thought better of it. The barman was right. If the questionable committee had it in for the Wild Hunt, then

Gabriel would be their number one target, and Gemma was with him.

"We will," Mike replied.

The barman nodded, retreating back behind the bar and beginning to wipe down the glossy brown wood. "There'll be no more trouble here tonight," he said, "but fear is a persistent plague. Watch yourselves out there."

A fire flickered in the grate of the Warren House Inn. It had burnt uninterrupted for one hundred and sixty-five years. Even when the previous pub building had burnt to the ground, a smouldering coal had been kept alight and transferred to the newly built fireplace. Or so the story goes.

Tonight there were three guests. The man nearest the fire was sat by himself. His name was Tom Dunn, and he was experienced in drinking alone. Every so often he attempted to scroll through his phone, but gave up after a few swipes. There was no signal on the high moor. There was almost nothing at all, come to mention it, other than the isolated pub, a scattering of hut circles, the wild sheep and the wind.

Tom rifled around in his pockets and produced an old dog-end, which he flicked onto the fire. He watched it flare up and then curl into ash. Then he got to his feet, stuck a freshly rolled cigarette to his lip, and went outside.

It was a cold, clear night. He might have picked out the distant constellations, if he was interested. Orion the Hunter and Canis Major wheeled above him, tracking their slow path across the autumn sky. But his attention was on the saggy cigarette and temperamental lighter.

"Bugger," he said, casting his eyes about for some shelter. There was a small outhouse next to the pub, and he leaned against the back wall out of the wind. At last, his rollie caught light, and he sucked at it contentedly, staring out into the darkness of the moor.

Something was moving out there. Tom's eyes narrowed with concentration as he tried to work out what it was. Drawing thoughtfully on the cigarette, his face flared red intermittently with an eerie glow.

"What are you then?" he taunted. The pale shape moved a little, and Tom took a good swig from his glass. Whatever it was, it didn't fade or move away as he slowly walked closer. "Well then-" he said, taking a last drag on the cigarette and flicking it onto the floor, "I'll be buggered."

Then there was someone behind him, and a cold blade at his throat.

"That was not my plan," said a silky voice. The grey horse looked on with interest.

"Take my wallet, take it! It's in my pocket!" Tom stuttered.

"I have no interest in your money."

Black and tan hounds melted out of the shadows, prowling and patient, their eyes flickering with infernal fire. Tom's thoughts were blurred by alcohol, but he clung to the idea that this was a mugging. He understood muggings.

"My car," he said, "take the keys. It's parked over there."

"I have no need for transport. I have a horse already, as you have seen."

"Well then, w-what do you want?"

"I want you to die, Thomas Dunn. I want you to know the darkness of the abyss, and those few fleeting seconds of despair while your soul bleeds out of your body."

Tom made a muffled squeaking sound. He had faced a broken bottle in a bar fight and a screaming drunkard with a knife. But this was different. This was worse.

"Please-" he managed to say. But any further begging came out as a gurgle.

Cabell took hold of Tom's glass, whilst letting his body slide to the floor. Blood bubbled out of the neat slice on the man's neck and the hounds pressed closer, their tongues lolling out in anticipation. Cabell wiped his dagger on his victim's shirt, and then took a small sip of port.

"Have at it," he said to the hounds.

10.
SANCTUARY

Owain looked at his reflection in the mirror. This evening he had been provided grey trousers, with a matching silk shirt and jacket. There were little skulls embroidered around the cuffs and along the line of the lapels. Some of them were deer, some were foxes, and some were hounds. But some of them were also fae. Or humans. The more he looked at the small skulls, the more a feeling of unease gathered in his stomach. It writhed like an eel, making him rush to the washstand and splash cold water over his face. He drew in deep, measured breaths. The swan wytch's words had stayed with him; *you, Apprentice, most of all*. But why did he need an ally now, more than ever?

He ran damp fingers through his red hair, pushing it back from his face. It was naturally straight, although it fell in a slight curl where it touched his shoulder. He thought back to how he had borrowed Gabriel's bloodstained hunt coat and practiced the rite of raising the hounds. It had been so exciting, and he had wanted nothing more than to lead the hunt himself. But the rogue hound had been deadly, and the binding ritual was a savage pledge. He had seen the truth, the horror in the Huntmaster's eyes, however well he tried to hide it.

Owain jumped at a knock on the door. He stood to open it, feeling his heart beating out a battle rhythm. He was relieved to see Gemma outside, even though she seemed agitated.

"Can I come in?" she asked.

"Of course." Owain flung the door wider and gestured her inside. Gemma's dress was grey as well, with

131

layers of fine fabric that fluttered like gossamer when she walked. She sat down heavily on the chair by the washstand.

"Has something happened?" he asked.

Gemma hesitated. Her lips paused half parted, the weight of words weighing heavy on her tongue. Should she tell Owain about her experience at the well? She trusted him, but Segain had sounded serious with her caution to secrecy. "Gabriel hasn't come back," she settled on saying.

Owain nodded. It was a relief to have a topic to direct his strange dread towards. "Not since last night?"

"He never came back at all. I haven't seen him since the feast. In fact," she added thoughtfully, "I've barely seen him."

"I know he has been speaking to the King." Owain folded cross legged onto the floor. He looked out of place there, in his fancy evening clothes, but the tightness of his body seemed to relax a little.

"About what?" Gemma asked.

"His sister. We will hear how she has been judged tonight."

"Judged?"

"For her crimes. After we met her on the moor she fled here and claimed sanctuary. That's what this whole gathering is really about; her fate," Owain explained.

Gemma tilted her head to one side. *Crimes* barely began to cover it. Asterra had tortured Fian and left him to be eaten. She had unleashed a hellhound to attack the people of Princetown. "What fates are on offer?" she asked.

Owain fiddled with his embroidered cuff. "She tried to kill Gabriel. The murder of fae kin is considered the highest crime."

"Will they kill her?" Gemma's eyes widened with dawning horror. Had she been told to eat well now, in preparation for watching Asterra die later?

Owain shook his head. "That would be considered a comparable crime. We are forbidden from killing our kin, except in battle. Although, there are worse punishments."

"Such as what?"

"Being banished to live as a mortal with all memories removed." Owain almost whispered, as if even uttering the words might somehow bring this fate upon him.

Gemma smoothed down the soft fabric of her dress. Her food waited untouched in her room, and she saw that Owain had paid no attention to his plate either. Asterra was a vicious predator, who would stop at nothing to get her own way. She had no problem hurting or killing a child, and Fian had only been reborn as a hound through some strange and unexplained magic. But still, Gemma had no desire to watch the woman die. "Is being human so bad?"

"No offence meant," flustered Owain, "Being mortal is fine. Probably better, actually. But losing your Clan and identity..."

"I do understand," Gemma replied. The fear lay alarmingly close. Even after her dip in the well, no recollection of any previous life as Elyn had returned. Gabriel was in love with a dead woman, and she was a watered-down substitute.

"Have you eaten?" asked Owain, gesturing towards his plate.

"No. I keep getting told I should."

"It would be a shame to waste their hospitality."

Gemma reluctantly agreed. She picked up the plate and set it between herself and Owain on the floor. It contained a selection of bread, cheese and preserved meats. It would have looked delicious, if her stomach

133

wasn't already turning.

Gabriel strode down the corridor, a black riding cloak billowing behind him. Guards jumped aside as he reached the door to Asterra's chamber. He knocked urgently. It was ignored. He knocked again and then, on hearing no answer, commanded the guards to open the door. They hesitated, but did as he asked.

Asterra sat with her back to him. She made no move to acknowledge his arrival. Her long blonde hair spilled in soft waves over her shoulders and down to her waist. The plain blue dress she wore ended at her ankles, and Gabriel could see her bare feet through the legs of the chair.

He walked over slowly, his soft footfalls seeming loud in the stillness of the room. Asterra remained motionless, her eyes fixed on the wall opposite her.

"Sister," said Gabriel, "the evening approaches. I could not face it, without speaking with you one last time."

Asterra stared fixedly ahead, the slow rise and fall of her chest the only proof she still lived.

Gabriel bowed his head, his tone low and urgent. "We both know the fate you will face. But you can still change that. Ask for their mercy Asterra, tell them you were not in your right mind. Tell them I drove you to madness with my neglect." He lay his hand over hers.

She made no move to acknowledge him, and her skin felt cold and thin beneath his fingers.

Gabriel crouched and looked up into her blank, blue eyes. "Blame me all you like. I beg you, for our bloodline and the bond between us, to speak out in defence. Tell them you will make amends. Humble yourself

134

to their mercy, and they may yet be swayed." His shoulders slumped and his forehead almost touched Asterra's hand. Silence stretched between them, deep and still as the Divide.

"There was a time," said Asterra slowly, "when your begging would have been sweet to me. Your misery might have tasted like fine wine, and I may have delighted in your return. But now there is no taste. Everything is made of dust, and I am indifferent to it." She pulled her hand from beneath his and folded her arm across her body.

"Please," replied Gabriel, "tell me what I must do."

Asterra laughed, a short, mirthless bark which sounded irreverent in the stillness of the room. "Renounce your human lover. Bring me her body as a gift. Repay me for all the years I have adored you."

Gabriel recoiled, his lips half pulled back in a snarl of disgust. "You ask the one thing I will not do."

"Then kill me." Asterra caught hold of his arm, her eyes flashing and frantic. "Release me from their cruel justice. Allow me that last dignity."

"I cannot."

Asterra held his gaze, her expression fierce and defiant, dangerous as a she-wolf starved by the winter. "Then you are not my brother." With these words she diminished, drawing back into herself, and settling into that same deathly stillness. Her eyes found their focus on the wall, and then faded to a glassy sheen.

Gabriel fell back and let out a howl which brought the guards running. Then he swept from the room, hands in trembling fists and eyes stinging with hot rage and despair.

Amergein found Gemma and Owain sitting on the floor, with a half empty plate between them. He shook his head at the sight of their fine garments being given such careless treatment.

"It is time," he said, gesturing elegantly towards the open door. Gemma fought down a sudden feeling of nausea. Did he sound more sombre than usual? He had abandoned his green attire and was dressed from head to toe in a dull gold, patterned all over with fern fronds. Across both shoulders were bronze epaulettes, covered in intricate knotwork depicting hounds and vines.

Owain scrambled to his feet, self-consciously dusting down his trousers.

"One moment," said Gemma. She hurried out and back to her own room, pushing open the door and scooping up a black fur stole. It had been hung with her dress, and she hoped it might help warm the strange chill in her bones. On the bed, Fian stretched his slender legs and flowed down onto the floor. He looked up at Gemma with steady, intelligent eyes. "Well, I don't see why not," she said, "Gabriel brought Fen yesterday."

Fian wagged his tail in approval, following her out into the corridor, where Amergein and Owain were waiting. Amergein nodded in greeting, and then led them down the corridor towards the hall.

Gemma wrapped the stole tightly around herself, glancing left and right with a nervous curiosity. Was it duller in the tunnels somehow? Did the candles burn lower, or was the light affected by the same strange dread she could feel? She glanced over at Owain, who smiled weakly in response. He could feel it too, clearly.

They were ushered into the feasting hall without ceremony, and Gemma and Owain took their same places on the top table. She tried not to stare, reminding herself that she was meant to be used to this spectacle. But the hall looked very different. The tables were draped with grey cloths and the thousands of candles had been replaced, each one burning as a bright flame atop a pillar of black wax.

A deeper hush fell as the King and Queen appeared in the doorway. With a nod of acknowledgement to their subjects, they took their places without any further announcement. The King was clad in resplendent golden armour, and his thistledown hair floated round his head like a halo. A sword hung at his side. The Queen wore a long black gown, gathered by a golden belt patterned with knotwork hounds.

Gemma realised that her shoulders had risen with tension, and she forced them back down. Gabriel's place was glaringly empty next to her. This fact had not been lost on the Queen, who leaned close to her husband and whispered in his ear. He nodded tiredly, one hand supporting his forehead.

Servants began to weave between the tables, filling glasses and goblets with wine. Gemma sipped hers experimentally. It was dark and syrupy sweet, with an earthy aftertaste she couldn't quite place.

Segain appeared, graceful as ever, and presented herself to the top table. She wore her swan feather cloak, as well as a feathered headdress with white tassels that obscured her eyes. The King nodded his consent, and the wytch turned, rising her hands to the gathered folk. She began to hum, low and melodic, her fingers tracing intricate shapes in the expectant air. Amergein joined in softly with his drum. The candles guttered in some unseen wind and the room seemed to shrink, until there was no separation and Gemma could hear Segain singing inside her own mind. Then there was a sudden exhalation. Gemma shook her head in confusion.

Gabriel threw open the ornate doors, stalking down the steps as if a storm followed him. He was dressed all in black, and his knee-high boots were speckled with mud. Wordlessly, he took his seat at the high table. Fen followed more sedately and hid under his chair. Gemma felt the rage burning off the Huntmaster's skin, smouldering like the embers of a fire. She turned to him, and he looked at her with inky eyes, shimmering with despair. The hairs rose on her arms, prickling with unease. What did Gabriel know? What was about to happen?

Segain picked up her humming. She gathered pace, bursting into almost a wail, as Amergein rode the rhythm with his drum. Faster and faster, the beat filled the room; a frantic heartbeat that rang through Gemma's chest and tightened her nails against the table. Then it stopped. The silence was almost painful. Gemma counted her breaths, willing her heart to steady. Next to her, Gabriel sat with both hands clasped in fists on the table. Fen whined softly at his feet.

The grand doors opened again. Asterra was escorted in by four guards. Her wrists and ankles were held in manacles, with each guard holding one of the trailing chains. Gemma recoiled as she noticed the blistering of Asterra's skin around the metal, and realized it must be iron. Fian growled and flattened his ears to his head.

Segain stepped to one side, so that Asterra could be held in the centre of the room. The guards took their places around her in neat formation. The chained wytch stood motionless between them, betraying no sign of the pain etched so clearly on her skin.

The Queen stood to deliver the accusation.

"Asterra, wytch of the Dartmoor Clan, you stand charged with the attempted murder of Gabriel, your brother. How do you plead?"

"Guilty," said Asterra.

"You are aware that murder of our own kin is considered the highest crime, and is punished accordingly?"

"I am." Asterra was eerily still. Her lips barely moved to form the words, and around them her face showed no sign of emotion.

"Then you are prepared to accept our decision, with no further defence? I must remind you, this is your last chance to speak out. Here, before our gathered Clan, you may defend yourself, and seek to divert this destiny. It is your right, having requested sanctuary." The Queen clasped her hands, waiting for Asterra's response.

"I have nothing more to say."

"Then it is time," said the King. He rose wearily, one hand lingering on his wine glass. "Asterra, you will be banished from your Clan and all others. You will have no memory of your heritage or power. For the rest of your days, you will live in isolation as a mortal, and we will never speak your name again."

Gabriel slammed his fist against the table, his lips curled into a snarl. Asterra bowed her head in acceptance. Segain pulled a bottle from her pouch and raised it for the King to inspect. Gemma recognised it as the same one she had seen the swan wytch fill from the strange, dark pool.

"Asterra," Segain said, "there will be no pain." She uncorked the bottle and lay an elegant hand on Asterra's cheek. "Are you ready?"

"I have a request," said Asterra.

"Speak now," said Segain.

"I want my brother to do it."

139

Segain lowered the bottle. She looked up at the Queen, who turned to Gabriel. The Huntmaster was deathly pale, his eyes black and shimmering. He stood, like a man facing the end of the world. Still in fists, his hands trembled, bloodied from where his nails bit into the skin. He gave the Queen the slightest of nods.

"Gabriel agrees," said the Queen.

Gemma watched with her hand across her mouth. There was a hush across the whole room as Gabriel stepped down from the high table and took the bottle of liquid from Segain. Asterra raised her face in preparation, blank eyes turned upwards to the ceiling.

Gabriel faced his sister. He leaned close, his lips almost brushing her ear. "Beg them. Beg them for mercy. Do it for me."

"I begged you once. I will never beg for anything, ever again. Do it. Just like you did for your brother," said Asterra, her voice a dry whisper.

Gabriel held her cheek, staring into her dull eyes. Where they had once been fierce, they held now only defeat and the reflection of his own despair. He tipped up her chin, and her mouth fell open. He pressed the bottle to her pale lips and poured the dark liquid.

Fen let out an unearthly howl. It filled the room, thrumming with raw pain. Fian melded his voice with hers, standing shoulder to shoulder in comfort. Gabriel caught Asterra when she fell, turning limp as the liquid burnt through her veins. The guards unlocked her manacles and lifted her body away from him. He remained on his knees as they carried her out of the room like a corpse. Then, slowly, he stood and returned to the table.

Gemma found herself standing, her arms stretched out towards him. She gathered him into an embrace without thinking, feeling the wetness of hot tears on his cheeks. His heartbeat echoed through her own chest, drumming out a quick beat. He pulled back, as if suddenly remembering himself, and she reached up to touch his face. There were no words for this horror, but she felt him lean for a moment into her hand. Then he sat back down, draining his glass of wine. She echoed him.

Quiet music started up and the servants returned to refill cups and lay out platters of food. Few of those who were gathered made any move to begin eating. The King was leaning in conversation with his Huntmaster, who stood out as suffering no loss of appetite. His Apprentice, keen to impress, was forcing small pastries into his mouth, although Gemma could tell he was struggling from the pallor of his skin.

"Something rousing," commanded the Queen, gesturing towards the musicians. Immediately, the tune turned triumphant, rolling across the room as a rich swell of sound. Very slowly, conversation returned.

Gemma leaned close to Gabriel. "I'm so sorry."

He took her hand under the table and held it tight. "There is nothing for you to be sorry for, Elyn."

She felt a familiar twinge of resentment at his use of the name, but she forced it back down. It was her title while she was here, after all. Fian rested his head against her thigh, and she snuck him a piece of meat under the table. Fen was curled up on Gabriel's feet, her head tucked into her body as if she had heard and seen enough for one night.

11.
DEFIANCE

It was the dark haired Huntmaster who now strode into the centre of the room. His Apprentice followed, carrying a black leather bag. The lively music lulled and then stopped, as the King once again rose to his feet. Nervous whispers spilled across the room, tightening the air and dragging the shadows closer. Segain joined the Huntmaster and he bowed to accept her kiss to his forehead.

"Connar is our Huntmaster," she told the seated guests, "gather close and show him honour."

There was a scraping of benches as everyone stood and began to make their way towards her. They formed a silent circle around the wytch and the Huntmaster. At a nod from the King, the rest of the high table did the same. Gemma took her place, clutching Gabriel's arm.

"I thought it was over," she hissed, "what's happening now?"

Gabriel's lips were set in a grim line. Gemma could feel his muscles, coiled tight beneath his clothes.

"You will not shield your eyes, Elyn," he said.

She glanced over to Owain, her mouth falling open in silent confusion. His lips twitched into the faintest smile of comfort and he stood a little closer, so that she could feel his shoulder next to hers.

"The Huntmaster gives his life to the task of our protection," Segain continued, "and in return we offer lives to him. Part of the pack, they never die."

"Part of the pack, they never die," the crowd echoed in answer.

Unlacing the leather bag, the blonde Apprentice

reached inside and paced the perimeter of the circle, sprinkling rich, black earth. As he did, Connar produced a fistful of bones from his pocket. He threw them, one by one. Where they touched the soil they began to swell, sprouting like seeds and spreading like tendrils of ivy. They snapped and unfurled into full skeletons of hounds, which shook themselves and grew a layer of grey fur.

They were long legged and lithe; the kind of creatures that might take down a wolf or a red deer. Moss tangled in their wiry coats and lichen speckled their damp, dark noses. Their eyes were the deep green of murky water. Connar eyed them proudly, and glanced over at Gabriel to note his reaction. Gabriel spared him a nod, for the magnificent hounds.

The crowd parted as a woman walked to the edge of the circle, clutching a bundle wrapped in black cloth. The air stilled, not even stirred by a breath, as Segain greeted her gravely. It was the first time Gemma had seen the swan wytch bow to anyone. The woman offered the bundle, and Segain took it. From the folds of cloth, a small hand reached out to grasp her finger. Gemma saw red rings round the eyes of the fae woman, too raw even for glamour to hide. Inside the circle, the hounds paced hungrily, tasting the air with their ragged tongues.

"One Master," said Segain, "one Apprentice, and the fortunate houndmarked to meld with the pack."

Gemma's eyes flew wide with horror. She realized now what was about to happen.

"Our safety is their legacy. Our protection is their purpose. Part of the pack, they never die." Segain lifted the baby boy and showed him to the crowd. They fell to one knee, bowing their heads in respect. The wytch gently pushed the material aside to reveal a red birth mark, of three parallel lines, on the child's shoulder. The King nodded formally, his face impassive, although Gemma noticed that he held the hand of the Queen. Had they offered a son in the same barbaric ritual?

"We are grateful," said the Queen.

Segain cradled the child close, humming a low lullaby. She rocked the little boy until his eyes flickered and shut, his small mouth relaxing into the half smile of sleep.

Connar raised his hands. He dragged them through the air slowly, as if pulling some great weight. Around him, his hounds sat to stiff attention. The air sizzled with expectation, and their green eyes burst into eldritch flame, glowing like a ghostlight on the wild stretches of the moor.

Gemma gripped Gabriel's arm so tight that her nails bit his skin. Her lips were already mouthing the word, over and over, but she whispered it out loud. "No."

"Remember yourself," Gabriel hissed through his teeth. Gemma's lip curled. There was that resentment again, burning like bile in her throat, twisting in her stomach like something turned sour. *Remember yourself*. By her side, Fian raised his head in defiance, a low growl rumbling in his throat.

Segain lay the sleeping baby down in the centre of the circle. Gemma trembled with rage. Her eyes darted left and right, taking in the sombre stillness of the crowd. No one was going to stop this; they were accepting it with a sort of docile misery. Very softly, there came the sound of sobbing, but it was quickly silenced.

Connar turned to Gabriel. An unpleasant smile clung to the corners of his lips. "It is custom," he said, "to give a visiting Huntmaster the honour of the kill."

"I ask no such honour," Gabriel replied.

"I insist," pressed Connar. The horrible smile

broadened.

This was a test. Gemma had no doubt of it. She saw Connar narrow his eyes as he waited for Gabriel to react. She looked up at Gabriel and for a second he caught her gaze. His facade flickered, and beneath the glamour and gore she saw fear, and a horror so deep it could swallow the sun. But then those midnight eyes stilled, until all that they held was her anxious reflection. Spines raised along Gabriel's forearm, piercing the fine cloth of his coat. Instinctively, Gemma dropped her hold on him. He didn't notice.

One hand curled towards Fen, beckoning her forward. She did as commanded, slipping into the same form she had taken at Grimspound. Her eyes blazed red as coals, turned up towards her Master in unquestioning loyalty. Gabriel pointed towards the centre of the circle. Fen bared dripping teeth, pushing up through rotten gums.

Owain held Gemma back, but she flung him off. Fen, the same Fen who had comforted her in the past, was about to kill a defenceless child. It was wrong. Screw all their stupid traditions! Elyn might have watched this spectacle, but she sure as hell wouldn't.

Fian was beside her. They strode past Gabriel and turned back to face him, blocking his view of the child. Fen barked a warning, but Fian matched her, squaring up in front of Gemma and issuing a guttural challenge.

"I've said it before," said Gemma, "Nothing else good dies."

Gabriel's eyes flashed with fury. "Step aside woman," he growled. He was all Huntmaster now. There was only duty, and death, and the hot rush of the kill.

"No." Gemma crouched and picked up the sleeping boy. He barely stirred, held in his deep sleep by Segain. Fian and Fen circled each other, white against black, testing for the first sign of weakness. Fian seemed larger somehow, and his fur held a strange shine, like the halo which wraps round the moon.

"Enough of this madness," snapped Connar, "speak with your woman."

"Stop this Elyn," Gabriel commanded.

That was it. The resentment which Gemma had pushed down and down into the core of her being began to boil. She allowed herself to feel it, focusing on that hard diamond of rage in her stomach. "Come and make me," she said. Fian snapped his sharp, white teeth at Fen.

Connar rolled his eyes and beckoned to his Apprentice. As one, his hounds lowered their heads and took a step forward. Gemma held the warm bundle closer, feeling the tiny heartbeat against her own chest. The grey hounds prowled nearer, until she could feel their hot breath while they licked their teeth with hunger. She threw Gabriel one final look of fury, and then she closed her eyes.

"Stop," said Segain. Connar glanced at her in confusion. There were strict demands of tradition that must be followed; not even the wytch could defy them. The crowd began to fidget, glancing nervously at those pressed next to them.

"Your woman is too wild," said Connar to Gabriel.

Segain turned on him like a viper. "Your tongue is too wild, Huntmaster." There was a ripple of shocked intakes of breath. Unsettled eyes moved between the wytch and the petulant Huntmaster, who massaged his cheek as if he'd been struck.

Segain watched the double doors expectantly. Straining her ears, Gemma could hear hurried footsteps ringing down the corridor. Seconds later, the doors burst open. Connar turned instinctively to protect the King and Queen. But it was an old man who ran down the steps, one hand pressed to his chest with the exertion of running. The crowd parted curiously.

The man threw himself at the feet of the King. A single hound limped stiffly after him, negotiating the steps with an arthritic caution.

"Bless this earth! I am in time!" cried the old man.

"Rise, please," said the Queen. The lean hound crouched low, supporting its master as he creaked to his feet. Two guards jogged down the steps, both breathing hard from running. Their faces coloured as they bowed to the King, glancing nervously between him and the old man. The aged Huntmaster had clearly taken them by surprise. With a wave of her hand, the Queen stood them down.

"What is the cause of this intrusion?" the King asked. His tone was formal, but his green eyes were kindly.

"Forgive me, I have not introduced myself. We have little chance to travel and have not attended gatherings for many years. I am Darragh, Huntmaster of the Antrim Clan."

"You are welcome, if unexpected, Darragh," the King replied.

"Bless you, bless you, may Boann look kindly on you all of your days." Darragh bowed as low as he was able. "I have come to beg for your aid. As you can see, I am old. My hounds hope for the earth, and the long sleep."

"You have years yet, Huntmaster," smiled the Queen.

"Perhaps, perhaps. But my bones ache. I have no Apprentice to train, and the learning takes many years. My Clan have borne no houndmarked sons. Who will protect my people when I grow too weary? Who will stand between them and the wild weight of the world?"

"My sympathy for your lack of Apprentice. Tell us how we may aid you," replied the King.

Gemma glanced over at Segain. The swan wytch caught her eye, and a small smile flickered between them.

Darragh raised his hands, palms upward in supplication. "Let me raise this child," he gestured to the bundle still gripped in Gemma's arms. "Let me take him as my Apprentice, where my own bloodline has failed." There were tears in the old man's eyes, and a longing in his outstretched, empty arms.

The King and Queen looked at each other. Gemma noticed that they still held hands.

"It is destiny," said Segain, stepping forward and lifting off her elaborate headdress. "Elyn sensed it. If it had not been for her foresight, then we might have failed our brothers in Antrim."

"The bards tell of it," said Amergein, "in Leitrim and Limerick, in Carlow and Cavan, there are tales of Clans raising other Clan's sons. They grew to be bold Apprentices and valiant Huntmasters, and they bonded their people with that blending of blood."

From the scabbard at his side, the King drew a bright, ornate sword. He stepped towards Gemma, the blade light in his grip. She felt her arms tremble, but a reassuring nod from Segain instructed her to stay still. The King touched the child with the edge of the sword. It rested on one tiny shoulder, where three red lines had marked the infant for sacrifice. The pressure was light, but where the sword had lay a tiny bead of blood blossomed to the surface. The King took it on his finger and offered it to the nearest of the hounds. At a nod from Connar, the creature licked away the red smear.

"This child is dead," said the King, "he has returned

149

to the pack."

"This child is reborn," said the Queen, "son to Darragh of Antrim."

Gemma felt hot tears spill down her cheeks. A woman ran from the crowd and threw her arms around Darragh, almost knocking him to the ground.

"His name is Oisin," she said, "he is healthy and strong. He was full of courage, from the moment he was born-" her words dissolved into sobs of gratitude, and Darragh pressed his forehead solemnly to hers.

"I will raise him as my own son. He will want for nothing, and when he is grown he will be a proud Master, leading our long legged hounds across the basalt bones of the cliffs."

Segain opened her arms and Gemma handed her the little bundle. As she cradled Oisin, his eyes flickered open, and he reached out towards Darragh with a carefree curiosity. The wytch placed the child into the arms of the Huntmaster. With the boy against his chest, he seemed to stand taller; the stoop disappeared from his back, and his grey hair settled into sleek curls. He gathered his glamour about him, and when he faced the King and Queen he was no longer an old man. "You have my eternal gratitude and unending loyalty," he told them.

"There is a blood tie between our Clans now," said the Queen, "we will not forget it."

Connar clicked his fingers and his hounds fell back to bones. His Apprentice busied himself collecting them, placing each one carefully into the black leather bag. Fian pressed his muzzle to Gemma's hand, and she rewarded him with a triumphant ear scratch. Somehow, they had won. They had stood in the way of two furious Huntmasters, and they had come out of it, not just alive, but miraculously victorious. Gemma's blood fizzed with adrenaline.

"Play on," said the Queen. The crowd dispersed back to their seats, and a quiet melody sprang up around them. Servants appeared and shared out more wine. Gemma caught Gabriel's eye, and the triumph withered in her chest. She took her place reluctantly, feeling helplessly exposed on the top table. Low, fast chatter sprung up all over the room, and more than one furtive glance was aimed in her direction. But she could see Darragh, sitting with Oisin and his mother, chatting like old friends over their platter of food.

"Excuse me," said Gemma, standing up and edging her way round Gabriel's chair. She could still feel his fury, pooling around him like the overspill of a winter river. She stopped to bow to the King and the Queen. "I would like to lie down. Please." She should have worded it better, and she caught a calculating expression from Connar on the edge of her vision, but she was suddenly exhausted. The consort of the Huntmaster should have the stomach for all this. But she didn't, and there was no good in prolonging her failure.

"Of course," said the Queen kindly.

Gemma turned at once, ignoring the heat of Gabriel's gaze and the sneer on the lips of Connar and his Apprentice. Segain was waiting by the doors, and she pushed one open as Gemma approached. In the corridor, the two swans curved their metal necks and displayed the countless candles held in their wings. The wytch caught hold of Gemma's arm. The touch was light, but it left Gemma powerless to anything except turn and look into the other woman's eyes.

"There is only one fit consort for Death," said Segain, "and that is Life herself."

Gemma opened her mouth to ask what on earth that was supposed to mean, but Segain had already released her. The wytch was slipping through the double doors, light footed and lithe, letting the swell of chatter rise and fall back away. Then Gemma was alone; more alone than she had felt in a very long time.

It seemed a long way back to her room. The grey dress was unbearably tight; ensnaring her feet on every other step and conspiring to trip her with gossamer cloth. Slamming the door at last, she pulled frantically at the lacing, and drew a deep breath as the garment came loose. She stepped out of it, as if it was contaminated. Her familiar jeans and jumper were waiting for her in the wardrobe, and she pulled them on eagerly. It was wrong to have come here. She should have told Gabriel just where to stick it. He could keep all his glamour, and his expectations, and his hands to himself.

There was the inevitable knock. She had been dreading it, and she held her breath in the hope he might leave. But the knock came again, and Gabriel called in from the corridor.

"Elyn," he said. Gemma's anger flared with renewed heat. "Elyn," he called. His voice was curt and cold, and suddenly Gemma wanted his fury; she wanted to match it with her own, before facing the embers of terror.

"That isn't my name."

Gabriel threw open the door. Spikes of bone still showed on his forearms, and his jaw was clenched beneath the white skin of his face. "What is this madness?" He shut the door behind him. It sounded very loud and very final.

"My name isn't Elyn. My name is Gemma." Her voice came out surprisingly steady and there was a rush of relief at admitting the truth out loud.

Gabriel shook his head. "You drank from the well-" he began.

"And nothing happened." Gemma faced him, brown eyes matching black. "There was nothing to remember, because there is no Elyn; not inside me and not anywhere else."

The Huntmaster shook his head again. The thought was too much to take in, and he seemed to discard it. "You defied me this evening. You know you could have died?"

Gemma was getting bored of death being bandied about as the consequence of everything. It had begun to lose any use as a threat, and she had seen enough to know it might not be so final. "And I'll defy you again, every time you try to murder something innocent."

"It was duty. It was never my choice!" Gabriel opened his hands, stretched his fingers in a gesture of pleading, and then flexed them back into trembling fists.

"Everybody has a choice. Maybe Elyn chose to stay dead, rather than put up with your ridiculous talk about duty." Gemma observed the effect of her words.

Gabriel reeled back, as if wounded. He staggered, shedding his usual elegance, and his eyes grew very wide.

"Maybe she never loved you," Gemma pressed, feeling powerful in her jeans and baggy jumper, as the Huntmaster shied away from her. She thought of Fen, with her hungry jaws, and the thickened flesh on Gabriel's back, which was raised in the shape of three parallel lines.

"She did. She said she did." Gabriel had one hand raised, as if to shield himself from a blow. His eyes darted wildly around the room, searching for some kind of solace. He spotted the grey dress, discarded like a rag on the floor, after he had taken time describing to Amergein exactly what his consort should wear. His arm lowered, and he

153

extended it to Gemma.

The scent of woodsmoke and honey rolled over her, clogging her throat and laying thick in her lungs. Gabriel was glowing. Gone were the spines and the inky eyes; his hair hung in golden waves down to his shoulders. He looked like the painting Elaine had showed her, what seemed like a lifetime ago. It was the figure who had turned his horse towards an oncoming car, saving the life of her mother, who stood in the room with her now. He was the angel who had driven a grown woman to madness.

His hand was open, palm up, only half a pace away. Gemma felt herself sway against the force of his will. It was the same nausea that had gripped her in the Plume of Feathers, when she had stood up and told Adrian that he was deluded. She was beckoned wordlessly into Gabriel's arms. The scent of honeysuckle smelt stiflingly sweet. One foot stirred beneath her, and she saw a satisfied smile spill onto the Huntmaster's lips. It appalled her.

"Stop," she managed to say. Gabriel was taken aback, and the strength of his glamour waned. The hag stone felt hot against Gemma's chest. She pressed her hand to it and breathed in the fading scent of honey. "If I really was Elyn, would you need to force me?"

Gabriel looked at his hands. His expression betrayed his surprise.

"She's been dead for hundreds of years. Get that into your head. You don't care about me, and you never have." Gemma crossed her arms. Her heart thudded against the bars of her ribs. But she felt lighter, as if she had been carrying the body of Elyn around the whole time, and she had finally managed to lay the corpse down.

The Huntmaster snarled, but Gemma stood her ground. "Get out," she said.

Gabriel glared at her, his eyes bleeding back to black, and then strode out of the room.

12.
DEBT

The kitchen smelt of fresh coffee and paint. Elaine stood by her easel. Wrapped in a thick cardigan, she gripped a mug with both hands.

"Alright," she said to the canvas, taking a steadying sip of her coffee, "I suppose it might be time."

Mike looked up from his laptop. He was writing the final few paragraphs of his article for *Legendary Dartmoor*. He smiled to himself, aware that Elaine wouldn't see. She looked a little better this morning, as if the long sleep had done her some good. There was a light dusting of pink to her cheeks, and her brushstrokes had been steady and smooth. Mike stood to look at the image filling the canvas.

Elaine sensed him behind her and reached out one slender hand. He took it, allowing himself to be drawn closer. A man fixed his acrylic eyes on them both, staring out from a background of dark hills and stars. His skin caught the pale light of the moon, and his face was framed by waves of dark hair. But it was the antlers that made Mike stare. They thrust out from that dark mane, curving upwards in multiple tines, crowning the figure with the strange weight of bone.

"Do you know him?" Elaine asked.

"I don't," Mike replied.

"I thought you might, with all of your stories." She put down her coffee, dipped a finger in paint, and traced a silver highlight down the antlered man's cheek.

"Do you?" Mike countered, hesitantly.

Elaine turned, lightly placing her hands on his upper arms. "Shall I tell you a story?" she asked.

"Please do," Mike nodded, and sat down in his chair. Elaine turned back to the painting, drew in a deep breath that rattled like winter twigs between her teeth, and then began to speak.

"Gwyn ap Nudd laid eyes on the maiden Creiddylad and swore to let nothing stand in the way of their union. But, the maiden was betrothed to another man; Gwythyr ap Greidawl, with the flaming red hair and eyes like the midday sun.

"Gwyn raised a great army against his rival. Gwythyr summoned his own men, and there was a long and bloody battle for the hand of Creiddylad. But in the end, it was Gwyn who was victorious. His dark eyes flashed in triumph as he surveyed the battlefield. Gwythyr's men were broken and fleeing. Many had already been taken prisoner.

"But Creiddylad was not such a simple prize to take. It is said that King Arthur heard of the animosity between Gwyn and Gwythyr, and of the further cruelties inflicted after the battle. He summoned the two men; Gwyn with his sloeblack eyes and the white tinge of frost on his skin, and Gwythr with golden eyes and skin that simmered with summer heat.

"Arthur judged the men's deeds and weighed up their crimes. He concluded that they must continue to do battle each May Day, through all the centuries, until Judgement Day itself. Only then, on that final day, would the winner claim the maiden."

Mike looked at the painting again. Was there a cruel set to the man's lips, or was he just imagining it? "I hadn't heard that one," he told Elaine.

"I always wondered," she leaned wearily on the back of an empty chair, "what Creiddylad thought of it all.

Apart from being an object of desire, the maiden barely gets a mention."

"I suppose she's better off without either of them."

Elaine laughed, shaking her head as if a thread of spidersilk had fallen against it. Then she reached for her coffee and took a slow sip. "I suppose she is."

A companionable silence settled between them. Mike half stretched out his hand, and then paused. Elaine was looking at the painting, in the strange way that she still seemed to look at her creations, despite her eyes having failed her. Her lips were drawn tight and her cheeks glistened with silent, salty tears.

Mike wanted to tell her that she made a baggy cardigan look elegant. He wanted to comment on how her hair fell perfectly, even with paint dried into it. He wanted to tell her that she was a bright light in a dark world, and that it killed him to see her flame flicker, as she fought something he didn't understand.

"Would you like more coffee?" he asked.

Elaine shook her head. She was preoccupied. A sudden shriek roused her, and she spun round, startled, in the direction of the noise. Adrian hopped into the room, clenching his fists and shaking one foot in the air.

"Who put that there?" he said, gesturing towards the doorframe.

Elaine allowed her shoulders to drop. "Are you hurt?" she asked.

"It's my toe. I bet it's broken."

Mike allowed himself a small chuckle. "Well, if you will go picking fights with doorframes..."

"I know, I know." Adrian picked up his phone and limped over to the sofa. As soon as he sat down he went back to scrolling urgently through something on the screen.

His forehead was gathered into creases of worry and his eyebrows were drawn close and low. The skin around his eyes had a grey pallor, which hadn't been there yesterday.

"What are you reading?" Mike asked.

Adrian looked up in confusion, as if shocked to find he wasn't alone in the room. Elaine reached out, and Mike took her hand.

"It's no surprise. We knew it already," she said.

Adrian walked carefully to the fridge and grabbed an energy drink. He flicked the can open and sat down at the table. Elaine lowered herself into the chair next to him.

"It's Cabell, is it?" guessed Mike.

Adrian nodded, his eyes back on the screen, and took a gulp from the can.

"That stuff's bad for you, you know," the storyteller added.

Adrian glanced up. There was the ghost of a teasing grin on the other man's face. "That's rich, coming from you."

"I'm a reformed soul," Mike said, putting one hand to his heart, "free of the drink and ready for whatever life throws at me."

"You're not ready for this," Adrian said darkly.

"Try me."

"Alright." Adrian put the phone to one side and drew in a deep breath. "Another death last night. Or a presumed death, at least. All they found was blood and a few scraps of clothing."

"Where was it?" Elaine asked.

"Next to the Warren House Inn."

Mike nodded. "I know that pub well. It's up on the high moor, right in the middle of nowhere. Was his name in the records?"

"Of course it was. *John Dunn, carpenter,*" Adrian

160

said.

"So his next victim might be a descendant of the blacksmith," Elaine theorised.

"Maybe. It depends how many descendants each of these people have, and if one victim from each family line is enough." Adrian shrugged helplessly. He tapped one foot against the floor in a fast rhythm.

"We can't protect every descendant. I'm not sure they'd take kindly to us turning up and warning them about a murderous demon. I'm not even sure if we could protect them, to be perfectly honest." Mike shook his head.

"There might only be one or two still living on the moor. If we could find them, then we could at least try," suggested Elaine.

"Try to what? Convince them they need a sudden overseas holiday?" Adrian asked.

"Perhaps I had a vision that they should," said the blind woman. She was only half joking.

"Well the first step is to find them," said Mike, turning suddenly business-like, "and I still think we should speak to this witch."

Adrian leaned back and took a long swig from the can of energy drink. Then he took another, and another, until it was empty. The murder of two men certainly troubled him, but it felt distant somehow, as if it was other people's grief. No one in the room was a descendant of the three men who had incarcerated Cabell's corpse, which meant the demon huntsman wasn't looking for them. But the Wild Hunt Investigation Committee were worryingly active, and if the comments beneath the news headlines were anything to go by, then they were gaining more members. Gabriel and Gemma were due back tonight, and Adrian was worried about what might be waiting for them.

"We should eat. No one has good ideas on an empty stomach," announced Mike. He was already up and reaching for his waxed jacket, which hung by the door.

"Would you mind if we drove somewhere? I could do with sorting something out," said Elaine, her voice sounding carefully offhand.

"Yes, I was thinking that," Mike agreed, before asking where.

"It's a little way, but we could have breakfast there. You haven't been to Glastonbury, have you Adrian?"

"No," he replied, suddenly brightening. For a moment, all of the weight lifted, and he could have been back in Elaine's studio, quizzing her about the best choice of tarot cards.

"You'll like it," she replied.

Two hours later, they were poring over a menu in the Hundred Monkeys. The restaurant was half full, with joyful chatter in a mix of languages filling the room around them. From the kitchen, there was the smell of fresh bread and food being baked.

Elaine ordered tea, but only drank half of it. She attempted the egg on toast which was brought out for her, but gave up after a couple of bites. Adrian ate with his laptop open beside him, and every so often he forgot about the fork raised halfway to his mouth. The crystal shops and incense suppliers outside were enticing, but somehow the appeal fell flat when he thought about Gemma. They should be going from shop to shop together, and she should be rolling her eyes while he asked about magic wands. He looked up, as Elaine rose to her feet.

"Would you walk with me a little way?" she asked Mike. He glanced over at Adrian, conflict tightening the corners of his mouth.

"I'll be fine here for a bit," Adrian assured him, gesturing around the room, "if there isn't someone here who can prod my soul back into place, then Elaine has mis-sold this whole town."

Elaine frowned with concern.

"I'm joking. Nothing's going to happen," Adrian assured her.

With a guilty backward glance, Mike took his place next to Elaine and guided her out of the restaurant. The sun was beginning to warm up, and in between clouds it carried the memory of summer. Elaine walked slowly, describing the way they should be going. Her memory of the High Street was perfect, except for the fact a few shops had changed.

"So you came here a lot, before you went blind?" Mike guessed. He hadn't felt right asking how it had happened, and Elaine had never offered an explanation.

"Too many times to count," she answered, squeezing Mike's arm to turn right at the top of the High Street. The high walls of the Abbey grounds reared up beside them, sagging in places under the weight of themselves. "Shall I tell you how I lost my sight?" Elaine asked.

"Only if you want to." Mike felt her lean a little more on his arm, as if the story was a burden that she carried.

"I want to, because I've never told anyone. Do you have any stories like that?"

"Sometimes I think so." Mike shivered, despite the sun. There was the memory of a white horse with bells, and the buzz of flies, and the taste of something that burnt when he swallowed.

"They weigh you down after a while, all of the secrets," Elaine combed her hair back with her fingers, "it was near here that I lost my sight. There was a man that I loved; I thought I loved him more than life itself. Of course, I was young, and I didn't. But, when he disappeared, I travelled to the Otherworld to find him."

Mike stopped walking. "You've been *there*?"

"Only once, and the journey cost me my sight." Elaine tugged Mike's arm gently, to remind him to keep moving.

"And your man?" he asked awkwardly.

"Oh, he had long forgotten about me! I was just another silly girl by then, and he sent me back here in a hurry. He couldn't fix my eyes. That's how it works you see; a price to every crossing."

"So Adrian's soul?"

"It might be similar. I'm going to try and find out," Elaine said.

"Is that where we're going?" Mike asked.

"Where I'm going," she corrected.

They passed Chalice Well, claiming to contain the ancient red spring of Avalon, and then turned left down a narrow lane. Mike guided Elaine over a rusty cattle grid, which sung with the sound of water rushing beneath. Elaine stopped, her free hand reaching out tentatively.

"There is a path," she said. Mike saw it. They walked uphill, passed through a kissing gate, and followed the well-worn path that led up to the Tor.

A robin watched their progress from the hedge. It had seen countless pilgrims, taking that same path, hoping to find something at Glastonbury Tor. Some of them left clooties; knotted ribbons that hung from the low branches of apple and thorn, while others poured wine on the ground and spoke words, in earnest, that the robin didn't understand. Still others came with drums and loud voices. These were the visitors that the robin liked least, but it would still flutter down, and eat the bread they left out for the gods.

Elaine paused at a curve in the path. She described a grassy track, worn short by walkers feet, and they followed it around the side of the steep hill. The ground was uneven, but Mike guided her around rabbit holes and fierce thistles with care. Her pace quickened. Her expression tight with determination as she recognised the lie of the land beneath her feet.

"We're here," she said.

Mike looked around for some sort of landmark. There was the tufty grass, grazed short in places by sheep, and further up the slope there stood a lone hawthorn tree. It was small and gnarled, its branches bandaged with tattered ribbons. The only other thing to be seen was a large stone.

"Have I missed something?" Mike asked.

"Undoubtedly," Elaine's tone was gentle, "would you just help me up to the Egg Stone?"

Mike eyed the boulder next to the tree doubtfully. He supposed it could be slightly egg shaped, at a push. Supporting Elaine, while scrambling for footholds himself, he climbed up to the boulder. The earth was worn bare around it, as if many visitors had made the same journey, for some inexplicable reason. Elaine lay her palm against the smooth curve of the stone. "Thank you."

"You're welcome. What now?"

"You come back in an hour," Elaine answered.

Mike reeled back in surprise. "But," he stuttered, glancing around at the treacherous terrain, "but-" he

165

struggled to phrase the cause of his concern.

"I won't move from this spot. I'd just like to sit here for a while, alone," she said.

"Well, if you aren't going anywhere-"

"Exactly. In an hour I'll still be right here, waiting for my knight in shining walking boots."

Mike chuckled, waving the compliment away with one hand. He was grateful that Elaine couldn't see him blush. "I'll see you in an hour then."

Adrian ordered another coffee and opened the notebook app on his phone. He had found the name of the blacksmith who worked on the Cabell tomb in the parish records. *Garrick, Garrick*, he mouthed to himself, as he scrolled through the online phonebook. He searched in Buckfastleigh first, before simply typing in 'Dartmoor', but the automated message remained the same. There was no one registered with the name of Garrick on the moor. But not everyone had their name in the phone book, of course.

The waitress arrived with his latte, and he leaned back in his chair to take the first sip. His fingers tapped thoughtfully against the mug. Was being a blacksmith still a thing? Lots of people had posh gates, he supposed, and there were always those tongs that you seemed to need for poking your fire. It was one of those traditional crafts which people liked to keep in the family. You might not pass on your great love for fishing, but you might take the time to teach magic that made metal sticks into art.

Adrian paused halfway through a sip. That could be it! He opened up a new tab and searched the local business directory. Six blacksmiths came up, although none of them were in Buckfastleigh. The nearest one was in Princetown.

It wasn't far from the Visitor Centre. He typed the number into his phone and waited as it rang.

"Hello?" said a female voice.

"Oh, hello, could I speak to the blacksmith please?" Adrian asked.

There was a short pause. "You're speaking to the blacksmith."

"I'm so sorry. I presumed it would be-"

"A man?"

"Yes. Sorry." Adrian covered his eyes with one hand. How was he already making such an enormous mess of this?

"Don't worry, most people do. But my brother is far more interested in computers."

"Your brother? Does he live with you?"

"No, he moved to Canada. How can I help you?"

"Um," replied Adrian, wishing he had thought of some excuse for calling, "do you sell those fire things?"

"You mean a companion set?" the woman chuckled.

"Probably. It isn't for me."

"I'd guessed that. I have a couple of fireside sets here, readymade."

"Great! Could I come and look at them?"

"Yes, of course. I'm open until five." There was still that amused tone in her voice. Adrian couldn't help feeling that he liked her.

"Thanks, I'll be over. What's your name by the way?"

"Kate."

"Your second name?"

"Blackwood. Why?"

"Err, I have no idea, to be honest. Sorry. I'm looking forward to seeing your pokers."

"Right you are," said Kate. Adrian caught a second

of laughter just before she hung up.

He turned his phone face down on the table. That had been in the top five awkward conversations in his life so far. It may well have been worse than when he came out to his grandparents. At least they were understanding, whereas Kate clearly thought he was insane. He was already dreading visiting her later. What was he going to say? *There's a demon huntmaster on the loose, and he might want to kill you, but then again, he might actually be after somebody else?* Hideous. He needed Gemma's help with all this; she would have known something normal to say.

There were five other blacksmiths on the list. He decided to wait for Mike before making more calls.

The robin watched a figure sitting on the grass. He was talking to himself, which was by no means unusual, but he seemed to be saying the same thing over and over again.

"Would you like to go for dinner?" Mike asked the empty air, and then shook his head. "I've booked a table at the Globe in Chagford. I thought we could get some food." He stood up and began to pace a small circuit on the turf. "How about dinner?" he tried, then stopped, and shook his head again. The robin lost interest, as the man showed no sign of throwing any bread on the floor.

Mike pulled his hands from his forehead down to his chin. How could he be lost for words, when he knew so many stories? He might have advised a bit of Dutch courage in the past, but these days that was out of the question. "Elaine," he addressed the empty field with a flourish of his hands, "I think I might love you."

Morgana reclined on the flat ledge of Vixen tor. Lower down the slope, lay a flat slab of granite marking a Bronze Age kistvaen. She watched a thrush crack open a snail on the lid of the tomb.

"You must show them no mercy," she said. The thrush wiped the soft innards of the snail on the grass before swallowing it down.

"Yes m'lady," said Cabell, hastily buttoning his waistcoat.

"Unleash your hunt against them. Remind these mortals why they once feared the night!" The wytch stretched out her pale fingers and a black and tan hound raised its head. She sat up to stroke it, and where her hand fell the fur peeled away to ash. "I want their screams to lull me to sleep."

"I will ride now," said Cabell. His hounds slunk from the long shadows cast by the tor. They clambered out from the rocks, tongues tasting the air at the promise of meat.

"My huntsman," Morgana purred, beckoning him close. He leaned in hesitantly. The hunger that burnt in her eyes was enough to consume worlds. "Do not fail me." She caught hold of his jacket and pressed her fierce red lips against his. The skin of his face hollowed and cracked, grey dust filling his lungs with the scent of the grave. He pulled away, gasping, and clenched his fists at the ache of flesh growing back. Morgana laughed and released him.

"M'lady," Cabell managed, bowing his head in submission.

She watched as he mounted his horse and led the pack of hounds streaming across the moor. Then she turned back to the thrush and watched it smash open the shell of another snail.

"Let us see how much Gabriel loves his precious mortals when they rise up against him," she told the songbird. It paused pecking the shell free and cocked its head to one side. "Then I will guide the Clan in judging his betrayal." A cruel smile curved the corners of her lips. The thrush turned its attention back to its prize.

13.
HEAT

Elaine knelt in front of the Egg Stone. Her knees pressed into the soft brown earth, and her palms rested lightly on the rough surface of the rock. Very softly, she began to hum. Her voice grew slowly stronger, as the half-forgotten melody returned to her. The tune tasted of autumn fruits, and the first frost and the sweet tang of honey wine.

Around her, the air stilled. Clooties hung motionless on the thin branches of the small hawthorn, and the distant sound of pilgrims climbing the path to the Tor faded away. A thin mist breathed from the pores of the earth. First, it entangled the grass, then it spread, velvety slow, to lap at the grey base of the Egg Stone. Elaine breathed in deeply. She felt the mist rise, licking up along her skin, and she shuffled backwards as the stone beneath her hands fell away into the earth. "Gwyn?" she whispered.

Then there were strong hands, lifting her up, and lingering on her elbows in a steadying hold. "Elaine," the man greeted her. His voice was deep and smooth.

"You remember my name. I'm grateful," she replied, pushing a stray strand of hair away from her face.

"How could I not remember? I see that time has touched you very little."

Elaine laughed. "And time has touched you not at all. I can't see, but I'm sure of it." She reached up hesitantly, her hand shaking as she reached for Gwyn's face.

He caught her fingers, holding her hand softly against his cheek. A few seconds passed, and he guided her hand back down to her side. "At our parting, I promised you one request. I asked you to save it for the darkest time in

171

your life. Is this time now?"

"I think so."

"Then speak, and let me think on the remedy."

"It's my friend-" Elaine began, clenching her fist in front of her. She explained how Adrian had been dragged back from the dead, and how a piece of his soul remained in the Otherworld.

Gwyn wrapped his strong fingers around her fist. There was a gentleness to him; the sure movement of muscles barely being used. "I cannot interfere with the agenda of another Huntmaster, it would be an aggressive act against his Clan."

"But perhaps you could tell me what to do? I will visit the Otherworld myself again, if I need to," Elaine pressed.

"Your next visit to the Otherworld will be your last. You will not return." He said this softly. It was not a threat; merely a fact that must be considered.

"Then someone else?"

"Perhaps. Have you spoken with Gabriel? Does he know the boy's soul is loose?"

"No." Elaine's shoulders sagged. She should have been wiser than to have believed that Gwyn would wade in and fix everything. "Gabriel is away. He already has a demon huntsman to deal with on his return."

"A demon huntsman?" Gwyn asked. His interest was roused.

"Squire Cabell. A man cursed to return from the dead with his hounds. He's killed twice already."

"So he is mortal?"

"He was," Elaine shrugged, "now he's something else."

"There is an imbalance here," said Gwyn

thoughtfully, "Gabriel and his Clan wytch should have wards drawn up to prevent any such thing laying foot on their lands."

"You think there's more to it, than Cabell's desire for revenge?"

"Perhaps. You say it has begun while Gabriel is away? That seems a strange coincidence, for this huntsman to appear when his Clan is most vulnerable."

"Can you help?" Elaine asked. Her hands were clasped in front of her, and Gwyn once again took hold of them. For a long moment they just stood, two figures in a soft world of mist. The air hung thick with magic and the echoes of Elaine's song. She couldn't see Gwyn's eyes widen with concern.

"Is there nothing else you wish to ask?" he said.

Elaine's jaw tightened. She thought of the hospital visits, the patient nurses and the disease which spread tendrils inside her. It was as natural as life. Who was she to be excused? "No," she replied.

Gwyn released her hands. The air turned damp and cold, clinging to clothes and settling on skin. Elaine shivered.

"I will think on it," he said sadly.

"Please do," her tone was curt. The memory of their love was irreversibly tarnished. It lay like the skeleton of some creature claimed by the winter, slowly returning to the earth.

"We may not meet again," said Gwyn.

Elaine nodded. There was a lump in her throat which she was afraid might escape if she opened her mouth. Her arms were crossed over her body, hugging herself tight in a cocoon of cardigan.

"But this is not a fitting final memory for us," he added. With a wave of his hand, the mist disappeared. It was a warm autumn day and the air was sweet with the scent of ripe apples. Elaine looked around incredulously. She could see!

Gwyn smiled at her. The years had washed over him without trace, and his hair still curled, raven black, to his shoulders. His strong jawline was shadowed with a few days of stubble and his eyes gleamed like ripe berries. Extending a hand, he led her through the ancient orchard. Some trees had half fallen under their burden of apples, and they now grew reclined, like sated guests at a feast. A lazy breeze carried the busy hum of insects feeding on the sweet, soft flesh of the fruit.

Elaine remembered this day. The orchard lay on the lower slopes of the Tor, and that autumn had seemed to stretch on forever, full of wild fruit and honey. She had met the Huntmaster, thinking him no more than a handsome stranger.

"When I first saw the sun fall on your hair, I believed you were one of the fair folk yourself," Gwyn told Elaine.

"Not quite," countered Elaine shyly. The memory was too bold; too saturated with colour. She knew it wasn't real, but she longed to give in all the same.

"Believe me. I vowed in that moment to make you mine."

"And you did. What chance did I have?" Elaine's tone turned light. The soft sun was irresistible, and the air was heavy with the scent of over-ripe fruit. She breathed in deeply, then bent down to throw off her shoes.

Gwyn reached up to pluck a perfect apple. It was red, and a green so light it was almost gold. He offered it to Elaine. She snatched it mischievously and spun away, dancing in circles on her bare feet. The grass felt warm and springy, as if all the layers of earth beneath existed for the sole purpose of holding her up. There was no pain.

"This is all glamour," Elaine said.

"Does it matter?" countered Gwyn. He lay on the grass, reclining with his head against a fallen bough. Extending his hand, he beckoned her over.

She sat down next to him and took a bite of the apple. It was sharp and sweet at the same time; the flesh filled with clear juice. "No, it doesn't matter," she said. Her thoughts were slowed by the hot air. She relaxed into the syrupy weight of the sun and rested her head on Gwyn's shoulder. "I never asked why we ended. I travelled to the Otherworld with the intention of asking, but I somehow never asked."

"What answer would you like?" Gwyn replied, reaching over to smooth down Elaine's hair.

"Don't demean me. I'm not a child who requires the truth dipped in sugar."

Gwyn looked up at the blue sky through lichen clad branches. They spread like cracks in the heavens, weighed down with mistletoe, but still stretching towards the stars. Even the old, dry log beneath him had pushed forth a few buds, and a scar in the bark bristled with spindly branches. "Facing eternity, I feel a love for the transient," he said.

"An apple is sweetest, just before it goes bad," Elaine said dreamily.

"The whole tree is beautiful, because I can see it is dying."

High above the Tor, a raven croaked to its mate. It wheeled easily through the hot air, scything the sky with wings made of midnight. In the tangled hedgerow, small creatures cowered and crept, gorging on berries in preparation for winter. Sleep claimed Elaine slowly. It

175

slowed the blood in her veins, dropping like sap to the slow roots of memory. Gwyn kissed her on the forehead.

Kate Blackwood flicked down the switch on the electric kettle and fell back into her seat behind the till. The shop had been busy this morning, but now was the lunchtime lull. Her phone sat on the table. It was still open on the Devon Live news page, and the article she had just read was lodged in her mind.

The kettle clicked, and she made coffee slowly. Outside the shop, the sun had gone in, and a sombre grey light was pouring through the windows. She was thinking of a story that her father used to tell. Sometimes she would stay up with him, while he worked late at the forge to finish up some urgent order. Perhaps a woman needed a bespoke weathervane for her husband's birthday, and it needed to depict their three gundogs. Or a barn conversion might be in dire need of a curved curtain pole, before some all-important dinner party. She smiled to herself. But the story would always be about making iron bars, in double thickness.

There's magic in the iron, her father would tell her, *and we use the fire to wake it*. Very occasionally, the village vicar would call and ask the local blacksmith to make something. It would be a matter of great secrecy, and no money would swap hands. But the blacksmith and his family, however heathen they might be, would never go hungry if times became hard. In the story, the vicar wanted bars for a sepulchre. He came late in the evening, with no time to waste, and Kate's ancestor worked through the night to fashion the bars. They were installed the next day, in the tomb of Richard Cabell.

"They say he was a devil," her father had told her, laying cherry red metal over the anvil, "but that good iron would keep his soul in. Even during the Second World War, when they were stripping metal from just about everywhere, the bars on that tomb were never touched."

Kate held the coffee to her chest. They were treating it as an act of vandalism; the desecration of Cabell's tomb. There were a few suggestions, in comments on the article, that it might be the work of the same Satanists who had burnt down the church. But Devon Live was barely interested in the story. What was making good news, were the two mysterious murders on the moor, where only scraps of clothing and flecks of blood had been found from the victims. Both Simon Holloway and Thomas Dunn appeared, for lack of a better explanation, to have been eaten.

But no one seemed to be making the connection. This witch and her amulets was clearly an absolute crook, out to make a name for herself in the papers. But Cabell's tomb, sealed shut for three hundred years, was open, and two people were already dead. Things were bound with stone, iron and wood for good reason. Although, it wasn't the image of someone being devoured by a pack of ravenous hounds which was unsettling Kate. It was the nagging feeling that those names were familiar. She finished her coffee and flipped over the sign in the window to read 'Having lunch. Back soon!'.

She walked into the back room, which housed the forge and the workshop. Everything was cool and quiet. A half-finished companion set lay on the bench, and Kate thought of her strange caller from earlier. She hoped he didn't come while she was on lunch, although there was a phone number in the window, so he could ring if his poker needs were really that desperate. Smiling to herself, she pulled a cheese sandwich from her bag and began to unwrap it. Taking a bite, she pressed her phone to her ear and listened to the call tone.

"Kate," answered a gruff voice.

"Hi dad, quick question."

"Fire away. Is the shop alright?"

"It's fine. I was just thinking about that story you used to tell me, the one about Cabell's tomb."

"That one," replied the voice hesitantly, pausing while the phone was switched to the other ear, "isn't a story to think about on your own."

"I know, and I'm not thinking too much. It's just bugging me, what were the names of the other people who built it?" Kate asked.

"The tomb? Blowed if I know. That's a strange question."

"Yeah, I know it is. I just thought you told me sometime."

"Well, let me think. Now you mention it, maybe I did know. I'll text you if I remember, alright?"

"Alright, thanks for that."

"Ring on your way home."

"I will. Bye." Kate pressed the screen and shoved the phone in her pocket. There were no windows in the workshop, and it felt chilly without the forge alight. She was just considering making another coffee, when there was a scratch at the back door. She stood still, straining her ears to make sense of the sound. It came again, and her heart quickened in her chest. It was the unmistakeable sound of sharp claws against old wood.

Her phone vibrated in her pocket. Her eyes still on the back door, she unlocked the device and read the

178

message.

Holloway, Dunn and Garrick. Stone, wood and iron. Drop by after work, I'm making stew x

They were the same names as in the news. She knew they would be. Ever since hearing the story of Cabell and his tomb as a child, part of her feared this would happen. Even the best made bars rust in the end. But Garrick was her maiden name, and the magic of the blacksmith ran in her blood. She took a half-finished poker from next to the forge.

The scratching had fallen silent, although she knew that was no reprieve. Cabell was here for her. Calling the Police would only mean needless bloodshed. Kate texted her husband a simple *I love you*, and then opened the back door. She stood, feet slightly apart in the little patch of scrubland which they loosely called a garden. It bordered a small field, and round the edge scrawny elders grew, tangled in a cobweb of bramble. There was no one else there.

"Cabell!" Kate called towards the thorny hedge. She gripped the poker with two hands. One end came to a sharp point, and the other was curled into an ornate swirl of iron. It was still black with soot from the fire. "Show yourself!" she demanded, turning a slow circle, as her eyes darted around, seeking any sign of movement.

Low in the hedge, leaves rustled. They were loosened by the change of seasons, and already turning brown. The brambles fell aside as a hound forced itself through the tangle. It could have been a stray foxhound, except for the fact that its eyes were on fire. Thorns had snagged its skin, and in places the fur parted to reveal lines of red lava, dulling to a grey ash round the edges. The inside

179

of the hound looked like the heart of the forge. But Kate was no stranger to fire.

"You're less frightening than I imagined," she said to the creature. It crouched low, lips pulled back over gums filled with jagged teeth. *Come on then*, Kate mouthed. The hound sprung, claws stretched towards her chest. She waited, watching the arc of the creature's spring, and on the downward curve she thrust hard with the poker. The weight of the hound fell against it, forcing the metal through its shoulder and out the other side. Kate crumpled to her knees with the impact, but managed to keep hold of her weapon.

She scrambled back to her feet, treading on the limp hound with one foot as she pulled the poker free from its body. Liquid fire oozed out of the wound, and the beast lay still. She spun round, ready for another. The poker felt hot in her hands, but she forced herself to ignore the pain. "Who else wants a ticket back to Hell?"

A second hound prowled in a circle, sniffing the sulphurous scent of its fallen companion. It made a dash for Kate. She dodged the first snap of its jaws, stepping aside as they closed on empty air. It turned again, dripping tongue lolling out from its mouth, and she dealt it a sharp blow to the side of the head. The iron poker tore away a line of skin. The raw edges curled up and turned grey, framing a gash which flickered and steamed. The hound shook its head, dislodging a few droplets. They fell on the grass and kept burning. It leaped at Kate again, but the wound was affecting its eye, and its aim was poor. She sidestepped it easily, spinning on the ball of her foot and bringing down the poker as the creature landed clumsily. The iron pierced through the ribcage with surprising ease, pinning the flailing hound to the ground. It snapped and whined, but soon fell silent. Kate removed the poker.

Two more hounds had appeared in the garden. They eyed her hungrily, muscles rippling beneath their black and tan skin. Kate gripped the iron rod with both hands. Her arm muscles were strong from working the forge and adrenalin made her feel light on her feet. Both hounds attacked at once. She kicked one out of the way and stabbed at the other with the poker. It leaped back with a small wound to the leg. The first hound came again, and she raised the poker quickly, batting it off course. But, as the beast spun in the air, it lunged for her shoulder, catching sharp canines on vulnerable flesh.

Kate staggered, losing strength in that arm for a moment. The hound landed hard, but scrambled up quickly, licking the taste of warm blood from its teeth. There was a sudden rush of pain. The wounded hound had darted forward and bit Kate's leg. She dropped to one knee, and impaled the ravenous creature with the poker while it tore at her calf. It slumped to one side. She pulled out the poker, with some difficulty, and then leaned on it as she tried to stand.

"You have guts. I think we might be about to see them," said a chilly voice. Squire Cabell had forced his horse through the thicket and sat watching with a languid interest.

"Three hundred years to work on it, and that's all you've got?" Kate countered. There was blood trickling down the inside of her jumper.

"Three hundred years, which felt like all of eternity," Cabell growled, spurring his horse forward, "you could not begin to imagine."

"Probably not." She was watching the remaining hound with one eye. It had dropped back, waiting for another command from its master. More hounds were pouring through the hedge, their noses low to the ground and tails held high in excitement. Kate got to more than forty, before she lost count.

"I see you have killed three of my hounds. How regrettable. The others did no such damage." Cabell dismounted from his horse and stalked closer. He moved with the same feral grace as his pack.

"You mean Simon and Thomas?"

"They were easy prey. Dispatching them lacked any excitement. But you... you have some fight in you."

Kate held her head high, lips slightly parted as she breathed through the pain. She was like a cornered vixen, her gaze darting between the hounds and their master. "I'm sorry about the tomb and all that, but if you come a step closer I'll kill you as well."

Cabell laughed. His eyes shone with genuine enjoyment. "Brave girl," he purred. With a flourish of his fingers, the three fallen hounds flared up and fell away into ash. Only scorched shapes on the grass remained where they had lay. "I must accept your invitation." He produced the dagger from inside his pocket.

The huntsman strode forward and Kate backed away, keeping the distance between them. She moved clumsily, fresh blood welling up from the wound in her leg. Her only chance was to lure Cabell close enough to get a good stab with the poker. She held the weapon at her side, one palm on the handle, ready to drive it home with all of her strength.

"You seem very eager to meet your end. Again," she taunted.

Cabell was playing with the dagger, spinning it from hand to hand. His slim fingers were unpleasantly nimble, giving the impression of a spider reeling in its victim. "On the contrary. This is only the beginning. There are so many vermin needing to be culled." He smiled broadly at the thought.

"I almost feel bad to stop you."

"Let me end those feelings forever." Cabell lunged forward, covering the three paces between them too fast for Kate to dodge. But the poker was already prepared, and as he stretched towards her, she angled it up and thrust towards his chest. Her damaged shoulder took some strength from the blow, but the sharp point of iron made contact, gouging a line into Cabell's forearm. He reeled back in surprise, staring at his torn jacket. Beneath the red cloth, blood oozed to the surface and bubbled with a strange heat. The wound scabbed over with a coating of ash. He inspected it curiously.

Kate realised it was the first time he had been injured. "Next time it won't be a warning," she forced her voice to sound confident, despite knowing she was no match for the huntsman.

"You know I could simply instruct these hounds to devour you?"

"But you won't, because you want to do it yourself."

"Brave and perceptive. This is almost a waste." He moved slowly this time, his lips parted in anticipation. Kate bent her knees slightly, grounding herself and gripping the poker. There was no theatrics with the dagger now. Cabell held it steady in front of him, both eyes fixed on his prize. He was perhaps an arm's length away. Kate needed him just a little closer to get a good strike. *Come on*, she mouthed.

Cabell struck. But the dagger was held high. Kate had guessed he wouldn't go for a killing blow to begin with. She jabbed forward with the poker, a wild cry tearing from her throat, as she put everything she had into the blow. The iron spike slid beneath Cabell's ribs. He froze, blade still raised, and looked down at the blood blossoming from around the puncture. There was the hiss of liquid on a hot surface, and a red glow spread along the length of the poker. Kate let go. She stared as the flesh around the hole tried to heal, but each time the ashy scab touched the iron it peeled back and had to begin again.

A hand caught hold of her shoulder. Kate's mouth fell open. Cabell dragged her closer, until she could feel the searing heat of the poker next to her skin. The arm with the dagger dropped and brought the blade down to her cheek. There was an unpleasant smell of burning flesh.

"Fine sport," Cabell murmured. The dagger fell away. It reappeared in the back of Kate's neck. She crumpled immediately. The huntsman took her weight, lowering her slowly to the ground. Grimacing, he placed both hands on the poker and pulled it free from his chest. Immediately, the wound began to scab over. He wiped the dagger on his own bloodstained breeches.

The hounds prowled close, sniffing the scent of blood on the air. Their jaws hung open, dripping with saliva. A couple lowered their muzzles towards Kate.

"Leave her," Cabell snapped. The hounds backed away sulkily, their tails between their legs. At a gesture from their master, they all turned as one, and went pouring back through the bramble hedge.

184

14.
DESTINY

"It's a reproduction," said Franz, turning the Iron Cross over in his hand.

"How can you tell?" Eva asked.

"Look at this marking on the pin. Can you see it has L/4 engraved into it? The numbering system started with L/10, so this cannot be original." He passed it back to a slightly stooped man in a flat cap, who was shaking his head incredulously.

"I was assured this was genuine," said the antiques dealer, resettling his cap in agitation.

Franz shrugged. "It is a good replica. Others might not notice."

"Do you know much about the Spear of Destiny?" Eva asked the old man.

He paused with his hand in the display case, where he was flattening the frayed ribbon on the medal.
"That isn't a piece handled by lowly dealers like me. I'm not even sure I'd want to come across it, if I'm honest. Fascinating, yes, but cursed so they say."

"What kind of curse?" Eva asked. Franz was busying himself looking at an assortment of pieces in another display cabinet. There was a small metal plane, with one wing bent from a life of rough use.

"Oh, I don't really pay much attention to these things," the antiques dealer explained, waving one hand dismissively through the air as he locked up the medal cabinet, "but the story goes that whoever wields the spear will be victorious in battle."

"Doesn't sound like much of a curse," Eva

interjected.

"Hear me out. The downside is that, should the owner ever lose or discard the spear, then their death will immediately follow! Take Hitler for example. American soldiers found the spear holed up in a wall, and less than an hour and a half later the Fuhrer was dead."

Eva nodded thoughtfully. She had pulled up the boot liner in the Range Rover and the spear was carefully stashed in that hollow. Most nights she would wake up with the sudden urge to check it was still there. Even thinking about it now made her palms itch with the desire to hold it.

"But it's a load of old tosh," the old man added, his cheeks slightly coloured with embarrassment as he sidled back behind his counter. "It's most likely fake anyway!" he directed this observation at Franz, who appeared to have lost interest in the new turn of conversation.

Franz looked up, the trace of a startled look in his eyes, as if he had been roused from the depths of a daydream. "How much is your plane?" he asked.

A few minutes later he and Eva were walking out of the antiques shop, each carrying an additional weight. Franz had the plane wrapped in tissue in his pocket, and Eva was weighed down with the story of the spear. Her thoughts were grey, like the clouds which rolled across the sky and threatened rain. A chilly wind was plucking at the leaves on the trees, which would soon be too loose to withstand its attentions. From an island in the middle of a small pond, a rather forlorn looking duck surveyed the car park.

Franz noticed Eva shivering. "Do you want coffee?" he asked her. There was a timber clad building nearby, with an A-frame outside proclaiming the high quality of their cream teas. The folded sun umbrellas seemed redundant beneath the gathering clouds, but the bold use of coloured chalk paint added a touch of cheer.

"Maybe," Eva conceded.

They pushed open the door to the tearoom. It was quiet, and pleasantly warm, with just one couple sharing a plate of scones in the corner. The walls were crowded with prints of cupcakes, and artificially aged metal signs advertising flour. Behind the counter, a woman with victory rolls and a gingham apron beamed at them.

"What can I get you?" she asked.

"Black coffee, and-" Franz turned to Eva.

Her eyes were glassy. "Earl Grey, please," she said, rubbing her forehead.

"Sure thing. Take a seat and I'll bring them over."

Eva dropped heavily into her chair. It was wooden, with a detachable cushion made from floral fabric. Franz sat more carefully, his hands clasped on the table in front of him.

"You look like you're about to question me," Eva laughed dryly.

"Are you feeling guilty?" Franz retorted. He watched Eva's face lose a little more colour.

"No more than usual," she replied. Her fingers played a nervous rhythm on the scrubbed wood, until the arrival of her drink brought a welcome distraction. She opened the lid of the pot and began to poke at the teabag with her spoon.

Franz blew on his coffee. "So what now?" he asked. There had been no discussion of what happened out on the moor, other than the brief allusion to it in Ashburton. But the pain of it followed them like a personal raincloud, and Eva was showing signs of her suffering. She struggled to sleep. She didn't eat enough, and her face had the hunted look of someone who was on the run.

"Get under the table," said Eva. Her eyes were wide with terror.

Franz obeyed her urgency without question, muscle memory folding him silently to the floor. Eva watched through the legs of her chair as a swaggering figure strode up to the counter.

"Tea please, takeaway," said the drawling voice of Blake. He was wearing a white Panama hat, which seemed inappropriate for the weather, and a grey suit. One shiny black and white shoe tapped impatiently on the floor.

"Coming up," said the woman, turning to the urn behind her.

Blake seemed distracted. He pushed up his sleeve and consulted a surprisingly modern looking watch. Whatever it showed him seemed to be dissatisfying, and he let the fabric drop with a scowl.

"Sugar?" the lady behind the counter asked.

"Four," replied Blake, almost snatching the cup from her hand when it was offered. He left the money on the counter and turned heel with an agitated shake of his head.

Ten seconds passed like an eternity. Finally, Eva clambered back onto her seat. The woman working in the shop watched her with some concern. Franz dusted off the knees of his trousers and took a generous sip of coffee. Eva lunged forward and grabbed his lapel, dragging him roughly across the table. He managed to steady his coffee cup. Her face was inches from his.

"He's following us," she hissed.

"I suspected that, since his last appearance," Franz said levelly. He closed his hand around Eva's and gently prised her fingers off his jacket. Slowly, he sat back down, motioning for Eva to do the same. She complied, although her expression remained terrified.

The lady who had served their teas bustled over, carrying a slice of Victoria sponge on a fine china plate. "Here, I'm never going to sell all of this today." She lay the cake in front of Eva, a motherly concern in her eyes.

"You are too kind," said Franz, dipping his head, "may we have takeaway cups for our drinks?"

"Of course." The woman bustled off again.

"Why didn't you say something?" Eva demanded.

"I couldn't be sure. But this proves it. I think he is tracking the credit card we were given."

"But it's in the car, and we haven't used it here."

"Which is why he knows we are nearby, but not exactly where. That is the only reason he has not contrived to bump into us yet."

Eva jumped to her feet. "The car! He can track the car!"

Franz narrowed his eyes. The vehicle had never been designed to blend in, and he had advised against it at the dealership. But Eva was adamant at the time. "Why does that matter in particular?" He poured his remaining coffee into a paper cup and reached over to do the same for her tea.

"Well, everything we own is in there," she said defensively.

Franz nodded, choosing to drop it. There was more to this, and it tied in with Eva's pale face and the way she mumbled in her sleep. He wrapped the cake in a napkin.

Outside, the wind had gathered force. Small ripples spread across the surface of the pond, and the duck had retired somewhere for shelter. Eva gripped Franz's arm as they hurried across the lawn, heads bowed to the weather.

"Let's get out of here," she said, risking a quick scan for any sign of Blake, "let's just drive."

"It will require a new credit card, which means an account and an address. But nothing is impossible, something can be done," muttered Franz, touching the model plane inside his pocket.

They crossed a small road and cut through a gravelled courtyard, crowded with rusting tools, headless statues and vintage clothes on rails. Multiple small shops spilled out of sheds and shipping containers onto the gravel, each claiming to be full of antique wonders. Eva's gaze lingered on a dingy shack crammed with taxidermy, dried insects and pickled organs in jars. There was a human skull leering out from the cobwebbed window. She hurried past, unsure if she was more afraid of it stirring, or of nothing happening at all.

In the far corner of the courtyard was a rickety bridge, spanning a slow and dirty stream. The green metal handrails were peeling and the worn footboards, which may have once served as scaffolding, were bowed with use. Their car waited for them on the other side. But the bridge was blocked.

Blake took off his hat with a flourish. He bowed as Franz and Eva came to a halt. "How fortunate to cross paths with you again!" he oozed.

"What do you want, Blake?" Eva snapped. Her fists were clenched so tight they were shaking.

"What do I want? Now that *is* a question. I'd hate to bore you with a full answer, especially as I often change my mind. But, as you were so kind to ask, I shall divulge a little secret to you," he looked theatrically from side to side, as if making sure this next utterance would not be overheard, "I want you to have your father back." He nodded seriously, extending his hands as Eva broke away from Franz.

"What do you mean?" she demanded.

"I lost my own father," Blake explained, reaching into his waistcoat for a gold pocket watch, "fine man. Casualty of war." He pressed the edge of the watch and it sprung open to reveal a clock face on one side, and a black and white photograph on the other.

Eva drifted closer, her eyes wide with the familiar weight of tears. "I'm sorry."

"I'm sorry too. It wasn't his time you see! Such a terrible waste, especially when he was so brave. All he wanted was to keep his family safe." Blake took a white handkerchief from his pocket and made a great show of dabbing at his eyes.

"Could you get him back?" Eva asked.

"Alas no. I didn't know people capable of such wonders at that time," Blake folded the handkerchief and returned it to his pocket, "but now I have friends who I feel you must meet. You know one of them already; he is taking wonderful care of your dear father's aeroplane."

"Maximillian?"

"Quite so. The fabled Collector himself. He is just one of a group of fine folk I'd like you to get to know. It would be my pleasure, in fact, my absolute honour, to introduce you to them."

Franz moved protectively to Eva's side. She stood with her toes resting on the warped planks of the bridge.

"Can they bring my father back to life?"

"My dear Evangeline," said Blake grandly, his hands raised reverently to the heavens, "there is nothing these men cannot do." He dropped his hands and reached into the inner pocket of his jacket. Opening an ornate silver case, he slid out another black business card and offered it to Eva. "Time is of the essence," he added.

Mike climbed the steep track up the side of the Tor. He had passed the hour quickly, wrestling with the best way to invite Elaine out for dinner. The robin had grown so bored of the repetition that it had found another field to observe.

"The table is already booked, it's nothing much," he muttered under his breath, feeling an ache in his calves as he hurried up the path. He had always been in the habit of taking long daily walks on the moor, but with Adrian to look after he found himself staying much nearer the house. There was something else as well; the faint sound of bells and the distant scent of carrion under the sun. It frightened him, in a way that even his encounters with the Beast never had.

He scaled the final grassy bank up to the Egg Stone. Expecting to see Elaine perched on the boulder, he paused in concern when there seemed to be no sign of her. "Elaine?" he called. A restless wind caught his voice and dragged it up, along the line of the hill, and sang it through the ruined tower that crowned the Tor. There was no reply. Scrambling the last few steps, he swung his head from left to right. The worn-down earth around the smooth stone was conspicuously empty. He turned his attention to the gnarled hawthorn tree. Purple, green and gold ribbons fluttered in the breeze, and small bells jangled from the thorny branches. A woman lay still on the ground beneath them.

Breaking into a jog, Mike covered the short distance to Elaine. He paused a pace away, suddenly afraid to get any closer. Her dark hair was spread on the grass like clambering vines, and her limp fingers curled around a half-eaten apple. The lingering expression on her face was serene, as if she could feel the sun on her face through the gathering clouds. Her shoes were placed next to her.

"Elaine?" he repeated. Was he imagining it, or did her eyelids flicker? He took the final step and fell to his knees. Her chest was rising and falling softly. Mike allowed his shoulders to drop, although his heart still beat fast. "Have you heard the tale of the man who fell asleep beneath a faerie thorn?"

Elaine stirred, rolling onto one side and half opening her eyes.

"He was spirited away to another world, and in that hollow hill he met the faerie Queen. She was the most beautiful woman he had ever laid eyes on," Mike said softly.

"What happened then?" Elaine asked drowsily.

"What would you like to happen?"

Elaine closed her fingers testingly on the apple in her hand. She felt about for her shoes, and then pulled them back over bright, mismatched socks. The wind was picking up, teething against the trees on the lower slopes, as it prepared to unleash a deeper chill.

"I suppose she might say something like; *a human lifetime is a terribly short while to get anything done. Let's not waste a moment longer. We shall go out for dinner, but you must choose the restaurant!*"

A beaming smile spread over Mike's face. He helped Elaine to her feet and grinned as she leaned on his arm. "What a wise woman," he chuckled. They descended slowly, avoiding rabbit holes and large, spiky thistles. "Did you sort out what you needed to do?" he asked.

Elaine's face darkened. "I'm not sure." She offered no further explanation, and Mike was content to drop it.

They walked the rest of the way back to the High Street in easy conversation about recommended restaurants and favourite foods.

Adrian glanced up as they walked into the Hundred Monkeys. He was halfway through writing a phone number on a napkin, and there were two empty cups lined up next to his laptop.

"Good walk?" he asked.

"Very good," Mike replied happily. He shifted his weight from one foot to the other, as if he could hardly contain a newfound energy.

Adrian dropped his gaze and completed copying the number for the amulet selling witch. Then he folded the laptop and tucked it under his arm. "Still up for paying some visits this afternoon?" he asked Mike.

The storyteller looked uneasily from Adrian to Elaine. "Yes, I reckon so. Just not in the evening."

"We can go now if you like," Adrian said.

It was mid-afternoon by the time they got back to Princetown. Elaine was tired, so they helped her into the house before making their visit to the blacksmith. It was a five-minute walk; past the Visitor Centre and across the carpark where Adrian and Gemma had arrived at the very start of all this. That day seemed a long while ago. Adrian comforted himself with the reminder that Gemma should be back by the evening.

The door to the shop and forge was closed. There was a note stuck to the glass which read: '*Having lunch, back soon.*'

"Seems a bit late for lunch," Mike observed.

"I phoned, so she is expecting me this afternoon.

Perhaps she forgot to take the note down?" Adrian cupped his hands and peered through the glass. The light was on in the shop and a mug of drink sat on the counter.

"What did you say on the phone?"

Adrian coloured. "You don't want to know." He rested his fingers on the door handle and pushed down gently. It gave way under the weight, and the door swung inwards.

"Maybe you are right about the note," said Mike.

"Hello?" Adrian called, as he stepped inside. He waited a moment, and then called again. "Kate? I phoned earlier about the fire stuff."

"What do you need a fire set for?" Mike asked.

"I don't, I just needed a reason to come here," Adrian whispered. "Kate?" he called again. The door to the back room was ajar, and Adrian could see a work bench laid out with tools and various pieces of metal.

"It all seems very quiet. Perhaps we should come back tomorrow," suggested Mike.

"She said she'd be here," Adrian shrugged, reaching towards the door of the workshop. He knocked sharply. There was no answer, so he pushed the door fully open. The forge was unlit and there was no sign of Kate, other than an open lunchbox and one half eaten sandwich on the bench. There was an unpleasant feeling to the room; a lingering prickle of fear which Adrian would have struggled to explain out loud. But he could feel it. A third door, leading out onto some rough sort of lawn, was also open. A shape on the grass drew all of Adrian's attention.

"Bloody hell!" he cried, breaking into a run. Mike followed at once, and they both skidded to a halt a few paces from Kate's motionless body. There were burn marks in the grass around her, and the air held the hum of congealing blood.

"Look at these," said Mike, tracing the edge of the scorch marks with his foot, "see the shape?"

"Hounds!" exclaimed Adrian, crouching to look, "they're the shape of hounds!" he stood quickly, pulling his jumper up over his mouth. He was trying not to look at Kate, with her brown eyes still open and staring blankly at the sky.

"It looks like she did a bit of damage before Cabell finally got her," Mike said sadly. There were three charred patches of grass. A metal poker lay close to her body.

"Why wasn't she eaten like the others?" Adrian asked, through his sleeve.

Mike shrugged. "I don't know." He was looking at Kate with sombre weariness. There was a wound to her shoulder, but the damage wasn't enough to have killed her. Bruising on the front of one calf told him there was a worse wound behind, but still not a deadly blow. He guessed there must be another, more subtle, injury.

"What do we do?" asked Adrian.

"I'm going to phone the police. I want you to go."

"What do you mean?"

"Look, I live here. It's not so strange that I might come in to check on a neighbour if I see her shop is quiet. Speak to the witch. Dealing with the police always takes a while," Mike said softly.

"Alright," Adrian agreed. He was beginning to feel lightheaded. The bodies at Grimspound had felt less real, because there was a crazy necromancer, and undead servants straight out of a low budget film. This was much more disturbing. It was a normal day, birds were singing in the hedgerow, and there was a woman lying dead on the grass. He turned back, halfway to the door. "How do you know about dealing with the police?"

"I told you before," said Mike, pulling his phone from his pocket, "people die out on the moor."

Adrian sat on the grey steps of the Visitor Centre and phoned the number on his napkin. A bright, slightly squeaky voice answered.

"Hello, Clara Merryweather, Professional Witch, how may I help you?"

"Oh, hello," said Adrian, praying inwardly not to turn into a blabbering weirdo on this phone call, "I was hoping to purchase one of your talismans."

"Well, how wonderful! I have lots to choose from online."

"The thing is, I live just up the road. I was wondering if I could, you know, come over and handle some," Adrian explained. He put one hand to his forehead as soon as the words fell out his mouth.

"I see," said Clara, in a voice which suggested raised eyebrows, "what did you say your name was?"

"Adrian."

"Alright Adrian, you come over and take a peek at my wares!" There was the echo of a giggle. Adrian wished he wasn't visiting alone. "I'll text you my address. And it's cash only, just to let you know," Clara added.

The keys to Adrian's Beetle hung on the rack just inside Mike's front door. There was no sign of Elaine in the kitchen, and Adrian guessed she must be sleeping upstairs. He unhooked the keys with a mix of excitement and worry. This would be the first time he had driven, since being technically dead, and coming back with inconvenient blackouts. But Mike was busy with the police, and Cabell had killed three people now. The witch was the only one who had survived, if you didn't count him and Mike hiding

197

in a bush, which meant she had to know something. It was just a case of getting that knowledge out of her.

He drove slowly to the address in the text message. It was a small house, down a nondescript road, on the edge of Buckfastleigh. There was a metal cat in the front garden, with marbles for eyes, and a doormat with a broomstick printed on it. Adrian rang the bell.

Clara opened the door with a flourish. She was wearing black harem pants, glittery slippers, and a sheer silk blouse printed with crescent moons and stars. Cluttered strings of beads hung from her neck, dripping with crystals in silver cages and small pouches marked out with runes. Her cheeks glowed with blusher.

"Adrian?" she asked. Her tone carried some disappointment.

"Yes, I'm here about the amulets."

"Of course you are. Come on in." She bustled through to a busy looking living room. There was a small table, painted like a Ouija board, and two chairs draped in black velvet cloth. "Will you have tea?"

"Yes please," he answered, attempting to take in the occult assault on his eyes.

"Do sit, make yourself at home," called Clara from the kitchen. Adrian suspected he had been saved from something by the virtue of being just a little too young.

The witch returned with a tray of tea making essentials. She had draped a black, tasselled shawl over her blouse and exchanged the sparkly slippers for more comfortable looking furry ones.

"Where did you hear about my amulets?" she asked.

"I read an article in the paper."

"Excellent. I thought that was worth doing. Now,

where are my manners?" She poured tea into two bone china cups and offered Adrian a plate piled with biscuits. He took two chocolate covered ones. Clara placed three on her own plate.

"Did the papers approach you?" Adrian asked.

"Yes, they read my blog and asked me to share my knowledge with their readers. People aren't used to these supernatural manifestations right under their noses. The Wild Hunt Investigation Committee are working flat out to research the phenomenon," Clara explained.

"You know them?"

"Of course. I am the local witch," she said, a little haughtily.

"I overheard them in the pub," Adrian told her, dunking half a biscuit in his tea, "they were talking about burning down Wistman's Wood."

"They were?" asked Clara, hesitating with her cup raised, "That's awful. Steven told me it was about gaining knowledge."

"As far as we could tell, it's about him getting free stuff, and delusions of power," said Adrian.

Clara put a whole custard cream in her mouth, many silver bracelets jangling forlornly with the movement. Her eyes were turned downwards, fixed on her empty teacup. "I see."

"He's very persuasive," Adrian added comfortingly, pouring the slightly deflated woman a fresh serving of tea. "Have you been a witch a long time?"

"Well," said Clara, rearranging a string of amber with some grandeur, "my great, great grandmother could cure warts on pigs, so I know the gift runs in my blood. After feeling the call myself, I have been following the ways of Hekate, Great Queen of witches for, ah, at least... two and a half moons now."

"Two and a half moons?"

"Months. Two and a half months," Clara admitted, crossing her arms in front of her.

"That's quite a while to stick at something new," Adrian told her kindly.

"It is?"

"Definitely. I gave up palm reading after three days. I realised I didn't really like hands."

"Oh, I know what you mean! Aren't sweaty hands just absolutely awful?" agreed Clara, regaining some of her enthusiasm. "May I show you the amulets now? I'd really like to."

"Please do," replied Adrian.

Clara stood up and rummaged deeply in the pocket of her baggy trousers. She found a small, silver key, and used it to unlock an Art Noveau display cabinet. There was a quite amateur painting of a naked man with antlers hung in a gold frame above it. Next to the cabinet was a ribbon clad broomstick, and a black mirror which had gathered a thin veil of dust.

"Here we are," said Clara proudly, spreading three clay charms across the palm of her hand. "I mix the clay with ashes and dried herbs for protection. The gemstones help to increase their power."

In a room full of clutter, the amulets were noticeably real. Clara's fingerprints were on the clay, and a layer of clear varnish did nothing to neaten the rough mix of ashes and crumbled leaves. One disc had a triple swirl carved into it, with a green stone in the centre. The others featured a well-endowed woman and an almost symmetrical pentagram. The raw nature of them was part of their power.

"I like these a lot," said Adrian.

"You do?" replied Clara brightly.

"How much are they?"

"I was thinking around the forty pound mark."

Adrian raised an eyebrow, but kept his lips pressed politely closed.

"Twenty pounds to you?" added Clara experimentally.

"Sold. I'll have the swirly one please." It was almost worth the money to just see the delight on Clara's face, but the necklace would also be a good welcome back gift for Gemma. The witch wrapped it carefully in purple tissue paper and stuck it down with a star shaped sticker. "What do you know about the Wild Hunt?" Adrian asked her.

Clara paused, a look of guilt ghosting across the curves of her face. "Not a lot," she admitted.

"But you told the newspaper that you met the hunt out on the moor?"

Clara looked from side to side, as if concerned that the china cats or the antlered man in the painting might overhear her admission. "That's what he told me to say. The man I met told me to warn the world about the Wild Hunt. He said that witches understood fear, which was why he didn't kill me."

"Can I tell you something Clara?" asked Adrian quietly. She nodded, pulling her chair a little closer to the table. "I've met the Master of the Wild Hunt myself. His name is Gabriel. I don't like him, but I do know that he has been away from here for the last three days."

"How do you know that?"

"My best friend is with him," Adrian explained.

"With him? As in dating him?" asked Clara, wide eyed.

201

"No! Well, not really. I bloody hope not, because he's an asshole," said Adrian, with some venom. Clara was still staring, her mouth a little open. "Anyway, the point is that the man you met is something else entirely. His name is Squire Cabell. You can look him up on Wikipedia," Adrian added quickly.

Clara was nodding slowly, as she attempted to digest this new information. "So why did he tell me to talk about the Wild Hunt?"

"I'm wondering that as well."

15.
REUNION

A shadow flitted from the fence to the holly tree. It lifted its head, a small scrap of black against the pressing wilderness of the moor, and began to sing. Dusk circled behind it, hungry and slow, but in that small square of garden the blackbird was king. He surveyed his domain with a generous pride. There was the lawn, left a touch too long and sprinkled with late wildflowers, and the little cracked patio where snail shells could be smashed if dropped from a height. Then there was the wooden table, with two matching chairs, and the figures that hunched, in silence, around it. He tolerated them graciously.

"We should go in," said Adrian.

Mike hesitated, his fingers round an empty glass. The evening air was cold, even with a coat. But going in was somehow admitting defeat, and accepting that the day was over. He had phoned The Globe to cancel his table. Elaine had not woken up, and he guessed she would sleep through until morning. There was still no sign of Gemma.

"You're probably right," he agreed, making no effort to move.

There was the faint sound of knocking. Adrian leaped up from his chair, sending the blackbird fluttering away in fright. He ran through the house, with Mike following close behind. Adrian slowed slightly in the kitchen, pausing enough for Mike to overtake him and pull open the door.

Gemma stood on the cracked garden path. She looked tired, but otherwise alright. Owain stood a pace behind her, hugging himself and looking grey.

"Turns out Owain gets seasick," Gemma said.

Mike ushered them both inside and put on the kettle. He bustled about busily, setting out cups and digging some fruit cake out of one of the cupboards. Fian sniffed at the counter with interest.

"You should have a sweet tea," he said to Owain, then stopped to think for a second, "do fairies drink tea?"

"Yes, thank you," said Owain. He gripped the edge of the table, as if the waves had followed him.

Adrian held out his arms and caught Gemma in a tight squeeze. Her clothes smelt strange. He breathed in the scent of sweet honey, overlaid on the stale musk of caves. "Was it bad?" he asked her.

"It would have been better if you were there," she replied. There was a smile on her lips, but a shadow clung to her eyes, as if things lodged there that couldn't be unseen. Adrian realised he must look the same. A lot had happened in three days.

"Are you allowed to tell us about your adventures?" Mike asked Gemma, forcing an unsteady lightness into his voice.

"I don't know," she answered, glancing at Owain.

"You're going to tell Adrian anyway," he mumbled, his head in both hands.

Gemma opened her mouth to argue, but decided it was pointless. The Apprentice was right; she was going to tell Adrian about *most* of it. So she did.

She skimmed over the music and the food and the hall full of candles. She mentioned the swan wytch, and the fate of Asterra. She stumbled a little over the baby boy, and the way his mother had sobbed in the silent room. "I thought of you Adrian, because standing in the way of those hounds was the most stupid thing I've ever done. But it was worth it."

"Sounds like those Irish faeries weren't ready for you!" grinned Mike. He had relaxed a little, finally taking a seat next to Adrian. Lifting the mug of tea to his lips, he realised, with surprise, it was empty.

"How have things been here?" Gemma asked. Mike and Adrian looked at each other.

"You're not going to believe this," Adrian told her. His face was serious, but there was that tell-tale glint in his eyes that told her this was to do with the supernatural. He mentioned the news reports, and the murders and the mysterious witch who was suddenly famous. He described the way the stone of the sepulchre had burned, and how the iron bars had melted down to liquid metal. When he got on to Kate, the light dimmed from his eyes, and he described the way they had found her with simple words. "But Elaine has been doing some painting, which is nice, and I did get you a gift." He produced the wrapped amulet from inside his pocket.

Gemma pressed two fingers to her forehead. "You say there's a witch going around, scaring people with stories about the Wild Hunt, while a demon huntsman is *simultaneously* out for murderous revenge?"

"It'd make a good story, if it wasn't so true," said Mike.

Adrian reached towards her, over the table, and pressed the wrapped bundle into her hand. "The witch said this was an amulet of protection. She's mostly mad, but she was nice when I met her."

"The Wild Hunt Investigation Committee. What does that mean?" asked Owain. His eyes were still turned down to the table.

"They mostly seem to drink," said Adrian.

205

"Although one of them had the bright idea of burning down Wistman's Wood," Mike added.

Owain's head shot up. He fixed Mike with a wild expression.

"The landlord gave them a good speaking to," Mike said reassuringly.

"And Clara, the witch, has vowed not to mention the Wild Hunt any more to the papers," said Adrian.

But Owain was already on his feet, coiling his leg muscles like a creature restless to run. "I need to tell Gabriel," he said. Mike nodded. The Apprentice threw a look at Gemma. It was somewhere between an apology and a promise. Then he was gone, racing out the door and turning towards the moor. There was the rumble of a large engine and the screech of tyres as a car took off at high speed.

"Is it weird how much Owain drives?" Adrian asked.

Gemma shrugged. "He does fae stuff as well." She unwrapped the little parcel held in her hand, and the amulet spilled onto her palm. It was the size of a large coin. "What is this supposed to do?" she asked Adrian.

"Protect you from the Wild Hunt."

"But I thought the demon huntsman was the problem?"

"Well, maybe it does both," Adrian suggested.

"Isn't one supernatural hunter enough for this place? I mean, why couldn't I have come back to the mystery chocolate gifter, or the strange tale of the free spa?" Gemma grumbled.

"That would be something," said Mike, stifling a large yawn. "I've changed the sheets. I'm happy on the sofa."

"Alright, let's make sense of this in the morning," suggested Gemma. She returned to the room which had grown familiar over the past month. The air felt different, as if she had been away for much longer than three days. But, there was a comfort to the worn out old sheets, and the tiny flowers embroidered on the edge of the pillow. She changed into her pyjamas and curled up under the chilly covers. They weren't the silk sheets of Newgrange, but they smelt of familiar washing powder and warmed up with the heat of her body. It was the closest thing to home.

She thought of her small flat, and the trinkets that filled it, which had once seemed so precious. They felt irrelevant now, as if their loss would be of little consequence. There was an email from the landlord waiting in her inbox. She hadn't dared open it yet, although she could imagine what it said. There was only so long that a seriously ill friend would stand as an excuse for not paying rent. Gemma made a silent promise to read and reply to that email tomorrow.

The heating was on. She could hear water gurgling in the ancient pipes. The wood framed window was open a crack, letting in fresh night air and the occasional hoot of an owl. Princetown was quiet, and the small noises of the moor seemed to creep onto the streets with the darkness. A dog barked a few roads away, and Fian sat up on his blanket. Another dog answered, responding with a mournful howl, and the white hound slunk up onto the foot of the bed. He curled contentedly around Gemma's feet. She could feel the weight of him; warm and reassuring in a world that felt very dark and very wide.

Gabriel was furious with her. The look in his eyes was hard to forget. For the whole ferry journey she had been wrestling with what to say to Owain, while he had been too sick to speak. But even on the car journey, when she drove and he looked out the window, she couldn't bring herself to repeat what she had said to the Huntmaster. Gabriel might be a monster, but the man in him was wounded.

He was probably speaking to Owain right now. They were probably both agreeing she was an absolute bitch. They were probably right. She was proud of protecting the child, but the way she was afterwards filled her with shame. Gabriel had already been hurting, but there was a thrill to the way her words sent him reeling, and she had struck and struck again. She added *apologise to Gabriel* beneath *reply to email* on her mental to do list.

Sleep came suddenly. She thought that guilt might keep her awake, but her body and mind were exhausted. Fian's breathing was soft and steady. Slowly, her own lungs fell into the same rhythm, until the room seemed disturbed by just one set of breath.

Owain sat in the half darkness of a flickering fire. It was lit over a black stain, left by the blaze which burned there before the journey to Grimspound. Gabriel had cooked a hare then. But Owain had nothing to heat, other than his hands.

Night gathered thickly outside, crowded with the small sounds of life on the moor. A shrew hurried through the moss, small groups of rabbits grazed on close cropped grass, and an owl watched with interest from a stump of old gorse. No trace of the fire could be seen from outside, and the cave entrance was hidden from any observer.

Owain stretched out his legs, enjoying the heat through the soles of his boots. Gabriel was due back some time before morning, but that was beginning to feel like a very long wait. There was no chance of sleeping. The worry of this witch, the Wild Hunt Investigation Committee and the murderous huntsman all played on his mind.

He shifted position again, warming his knees and palms. The memory of cooked hare was making his stomach grumble. Catching a rabbit of two wouldn't take long, and Gabriel was bound to be hungry when he got back. What better welcome could he give, than a freshly caught rabbit, roasted over the fire? Owain glanced around the empty cave. There was no one to disagree.

Night welcomed him like an old friend. It pressed silky lips to his skin, tasting him with the velvety softness of shadow. The same wild magic ran through them both, and soon the first frost would strip leaves from the trees and freeze branches to sleep. Come one more cycle of the moon, and Samhain would be upon them. The hunt would be called to ride out in full cry; sharp hooves piercing the earth, frenzied hounds howling and a master leading as winter incarnate.

With Gabriel absent, Owain felt the longing of the soil directed at him. As Huntmaster, it was impossible to resist. The land and the master were one; sharp teeth for the fertile earth. But Owain was still an Apprentice, and the call was a thrill he could simply enjoy. It filled him with energy, and he felt the darkness bend softly around him, malleable to his will.

There was a skill which he needed to practice. Each of the houndmarked were born with various abilities, and Owain was already good at using his hagstone for dowsing. Some fae wouldn't touch one, but he found that it focused his mind. His other talent was slightly more unsettling. If Mike was there, he might have reeled off an example of the Wild Hunt pinning their prey to the spot with sheer terror. But Owain didn't think of it like that; it was more of a slowing things down, and he could convince other creatures to pause when he looked at them. It was very useful when hunting for rabbits.

Stalking silently through the gorse, he allowed his thoughts to still. Slowly, his awareness spread, tracking like slow tendrils of mist across the moor. There were three rabbits gathered on a mound nearby. Turning his feet towards them, his eyes widened, catching the pale half-light of the moon. One animal stirred, tensed muscles ready to run. But Owain held it. The others looked up, noses twitching for the scent of a predator.

The Apprentice spread his arms. Night swirled around him, placid and inevitable. The rabbits watched him come closer, startled eyes softening into dull acceptance. Two were of a good size, but the third was smaller. Effortlessly, Owain released his gaze on the young one. It leaped up and darted off into the heather. The others remained, eyes fixed on the figure that approached.

He snapped their necks with ease. Quick hands emptied them of innards, and Owain cast the entrails onto the grass for the crows. The moon looked on with silvery indifference. Turning back towards the cave, he held the pair of rabbits by their back legs and walked with a swagger of pride.

"I am impressed," called a smooth voice.

Owain spun round, cursing himself for not noticing the presence of another. "Morgana," he said.

"Your skills are growing, Apprentice," she purred, melting from the night in a midnight black gown.

"Thank you, I think."

"One day you will lead the hounds. I suspect you will be glorious."

"Well, that won't be for a long time," Owain said,

shifting the rabbits over into his other hand, "Gabriel is still in his prime, and I have a lot left to learn."

"You might think that, but leading the hunt is in your blood. Can you not feel the call of the land? She knows you already. She will whisper what to do," said Morgana.

Owain could feel it. It sang in his veins even now, ancient and wild, fierce and wonderful as a winter storm. But he shook his head, pushing the energy down, and backing away from the wytch. "I know I am not ready."

Morgana laughed, swiping the air with her long nails. "What are you so afraid of?"

"You frighten me a little," answered Owain, taking another step backwards.

"And the hounds? The deep earth of Houndain, full of a thousand bones? Do they frighten you?"

"No."

"Then do you fear the sacrifice? Do you dread the heavy heat of that much blood on your hands?" Morgana pressed. Her eyes shimmered with a striking amber, betraying the fact that she had recently shifted.

"None of that scares me," he lied defiantly. But it wasn't the blood of a deer, or a fine fox, which bothered him. There was a far greater sacrifice required of every Huntmaster. He had watched Gabriel lose a little more of himself with every time he led the hunt. The land was a demanding mistress, and the winter was cruel, and there was only so long you could keep the chill from seeping into your bones.

"Brave Apprentice," chuckled Morgana, stripping leaves from a twig of Hawthorn, "so proud of your brace of dead rabbits."

"Goodnight, wytch," said Owain, walking purposefully away.

"Greet Gabriel for me, will you?" she called after him.

Owain left her words hanging on the night air. He strode nimbly through the rough heather, stepping between occasional lumps of granite, strewn over the uneven ground. Slipping gratefully through the secret entrance to the cave, he finally let the tension fall from his shoulders. It was a bold move, turning your back on a wytch. Morgana was filling the role which Asterra once had, even though the Clan had not voted on her appointment. But there was no other budding wytch, and no fae child for her to teach.

He put fresh logs on the fire and skinned one of the rabbits. Soon the smell of roasting meat began to fill the small, stone hideaway. Outside, the darkness deepened, stretching into the stillness that came after midnight.

Owain ate the first rabbit. He skinned and cooked the second one, meaning to leave it for Gabriel. Just before dawn, he ate that one as well. There was no sign of the Huntmaster.

Emerging into the first pale light of morning, Owain zipped up his waxed jacket. There was always a set of clothes kept in the cave, but he hadn't changed out of human attire. The light prints of a fox crisscrossed the springy turf, and near a low mound the earth was disturbed by the digging of rabbits. Tangled stems of brown heather glistened wetly with dew, and fine spider webs were adorned with crystal droplets. This was the pause before day, when nothing was quite yet decided, and the hours ahead were full of possibility.

Gabriel should have returned. Owain paced restlessly, his route leaving a darkened track on the grass. His Clan needed to be made aware of the threat from the

Wild Hunt Investigation Committee, and there was the demon huntsman to deal with as well. But it was the Master who should bring them news, not the Apprentice. He glanced up to the greying sky, where the edges of clouds were turning a washed-out shade of yellow. Something felt out of balance; the earth told him that through his feet. With the sunrise behind him, he turned and hurried towards Wistman's Wood.

16.
DUTY

Dawn spread slowly, spilling across the moor and trickling down to the grey streets of town. Slate roofs caught the light, glistening damply with a cold skin of dew. Elaine had been up for some time, and her hands worked the canvas in that still time before day.

She paused, reaching for her coffee. There was red paint on her cheek, and smeared in a gory stain from fingers to wrist. Her hair had the wild look of someone who had slept restlessly, and never bothered to brush it. The painting in front of her was a furious swirl of crimson and black, with tangled shapes overlapping and fading out into fire. She shook her head angrily, as if the two figures on horseback in the image could see her.

"This isn't how it was meant to go," she said, clinking her mug back down on the table, "It isn't fair. You know he isn't ready." The room settled back into stillness. If the universe, or any listening gods, had heard her, then they remained stubbornly silent.

She pursed her lips, a flush of pink defiance spreading onto her cheeks. Dipping two fingers into the thick red paint, she raised her hand to the canvas and daubed out one of the horsemen. Pressing acrylic into the cloth, she envisioned another ending, praying for Owain to be spared. But the painting felt hot. She snatched her hand back, curling up her burnt fingers protectively. The smear of paint bubbled and boiled, peeling back from the figure beneath and dripping like blood from the skin of the canvas.

There was nothing she could do. She stood by the sink and ran cold water on her hand. For the past years she had been content to not intervene, and simply pass on the messages that she saw in her paintings. Sometimes it was hard. Change was always frightening, and death was perhaps the biggest change of all. But it was natural. It formed the ebb and flow of life, which washed in and out, building bodies to house spirit and stripping flesh back from bones. But this time was different. There was nothing natural about it.

"You're up early," said Mike.

Elaine turned towards the sound of his voice, lifting dripping red hands out from the sink.

"What the hell happened?" Mike cried, in surprise.

"It's paint, it's just paint," Elaine reassured him.

"Sorry, I should have thought of that," Mike grinned, crossing the room towards the kitchen. "Lots of red in this one then, I take it?"

"Too much red," said Elaine.

Mike stopped by the easel. The painting was a swirl of hounds and fire, with two figures facing each other in the centre. They were both wearing crimson. "Two Huntmasters?" he asked.

"One is Cabell."

"Then the other is Gabriel, I suppose. I thought they might fight it out."

Elaine shook her head, stained hands clutching restlessly at each other. "Gabriel is gone. I don't know any more than that. The second figure is Owain."

"But he's just a boy. He can't lead the hunt!" said Mike.

"I know. But it's going to happen anyway."

There was a sharp rap on the door. Mike dragged his eyes away from the painting, and strode across the kitchen. Elaine gripped the back of a chair, her knuckles white with the effort. Owain was standing outside. His arms were crossed over his body, as if he was cold, even though he still wore the same jacket as yesterday. He had the red eyes of someone who hadn't slept.

"What is it Owain?" asked Mike, stepping aside to usher the Apprentice indoors.

"It's Gabriel. He hasn't returned."

Elaine edged round the table, her right hand remaining on the chair backs to steady her. "I knew something had happened," she said softly, gesturing towards the painting, "because I woke early with this in my head."

Owain walked over to look at the picture. His eyes darted from figure to figure. "What does it mean?"

"What does your gut say?" Elaine asked.

Owain dropped his eyes to the ground. There were too many signs for him to ignore. The earth did not desire one particular Huntmaster, but it did demand a figure to take on that role. He felt it calling him, with a strength that was new and alarming.

"Something is very wrong," he replied, thinking back to the unsettling delight in Morgana's eyes as she talked about him leading the hounds. Had she sensed something too? Did she foresee this disaster?

"Do you have any idea why Gabriel might have disappeared?" Mike asked.

Owain was staring at the painting again. One mounted figure had brown hair, and the other had red. Why would Gabriel vanish, when his Clan needed him the most? Although he didn't know that, of course. This demon huntsman had appeared suddenly, and just at the time their Huntmaster was most distracted.

"I might have the answer to that," said Gemma

sheepishly. She was wrapped in a dressing gown, although her feet were still bare.

"What do you mean?" asked Owain.

She hovered on the threshold, swaying slightly as she gathered the courage to step into the room. "I think it might be my fault. I think I upset Gabriel. A lot."

Mike refilled the kettle. If he couldn't face this confession with the assistance of alcohol, then at least he would be holding a large mug of tea.

"Go on," said Elaine.

"We argued just before I came back from Ireland. I told him to get out," Gemma said.

"That wouldn't have-" Owain began.

"No wait," Gemma pressed. "I told him Elyn would prefer to stay dead than hear him talk about duty. I told him that I wasn't her, and I never would be, and that she never loved him."

Owain slowly sank down into a chair. He was nodding to himself, mouth tight as if tasting something bitter. "I see."

"I wanted to tell you about it on the way home, but I didn't know what to say." Gemma pressed both hands to her forehead, rubbing her temples in remorse. "I took it way too far, and he was already gone!"

"Who is Elyn?" asked Elaine.

"I may have missed that bit out," Gemma answered awkwardly, "she's the real reason that Gabriel was so interested in me. He thought that I was her, reborn in a human body by some strange magic."

"But you really aren't?" checked Owain.

"I'm really not," she said firmly.

"So she's the reason that your angel Gabriel was so keen to protect your family line," concluded Elaine.

"Yes, he was waiting. Daughter of her daughter's daughter, or something like that," Gemma said.

"Except something went wrong," added Mike.

Gemma nodded sadly. There was a part of her, and she suspected that it had always been there, that wished she could be what Gabriel so desired. But all the glamour in the world couldn't hide her lack, and she couldn't bear to go on pretending.

Owain was noticeably quiet. His eyes had the glossy sheen of a wild creature looking into the headlights of an oncoming lorry. Gabriel's disappearance was beginning to make terrible sense. He was grieving the loss of a hundred years of love, and facing the death of Elyn for a second time. Dealing with Cabell was the least of his concerns.

"I know what you fear," said Elaine gently, reaching towards the Apprentice, "I have already seen it."

"The hunt. My destiny since the day I was born," said Owain dully.

Elaine nodded. Mike poured hot water into four mugs. He had no idea how old Owain was in human years, or how that worked compared to faerie ageing, but he might have said he looked nineteen. Yes, boys had gone off to war far younger than that, but death was a small part of the horror of the hunt. Then it was there again; that weight of knowledge that pressed at his forehead and made his brain ache. *I know something about this.* "I know something about this!"

The second utterance was out loud, and everyone turned their heads towards him. Mike's cheeks coloured. "I'm sorry about that."

"Hang on," said Gemma, jumping up from her seat, "I have something for you!" She ran upstairs, pounding along the groaning floorboards, before racing back down with the gift in her hand.

"My water bottle," said Mike, recognising the metal container, "I'm glad it survived. But you can keep it, if you like."

"There's something in it for you. I filled it up in the Well of Memory."

Owain stared incredulously. "How did you do that?"

"Don't make me tell you. You'll hate me even more," said Gemma, half smiling. The sight of those mossclad bones, peeling away from the side of the pool, was not a memory she wanted to dwell on.

"Does it do what it says on the tin?" asked Mike, handling the scratched bottle like it was either a relic, or a grenade.

"One way to find out," shrugged Gemma.

The early rush of commuters had been and gone, leaving Epping station grey and quiet. Eva stood next to Franz on the platform. She had barely slept last night, and her careful use of makeup couldn't cover all of the evidence. But there was a fierce, feverish smile on her lips, and the hand in her pocket held the black business card in a vice-like grip.

A red and white tube train rolled into the platform. It halted, greeting potential passengers with an automated warning to mind the gap. Franz eyed the machine with interest.

"This train is electric?" he asked.

"Of course," replied Eva offhandedly.

Franz began to wander down the side of the train, appreciating the smooth lines of the carriages. It reminded him of the Fliegende Züge, which he recalled in bright colours, displayed on posters with pride. He touched the glossy paintwork tentatively, half transported in a glorious dream. The railway was racing ahead, a model of modern industry, powering the rise of 'Greater Germany!'

But then there was the war. Fast trains were forgotten. Priority shifted to military transport, and the engines were converted into makeshift power generators. The daydream turned sour. Franz dropped his eyes to the ground.

Eva grabbed his elbow and pulled him towards a set of open doors. "It'll go without us!" she cried.

There was an urgency to her voice which made Franz feel suddenly unsteady. He gripped her arm, caught for a moment in the strange fervour. Faces swam past him, grey with the halfmist of memory, and all with their eyes fixed upwards in adoration. Some of them he knew, many he had only seen in passing, though they all saw his uniform and cheered him as a hero. He clutched at the brown wool of his suit, afraid it might have somehow turned black.

"Come on!" Eva half pulled him into the carriage. They sat by the window, watching the station slip away as the train picked up speed. "The electricity comes from the tracks," Eva said, sitting very straight, "if you step on them you die."

Franz nodded. He understood how the train worked, but he couldn't shake the chill from his bones. It was the hope that frightened him; he had already seen it, given to the masses and honed as a weapon. Blake wasn't the kind of character to promise a huge feat of necromancy and expect nothing in return.

"I have never been to London," he told Eva.

"I've been lots of times. My father would drag me to all manner of stuffy old antique auctions. But sometimes there was free champagne, or at least chocolate." She shifted to find a better angle in her seat.

"Did he ever mention these people we're going to meet?"

"No, I don't think so. He only ever spoke about the Collector, who wanted the dagger from Dartmoor."

Fields were slowly replaced by factories and sprawling shopping centres. Patches of woodland gave way to crowded streets of houses, and the carriage around them began to fill up. The air subtly changed; it thickened with the hum of activity that filled the suburbs. After a while, the train dropped underground.

Despite his reservations about their visit, Franz couldn't help falling into a good mood. Even the grey, dilapidated stations were full of life. He didn't recognise any of their names, but the litter and the graffiti spoke of careless nights spent with friends. The lurid paint clashed with the old-fashioned brickwork, but the brazen contrast offered him a strange sense of ease. He could blend in here. He could push back the burden of the past, for a little while.

"The next stop is ours," said Eva. Franz watched lights flash past in the darkness, his body swaying with the rocking rhythm of the rails. The train slowed, and a sign identifying the station as *Holborn* came into view.

Eva jumped up as soon as the train stopped, leading Franz through the flow of purposeful people and up into the fresh air of the street. The escalator earned his approval. It was easy to forget the season in the unchanging warmth of the underground, but outside the station the wind blew with a brisk chill. Eva fiddled with a map on her phone, double checking the destination against the address on the business card. She turned to Franz and shrugged.

"My phone is adamant we're going to a bookshop," she said.

"Let's go to a bookshop then," replied Franz.

The moving map led them down smaller and smaller streets, many of them scented with the enticing smell of fresh coffee. Eva clocked the small, elegant cafés for later exploration. Bloomsbury had always been affluent, as far as Eva could remember, and she recalled her father selling something to one of the occult bookshops once. But they found themselves standing outside a shop she didn't know. She would have missed it entirely, with the small, dingy window and the narrow door covered in peeling paint. But it was definitely the address on the business card.

"Alright," she said, more to herself than Franz, and pushed open the door. The room inside was cluttered and still. It smelt of dust and old paper, with the underlying aroma of dry leather binding. A little bell rang as the door opened and shut.

"Can I help you?" asked a reedy voice. A small man, dusty and old as the books that surrounded him, stood up from behind the wood panelled counter.

"Yes please, I hope you can," replied Eva, putting on her best beaming smile, "I was directed here by a friend." She strode over and presented the business card. The old man took it, without surprise. He flipped it over in his hand, examining it with the delicacy due to unearthed treasure. There was a precise care to his movement that made Eva think he had touched many precious things in his lifetime. She wouldn't have been surprised if he came out with some niche fact about the paper, or the pigment used in the ink. But he didn't. He popped the card into his waistcoat pocket and smiled up at Eva.

"Please wait while I make a call," he said.

Franz had already drifted towards the shelves. He could read well in English, and the shop was crammed with the type of books he would have given anything to find while studying. It was his knowledge of folklore and myths which had first brought him to the attention of the Reich, and they had permitted him to continue, with a few new instructions. Anything he discovered that related to the raising of the dead or gifting of superhuman powers must be passed on immediately. So he had sat, in his tiny apartment, mailing letters about faeries, magical cauldrons and occult rituals to high up members of the SS.

But now he was free to read without their agenda. He picked up a book with a promising title: '*Silent as the Trees: Devonshire Witchcraft, Folklore & Magic*' and began to leaf through. The leaves fell open at page one hundred and fifty-two, as if someone had pressed them down to read this passage in particular.

'Wistman' also appears interestingly to be a local name for the Devil; a most traditional candidate for the Wild Hunt's leadership.'

"What are you reading?" Eva asked. Franz shut the book quickly, aware that any mention of the Wild Hunt was likely to turn her mood for the worse.

"Just a little folklore. It reminds me of my time as a student," he replied.

"Do you miss it? Your own time, I mean?" she asked in a low voice, which made Franz feel like he was in a library.

"I try not to think about it," he replied. There was a small model plane in both of his pockets now, as if the one he carried for his brother was accumulating interest.

The old man shuffled back through a doorway behind his counter. "Apologies for that," he said, disappearing behind the books piled on most of the surface. There was the sound of stiff drawers being opened and shut. At last, he emerged with an envelope.

"Here we are!" he said, offering it to Eva. Her name was written in neat, swirling lettering on the front. "We've been expecting you," he smiled.

"Alright," said Mike, placing the metal flask next to the kettle, "I'll get on the magic water later." His tone was light, but there was fear in his eyes. The weight of memory was so vast that he couldn't help wondering whether his mind could hold it. Once those floodgates were opened, there'd be no going back, and nothing withstands a river in spate.

"How can we help you Owain?" asked Elaine. The Apprentice was staring out the kitchen window, both palms flat on the wooden table.

"I suppose, I will need to bind the hounds." He had played at the ritual, borrowing Gabriel's gore covered hunt coat to imagine he was the master. But then there was the fear that the rogue hound was his doing, and people had been dying, and Owain lost the desire to visit Houndain alone.

"It's a bit gross, but I think you're up to it," said Gemma cheerfully.

"You saw Gabriel remake his bonds. He is already a strong Huntmaster, and the hounds know him. This is my virgin binding, and I must call up the hounds in new bodies," said Owain. His eyes were glazed, and still fixed on some point outside.

"Is there a set ritual for your first time?" asked Elaine.

"The ritual is the same. But I would be blooded by my master, and the Clan would be there to hold me," Owain said.

"So they hold space, they hold energy, while you perform the binding?" Elaine clarified.

"Yes."

"Well we can do that for you," said Elaine, her tone turning business-like, "we have some experience between us."

"Speak for yourself," said Mike, "why can't your Clan be there to help you?"

Owain pulled his eyes away from the window and dragged both hands together on the table. "I thought about it most of last night. In the early hours, I walked back to Wistman's Wood, with every intention of warning them." He looked pleadingly at Mike. "But I couldn't do it. If I tell them Gabriel has disappeared, then there will be questions about his leadership. Asterra has already stirred doubts about his capability as Huntmaster."

"But they know what she did! Surely they've heard how she treated Fian?" Gemma exclaimed.

"They know that. They know she tried to kill her brother. But some of what she said rang true," said Owain. He gazed at Gemma gently, an apology lacing the pink of his lips, "we aren't meant to care about mortals. Gabriel risked the Clan's safety to see you."

"Then we owe him. I owe him. Again," Gemma said sadly.

"Who owes who?" asked Adrian, stretching as he strolled across the carpet.

"Get a drink, you're going to need it!" said Mike.

226

Adrian looked from Owain, to Gemma and Elaine. "Is this an energy drink for breakfast kind of morning?" he asked, already aware of the answer.

"It's something like that," said Elaine.

"Alright then," said Adrian, reaching into the fridge and selecting a dark purple can. He popped the ring pull with a slow hiss. "Hit me."

"Gabriel's gone so Owain will lead the hounds to fight Cabell. We're just working out the finer details," said Gemma.

Adrian paused with the can half raised to his lips. "What do you mean, gone?"

Owain shrugged. "He didn't come back from Ireland. We think he might be upset."

"About what? Being bad mouthed by a witch?" asked Adrian.

"No, this is my fault," said Gemma, "he doesn't know about that."

"She gave him the cold shoulder, and he didn't like it," explained Mike, glossing over the details.

"Well, good for you!" Adrian applauded.

"No. Not good for me. Not good for any of us, and especially not Owain." Gemma glanced over at the Apprentice, guilt brewing inside her. "I could have done it kindly."

"What's done is done," said Mike, placing mugs of tea pointedly on the table, "it's where we go now that matters."

"Where do we go now?" asked Adrian.

"To Houndain," said Owain.

17.
RITUAL

Damp ground angled down towards the hawthorn ringed hollow. Fleshy fern stems were flecked over with brown, bending at strange angles like broken bones. Mossy turf spread, springy and yielding underfoot, as if Owain and the others trod on the very thinnest skin of the earth. Beneath that there were the roots, and the brown soil made from millennia of death. And there were the hounds.

"Slow down, will you?" called Mike, from a little way behind. He was no stranger to walking, but he wasn't used to carrying half a sheep in a bin bag at the same time. It had seemed a good idea in the butchers, but now he was rethinking his generosity. Perhaps a large chicken would have been fine.

Owain paused at the lip of the hollow. The earth fell away steeply, and shade gathered thick round the tangle of trees. Around him, the air hung still, though beneath his feet the pulse of the land throbbed as an ancient heartbeat. It longed for him to pierce through that fragile surface and release the roiling liquid beneath, overspilling like bile; birthing rotten bones back into flesh. He rocked on the balls of his feet. Fear mixed with helpless desire.

"Do you feel ok?" Gemma asked him.

"Mostly," he replied, through gritted teeth.

"You just tell us what to do," prompted Elaine. She was leaning heavily on Adrian, the walk having caused her considerable pain. But nothing would make her acknowledge it.

"Do you need to rest?" Adrian asked her, for

229

probably the seventh time.

"Absolutely not!" came the stern reply. Her jaw was set fiercely against any failing of her body. "I'm the least of everyone's concerns."

"Stay on the edge of the hollow. Do not step into the bowl," said Owain. Mike uncovered the carcass and handed it over.

"We're holding space," said Elaine. She allowed Adrian to lead her to a safe spot, and then shook off his hand. There was a narrow path inside the ring of trees, just wide enough for one person to stand on. "Spread out equally," she instructed, spreading her fingers in the air, "imagine a rope of gold light, stretching between us."

"What's going to happen?" asked Adrian.

"I will place the sacrifice, then I will make a small cut and draw a circle with my blood. Then I pledge my loyalty to my Clan-" Owain paused here, biting his lip.

"For now, we are your Clan," said Elaine, "but we have no doubt of your other loyalties."

The Apprentice nodded in nervous gratitude. "Then I call up the hounds by name. If all goes well, they will cross the circle of blood, accept my leadership, and eat the meat."

"If it goes badly?" Adrian asked.

"They might eat all of us," answered Owain.

"Lovely. I thought I hadn't died horrifically enough!" Adrian said, but there was an encouraging smile on his face.

"You've got this, Owain," said Gemma. Her hands were outstretched, mirroring Elaine's, and her voice carried the strength of conviction.

"Very well," said Owain. He hefted the half carcass over his shoulder and walked carefully down the slope. The sodden earth squelched beneath his feet, rising up and sucking at the leather of his soles. His eyes were fixed on the ground, partly to watch his footing, but also to delay the moment that he faced the stone altar in the middle of the crater. Sticky sweat laced his skin, even though the day was cool. His heart rattled hard against his ribs, beating fast with painful anticipation. The altar was now too close to ignore.

Owain looked down at the grey stone, cleaned of any old stains by wild animals and the weather. He threw his sacrifice across it, glad to be free of the weight of the meat. He thought of Gabriel's glorious offering; what could make a better show of strength than murdering an entire human hunt? Their blood and bones still lay in the hollow, mingled with mud and awaiting his call. Would they want to rise up for an oversized lamb chop? He hadn't even killed the creature himself, and after hanging for a week there was little blood in the carcass. Owain tried to shake these thoughts from his head. His will was the key here, and he needed to focus.

There was a small knife in the pocket of his jacket. He had used it to gut the rabbits earlier, and he unsheathed it now in the shade of the hollow. Holding the blade out in front of him, he observed the shake of his hand.

"You look suitably creepy!" called Gemma, by way of encouragement. Owain glanced up at her, a grateful smile blooming across his face. He didn't feel creepy; he felt very plain. But there was a way to improve that.

He lay the knife on the ribs of the sheep. Then he pressed one palm flat to the earth. Crouching down, he allowed his eyes to fall closed. The call of the land was loud and impatient, thrumming up through his feet and spreading into his blood. Beneath his hand, the yielding earth heaved, spilling peatblack water between his fingers.

He realised he had been resisting, and there was no time for that. His lips parted a little, as he let down his barriers, and promised to serve. The soil opened up, and his arm disappeared down to the elbow.

"That's disgusting," said Adrian.

Owain's fingers closed around something solid. He gripped with his nails, heaving the object out from the earth. The wool was still red, though burial had stained it. Rips and tears in the cloth were surrounded by ironbrown smears. But it was Gabriel's hunt coat, and it still smelt of death. The Apprentice put it on.

"It suits you," said Mike. He felt slightly nauseous. It wasn't the carcass, or the stale smell on the air. It was the sheer weight of memory, swelling like a blister in the back of his mind. None of it was accessible, but the pressure was displacing normal thoughts all the same. It seemed like there was something he needed to say, but he didn't know, for the life of him, what it was.

The coat felt heavy on Owain's shoulders. It was soaked with the dark water of Houndain, smelling of soil made rich by bones and flesh. But it felt right. He drew that scent deep down into his lungs. The impatient earth pressed at his feet.

"I am your Huntmaster," the words rolled, unbidden, off his tongue. They felt strange and exciting. He pushed up one sleeve and sliced a red line with the blade of his knife. Blood began to flow in a slow drip, and he paced a circle around the laden altar. The air turned thick when the shape was complete. It crackled with energy, poised to clothe bones in new, eldritch flesh.

"We're holding it!" called Elaine, the gold rope that she visualised was tight with the strain.

Owain nodded, only half aware of her voice. He

strode towards the raised stone and buried his knife in the carcass. The skin yielded, but no blood flowed from the opening. He raised the dagger again, stabbing the meat until the surface was in tatters, and the point of the blade was made blunt by the altar.

Gemma squirmed, but kept her arms outstretched. This wasn't the Owain she knew, and the violence in his movement made her stomach turn. He had sat on her bed and been awkward about talking to her. Now he was butchering an animal with horrible urgency.

Blood finally began to trickle down the sides of the altar. It was a thin stream, but it flowed towards the moss climbing the base of the stone.

"Come to me Gelert, in a form made my own. Come Skriker and Valefor and accept your new Master." Owain dropped the knife and raised up his hands. The earth trembled around him, sucking back like breath between teeth, before bubbling over with brackish water. Two patches of moss began to swell. Adrian watched, in abject horror, as three hounds clawed up out of the earth. They were lean and grey, with skin stretched tight over exaggerated ribcages. Their eyes glowed an awful, drowned blue.

"Rise up Guinefort, Barghest and Shuck!" cried Owain. Gemma remembered the names in Gabriel's voice, but they answered to Owain. Dragging long limbs from the putrid peat, they came creeping towards the altar, moving with the crunch of cracking bone.

"Come Gytrash and Sirius. Come now Fenrir," he spoke Fen's name softly, as if it were especially sacred. Four more hounds shook earth free from their fur. Gemma counted them. There were seven in total.

"Sirius won't come, he got mixed into Fian," she

called down into the crater. The white hound was at home, probably sleeping under the radiator. "Fen is with Gabriel, wherever he is."

Adrian was shaking his head. Seven hounds against fifty weren't odds that appealed. "Can't new hounds get made?"

"Let me try," said Owain. He looked taller, in the halflight of the hollow. He had learned the names of the hounds by heart, and he had seen Gabriel summon them multiple times. But he had never seen a new hound created; other than Fian, of course.

"Come to me Grim, sleek as the night. Come now with teeth, sharper than frost. Come now with claws, like blackthorn in winter." The name sang on his tongue and sent shivers across the surface of the earth. Owain clenched his fists, dragging at the air as if gripping reins. Something stirred at the base of the slope.

Mike held his breath. Every sense in his body was screaming a warning. But what was he missing? What words could he feel, clawing through the thick webs of his mind? "Owain!" he cried.

The Apprentice didn't hear him. Owain's will was all focused on the bulge in the earth. The surface cracked, mud slid aside, and a skull blossomed up through the soil. It was half fleshed, large as a horse, and covered in patches of dripping, grey fur. Grim shook his head. Huge teeth ran with saliva, wrapped round with stems of half rotten grass. The beast fixed blue eyes on Owain.

"Serve me, and take your share of the meat." The seven smaller hounds sniffed at the circle, drawn out with blood. But Grim raised his head, tasting the air. The carcass on the altar was stale, but nearby there were hot, beating hearts.

"That doesn't look good!" cried Adrian. The creature moved in slow motion, eyes upturned towards him.

"Do as I command," yelled Owain. But his shoulders were sagging under the weight of the hunt coat. Grim flicked off his words like a fly on the ear, and stalked purposefully up the slope of the hollow. He would get to Adrian first. Next would be Elaine.

Mike screwed his eyes shut and grimaced in fury. There was a fragment of this ritual missing, and it was lodged in his memory. But it lay under the sediment of forty years spent in pubs. "Elaine, can you hold this without me?"

She nodded. Gemma felt the invisible rope flex, but it settled and held. Mike circled his wrists, then patted his pockets for the penknife he carried. His hand fell on the shape of the old metal flask. *I filled it up in the Well of Memory*. Right now, anything was worth trying. He pulled out the container and unscrewed the lid.

"Is now really the time?" Adrian squealed.

"That isn't just water," said Gemma, her eyes widening with hope, "it's all of his memories, if it works like it's meant to."

Mike upturned the flask. He swallowed in large gulps, like a man used to drinking. A little of the liquid ran over his chin. Then he lowered the bottle, and let it drop from his hand.

Grim watched it roll down to the base of the hollow. His jaws were held open; rust coloured tongue hanging over his teeth. Flesh peeled back between tangles of fur, glistening and pale from lying in water. A rumbling growl poured out from his throat, carrying with it the scent of decay.

"Not on my watch," said Mike. He pulled off his

235

jacket and rolled up both sleeves. Black liquid ran, in long lines, over his skin. Covering his arms, and up to his neck, a tangle of tattooed keys writhed in torment. They bubbled and boiled, like water dropped on hot metal, as his body began to force the ink out.

"The keys, they're melting!" observed Adrian.

"He doesn't need them," said Gemma. Her eyes followed Mike as he strode down the slope. His movements were easy and fluid, as if the altar and Houndain were nothing out of the ordinary. Had she noticed that he was taller than Owain? She couldn't remember.

Eight pairs of eyes watched him with interest. They were the cold blue of old ice, that lays in the deepest hollows never touched by the sun. An awful light flickered within them, like the sky seen through water.

"Houndmarked, do you remember becoming an Apprentice?" Mike asked urgently.

Owain turned, dragging his gaze away from the hounds. "Gabriel marked me with blood. It was a blessing."

"I will mark you again." Mike reached for the carcass and smeared gore on his fingers.

"But- you aren't," stammered Owain.

"Huntmaster? No I'm not." He raised his hand towards Owain's forehead. The storyteller's eyes were clear and serious. "But you know what I am. You've known all these years."

Owain bowed his head. Mike touched two fingers to his hairline and drew downwards in blood.

"You are the sacrifice. To lead the hounds is to give up yourself. Are you ready to die?"

Owain looked up at him. Tears pooled in the corners of his eyes. "I don't know."

Grim dropped his shoulder and swung away from

Adrian, half rotten muzzle turned towards the figures in the base of the bowl. The other hounds backed off, heads dipped to the earth, whining a low dirge.

Mike glanced round at the approaching monster, then turned back to Owain. His eyes were kind, but he shook his head with a stiff sorrow. "Are you ready to die?" he repeated. Grim sniffed at the blood which circled the altar.

Owain sobbed, and jerkily nodded his head. "Yes," he said. Tears overflowed and tracked down his cheeks.

Mike witnessed Owain's fear without flinching. "Then face death, Apprentice."

Owain turned slowly to face the freshly made hound. On the edge of the circle, two people held their breath. Elaine swayed softly, eyes closed and jaw clenched. Grim flared his nostrils, sucking in the strange scent of Owain. The huge claws that curved from his paws pressed against the barrier of blood.

Raising his arms, Owain spread out his fingers, turning up his face to look the hound in the eyes. "Come to me," he murmured. Grim flexed one foreleg, then stepped into the circle. The air crackled and fizzed. Gemma felt her stomach drop. The seven other hounds threw up their heads and howled.

In that last moment, Owain turned to look at her. His lips moved, forming a phrase which only she saw. It cut like the blade which still lay on the floor. Forgetting the rope, she reached out towards him, eyes stinging with salt. But his expression had shifted. His pupils bled into black and the skin stretched tight over the bones of his face. A guttural cry tore from his throat, as fierce spikes pierced through the flesh of his forearms and spine. Grim tore a chunk of meat from the carcass.

It was horrible. Gemma watched the other hounds join in the feast. But none of it was as bad as the image of Owain, mouthing *help me*, when there was nothing she could do.

Elaine crumpled quietly to the ground. Mike and Adrian both raced to her side, propping her up and checking her breathing. Her chest rose and fell softly; she was simply exhausted.

Gemma kept her eyes on Owain. The energy that had arced through the air drew back to the base of the hollow. It settled like snow, slowly sinking to rest with the bones in the soil. The newly made Huntmaster was inspecting his hounds. Gemma wondered if Gabriel could sense this somehow, wherever he was. Was he feeling betrayed? Or was he feeling relieved?

"Your Clan honours you," said Mike to Owain, as he left Elaine's side to stride back down the slope. "Now is the time to ride out. Squire Cabell threatens our secrecy with his wanton killing. Restore the balance. Return him to his grave."

Owain nodded. He reached out his hand, and a horse heaved itself up from the earth. Gemma noticed how he clothed it with glamour; stained bones were hidden behind a facade of fine flesh. The hounds were the same. Grim has shrunk to almost the same size as the others, and all of them were covered in glossy, grey fur. This wasn't the macabre display that Gabriel put on. Owain had even managed to make the hunt coat look tidy.   Somehow, all of this didn't make the Wild Hunt any less threatening. If anything, it made it worse. She now knew that Owain could consider murder at the same time as cleaning his clothes.

Hounds poured up the side of the hollow, slipping

through the tangle of branches, regardless of thorns. Owain sprung onto the horse, turning towards the gap in the trees. He looked back, sloeblack eyes falling on the scraps of bone and tattered moss of the hollow. Gemma searched his face for something she recognised. But there was only duty, and a horrible half smile, on lips that promised to take pleasure in the hunt and the kill. He turned away, steering his horse onto the open moor.

Mike fell heavily to his knees. He seemed unconcerned about the stagnant water that seeped through his trousers, staining them black. Adrian still sat with Elaine, whose eyes flickered as if she was dreaming. Gemma slid down the slope to crouch next to Mike.

"I'm guessing the water worked," she said softly.

Mike looked up, his eyes laced with tears. "A lot of things make sense now. But some things, make less sense than before."

"Although you knew what do to with the ritual. You saved all our lives!"

"I wasn't sure that would work. It should be the Huntmaster who bloods the Apprentice. I hoped I'd be close enough."

"What does that mean? You said something to Owain as well. You said he knew what you were."

Mike nodded slowly. He scratched at his arm where the keys used to be. "We share the same blood, Gabriel and I."

"You what? You mean- you're telling me that you're fae as well?"

"I'm his brother," said Mike.

239

18.
ALLEGIANCE

Eva eyed the selection of dresses with doubt. "Do I really have to?"

"It says evening wear on the invite. I know these kind of dinners," Franz said. He had been to more than he cared to remember; each one a long evening where he barely spoke and various men droned on about glory.

"My father went to them sometimes. His clients would hold them, mainly to show off. He said they spoke about business."

"I think this will be similar. The blue dress would look good on you."

Eva lifted the garment off from the rail. It was calf length, with cornflower folds gathered at the waist. "It's a bit old fashioned."

"I'm old fashioned," replied Franz. He was examining the small selection of suits with a frown.

"Don't you like them?" Eva rested one hand on his back, peering past him at the jackets on display.

"I would just-" he paused, pulling one out and holding it up to the light, "I would just rather not black."

Eva glanced round the formal section of the large department store. "Shall we go somewhere else?"

The street outside was bustling with people. Eva linked arms with Franz, steering him through the crowds at a purposeful pace. "I'm glad you're with me," she said, with a squeeze.

The model planes felt heavy in his pockets. He inclined his head and offered a smile that didn't spread to his eyes. "Well, I am your brother." He remembered the cracked concrete of the airfield, and the cans of drink they had allowed to get hot in the sun. Eva had told Blake they were brother and sister. She said they practically were, having both been reborn from the boiling water of the moor.

Franz had no memory of crawling out of the earth. The first thing he'd seen, since the inside of his plane, was a skeletal grey monster stretching towards Eva's throat. He went for his gun. It was the first time he had shot anything, other than a target.

"You are," replied Eva, squeezing his arm again. There was an energy to her steps, as if the heavy thoughts which had plagued her were at last cast aside. The crowds around them thinned. A few businessmen walked past, eyes fixed on their phones. Small groups gathered outside coffee shop windows, their backs turned to the wind as they smoked cigarettes.

Franz looked up at the grey sky. It was the same sky that had hung over all the triumphs and horrors of history. "Why did you ask about the Spear of Destiny?"

Eva tensed. He felt it through her arm. "I was just curious. It keeps coming up."

"Maximillian asked us about it. Your father sourced artifacts for wealthy collectors. Is it possible that he had been tasked with locating it?"

Eva peered into the shop windows to her right, but Franz watched her free hand move to tap at her chest. It wasn't the first time he'd noticed the habit. "He never said anything."

Franz shrugged, slipping his hand into his pocket and gripping the small metal plane. Eva was the closest thing he had to family. But she wasn't the woman who had sat with him on the airfield anymore. Since failing to reanimate her father, she had slipped into long periods of silence. The easy humour between them was gone, and a frantic expression sometimes accompanied the tapping at her chest. "We must be very careful tonight," he said quietly.

"Careful? Why?"

"These men do not deal in trinkets. If they are used to business, then there will be a cost attached to their help." Franz halted amidst the flow of people, turning to grip Eva by both upper arms. "Are you prepared for that?"

She paused for a moment, her weight pressed into his hands. Pedestrians poured around them, too caught up in their own lives to intrude on an exchange between strangers. For a couple of slow seconds, they were the only still point in a river of humanity, parting around them like water avoiding a rock. "I'm not prepared for anything." Eva caught Franz's hands and peeled them away. "But my father will live, and the Huntmaster will die."

"I thought you might say that."

On the edge of Houndain, Adrian still held Elaine. Her breathing was shallow, but regular, and her flickering eyelids had subsided to stillness.

"She's not walking anywhere, anytime soon," Adrian announced.

"I can see that," replied Mike. He glanced at the half moon shaped scars left in the turf. It was a shame he couldn't magic up a horse from the ground. Scrambling up the side of the slope, he thought through a more mundane solution. "Would you phone for an ambulance?"

Adrian nodded, pulling his phone from his pocket. "As soon as I have signal."

Mike gently slid his arms under Elaine. Lifting her up, he was surprised by her lightness. He carried her carefully, back turned to the branches of hawthorn encircling the crater. They snagged at his shirt, dragging threads from the worn-out old cotton, but he barely noticed the thorns. The wind came in gusts, bending the stems of browning bracken, and singing across the open mouths of abandoned mineshafts. It smelt of damp earth, and the slow sacrifice of summer to autumn.

"You alright with her?" Adrian asked.

"She isn't heavy," replied Mike.

Gemma followed the strange procession away from Houndain, through the hidden ravine, and onto the wider path that wound back towards Hound Tor. Adrian dialled for an ambulance and stayed on the phone.

The grey sky had discouraged casual walkers, and picnickers had found more sheltered spots for their feasts. There were five other cars in the car park, though their occupants were long lost to the wilds of the moor. Hound of the Basket Meals was shut. The white paint of the trailer was tinged with a coating of green.

"Will she be OK?" Gemma asked no one in particular.

Mike had propped Elaine up on the back seat of his Land Rover. Her head was cushioned by an old jumper, and Mike was carefully tucking a sun-bleached beige blanket around her. "I'm sure she will." The strain in his voice betrayed doubt.

"You took her to the hospital. Do you think there's something she's not telling us?" Adrian asked.

Mike perched in the passenger seat, leaning his elbow on the cubby box as he looked into the back. Elaine's face was pale, and every so often her eyelids creased with some memory of pain. "I think there's a lot she's not telling us."

The voice on the phone asked Adrian for an update. It assured him that an ambulance was coming. Gemma watched the lines deepen on Mike's forehead. "Can you do magic?" she asked.

"Excuse me?"

"Sorry, that did sound weird. I meant, can you do fae things, like Gabriel and Owain?"

"Fae things?" Mike chuckled darkly, "I suppose I can. But nothing much to help with this. I could make her cheeks rosy again, but it would just be an illusion."

"Do you miss your tattoos?"

"No. They were pretty embarrassing."

"I never thought that. I did think you were strange, when we first met you-"

"Well you weren't wrong about that!"

"No, you really are strange. But, what I wanted to say is, that it turns out we're strange as well. In fact, Adrian was always strange. But I'm strange too, I just wasn't admitting it." Gemma rubbed her eyes with her palms. "Thank you for everything," she added.

Mike smiled. For a moment, it wasn't the forced smile of a man masking his fear. "Thank *you*," he said. Then he dropped his voice and leaned closer through the open car door, "for my life back. Even if it is strange."

The wail of a siren echoed off the granite peak of Hound Tor, heralding the arrival of a bright yellow ambulance. It parked alongside them, spilling out two smiling paramedics.

"History of illness?" asked one, as the other began to examine Elaine.

"I think so," said Mike, "but she wouldn't tell me

what." He paced up and down next to the car, his hands pushed deep into his pockets. The paramedic nodded and asked a couple more questions. Elaine was moved into the ambulance. Mike asked if they could follow and was given a hospital address in Newton Abbot. None of it felt very real.

"I mean, she was alright," Adrian repeated, rubbing at a dust mark on the black paint of Mike's car, "well, not totally alright. But not ambulance level of not alright. Right?"

Gemma nodded. "I didn't think it was that bad. Whatever it is."

"The ritual overstretched her," Mike asserted quietly, watching the ambulance pull out of the car park. "We've been doing too much, with not enough help."

"Maybe this is getting too big for us," Gemma admitted.

Adrian pressed his phone to his ear. His face fell further as he listened to the voicemail. "Bloody hell!" he exclaimed.

"What is it?" asked Gemma.

"It's Clara. The witch. Talk about worst possible timing!"

"What's she done?" Mike asked.

"Grown a conscience. A bit suddenly and a bit late! She's very sorry about spreading rumours about the Wild Hunt, and she's going to deal with Cabell by herself," Adrian exclaimed.

"Is she mad?" cried Mike, throwing his hand to his forehead in exasperation.

"Well, yes," said Adrian, "but not like that. I didn't think she had a death wish."

"What's she going to do when she meets Cabell?" Gemma asked, hugging her arms tight across her body.

246

There were sharp teeth to the wind, and the open car park offered no barrier to the chill.

"Die," said Mike grimly, "That's what she's going to do." He glanced round at the road the ambulance had disappeared down. Then he looked at his muddy Land Rover. "Get in," he said.

High banks sped past either side of them, bristling with bracken. The creaky suspension rolled over bumps in the road like a boat in a storm. Gemma braced herself against the back of Mike's seat. *Elaine will understand*, she repeated silently, the movement of her lips masked by the jolting of the car.

"If you were a witch, with limited ability, and you wanted to summon Squire Cabell, where would you go?" Adrian yelled, over the rumble of the engine.

"To his tomb," replied Mike, taking the turning towards Buckfastleigh.

Clara inspected the tools laid out in front of her. There was a small dagger with a velvet wrapped handle, a half-burnt bundle of sage and a pork chop which was definitely on the turn. There was also a scattering of crystals, and a candle, just for good measure. Tucked into her bra was her, now rather tattered, copy of *Practical Spells for Teenage Witches*. She had read up a little about banishing spells online, but they all seemed to recommend certain phases of the moon, or the use of poppets, or jars full of white vinegar. There wasn't time for any of that, and the spell for getting over an ex-boyfriend sounded much simpler. She would just need to change a couple of words.

"Right!" she exclaimed, to the empty graveyard.

The warning tape was tangled in clumps around the plastic posts blocking Cabell's tomb. Half of the stakes were on their side, and a number of the others had melted. No one had bothered to come and redo them. Clara peered into the sepulchre, noting how the heavy lid had been thrown off the tomb, and that it now lay cracked in two on the floor. It would have taken two powerful men to move that slab. Or one inhuman thing, perhaps.

The stone itself was blackened by fire, and the remnants of metal bars pooled in contorted shapes on the floor. Around the tomb, grass lay trampled and parched, split by a maze of cracks in the earth. Clara wondered what temperature iron bars melted at. Suddenly feeling the chill, she wrapped her black shawl a little tighter around her shoulders. The movement caused one of her clay amulets to get tangled with the string of black tourmaline and rune pouch she wore round her neck. By the time all her jewellery was extricated, she had successfully put the image of the gaping tomb near the back of her mind.

"Let's see now," she pulled the book from her left cup with a confident flourish, "black candle, piece of paper," she referred back to the marked page, "and a lighter." Pulling each of these items from her pocket, she checked them off on the list. Now it was a simple case of giving the demon huntsman a call, so that she could order him to get lost. There wasn't much on demons in *Practical Spells for Teenage Witches* but there were five different spells for bringing back an ex-lover (FAST RESULTS). As she didn't have a photo of Squire Cabell, she had done her best to sketch him in pencil. This had led to the discovery that she was far better at witchcraft than drawing. But it would have to do.

Drawing a rough circle around herself with the

blade of the athame, she sprinkled a trail of salt mixed with charcoal. Then she smudged the area liberally with sage. This had the dual purpose of cleansing her spiritual space, and also going some way to masking the smell of the pork chop, which was suffering further from being out of the fridge. Pulling a purple chalk from one of her pockets, she lay down her drawing and knelt next to it.

"My sweet-" she shook her head, that didn't sound right, "My, uh, demon huntsman, my soul- no- my pork chop is ready to welcome your return to my life." She drew a circle in chalk around her mounted stick man. "My sweet, sod it, demon huntsman, my pork chop is ready to welcome your return to my life," she repeated. Was the wind getting up? Did the yew tree hedge look like it was stirring? "My demon huntsman-" there was definitely movement in the hedge line- "my sweet pork chop is ready to welcome you." Clara glanced around nervously. The four candles she had placed for the cardinal directions guttered in the breeze. She drew another circle around the image on her paper. "My sweet pork chop, my demon huntsman is ready to welcome your return to my life," she said shakily, eyes darting between the drawing and the trees.

A single hound leapt over the wall. It raised its head, tail held high, sniffing the air. Lines of red magma glowed where neck muscles should have been.

"My demon huntsman," intoned Clara, "my sacrifice summons you to return." Her voice had dropped, turning soft and steady. She circled her drawing with another layer of chalk, and the air around her began to buzz. Another hound cleared the churchyard wall.

Clara stretched up to her full height, which may have intimidated more shy types of wildlife. But confidence crackled around her as she repeated the summons one final time. The purple chalk tore through the paper, and Cabell spurred his horse over the closed gate.

"Witch!" he called, pulling his mount to a halt.

"Squire Cabell," she replied, placing her hands on her hips, like she might when speaking to a troublesome student, "I hear you have been misbehaving."

The huntsman was momentarily taken aback. All of his lives, he had obviously been misbehaving. It was what he did. "Have you summoned me with a pork chop?" he asked, with disgust.

"Erm, yes. Would you like it?"

"No. It smells off."

Clara shrugged. "Suit yourself. Thanks for coming, although I do need to banish you now. You're sure you don't want the pork chop?" She pulled the lighter, black candle and scrap of paper from her pocket.

An unpleasant smile curled Cabell's lips. Hounds were pouring through the yew hedge now, gathering three deep around the edge of the salt circle. He watched with interest as Clara brandished a small piece of paper with his name written on it. "You mean to banish me?" he asked.

"Yes Richard, I do. Or do you prefer Dick?"

Cabell's eyes narrowed. Clara flicked the lighter. She held the candle over it, waiting for the fresh wick to catch. Eventually it did, and she raised the black candle aloft, her wrists jangling with the clatter of bracelets.

"Go back to your grave," she said.

Cabell's horse snorted, shying back from the flickering flame. He applied his spurs harder, metal spikes piercing through skin to the hot liquid beneath.

"I must decline," he purred, unwrapping the long leather thong from his antler handled whip.

"Go back to your grave," Clara repeated, "harm

nobody else." She pushed the paper into the candle flame and one edge caught light, curling up as it blackened to ash. She turned the scrap until all the edges were charred. A couple of the hounds began to whine.

"Return now to Hell," commanded Clara, holding the remaining piece of paper in the heat of the flame. It was only the scrap bearing Cabell's name which remained. "You have no power here!" silver clanked against silver in righteous indignation. The hedge rustled, and the candle blew out.

"Quite the contrary," observed Cabell, as he climbed down from his horse.

Clara frantically clicked the lighter, but the fragile flame flickered out in the wind. She glanced between the huntsman and her shaking hands. "You can't cross the black salt," she said, as firmly as she could muster.

"You talk a lot witch. I hoped your loose tongue would have been of more use."

"What does that mean?" asked Clara, affronted.

"I see no sign of your townsfolk rising up against the Wild Hunt. In fact, I kill them and they still seem to do nothing. When did the world get so weak?"

Clara planted her feet a little further apart. The ground beneath her was firm and flat, filled with the bones of people who had worked and loved this land. "I don't think you understand weakness," she said.

"I think I see it right now. I think you reek of it." Cabell stepped forward, his hounds parting as he approached. The toe of one of his shiny black boots pressed against the circle of salt.

Clara was shaking. But she was shaking with rage. She flicked the lighter again and the flame caught, igniting the wick of the candle. "I've seen people like you. I deal

251

with bullies in school all the time. They think that they can get the new crayons because they're bigger, or stronger, or angrier than other children. They think that they're somehow entitled to get what they want, because maybe their dad has a sports car. But everyone gets the same crayons in my classroom. Except you, Dick. You're losing your colouring time!" She pressed the scrap of paper into the flame of the candle. It caught light immediately, flaring up as the ink faded under a bloom of red ember.

Cabell shielded his face. The four candles flickered and spat, while around them the air gathered thick with Clara's will. "Go back to your grave," she repeated. The scrap of paper turned grey, and light as a feather. It was caught by the breeze, and forty hounds watched it disintegrate as it drifted up over the graveyard. They dropped to their bellies, fiery eyes rolling towards their master. Cabell slowly lowered his hand. His lips curled into a sneer.

"Fighting fire with fire, how foolish." He flicked his hands upwards and the candle flames streamed skyward like tapers. The black candle in Clara's hand was suddenly a flare, announcing her failure to the heavens. She dropped it and blew on her fingers. One of the hounds lowered its muzzle and licked up the charcoal and salt. "I expected more from a witch!"

Cabell stepped into the circle. Spitting candles streamed wax in liquid pools onto the ground. The grass, already scorched once, caught light for a second time. Clara edged backwards, her heel sliding on the slippery pork chop, and sending her to the floor with a bump. The huntsman towered over her. One pale hand tapped the hunt whip against his boot, and the other was raised as a signal to the hounds. They stretched open steaming jaws expectantly.

"What did you expect?" Clara asked, shuffling closer to the piece of rather sorry meat.

"You were meant to inspire the villagers to rise up against the Wild Hunt and burn Wistman's Wood to the ground."

"Why would anyone do that?" Clara stalled, her fingers closing on something warm and slimy.

Cabell shrugged. "Why not?" He sounded bored. His index finger curled towards his palm, and one of the black and tan hounds stepped into the circle. Clara grabbed the half-burnt bundle of sage from the floor next to her, thrusting it into the nearest candle. The advancing hound shook its head in discomfort, as heavily scented smoke filled the air.

"Have some of that!" Clara cried, wafting the burning leaves in the direction of the creature. Squire Cabell clamped his sleeve over his nose with disgust.

"What is that smell?" he demanded.

"White sage," explained Clara, in a matter-of-fact tone, as she drove the burning bundle into the forehead of the distracted hound. It yelped, turning heel and stumbling blindly back to its companions. They snapped angrily as it careered into them, knocking two aside. "Best thing for dealing with bad vibes," the witch added.

"Enough of this," snarled Cabell, striding forward. His nimble fingers gripped the dagger.

Clara aimed the chop. She threw it with the accuracy of a woman who intercepts flung teddies ten times a day. The off meat hit Squire Cabell square on the nose. Clara made a run for the hedge line.

But she had only earned a seconds reprieve. Hounds poured around her, snapping and snarling as they raced for the yew hedge, turning to pen her in. Squire Cabell followed at a slow walk. When Clara glanced back, she just caught him finishing wiping his face with a handkerchief. Patches of grass were alight behind him, and the four candles had melted into puddles of wax.

"Time to die, witch," he said.

Clara clenched her fists. The hounds stank of stale meat and blood, their breath hanging hot and rancid on the air. If anyone had asked her how she might have felt in this situation, she would have said afraid. But, on actually finding herself here, she was angry instead. She didn't approve of bullies getting their own way. Cabell was far too used to throwing his supernatural weight around and getting what he wanted. It wasn't fair.

"You can't touch me," she cried, brandishing her own pendant of protection. She vaguely wondered if she should have tested it before selling one to that nice boy, Adrian.

"What is this tripe?" the huntsman strode forward, whip raised to strike the amulet from Clara's hand. But, as the antler handle swung downwards towards her fingers, the air crackled with a jolt of electricity. Cabell's arm flew back and, just for a moment, a look of shock appeared on his face. Clara was almost equally surprised. The amulet had worked!

"Begone, fiend!" she demanded, a little smugly. But the look of surprise on Cabell's face was rapidly replaced by his usual malicious smile.

"Have at it," he told the hounds. They turned as one, blazing eyes fixed on their prey. Clara's hand with the amulet began to tremble. A rough, hot nose pressed against her calf and drank in her scent with an obvious hunger. She closed her eyes. The hounds yipped and hollered, building themselves into a frenzy. So this was it. What a pity! She was just enjoying getting a hang of the whole witch thing.

19.
DEWERSTONE

The barking grew louder, underlined with a deeper, guttural snarl. The low, grey clouds pushed close to the desolate churchyard and the air took on an icy chill. One hound howled, staining the gusting wind with a sharp note of pain.

"Turn them all back to shadow!" cried a cold voice. Owain urged his horse forward, lithe hounds racing ahead of him. Cabell's pack turned in reply, hackles raised and skin shedding sparks. One black and tan body already struggled weakly beneath the paws of Owain's largest hound. Grim lowered his head and ripped out its throat.

Cabell turned slowly, gesturing for two hounds to watch Clara. "So you have come. I am honoured to have the Wild Hunt attend me."

"There is no honour intended," snarled Owain, "go back to Hell."

The huntsman smiled. It was the smile of a man who revels in carnage, and it promised blood and damnation. "Come and make me."

Owain jumped down from his horse. Glamour flashed around him, flickering as his will was directed elsewhere. One moment his red hunt coat was pristine and whole; the next it was tattered and stiffened with gore. Grim threw the broken body of the tan hound aside. The carcass ignited, spewing tongues of bright flame.

Cabell toyed with his dagger, shifting it fluidly between one hand and the other. The hunt whip was tucked into his boot. His hounds gathered by his side, shifting impatiently as they sniffed the sulphurous air, laced with the scent of their fallen companion.

"Take him," said Owain. Eight hounds sprung, mouths open, teeth dripping with peatblack ooze. The large pack swarmed forward in response, snapping and snarling, steam swirling from their lolling tongues. They were slightly smaller than Owain's hounds, but there were far more of them. Lunging for tendons and throats, they struck swiftly, then pulled back out of range from responding jaws.

Valefor was weighed down under three black and tan bodies; each time he flung one off another would jump to take its place. He caught the closest by the chest, ripping back a long strip of soft skin. It revealed gaping ribs, overspilling with the slow flow of thick magma. Valefor whined as the fiery blood scorched his gums and set fire to his fur. The other two hounds pressed their advantage, burying sharp teeth in his neck and flank.

Nearby, Shuck fought off five of the foxhounds, his paws blackened with the ash of two he had slain. Blue marshlight flickered from his eyes as his body twisted into impossible angles, teeth seeking out weakness in his nimble foes.

Cabell strode nonchalantly through the conflict. He noted his fallen hounds with a sneer of disappointment, but it did nothing to tarnish his confidence. "There are too many," he told Owain, "admit you are outmatched."

"I am inevitable, unbending as winter." Owain's pale skin took on a frosty sheen, catching the light like fresh snowfall. His eyes were blacker than midnight, swallowing even the yellow glow from the flames.

Clara slowly swung her gaze between the hounds either side of her. They hadn't stirred, but their attention was fixed on the battle. Very carefully, she began to shuffle her right foot outwards, her cheek tilting towards the yew hedge behind her. One of her guards snapped a warning, and she felt sharp teeth graze her thigh. The fiery eyes of the hound were upturned with obedient hatred, and as she gazed back fear tangled tight in her stomach. There was nothing to reason with here. Words would break on Cabell like cheap china in a dishwasher. Her only hope was the Wild Hunt.

The witch watched the Huntmaster with her lips pressed together. He looked young; younger than she might have imagined. But his face was hard, set in strong lines like shapes made in ice. Though it was his eyes that were strangest; glossy like tar and deep as forever. Horror crept over her skin, raising small hairs with a feeling of prickling flesh. She lost the power to move.

"Ice is no match for flame!" Cabell twirled the dagger, point facing skywards, and the metal glowed cherry red. Hot as the forge, small flames licked along it, frantic as terriers tasting blood on the grass. Then he threw it. The movement was fast and fluid.

Owain watched the blade bloom from his chest. A small plume of smoke curled up from the wound, which hissed as hot metal was quenched in cold flesh. Grim threw off the last foxhound. Seven now lay dismembered around him, their bodies slowly crumbling into embers and ash. He bounded to the side of his master, shaggy grey fur matted with marshwater and blood. With a whine of concern, he pushed his snout into Owain's limp fingers, pressing upwards against his palm with surprising tenderness. An iron hued stain was spreading slowly around the handle of the dagger. Owain's glamour had failed, and the hunt coat was marked by the last moments of others. A rumbling growl gathered in Grim's throat. It poured out past his teeth, guttural and putrid, heavy with the taste of old meat and earth.

Cabell dodged the first strike, summoning his hounds to close rank around him. They swarmed like rats, pulling at Grim with ravenous teeth. The grey hound stumbled once, but pulled himself back up, shaking loose his assailants with a wild yelp of fury.

Clara clenched her fists. It felt like the soles of her feet had taken root in the soil. All she could do was watch with wide eyed helplessness. She was out of her depth, and she was coming to terms with admitting it. Adrian must have listened to her voice message and thought she was out of her mind. *Adrian!* She mouthed, a crackle of hope catching her thoughts. If he was pally with the Wild Hunt, might he appear now as well? Might it be best if he didn't?

The two hounds beside her bared their teeth, tearing at the grass with impatient claws. At last, they were released, racing off to join the fray, their eyes alight with unpleasant eagerness. The grey beasts fought, surrounded by swirling shapes of tan fur and magma. The sacred circle was obliterated and the dry grass was on fire. But the Wild Hunt was winning.

Cabell vaulted onto his horse with a snarl, pale breeches smeared with the soot of vanquished hounds. Half of his pack had fallen. The hounds of this newcomer showed no sign of tiring. The huntsman pulled sharply on the bit, making merciless use of spiked silver spurs. His horse wheeled round, flaming eyes rolling and nostrils snorting plumes of grey smoke. He turned it towards the stone wall.

But, at the last moment, the animal shied, reeling back at the screech of tyres and scent of burnt diesel. Mike's Land Rover pulled up outside the churchyard, and he flung open the door.

"Not today, Cabell!" Mike cried.

Cabell turned his horse again, trapped between the advancing Wild Hunt and the large vehicle. For the first time, his face betrayed a faint touch of fear. Beneath him, his horse stumbled, and his eyes flew wide as two grey hounds tore out its tendons. The animal crumpled, spilling black bones and coal.

Owain was in no hurry. The dagger remained lodged in his chest, but the wound had stopped bleeding. He strode closer to Cabell, through a churchyard littered with still burning bodies. There was an elegance to his pace which was almost mesmerising. He was winter. Sure as the seasons, inevitable as the slow cycles of the earth. The demon huntsman stepped back, feeling the brittle remains of his horse crunch under his feet.

"Die," said Owain. His tone was measured. It was not a threat, it was a simple fact. Cabell turned his face upwards. The clouds were thick and grey; the kind that hang heavy and close to the earth. They were also utterly uninterested. His lips formed a name, and he remembered the fear and that dusk in the forest. *In your waking and sleeping, your living and dying, it shall be on your tongue*. He called it aloud, as his flesh fell from dry bones and his tongue shrivelled in his mouth. Dropping to all fours, he flashed amber eyes, turning to flee in the form of a fox. But Grim was too fast.

In the heart of Wistman's Wood, Morgana shrieked. It was a keening wail that cut through the air and drowned out the low crackle of fire. Her eyes blazed amber; for a moment the form of a fox loomed up in black smoke. But the fire settled, the shape dispersed, and the wytch was left gasping with a chill in her blood.

"You did it!" cried Mike, striding towards Owain with open arms. Clara teetered on the spot, but then Adrian was beside her, offering his arm. Gemma carefully picked her way between the black patches of ground that used to be hounds. Fian followed her closely, white fur raised along the length of his spine. The last few of the strange foxhounds were still twitching on the grass, power ebbing out of them. Only one remained standing, shaking its head in confusion at the sudden lack of command. Sniffing the air, it lumbered towards Adrian, mouth half open and gently steaming. With only a split second of indecision, Adrian stepped in front of Clara. His hands were stretched out, more in warning than defence, palms forward and fingers spread.

"Mike, some help here," he said, from the side of his mouth. He hadn't thought any further ahead than blocking access to Clara. Mike spun round, his eyes widening with horror.

"Over here!" he called, snatching a blackened stone from the ground and flinging it towards the animal. It didn't seem to notice the impact. Both burning eyes were focused on Adrian.

"Good dog?" Adrian tried. The hound stretched out its neck, pushing its drought cracked nose closer. "Who's a good boy?" he added experimentally. The demonic foxhound licked his hand. Then it whined and collapsed into ash.

Clara breathed an audible sigh of relief. Then she sat down, very abruptly. Adrian stood, turning his hands over in front of him. Slowly, he closed them into fists, looking at the black mark which still marred his fingers. It was recognition. One unholy thing to another. The world began to turn blurry. On the edge of his vision, the yew hedge softened and swirled, grey sky pressing so low that it turned into mist.

"No, no, no!" cried Gemma, leaping a burnt patch to run towards Adrian. She caught him by both arms, shaking him gently. "Adrian, we need you here. Can you hear me? Adrian?"

Before his eyes, the dull greens and greys of the churchyard were receding, replaced by a far darker tide. The air was thick with shadow, cold and still, clinging to his skin like cobwebs too fine to see. The night landscape was unmarked by features, and a black sky blended with black soil beneath his feet. He turned around, scraping a full circle with the soles of his shoes. Then he saw it. It didn't appear, it was as if it had always been there, he just hadn't noticed it. There were two fossilised trees, their brittle branches entwined, forming what felt like a doorway. It felt like a doorway, rather than looked like one, because there was nothing to be seen beyond it, other than the same black soil stretching on into the distance. But Adrian felt sure he would see something different if he stepped between the trunks.

The longing to do so was overwhelming. Before the thought had fully formed in his mind, he found his feet carrying him closer to the trees. Somewhere distant, and hopelessly distorted by static, a voice was calling his name. He shook his head, attempting to shed the irritation. Almost stumbling in his eagerness, he marched towards the strange archway. The air seemed to thrum, thick with an energy that matched the rising rhythm of his heart.

Stretching out with blackened fingers, he reached for the invisible skin that stretched between the trunks. His breath hung as mist on the air. There was an intoxicating sense of peace.

Then, something caught hold of him. He spun around angrily, identifying the something as a hand. It belonged to Gabriel.

"Go back," said the Huntmaster.

There was a blow to Adrian's chest. He lost his footing on the black soil and overbalanced. Next moment he was gasping for breath, air flooding fast into aching lungs. Gemma crouched over him.

"Adrian!" she cried, tears dripping off her chin.

"I saw Gabriel," he said.

"What?" she replied.

But Mike was backing up towards them, his eyes darting between Owain and the still seated Clara. "No time to chat," he said, "time to be going."

Gemma glanced up at Owain. He was unrecognisable. She felt the small hairs on her arms rise as she took in black eyes and paperwhite skin. Dragging Adrian to his feet, she turned to Clara, offering the witch a hand.

"I'm good. I think," Clara said, rising cautiously with the sound of jangling jewellery.

"Nice and slow, get in the car," Mike instructed. His gaze matched Owain's and an unseen electricity seemed to crackle between them.

The Huntmaster advanced through the carnage, grey hounds gathered beside him. The outer two peeled off, noses to the ground, moving to flank the mortals in front of them.

"Get in the car!" Mike yelled. Fian barked back a

challenge. Gemma's legs obeyed. She pulled Adrian with her, but he was weak. He only managed a few steps before falling to his knees. She crouched beside him, linking her arms through his and pulling upwards with fierce resolve. But he was a dead weight. His eyes turned up to hers, bright and imploring.

"Go," he said.

Gemma shook her head. There was ash smeared on her face, but clean stripes beneath both her eyes. "Not without you."

"I've got this."

"Don't be so bloody ridiculous," she sobbed.

"Gemma, in the car! Now!" Mike commanded. She felt the subtle weight of his will on her mind and was reminded how Gabriel had influenced her. Her eyes narrowed a little. It felt like a betrayal. But, her feet were taking her towards the Land Rover.

"The other seat!" Mike added.

Gemma climbed over the cubby box and into the driver's seat. The keys were still in the ignition.

"Now drive!" shouted Mike.

Her shaking hand reached towards the keys. Tears streamed down her face as the engine rumbled into life, the whole vehicle thrumming beneath her. Against every screaming desire, she kicked her foot to the floor.

The bulky car sprung away with surprising speed, lurching on its tyres as she aimed it down the narrow country lane. She had no idea where she was heading, but adrenaline burnt through her blood, blooming as red blotches on her salt-stained cheeks. Owain was not the boy who had wordlessly told her to be brave in Newgrange. He wasn't the young man who had coloured at Amergein's teasing. He was Huntmaster now.

Signs flashed past on either side, too quick for Gemma to read. She drove in a haze of panic, taking turnings at random and meeting corners too fast. But, eventually, her blood began to cool. The wheels beneath her slowed, as wide roads dwindled into tree lined tracks. She had no idea where she was. This wasn't the moor; the foliage was too lush and green, and the fields she had passed were well worked and tidy.

Movement in the wing mirror caught her eye. She turned sharply, glimpsing a blur of grey fur. Her fingers clenched the wheel, then dragged it impulsively to one side. The Land Rover lurched, rolling clumsily on its suspension, and careered towards the verge.

The impact threw Gemma forward, seatbelt biting into her chest with enough force to bruise. She gulped air, attempting to fill lungs emptied by the collision. Everything was pain. But an urgent thought screamed for attention amongst the chaos. *The Wild Hunt is coming!*

It took two shaking hands to click free of the seatbelt. Pushing open the driver's door, she half stumbled out, catching herself on the arm of the cracked mirror. Steam rose from the bonnet of the Land Rover, as the last of the water poured from the radiator. The stranded vehicle was caught between two saplings; one splintered under its axles and the other buried through what had been the grille.

"Shit," slurred Gemma. A yelp of excitement rang through the air. She pushed herself away from the car, allowing the momentum to carry her on into the woods. Crossing a small parking area, which was almost empty, she ran towards the sound of running water. Her legs worked mechanically. Could she cover her scent, somehow, if the river was big enough?

A wooden bridge spanned the water ahead. The river was wide, but it seemed to run shallow here. Darting to the right, Gemma jogged along the bank until she saw a spot to scramble down. The water hit her, shockingly cold, and her bruised chest clenched painfully. But she caught her hand in a tangle of roots, dragging herself along in the shadow of the high bank. Beneath the bridge, silt gathered thick as the water slowed round the sodden supports. Like a fox gone to ground, she dug into the soft earth, and curled up beneath the beams of the bridge.

Within moments, there was the click, click of claws on the wood above her. She clamped a hand over her mouth, in a bid to disguise her ragged breathing. From the corner of her eye, she saw grey hounds sniffing at the spot where she had slid into the water. One stopped to drink, its pink tongue flecked with specks of blood.

"Seek her out!" commanded a cold voice. Gemma recognised it as Owain's. She pressed deeper into the earth, willing herself to disappear. Were the others already dead? Had the hounds devoured Adrian like they had their sacrifice? Searing tears snaked down her dirty cheeks. Her face muscles ached from holding back sobs. This was the reality of it all. The beauty and the grace were nothing but glamour, and the truth of the hunt was the chase and the kill. Mortals were worthless, fit only for playthings. Wasn't that what the fae really thought?

Gemma was suddenly ashamed. Why was she trembling in the mud, when her friends had fought to protect her? What use was it anyway, if Adrian was already dead? She climbed out from the bank, chill water rushing past her in its hurry to the sea. If she had been looking, she would have seen the silver glint of tin in the smooth stones of the Plym. But her eyes had clouded over. She climbed up out of the river only by feel.

She presented herself to the path, expecting the sting of sharp teeth. But the bridge was deserted. The hunt had moved on. Her shoulders sagged with disappointment, and secret relief. Turning back to the car was no use, and the bare stretch of the road would leave her exposed. But the forest was old, littered with boulders tangled in curled ferns and moss, and it promised dark places to hide, if Gemma looked hard enough.

Crossing the bridge, she followed a path that bent right. It was well trodden and reinforced with flat rocks to slow down erosion. But no walkers used it now, despite the few cars left in the car park. Unwillingly, Gemma imagined what might happen to an unsuspecting couple of tourists who crossed paths with the Wild Hunt. It was bound to be unpleasant. But then, she pondered, there would be no stories if no one ever survived.

A scream rang from some way along the river. Gemma's whole body tensed, her strained muscles coiling tighter with fright. Fixing her gaze ahead, she broke into a run. The wail continued behind her, stopping for a moment, then rising with renewed resolve. It bounced off the great rocks that punctured the valley, echoing back until it seemed the whole forest was screaming. Gemma risked a glance back. Every shadow was shaped like a hound. The track split ahead, and she hesitated, before darting right along the wider fork. She regretted it almost immediately. The ground rose up steeply and the thick swathes of bracken began to grow sparse. Clutching her chest, she threw another quick look behind her, and veered off the path.

The soil was soft and black. Low, creeping plants clung to the ground, and Gemma used them as handholds to scramble up the slope. The screaming had stopped. She could only presume that this was because another life had been added to the checklist of loss. Anger boiled up again. It felt like the last rage she could muster, and she clung to it tightly.

At the very top of the rise, there was a small plateau. It was more rock than soil, although trees clung to cracks with their roots. A jagged outcrop stretched rain smoothed rock to the sky, and beyond it the ground gave way to oblivion. Gemma leaned, pressing her forehead against the rock. A yap and holler rolled upwards on the air. The noise spread like mist, collecting in hollows and the shallow dip of her collarbones. It flowed round her like water, licking her limbs and then pouring off the edge of the rock to the river below.

"Owain," said Gemma. She didn't look up, but she could feel him like winter. A howl rose, mournful and close, before simmering down to a throaty growl.

"Mortal," the Huntmaster replied. A strange fog roiled around him, as if the earth had turned putrid to match his disgust.

Gemma raised her head in indignation. After all that had happened, could he not use her name? This was the boy who had been too shy to dance. This was the boy who was clumsy at dinner. "You know who I am."

Owain shrugged. It was unimportant. He gestured Grim forward, and the hound split away from the pack. Huge paws turned up tendrils of mist, which twisted and settled like a tangle of snakes. The air had turned thick; tasting moist on the tongue. Gemma edged along the rock, her back scraping over the stone. A pale blue light flickered from the eyes of the hound, and Owain's eyes remained empty and black.

269

Gemma dragged at the anger, pulling it up from within and gripping it like a weapon. "Aren't you ashamed?" she spat, "Aren't there some fae rules about betraying your friends?"

Owain made no answer.

"Aren't you worried about Gabriel? He's going to be furious!" Gemma's voice cracked. The anger was spent, fading away like the last light of evening. Gabriel was gone. It was likely her fault. Elyn was dead, and she was about to join her.

A little wiry grass clung to the edge of the precipice. Bare stone dwindled to a narrow ledge. Somewhere below, the river Plym rushed over boulders and stirred up glinting stones veined with tin. But the mist masked it now, thick and grey on the air. Grim stalked forward, fierce as the night, sure as the seasons, his blue eyes glowing like a pair of corpse candles. Gemma stepped back. There was nothing to hold her.

20.
DIVIDE

Newton Abbott Community Hospital was very modern. It had been designed by someone who liked angles and glass, with grey panels giving way to smooth stainless steel and wall length windows. A well-kept lawn stretched out from the front, framing an equally modern piece of art. It may have depicted DNA, or even the far older twin serpents of the medical profession. Either way, there were the faint first signs of rust round the base of the sculpture.

Elaine shared a four bed bay with two other patients. The large windows at the end of the ward looked out over the tidy lawn and a row of young trees. She had watched their leaves move in the wind, following the occasional one that broke loose and fluttered away. But after a while the painkillers made her eyes tired, and she gave in to soft darkness, filled with the low bleeps and clicks of watchful machines.

Once or twice, she half stirred at the sound of ambulance sirens, but even that wail was turned gentle by the medicine in her blood. There was a slow thickness to the air of the ward; not quite stale, and strangely comforting. It shared a small sense of the sacred with deep forest glades and old, rural churches. This was a place of transition. The brushed steel beams and elegant glass were a thin skin over the deep, hallowed earth, brimming with the bones and dreams of the ancestors.

A nurse came in with a plate of hot food and spoke words that slipped away before Elaine could catch them. But there was a sense of kindness, which was pleasant, and Elaine pulled it close like the soft cloth of her sheets. The nurse nodded to herself, making a neat note on the paperwork clipped to the end of the bed. Twenty minutes later she returned and took the untouched plate away.

Elaine stayed in her darkness. She wasn't afraid. Above her, there stretched a great black sky, pricked all over with small, dancing stars. Under her feet, the black sand caught the starlight, and reflected back glinting specks, until there was no separation between two halves of velvet night. In the distance, there was an archway formed from two trees. But there were also memories of grey hounds, and strong hands and the sea salt smell of tears. She shifted in her sleep and turned her back to the window.

Clara's car smelt of lavender and old lattes. It also smelt slightly of burning, as it screeched into the car park near the base of the Dewerstone. Mike clutched the door handle and his phone, which was flashing as it tracked the location of his Land Rover.

"I thought it might get stolen," he said, "but never this." He'd taken in the smashed wing mirror and cracked radiator with a grim glance, and then turned away quickly.

"No sign of her in the car," reported Adrian, out of breath from his dash back to the road. He stumbled, and the world span sickeningly for a moment, but he clenched his fists and thought about Gemma. The grey tinge to the air slowly drew back.

"So what now?" Clara asked, "the tracker only finds us the car."

Fian barked, his head raised upwards towards the forest. His lithe limbs danced impatiently over the well-trodden earth.

"Of course. Track Gemma, you can do it!" Adrian

cried to the hound, gesturing for him to sniff the driver's seat. The animal lowered his nose to the ground and trotted off, tail held taut in concentration.

Adrian darted after him. Mike followed and Clara came last, silently cursing her fashionable boots. They had been advertised as having witchy chic, but Clara was coming to the conclusion that witching didn't involve nearly as much sitting around reading tea leaves as she'd originally thought. Come to think of it, dealing with demonic huntsmen and flammable hounds hadn't been mentioned in *Practical Spells for Teenage Witches* at all. She made a mental note to purchase more books.

Fian rushed along the riverbank, doubled back, and then caught Gemma's scent on the bridge. He whined, smelling her fear and the earthy memory of Owain and his pack. But her scent carried on, and he tracked up the path until her trail veered abruptly off into the woods. Turning an impatient circle on the path, he yipped sharply for the others to hurry. His frantic pace had turned up the earth and his white fur was speckled with flecks of brown leaf litter. Twenty sharp claws caught on the mismatched stones and left a cobweb of white scratches.

Mike caught up first, shortly followed by Adrian. Clara took longer and was nursing a stitch.

"I'm fine," she said, batting away Adrian's look of concern. "Too many biscuits. All my own fault."

Fian slipped cautiously between the trees. He moved slower now, zigzagging and looping round to catch the scent. Traces of mist lay snagged near the ground, despite no other sign of bad weather. Mike stopped for a moment, kneeling to examine an uprooted tendril of ivy and the scuff from a shoe. He spread out his hand near an enormous pawprint.

"They found her," he said softly.

Adrian broke into a run. Adrenaline carried him up the steep slope at a pace that came close to matching Fian. Large pawprints converged, pressed deep into the soft earth, leading up towards the peak of the Dewerstone. There was also a single set of half-moon hoofprints, cut sharply into the soil where the horse had struggled.

Fian let loose a howl, turning his pale snout up to the watery sun that filtered through browning leaves. Then he ran a circuit of the plateau, sniffing out shadows and testing the sparse grass for more clues on his quarry. Adrian followed slowly now, placing one foot in front of each other with aching precision. It felt very still. There was no cry of greeting, no grateful shout of *you're just in time!* There was no sign of Gemma at all. The hound finished his fruitless search and paused, hackles raised, peering over the edge of the precipice. Adrian shuffled to join Fian, dropping to his stomach when his legs shook too hard.

It was a sheer drop. Perhaps a hundred and fifty metres. The river raced past below, muttering to itself in an ominous gurgle. A few wisps of mist hung over the water.

"Is there another way down?" Adrian asked the autumn air. Fian whined, and half-heartedly began to search again.

"I've remembered it!" said Mike, emerging gratefully onto flat ground, "there's a story about this rock."

"Not the time," said Adrian.

"You're right," replied Clara, leaning on a boulder as she sucked in lungfuls of air, "I read it."

"This isn't the time for a bloody story. No more stories!" Adrian wriggled backwards and pushed himself onto his knees. His cheeks were red and glistened with tears. "Is there another way down?"

"I don't know," said Mike softly.

"Because it doesn't bloody look like it. It looks like there's the way we came up, or there's that!" Adrian stretched a trembling arm towards the edge of the rock. From where Mike was standing, there was nothing to see beyond it, except the wide, cloudflecked sky. He pushed his hands into his pockets and strode closer. Then he stood on the very edge and leaned over.

"Climbers use this rock. There are handholds all the way down," Mike said.

"It looks impossible," said Adrian.

"Look down. Do you see a body?"

Adrian craned his neck to look. "No."

"Well then, let's not give up yet." Mike lay his palm on Adrian's shoulder. There was a pause, and then Adrian matched the gesture. A few yellow leaves worked loose from the trees and spiralled away over the drop. Both men nodded to each other.

"Do you want to look?" Mike asked Clara.

"I'll take your word for it," she replied, still clinging to her rock.

The same hoofprints led back down the slope, with the marks of paws running along either side of them.

"No footprints coming back," Adrian said.

"That might not mean anything," said Mike.

"What does Owain even want?"

Mike shook his head, pausing for a moment to crouch and press his fingers into the indent of one monstrous paw. "I'm thinking on that." He pinched a little earth between his fingers and rubbed them under his nose. There was a faint smell of sulphur, from the fight with Cabell, and beneath that the scent of marsh water and bones. The soil was also cold, as if frost lay upon it not long ago. "We need to hurry."

The base of the Dewerstone was a mix of rich soil and a scattering of shed rocks from above. There was no body, and no sign of a struggle.

"That was it," said Clara, "A local man went walking through the forest one winter. He stumbled across a broken corpse at the base of the Dewerstone, and all around it were the pawprints of enormous hounds."

"They say Dewer and the Devil are one and the same," added Mike, "and that he chases poor souls off the edge of the rock. His great hounds run them down, and then tear the bruised flesh from shattered bones."

"Yes, thank you for that," said Adrian, testing his weight on a well-worn foothold.

"The villager ran back for help," continued Clara, "and four more men came back with the coffin cart. But the body was gone. There was just a little tattered cloth, the marks of those paws and a smearing of red blood on the snow." The witch spread her fingers and wiggled them dramatically, waiting for the usual gasp from her audience. But the performance was lost on Adrian. He had found a handhold and was pulling himself up the rock.

"I don't know how they do this," he panted.

"Something to do with chalk powder?" Clara suggested helpfully.

"It's no good!" Adrian let go abruptly, landing with a heavy thud. "There's no way she could have climbed down. My arms are already aching."

"It's surprising what we're capable of. Think of you and the necromancer," Mike said softly.

"I remember it well," snapped Adrian, "it was that one time I died."

Mike drew back, hands raised against the onslaught of words. His shirt was rolled up to the elbow, revealing pale arms with no trace of ink. "I do understand."

"How? How can you understand?" Adrian lashed out at the stone with his fist, then recoiled as pain bloomed up his arm. "You're one of *them*. You were always one of *them*!"

"You think that's stopped me getting hurt?" Mike's fingers closed into his palm. His shoulders were shaking and his lips had turned pale. "You think that means I don't care?"

"Gabriel is a monster. Owain is a monster. This whole damn place has so many murderous huntsmen I'm surprised anyone else can move! This one likes to chase people off a cliff. This other chap murders babies and gives them as gifts. This guy over here? He just likes to burn things, and his hounds eat what's left! Do you *psychopaths* have nothing better to do?" Adrian shook his fist at the forest, and his words echoed off the flat face of the Dewerstone, repeating themselves until they were dashed apart on the trees. *Nothing,* they whispered, *nothing. You have. Nothing.*

"I am not a monster," said Mike.

"Well congratulations, black sheep of the family."

"And neither are they."

Adrian dropped his arms incredulously. "How can you say that?"

"They're doing their job. They're doing the job they have to do."

"What, murdering people? And I thought wasps were pointless!"

"Listen to me. Being huntsman is no holiday. The Master is bound to the pack, for better or worse. They are

277

protector of the Clan. They are the bridge between worlds; hated and feared; the last guide to the soul," Mike growled. His voice trembled. "And there must be a Master." The dappled shade turned a touch darker and a crow cackled somewhere high in the trees.

"And the killing?"

"It is a corruption," said Mike, "We've caught fear off your kind."

Adrian turned abruptly away. Clara had already shuffled back from the men and was busy observing some moss. She poured all her attention onto it, even down to giving it a tentative poke. It always amazed her how this green stuff clung onto the bare rock, drying out as if dead, but always reviving in time to fall off her roof in the winter.

The smell of rotting wood drifted up from the earth, disturbed by the passage of impatient feet. Tall trees tangled together and a grey dullness began to overpower the green. Adrian shook his head. It was getting worse, whatever it was. He found it harder and harder to pull himself back.

"A bridge?" he managed to ask.

"The Huntmaster crosses over without having to die. It's how Gabriel brought you back," Mike explained.

"The Otherworld. I've been there."

"I know."

"No, more times than that. I was there in the graveyard. When I pass out I go back, and it's easier and easier."

"Like Elaine said, there's a bit of you left there."

"But last time, last time I think I would have been gone. It was cold. There was this doorway made of two dead trees, and there was black sand and black sky going on forever, and if I went through the gateway-"

"Then that would be it," finished Clara. "I've dreamed of it. When my mum died, I saw it every night for two weeks. Did you say you've come back from the dead?" She was clutching a black pendant that hung from her neck. It was worn smooth from years of fidgeting fingers.

"We call that the Divide," said Mike softly.

"What does that mean?" Clara asked.

"No man's land. The buffer, between this world and the next," explained Mike.

"He was there," Adrian said, one hand pressed to his temples, "I saw Gabriel there."

"What?" demanded Mike, taking two huge strides that consumed the space between them. He caught Adrian as he turned, catching him in a gaze like the beam from a lighthouse.

"It was him who sent me back," Adrian admitted.

"Then this all makes sense." Mike began to pace back and forth. His hands were pressed deep into the pockets of his gilet and his tanned forehead was creased beneath the burden of thought.

"Just wait," said Clara, "if I'm honest, I'm not quite past the point where you said you'd died once and come back. And Mike, you're a faerie too?" Her hands were placed on her hips and one pointy boot tapped a fast beat on the soil. She was losing it, she had to be. Exactly what she was losing, well that was hard to put into words, but things had taken a strange turn very fast. Of course she had wanted this, with the candles, and the charms and the crystals tucked down her bra, but when she had daydreamed of magic it had been more, well, magical. This was mostly blood and a surprising selection of ways to die.

"He is, and I'll explain the other one later. Great work on the protective charms by the way," Adrian said.

A smile creased the corners of Clara's mouth, and her cheeks plumped like ripe apples. She began to rearrange her necklaces, with a regal indifference. The clay pendants worked. The dark huntsman had been turned away. And it was real; all the fear and the folklore and the deep kind of magic that was fierce only when needed. Tea leaves were fine, but they did lack this excitement.

"Owain never had a chance," said Mike, shaking his head.

"I'm more concerned about Gemma," Adrian interjected. His arms were stiff by his sides. He rocked forward and back on the balls of his feet.

"I know." Mike's eyes were kind, but there was a hardness behind that hadn't been there before. "The hunt must have a master. It's close to Samhain, when the Wild Hunt gathers up all wandering souls. Before you say it, they don't kill them."

"They're already dead," said Clara. "I read an article. The hunt comes for souls that have got lost on their way."

"With Gabriel gone from this world, Owain isn't just borrowing the pack. The land demands that a duty is done." Mike looked down at the half-decayed leaves. "He isn't ready."

A sudden mist gripped the grounds of the Community Hospital. This type of weather was well known on the moor, and the nurse in attendance closed the curtains without comment. The small ward was quiet. Two patients slept, while the third sat propped up with some knitting. The needles moved jerkily, and the woman's hands shook, but slowly the shape of a small jumper was appearing.

"For my granddaughter," the woman explained,

"she's being born any day."

The nurse praised the softness and pale pink of the wool, then reread the notes that said *nil by mouth*. She silently hoped that the baby came early.

In the opposite bed, the lady with dark hair was fitfully sleeping. Morphine kept her thoughts slow and drowsy, masking the pain that burnt through her body. Handover said she'd been walking that morning, even if every journal said it shouldn't be possible. The nurse shook her head. Human willpower was amazing.

A bleep from her belt told her she was needed elsewhere. With a last sweeping glance, she assured herself all was well, and strode off into the bustle of the main hospital.

Elaine turned over in bed. Her mouth was dry but tasted faintly of apples. Mist lapped at the windows, condensing in droplets like breath on a mirror. The latch rattled once and then smoothly unlocked. Greyness poured in, throwing aside the white curtains and large French doors. The thin cloth hung on the air, billowing like sails on a strange, silent wind. Elaine half woke and leaned on one elbow. She could hear the woman opposite patiently knitting. The man in the bed nearest snored very softly. But the air was different; it was laced now with ripe fruit, with rich earth and the smell of the forest after a shower of rain.

Hooves clicked on the hospital floor.

"Summer lies dying," said a melodic voice.

Elaine opened her eyes. A soft skin of mist spread over the floor. The room around her was paler than she had imagined, as if viewed through dirty glass. But the figure before her was vivid as ever.

"Gwyn," Elaine eased her legs off the side of the bed and tentatively found the floor, "I'm in no state for a

281

visit." She was tired; not just in her bones, but somewhere far deeper. The autumn fruit still smelt sweet, but his words speckled rot on the ripe harvest of memory. Old vows were worth nothing. Thinking on things was no use.

"I know." There were no hounds beside him and his white mare was as pale as the light of the moon. An ornate golden horn hung from a strap at his waist. Somewhere, worlds way, hospital machines beeped and an old woman was knitting.

"Why have you come?"

"Your last request was a waste."

"Helping my friends was a waste?" Elaine stood carefully, her lips set in a fierce line. "This has always been it. You don't understand." She pushed herself away from the bed and turned to face Gwyn. Her feet turned up wisps of fine mist.

"I have watched you suffer," the Huntmaster said. The reins of his horse hung loose and both hands were raised.

Elaine narrowed her eyes. Black brambles were embroidered on the collar of his coat, twisting back on each other in knots filled with thorns. "And done nothing, I know-"

"I have watched you suffer," Gwyn repeated firmly, "I have watched you triumph and strive." He leapt down from the horse and took two quick paces closer.

Elaine curled in on herself, hands clenching weakly and shoulders drawing in. "Please don't."

"I have seen your wonders on canvas. I have heard you guide others with the visions you see. There are not many mortals who would make such use of their gift. All this without grandeur, and free from regret! How could I dishonour this wild woman, with help neither asked nor

282

required?"

Glistening tears traced down Elaine's cheeks, glinting silver like cobwebs covered in frost. Her shoulders shook and she clenched her teeth against shuddering sobs. "Gemma's painting. I read it all wrong."

"Right and wrong," mused Gwyn, "both words taste so similar. What if there is life, and the ride, and the choices you make?"

Elaine looked up at him, eyes wide with bright hope and horror. Tributaries of tears graced her cheekbones with a latticework of salt lace. Wet skin caught the light, glowing with the lustre of gold. Softer than spider silk, the golden lines spread, splitting like roots in the depths of the earth. Elaine looked on in wonder. The web stretched between them, piercing Gwyn's chest and still rushing on. She stared at her hands. Golden lines linked her to the woman with knitting and the man still asleep. Other threads thrust through the ceiling and down through the floor. "What is this?" she asked.

"You are seeing the web. Everything you do sings through these strands." He walked forward slowly, without disturbing the pattern. The thread that linked him to Elaine was thicker than the others.

"Gwyn, am I dying?"

"Only like the summer," the Huntmaster replied. Half a pace lay between them and Elaine could smell the sweet musk of his skin.

"But Cabell. And Adrian's soul-"

Gwyn stepped closer and whispered softly into her ear. Elaine's eyes widened and her mouth dropped gently open. Then he drew back, stretching out his hand. The pale mare whickered softly, prancing out a slow beat with her hooves. Elaine glanced back at the thin sheets of her hospital bed.

"With your permission," he said.

Elaine gripped his hand.

21.
MEDICINE

Eva examined herself in the mirror, ignoring the disapproving glance from a blonde businesswoman hurrying out of the bathroom. "Can you do up the back?" she asked Franz.

He moved behind her, finding the small zip and pulling it slowly, so as not to pinch her skin. The mirror framed their likeness, catching the strange scene in harsh electric light. Eva wore a red dress with a fitted waist and full skirt. Franz had settled on a dark green suit with a neat black bowtie. The colours clashed, and yet there was a raw elegance to them, there in the coffee shop toilet.

"What about our old clothes?" Franz asked.

Eva shrugged. "We can buy more." She leaned closer to the smeared mirror and began to apply a second layer of foundation. The grey beneath her eyes still showed, but was diluted to just a few sleepless nights.

"Will you be cold?" Franz made it sound offhand, but his gaze caught on the deep hollows above Eva's collarbones. Her body was constantly caught in some agitated movement, and she patted at her flesh as if fearing something lost. She seemed not to hear him. Her eyes were fixed on her reflection, as she added mascara and the pink blush of powder. "Almost time to go," he added.

Eva spun round to face him, a now familiar wild look in her eyes. She gripped his forearm with sudden fervour. "You've faced death. Were you afraid?"

Franz thought of his last seconds, strapped into the plane as it plunged from the sky. If anything, there was a strange calm, as he released all hold on the future. At the very last, he arrived fully in the moment. His heartbeat was surprisingly loud and it was wonderous, the way his lungs filled up with air. There was no time for disappointment, but as he thought of his brother there was the fierce heat of love. "No," he replied.

"Did you have regrets?" Eva pressed. She was almost as tall as him in heels, and he felt each of her nails pressed into his arm.

"Yes."

"Would you change things, given your chance to return?" Eva spoke it as a challenge. Franz recognised the rallying tone in her voice. Beneath her words lay the dark depths of duty, and allegiance and an expectation that he would follow with obedience. He was familiar with it all. "Would you?" she pressed.

Franz straightened his bow tie with a patient precision. He looked at his face in the mirror; the features frozen in time since 1945. "I have thought on that often," he replied.

"And?"

"I think I will be more kind."

Eva turned away, releasing his arm with a hiss of frustration. "I wonder if you buried your balls in that churchyard," she said.

"That would not have been practical," answered Franz, gently testing the fingermarks that still stung on his arm.

"Oh, here we go again. Practical this, patience for that. I'm done, Franz. Do you hear me? Done." Eva kicked her old clothes carelessly towards the corner of the room and glared fiercely for a moment into the mirror. Then she strode out.

Franz gathered up the garments and folded them

neatly next to the sink. Then he reached into his pockets for the two model planes. Closing his eyes, he focused on the feeling of metal in his palm, tracing the dull edges of wings with his fingers. *Just borrow it and bring it back*. Hot tears pressed against the inside of his eyelids. The world was no different, and yet everything was missing.

He grit his teeth, lips peeling back in a silent snarl of anguish. The weight of the toys was an unbearable burden. Bowing over the sink, he leaned on one fist, eyes rolling under their lids with the onslaught of memory. There was the sound of marching, and crying, and the heavy thrum from the engine of a bomber. He shook his head. But the sounds continued, harsh and crackly, like old footage locked away for too long.

"Stop!" Franz cried, slamming his second fist down. His eyes flew open, and he stared in horror at the silvery glass. The reflection was piercing his tie with a pin, before taking a moment to adjust his black cap in the mirror. It was the evening of his first formal dinner. He would be giving a short report on his research to Himmler and the others. His uniform felt stiff, made of heavy black wool. He had avoided ever putting it on until now. Glancing side to side, he drew himself up tall and practiced a salute. Franz raised his hand in response. Then he recoiled, aiming his fist at the glass. The wing of the plane caught the mirror and it shattered.

Staggering backwards, Franz patted himself down in panic. He was still wearing the green suit. But there was glass and blood in the sink, plus the rhythm of footsteps approaching the door. He shoved both hands in his pockets, double checked his face in the facets of the mirror, and then strode out with his eyes on the floor. A woman stepped aside to let him pass. He was already some way down the street by the time she was complaining to management.

Eva slowed her pace as she approached the first turning. Someone was running behind her. She stopped, stretching out one hand without looking back. Franz caught her, still running, and dragged her along until a couple of streets had been lost to the twilight behind them.

"What's the rush?" Eva asked breathlessly. She leaned to one side and massaged her thigh.

"Nothing," Franz replied.

She looked at him, lips parted as she sucked in ragged breaths. "You're keeping secrets."

"So are you," Franz replied. He matched her gaze, fear for fury, until Eva finally looked away. She unlocked her phone and pulled the envelope from her bra.

"Maps says the address is down that street over there." She pointed to a road crowded with regal townhouses. "Number seventy-seven."

The door of the house was glossy black, with a chunky gold knocker hanging above the tiny letterbox. Eva smoothed down her dress and returned her phone to the safety of her underwear. Franz hung back a pace, his eyes drawn to the flaming sun and triangle motif on the knocker. His skin prickled beneath the sleeves of his shirt.

Eva knocked. There was the sound of slow footfalls from inside. Franz fought to ignore the tightness that drew up both his shoulders. This was all too familiar. But, just like last time, there was no other choice. For a moment, he closed his eyes and sank back into the darkness of memory. For many nights he had tried to recall what there was before he climbed out from the bog and aimed his gun at the feral. But there was nothing, only velvety nothing, and the knowledge that the life that possessed him was borrowed.

"Welcome," said a soft voice.

Franz opened his eyes. A grey-haired gentleman stood in the doorway. He was wearing a modern dinner suit and a pair of gold wire glasses.

"We have an invite," explained Eva, offering up the paper printed with the address.

"Of course you do," the old man smiled.
Franz narrowed his eyes and dared to edge a little bit closer. It was the very same man from the bookshop.

"We have met in your workplace. You keep yourself busy," Franz observed lightly. He summoned all his strength to force a confident smile.

"Well, one must," the man answered warmly, gesturing for the two guests to follow him inside. "The Devil makes work for idle hands, isn't what they say?" he added, turning back to grin conspiratorially at them.

Eva's heels clicked loudly against the marble tiles of the floor. She was used to being dragged around rich people's houses, but the grandeur of this one snared her attention. High ceilings were lit with ornate golden fixtures, the soft glow spilling through Art Deco designs. Lowboys lined the halls, inlaid with exotic woods, and supporting glass cabinets brimming with artifacts. She paused to look more closely at one.

"Gold heart scarab, inlaid with lapis lazuli and malachite, found amongst the burial treasures of Amenhotep III," the bookseller explained. Eva nodded. She had some idea of the value of such things from her father's dealings.

Franz paused by a deep frame on the wall, hands

289

clasped tightly behind his back.

"From the Battle of Britain," said the old man, turning on one heel with an obvious glee, "it's part of a Spitfire. Can you see the kill marks the pilot painted on it?"

Franz stared at the twisted piece of metal, glaringly out of place amongst priceless works of art. There wasn't a speck of dust on the white wooden frame. Like everything else in the long hallway, the mangled piece of wreckage was frozen in time within a cage of clear glass. "Clearly," he replied.

Music carried softly from somewhere ahead. The bookseller inclined his head politely to his guests and turned the knob of a white wooden door. At once, the sound doubled, and Eva's eyes were drawn to the sparkle of cut crystal chandeliers. She and Franz were ushered into the dining room. Two chairs were pulled out, by smartly dressed servers, and a choice of wine was offered for their approval.

Franz stared at his napkin, which was folded into the shape of a swan. He could feel eyes on him; bright, curious eyes that were assessing just how he could be used.

"Welcome, to our final, honoured guests," said the silver haired man at the head of the table. He stood and raised a glass of red wine. Eva recognised him at once. He was Maximillian Early, the eccentric collector who had made her and Franz millionaires. She wondered if he had ever flown the Messerschmitt, or if it had simply sat in a hangar and gained a grey skin of dust. Nine faces turned obediently towards her, promptly followed by raised glasses in reply. She recognised many of them; vague characters from the news, politicians and businesswomen who pulled the strings backstage to the world.

"To Eva, and Franz!" The Collector's voice was

smooth, like thick, golden treacle. The seated guests echoed his call, and then blessed the statement with a sip of their drinks.

Franz had flattened his swan and couldn't work out how to refold it. He hid both sweaty palms beneath the table and forced his face into a courteous smile.

"Have I missed much?" drawled a voice from the far side of the room. Blake sauntered over and pulled out the last empty chair. A waiter appeared with white wine, but Blake pushed the bottle away in disgust. "The good stuff, if you please," he demanded, stabbing a finger at the small glass of gold liquid he had sourced elsewhere in the house.

"Our last guests have arrived," Maximillian replied, gesturing with a sweep of his hand.

"See, just as I said," Blake said with pride, raising his glass in Eva's direction. "I never let you down."

"Quite. Now, onto business. I shall not presume to bore you with too much detail, as we all know just why we are here." Maximillian opened his arms warmly to the table and nodded with mutual understanding. "The world has become sick. No matter how sweet the wine, the sour taste of rot remains in my mouth. You've all seen it for yourselves."

"Violent crime is up," said a moustached man near the end of the table. "Our prisons are full."

"Trade is barely profitable. We're falling behind," said a woman with dark, steady eyes.

"What type of world no longer finds time for God?" questioned a small man, clasping his hands.

Maximillian nodded with gracious concern. "We sense how this cycle comes close to the end. Like an arthritic hound, it labours over the tasks that once came so

291

easy. The fox has been left free to feast on the hens. We live in a world where we can no longer protect the ones that we love." He caught Eva's eye kindly and held it a moment.

"We can't bring them back. But we can change the world in their memory!" cried a blonde woman, her eyes bright with tears.

"We can do better than that," Maximillian said solemnly. "We can build a new era in their honour. Their sacrifice is the foundation on which we raise the next age. But first, my dear friends, this wound must be cleaned. The rot must be burnt out before the healing can begin. It is a kind master who takes his old dog to the green fields and shoots it. The time has come when, we too, must be kind. We must end the suffering of this dying world." He paused for a moment, with a hand on his chest. As if by some secret cue, the smartly dressed waiters reappeared and silently began to serve smoked salmon and artichoke hearts.

Eva jumped as the plate was placed down before her. She glanced round the table, and gently touched her wet cheeks with a finger. The blonde woman was being comforted by a slim man with glasses, and the other guests were nodding to each other. Her heart had grown too full for her chest, and for a moment she worried her ribs couldn't hold it. But it settled, enlarged, and beat like a drum.

"Wasn't that wonderful?" she turned and asked Franz. He had cut the artichoke into very small pieces and was studiously shifting them around on his plate. "Wasn't it?" Eva repeated fervently. Franz looked up. His eyes were bright, like rock pools caught in the sun.

"Do you think so?" he replied quietly.

"Well, yes. He understands, he really understands." Eva reached out and lay her hand on Franz's wrist. It was the hand with the knife, and he paused in his dissection of smoked salmon to face the searchlight of her gaze. Her eye makeup was smudged and her prominent collarbones were framed by expensive red silk. Beneath all the concealer, her cheeks were flushed red with excitement and hope.

"What does he understand?" Franz questioned carefully.

"That this world has gone wrong. Can't you feel it? I've felt it my whole life, but I never knew what it was."

"How can rock and earth be wrong? It is people. People can be wrong."

Eva gripped Franz's wrist. Her bright eyes held pity, but also a fierce, feverish heat. "Don't you understand?"

"I think I understand perfectly." Franz peeled his hand away. "None of this is anything new. I have heard so many men explain how they will save the world, at a cost. Are you really so caught up in this, when you have not been told the price?"

Eva blinked, disorientated. "But, we must be kind," she murmured, suddenly feeling a little bit lost. She was surrounded by a table of strangers, and Franz was frightened and angry. His eyes were sea glass blue and his cheeks were pale at the prospect of drowning. "Franz?"

But the plates were cleared with a sudden brisk energy, and Maximillian was standing, a smile on his face. "I trust that the starter was to all of your tastes?" he enquired, as more wine was poured. Many of the guests nodded with enthusiasm. Eva watched how their eyes were fixed on the Collector with reverence. "As always, I promise not to take your attention for too long. You honour me with your company, and through the trials you have shared with me. I have not forgotten about you for one single moment, and the time now feels right to share a deep truth of my

293

own."

He bowed his head for a moment in thought, and Eva's eyes were drawn to the strange item mounted on the wall behind him. It looked like the ships wheel from some ancient galleon and had nine wooden spokes speckled with holes from woodworm. She recalled the cufflinks Maximillian had worn when they sold him the plane and glanced at his cuffs with slow curiosity. They were the same golden, nine spoked wheels.

"My father was a great man," Maximillian began. "He fought for his country in the Second World War. He believed in us, and in freedom, and in many other wonderful things. He told me that, even in times of great darkness, things would come right, because nature has always sought balance. Dictators would die, grief would be forgotten, and people would find kindness in their hearts. He was wrong."

There was a low murmur of agreement round the table and Maximillian acknowledged it with a gentle nod. "His plane was shot down in 1944. There were no survivors. There was no kind heart to save him as he fell from the sky." The Collector's face was tight with emotion, and his usual elegant demeanour was twisted by the fierce heat of loss. Franz stared at the handle of his knife, noting how the room was distorted into strange shapes on the bright curve of silver.

"He believed that things would get better if we waited it out. He died waiting. I am not here to make the same mistake." Maximillian reached out to the seated guests, gold cufflinks catching the glow from ornate candelabras. "I have gathered you here with me, because you are people who can change the world. We are the medicine. We can heal the sickness that grips us, together.

My father was right about something very important; nature does seek balance. She calls us now to be her doctors, at this time of rebirth. Yes, there will be pain, but this is only natural, and a good midwife will not shy away from it!"

The blonde woman was in tears again, but other faces were stern and fixed in fierce resolve. They had each known pain, and it pulsed through their veins like the memory of poison. The world was sick, but they were survivors, and they understood that healing would hurt.

"How?" asked Eva, suddenly standing, "how can we change the world?" Her eyes were bright, but her hand hovered over her thigh as if an old injury troubled her.

"Perhaps you can change it most of all." Maximillian fixed her with his honeythick gaze. "We have been given all the tools we need. Great minds have paved the way and all that is left now is for us to act. Look at this." He picked up two napkins and curled both into cones. Raising one, he displayed it to the table. "This is our current cycle, and we are here," he gestured towards the narrowest end of the cone, "near the final point of decay. These are the end times, and very soon..." Maximillian let his finger travel off the edge of the napkin. "But Yeats taught us about the great gyres, so that we could all have hope."

Eva narrowed her eyes in confusion. She had never heard of a gyre before. The Collector caught her expression and turned to her kindly.

"A gyre is what we call these decreasing spirals that represent each cycle of the earth. The most wonderful thing about them, is that they never exist alone." He placed the second napkin behind the first, so that the widest point of that cone lay behind the narrow tip of the first one. "As one gyre comes to an end, another always begins. In this way, death is always rebirth, and the end is, by necessity, the beginning."

Once again, waiters appeared without warning and served steaming plates of dark meat and vegetables. There was a thick red sauce, which glistened in the light. Maximillian gestured amiably for his guests to eat and reminded his staff to offer more wine.

"Have you heard of this before?" Eva whispered to Franz.

"Something very similar," he said.

"And? Is it true?" Her hands were clenched into fists, and they shook slightly where they lay on the white linen tablecloth. The hollows above her cheekbones seemed deeper than ever, but her skin was aflame with a feverish glow. "Is it?"

Franz folded his napkin with a careful precision. "I have read prophecies from all over the globe. I have read about Ragnarok and I have read Revelations. From almost the very beginning, mankind has had a strange occupation with how the world will come to an end."

"But which one is true?"

"None of them. All of them. How can we know? They had me scour myth for the key to immortality; for magic that would make an unstoppable soldier. They searched for the treasures from the stories; the Cauldron of Rebirth, the Holy Grail and the Philosopher's Stone."

Eva's eyes widened, sparkling with memory. She smelt her mother's perfume, and the earthy scent of her horses. She heard her father laughing, while they drank champagne in the one room that was heated.

"But they never found them. Listen to me," Franz caught her hand and gripped it. "Men became so caught up in chasing myths that they lost sight of themselves. Eva, the horrors that have been carried out, all in the name of fixing the world!"

"They haven't found them... yet," she replied softly. Her hand settled to stillness and her breath became rhythmic. Her heart pressed eagerly towards her throat.

"Yet?" Franz withdrew his hand in defeat.

"You found me," Eva said.

"Well," said Maximillian, easing onto his feet, "I hope you will agree that meal was superb. Venison from Windsor Great Park, if I may brag just a little."

There were nods of agreement, and the man with the moustache raised his glass of red wine.

"But I have spoken more than enough. Now I must hand over to you. Is there anything you wish to ask?"

Blake raised an arm.

"The whiskey is in the decanter," Maximillian told him.

The man with the wine and the moustache loosened his tie just a little and looked up at the Collector. "These gyres," he said, testing the new word on his tongue, "you say they overlap?"

Maximillian nodded, hands clasped in front of him.

"Then, won't they reset, so to speak, without any help from us?"

"I'm so glad you asked that," Maximillian replied smoothly, picking up his two folded napkins again. "You are quite right in noticing that the very end of one gyre aligns exactly with maximum burst of energy that heralds the beginning of the next. This is the point of recreation, which comes naturally at the most dire point of destruction. As we are here," he touched his finger to a point near the end of the napkin again, "and there is a little way to go until the darkest of hours, my proposal is this; we do not prolong the suffering. We intervene, and switch onto the fresh gyre before the sickness is fatal."

"You said that nature seeks balance" said the slim man with glasses, "does this go against it?"

"Quite the opposite. In nature the sick are culled at the first sign of weakness," the Collector replied.

"How do we do it? How do we hurry up the next phase of the world?" asked the dark eyed woman hungrily.

"It's very simple really, we bring forward the end credits; give the energetic signal that this cycle is done," Maximillian said.

"You're talking about the end of the world," drawled Blake, raising a wineglass full of whiskey.

"Now, now, you should know better Edward," Maximillian chided, "I'm talking about the *rebirth* of the world. Quite the difference there."

"Either way, it has to be an improvement," Blake shrugged.

"All of you will be protected. Everyone you love will be safe. This is the cleansing of the earth; the disinfectant in the wound. Our methods will be quick and kind," Maximillian said urgently, his face tilted upwards with sharp edged determination. Belief rolled off him like smoke, thick and enchanting, sweet like the smell of a room full of lilies.

Eva drained her glass and placed it down on the table. "Blake said you could bring back my father."

The Collector turned and opened his arms, summoning her to him like a long absent child. "In the new age, anything is possible."

22.
CURSE

A chill wind whistled through Widecombe in the Moor. It swirled around stone cottages and climbed the Gothic tower of the village church. Rattling the stained glass, it sang of old mine shafts and the sweat of pit ponies, as it taunted the tinners rabbits carved in the eaves.

Clara parked in a lay-by just out of town. The moor stretched out around her, crumpled and folded like an old patchwork blanket. Heather gathered in blotches over tufty green grass and swathes of dying bracken bared brown, broken stems. The witch retied her black scarf more tightly.

"Are you sure about this?" she asked Adrian.

"No," he replied, throwing his car door open. The air was fresh and sharp. He breathed in until his lungs stung and his head almost stopped spinning.

There was the sound of hooves falling on tarmac. Clara leaned out her window, watching the white mare climb the last curve of the road. Mike sat astride it, seemingly at ease in the saddle.

Adrian leaned heavily against the little purple car. Everything was tainted with that strange black sand, speckling over his thoughts like the first growth of mould. They were here to find Gemma. To find Gemma, they must find Owain. And Mike had a plan.

"There we go, girl," said Mike to the horse, patting the shaggy fur of her neck. The animal sniffed Clara's wing mirror with muted interest.

"You're outrunning the Wild Hunt with that?" Clara asked sceptically.

"I don't need to outrun them. That's the whole

point," Mike replied.

"But the story-" said Adrian through gritted teeth.

"Doesn't tell of any danger to me. I'm just a simple farmer, riding home from the Widecombe Fair," said Mike.

"You're drunk, don't forget," added Clara.

"Yes. I won't forget. I'm a simple, drunk farmer, riding home from the fair, who has the terrible misfortune to cross paths with the Dark Huntsman."

"This is mad," said Adrian.

Clara frowned, fingers straying to the stone amulet hung round her neck. "He's right. This is a terrible plan."

"We haven't got time for another. The light's fading already," Mike said softly.

Adrian glanced around, his gaze straying to the sharp tors silhouetted in the distance. It had been twilight for him for some hours already. Was this how Gemma felt while he was food for the ravenous undead? Had she known this same numb horror, that turned limbs to lead and begged eyes to close? *It's too late*, whispered the darkness, *come rest, come and rest.*

"No!" Adrian cried, pushing away from the car with all the strength he could muster. "There's still time."

"That's the spirit," said Mike.

"What should I do?" asked Clara.

"You stay here with Adrian. I'm no more than a passing distraction for Owain. I will deliver the message and find out if Gemma is with him."

"There's more to that story," Clara said with a sigh, "you know what the huntsman gives the farmer, wrapped up in a bundle?"

"Huntsman, give us zum of yer game..." mumbled Adrian darkly.

"I know the story," Mike said, "and Owain is lost in

it. I should never have let him raise the hounds."

"I don't know that much about faeries, or hounds or even the Wild Hunt," said Clara, untangling the cord of her black amulet from countless other necklaces. "But I do know a little bit about difficult choices. I know that there are times when we want to carry other people, but we can't." She pulled the cord off overhead, only catching it once on her pentagram earrings. "My mum taught me that. At the very end, when she was all tied up with tubes and machines." Clara raised her palm towards Mike. The charm necklace lay curled in her hand. "Take it. It's tourmaline."

"The story is telling him, forcing him to become all that he feared he would! He was afraid. That's how it gets in." Mike's horse shifted her weight from one hoof to the other. The edges of the sky bled towards black, and the wind wailed like a fox in a snare.

"He will come," muttered Adrian. He swayed unsteadily, eyes rolling as he batted away the words that swarmed suddenly around him. They gathered like starlings, chattering with centuries of discordant voices, undulating in patterns of horsemen and hounds. Two dead trees reached towards him with their branches.

"We make our own choices," Clara said firmly. She was far too distracted to spare a thought for how she looked, but if she had stepped back and seen from a distance, she would have been pleasantly surprised. The restless wind caught her black scarf and it whipped round her like tatters of midnight. Her back was straight, and the glint of countless silver bangles was overshadowed by the fierce gleam in her eyes. On the wild moor, with stems of heather snagged in her dress, she was more of a witch than the author of 'Practical Spells for Teenage Witches' had ever hoped. "Now take the bloody necklace."

Mike reached down and took it. He nodded stiffly in thanks. Then he turned the old mare and coaxed her into a trot. Adrian and Clara listened to the rhythm of hooves until it stopped, and they both knew that Mike had crossed onto the moor.

There was a dull thud.

"Adrian!" Clara cried, rushing back to the car. He had slid down the door, and was now sitting with his back braced against the purple paintwork.

"I'm fine. Let's get on with this," he mumbled.

Clara glanced back towards the empty road, and then clasped her hands and she leaned towards him. "Tell me what to do."

"Just help me onto the grass."

Adrian was light, even as a dead weight. He gripped her shoulder weakly and she half dragged, and half carried him away from the lay-by onto short, mossy turf.

"Now what?" Clara whispered.

"Lay me here,"

"But it's wet!"

Adrian managed a hoarse chuckle. "That's literally the least of our worries." He lay down without flinching, even as he felt the cold water seeping through his jacket and trousers. The moor was a giant sponge, and beneath the soft turf lay sodden peat and a complex web of underground streams. Adrian felt them now, the rush of water ringing through him, matching the flow of blood through his veins. Going would be so easy, but the return, that was more tricky.

"You're sure he'll be there?" asked Clara. Her voice sounded distant and increasingly irrelevant. The ground beneath him was cold. He pressed his fingertips into it, and felt the soft shift of fine sand. It was a relief; his body had felt so heavy, but here his movements were easy. He rolled onto his knees and looked up. The black sand stretched, without any horizon, until it blended with a black sky sprinkled over with stars. All the constellations that ever were or would be watched over the empty dreamscape of the Divide. Orion, who had looked on while Cabell's hounds devoured Tom Dunn outside the Warren House Inn, shone most brightly of all.

"Gabriel!" cried Adrian, cupping his hands around his mouth. The sound carried over the featureless sand until it faded out. "Gabriel!" Adrian called again, scrambling to his feet and turning a slow arc. There was nothing. Even his own footprints faded after a couple of moments. He watched them disappear one by one, black sand flowing in to heal over the wound. An amount of time passed before he realised he was walking backwards. Clenching his fists, he forced himself to stop, feeling his feet twitching treacherously beneath him. There was no need to look behind him to know exactly what would be there. "Gabriel, please!" he tried again, through gritted teeth.

There was the low groan of wood under strain. Something brushed his shoulder, and a thin twig stretched over his chest. Adrian's eyes widened with horror as he watched buds swell and the branch thicken with impossible speed. "Huntmaster!" his voice came out as a scream, sharp and raw in the endless nothing, "Gemma might be dead!"

Bark snapped and splintered, unable to contain growing limbs, as sap spread through a web of new branches. There was no way forward through the tangle. Adrian turned around slowly.

Clara straightened her rings for the twenty fourth time. Adrian lay still as death, except for his eyes, which rolled restlessly beneath the thin skin of their lids. Had they all gone mad? Did they really believe that Gabriel would come back, simply because Adrian asked him? She pulled out her copy of '*Practical Spells for Teenage Witches*'. The bright pink cover was covered in sooty fingerprints and dog eared at the edges. It had seemed exciting, and a little bit dangerous, when she first looked at it, but now the girl with the black cat seemed woefully out of touch. The short skirt would be hopeless for a chilly day on the moor, and those pointy toed boots had proved to be painful! And as for the cat, well, they just weren't that stupid.

She flicked through to a page which contained a spell for good luck. She skimmed it half-heartedly, noting that the examples given included going on a date and doing well in a test. Her shoulders slumped forward, and she tossed the book aside in frustration. It hit the turf with a soft *flump*, and immediately began to absorb water. The cover arched open as the pages started to swell. But Clara's attention was elsewhere, and her face was forming an expression of mixed fascination and disgust.

In a ring around Adrian, mushrooms appeared to be blooming. They weren't the mushrooms that appear overnight in the hedgerow, although they were similarly pale. Pushing up through the soft earth, they parted moss with all the unstoppable force of decay. The largest one rose clear of the turf and shook itself. Cracks spread through the ground around it, and brown water bubbled up from the peat. Clara went to grip her piece of tourmaline and remembered she had given it to Mike.

She watched in mute horror as the skeleton of a small pony extricated itself from the soil. It was followed by a fox, a roe deer, three rabbits, a hedgehog and a vole. The bones of the vole were so tiny that it looked like a small, levitating skull. The fox had broken ribs on one side and the deer was missing an antler. Clara glanced at the road, and its signage begging drivers to 'take moor care'. The skeletons being there made some sense. The fact that they were now gathered in a circle, looking down at Adrian, didn't.

"Shoo?" said Clara experimentally. The hedgehog gave her what felt like a withering glance. She looked down at '*Practical Spells for Teenage Witches*', which was now looking very sorry for itself indeed. *Good luck in a test*, she recalled, perhaps it could work. If this wasn't some kind of test, well goodness knows what was. She crouched down to pick up the book, grimacing as she tried to peel apart the sodden pages. It was no use; her only guide to witchcraft was moments away from becoming a paper mache project.

"This isn't fair!" she shouted, waving her fist at the moor in general. "I know I messed up. Selling those amulets was greedy. *Although they did work*," she added under her breath. "But I told Cabell to stick it. And none of this was Adrian's fault." She shook her head slowly, and her hands clenched into balls. The chill wind caught the tears on her cheeks and they stung. Mike was somewhere out on the moor, risking his life to get Owain's attention. Adrian was lost in the dark, looking for someone who apparently disliked him. And here she was, crying in the company of a wet book.

There was a scraping sound from nearby. Clara looked up and saw that the empty eye sockets of the deer were fixed on her. It dipped its head, scratching at the turf with its hoof. She walked over hesitantly. The earth around Adrian had been turned up by agitated feet. She leaned closer, being very careful not to step on the vole. There was the click of bone on bone as the creatures around her shifted impatiently. Then she saw it! Fine fronds of frost curled over Adrian's cheek. There were tiny crystals of ice on his eyelashes, and the faint breath that rose from his lips came as wisps of pale mist.

"This isn't right," she whispered to the gathered bones. This was some kind of sign, and not a good one. She cast her mind back to their fruitless search of the Dewerstone. The earth had been cold where the Wild Hunt left prints. It was because they could cross, Mike had said, into the Divide and back. But it left its mark on them, and in that in-between place it was always cold. The Huntmaster could cross and come back, but no one else could. If Owain was master now, could Gabriel even return?

Clara leaned over Adrian, her hands clasping his upper arms. He felt cold, and very still.

"Time to come back," she said, "you've tried, and that's enough." Adrian showed no sign of stirring. "Come back, please!" she shook him gently. "Come back Adrian!" she shook him roughly this time, and he lolled side to side like an oversized doll. The tears came thickly now, dripping down her chin and coating her lips with the sharp taste of salt. She grabbed his limp hands and tried to warm them with her own. Intricate swirls of ice crept down from his cuff and spread over his palms, filling the shallow crease of his lifeline with frost. *Only the Huntmaster can cross and come back.* This was one of those old-fashioned fairy tales, where there was no happy ending. "I'm so sorry." Clara hung her head in defeat. Tears dripped onto Adrian's jacket, where they almost immediately froze.

Then there was a sizzling sound. It sounded very much like water on a hot pan. Clara looked up at the deer accusingly, but it simply cocked its head. Then she looked at the fox, who seemed guilty, but she suspected that this was more to do with the step it took closer to the rabbits every minute or so. A faint trail of steam curled up on the air. Clara looked down at Adrian's hands. One of them was completely covered in a delicate pattern of frost, but the other, the one with two burnt fingers, was very gently steaming. Each time the frost tried to spread close to the black marks it immediately melted.

A few things fell into place at once. Mike had filled her in on what happened with the fire and the tomb. Cabell's last remaining hound had sniffed Adrian's hand and not attacked. The demon huntsman was cursed never to cross into the Otherworld; to remain undead and scour the earth with his hounds. And a bit of the curse had somehow crossed over to Adrian. He wasn't fully all lava and stuff, but it was enough!

"Hang in there!" Clara commanded.

Mike coaxed the old horse into a slow, rhythmic canter. The wind caught his brown curls, revealing faint streaks of grey, and the pale mane of the horse stirred with each stride. Smeared across the horizon, the sun marked the end of the day with all the colours it could muster. The sky briefly blazed fierce red and amber, before being obscured by the rising grey mist.

"There once was a farmer, riding home from Widecombe Fair," Mike said to the horse, "it had been a good day, and he stopped at the pub for a drink." His cheeks coloured, and he felt glad that he was, for now, alone. Drink had eased him through a life made of sharp fragments, but now his memories had returned, and he finally felt almost whole. He carefully pushed the memory of Elaine being carried into the ambulance to the back of his mind. "By the time the farmer was riding home, night had already fallen on the moor." As if on cue, an owl hooted somewhere out in the shadows. "But he was not the only traveller that night-" Mike's voice faltered, and his horse shied beneath him, tossing her head as she felt his limbs tense. *Tell the story. Never let it tell you*.

"The cries of hounds rang through the darkness, a chorus of hunger that gave teeth to the wind. The farmer heard them, and he kicked his horse to go faster." As if she understood, Mike's horse picked up speed. The night was cold and wild, but she felt suddenly young, and something compelled her to race over the moor. "But the hounds were soon upon him," said Mike. Then he listened. A few moments seemed to stretch out impossibly long, filled only with the sound of thudding hooves, and the quiet trickle of ever shifting water. But it came. A single howl; rising up from the gorse. It was joined by others; yips and hollers of excitement rolling out from panting jaws.

"That's it," murmured Mike, "come for me, the story demands it." He let go of the reins, freeing the mare to choose her own path. He raised his arms, palms upwards, and closed his eyes. All of his imagination, he poured into picturing the hounds, racing alongside him like ravenous shadows. Soon he could smell them; old death and damp bone. They were here.

Then his horse stumbled. She let out a squeal of terror as the ground fell away beneath her, the grass turning to a treacherous bog. Mike was thrown clear. He rolled, cursing, and began to crawl back towards the animal, testing the ground ahead with his hands. But there were snapping teeth everywhere, and the horse was screaming as black shapes leaped for its throat. This wasn't the story. This wasn't how it was meant to go at all!

Mike's hand sank in front of him, and he quickly snatched it back. He couldn't get any closer without being sucked down himself, although the mire was even stopping the lithe hounds. For now. The horse thrashed helplessly, now shoulder deep in muddy water. "Shh," he tried to reassure her, but his voice was drowned out by barking.

He felt Owain arrive before he saw him. The darkness grew thicker, and the hounds backed away with muzzles low to the ground. Against all his instincts, Mike closed his eyes again. Hold onto the story. *It's the only control you have*. "There once was a farmer, riding home from Widecombe Fair," he murmured quickly, "It had been a good day, and he stopped at the pub for a drink. By the time the farmer was riding home, night had already fallen on the moor. But he was not the only traveller that night. The cries of hounds rang through the darkness, a chorus of hunger that gave teeth to the wind. The farmer heard them, and he kicked his horse to go faster. But the hounds were soon upon him-" Mike drew a breath, the freezing air making his lungs ache, "-and so was their Master."

A horse snorted behind him, sharp hooves tearing restlessly at the turf. Mike turned around very slowly. Owain was dressed all in black. A cloak billowed around him, and the first weak moonlight glinted off the spurs on his boots. His pale features were twisted into a sneer of disgust.

"Huntsman," Mike hailed him, "give me some of your game."

Owain reeled back, confusion widening his eyes. The air buzzed with the faint chatter of starlings, and the grip of the story grew tighter. There was something he should have done. Something terrible. His huge black horse snorted and snatched at the reins. Owain blinked, and for a moment Mike saw the Apprentice again; young, and very frightened.

"Gabriel needs you. He's lost in the Divide," Mike said quickly. Owain's eyes rolled and his face tilted skyward. He looked like a grotesque puppet. "Have you seen Gemma?" Mike pressed.

Owain stared upwards, his mouth slightly open. Around him, the hounds slunk slowly back to his side, gathering like a pack of black storm clouds.

"Gemma," Mike repeated, almost yelling now, "is she alive?" He pressed his hands to his ears as the air prickled with hundreds of high-pitched voices. A thousand years of folklore writhed in the air around them, waiting for a way in. Owain reached down into his saddlebag, expecting to feel cold flesh wrapped in cloth. He felt the blood on him; tiny, damp flecks cooled by the night air. There was the dark of a sparse room and a single, small cry that was easily silenced. Tears welled up and began to spill down his face, tracing trails of faint silver which glistened like spider silk. His fingers closed on nothing. The saddlebag was empty.

The chattering stopped abruptly. Owain turned to Mike with a speed that should have broken his neck. The Huntsman reached out and dropped nothing into the farmers outstretched hands.

"The story," murmured Owain incredulously, "it can be changed." He turned the horse with one hand, a triumphant smile curling up the corners of his lips. The hounds surged forward, Grim in the lead, their eager eyes leaving comet trails of blazing blue light. The night seethed with shapes and then, like frost after sunrise, they were gone.

Mike edged back over to the distressed horse. "There now my beauty," he half spoke and half sang, "that's the worst of it over." Then he got out his phone, praised the one bar of signal, and called Search and Rescue.

Adrian watched his fingertips with fascinated horror. The pull from the doorway had been irresistible, and he had turned to face it like a road weary pilgrim. The tangle of twigs blocked any path of retreat, but his thoughts had slowed down and leaving was forgotten. There was only the sand, jewelblack and brilliant, and the quiet demand that he walked through the archway. He had tried. But there was a loud sizzle, and he was spat quite resolutely back.

Since then, he had spent a good few minutes prodding the air between the two trees with his fingers. Each attempt produced a spark, and his hand was pushed away. Both burnt fingertips glowed like angry embers. "Interesting," he said to himself.

"It is," said a voice.

Adrian screamed, because someone had answered him while he was trapped in an endless world of nothing. Then he spun round. It was Owain.

"Are you still evil?" Adrian asked carefully.

Owain looked down at the ground and began to kick at the sand with one black leather boot. "I think I'm mostly myself again," he said.

"Is Gemma alright?"

"Well, I don't think she's dead, if that's what you are asking."

Adrian scanned Owain's face for any trace of a lie.

311

He looked pale, and tired, and somehow a year older than he had been a few days ago. "Do you know where she is?"

Owain shook his head and began to pick some dried mud from the cuff of his coat. "We need to find Gabriel. He can fix all this."

"I've called him," said Adrian, glancing around again just in case, "but nothing."

"I think maybe if I call him, as-" Owain faltered with embarrassment, "-as Huntmaster, then he will have to come."

Adrian nodded. "Try it."

"Don't be afraid. Please."

"I can't promise that," said Adrian. Even in the permanent twilight of the Divide, pink began to appear on Owain's cheeks. It clashed terribly with his red hair, and Adrian relented. "I'm tired and I've probably used up at least five lifetimes of dramatic reactions. Alright?" He managed a watery smile.

The two trees had gone. It wasn't quite that they'd disappeared but, between one blink and another, they had chosen to be elsewhere. Or they were still there, Adrian mused, but just not visible anymore. He looked down at his burnt fingers. They were scabbed black again and felt a bit sore if he pressed them.

"Come to me Grim," Owain demanded. Adrian stepped back instinctively. A patch of sand began to rise, and a hound shook itself free. "Come to me Gelert, come Skriker and Shuck. Come Gytrash and Guinefort, come Valefor and Barghest."

The black sand seethed, spitting out shapes that settled in the form of black hounds. Owain narrowed his eyes as he inspected the animals, and Adrian wondered if he was counting them. But the Huntmaster was concentrating; hands balled into fists and teeth bared like a fox brought to bay.   Suddenly the air was alive, filled with the high-pitched chatter of voices. Adrian clamped his hands to his ears and curled in on himself, trying to block out the onslaught of words. But the voices were ancient and determined. *Skriker...* whispered one... *so named for the shrieking sound he makes. Barghest...* sighed another... *the omen of death.*

"What's happening?" Adrian demanded, but his voice was drowned in the thousands of others. His knees hit the ground with a dull thud.

Grim... sang the voices... *first soul in the churchyard. Last sight of the traveller. You saw the Grim, my dear. Death within a week, that's what they say.*

"No!" shouted Owain. The whispers drew back a little, words flocking together like starlings.

Guardian of graves. They call this folkloric custom immurement; horrible practice... the voices pressed on, but they crackled like a radio with failing reception. *If you see the Grim. A great black dog. He guards souls from the Devil, though I can't think why, seen as they buried him alive. The northernmost corner.* The sound faltered and faded to a low hiss. *The Grim, you say? Leave him alone gel, and ye'll bide just fine.*

"Stop," Owain said. There was a final, unintelligible crackle, and the whispers were gone. Adrian stood up, dusting sand from his trousers. He was about to treat Owain to some choice vocabulary, but his eyes advised him to rethink it.

Owain had turned the hounds back to his favoured grey. He stood among them now, dark eyes glinting with deadly approval. Adrian hadn't seen Gabriel undergo the transformation, but what happened to Owain was just as

313

Gemma had described. His skin was pale in the starlight and stretched just a little too tight over the bones of his face. His red hair had the gleam of freshly spilled blood.

"We tell the story. It does not tell us," said Owain. It was his normal voice. Or as normal as the fae got, anyway. Adrian let out a breath he hadn't known he was holding. Owain was in control and, whatever the disembodied voices were, they were gone. Grim submitted to a pat from his Master, and Adrian's mouth dropped open in realisation. Stories had life. They hung on, after their tellers had died, and they waited for ways to get themselves repeated. And every tale ever told remembered itself.

"Gabriel," said Owain softly. There was a moments pause, and then-

"What have you done?" Gabriel snarled.

23.
EDEN

Eva stood up slowly. The whole table watched as she picked out a sharp knife and hitched up her dress. There was the crisp sound of cutting, and something came free.

"No!" cried Franz. He was silenced by Eva's raised palm. He clawed at his mouth, nostrils flared in panic, but his lips were sealed shut. Her will held him like a snare.

The Collector's eyes gleamed in triumph. His arms remained outstretched, like some forgiving and benevolent god.

"It's the Spear of bloody Destiny!" cried Blake, "I have a sixth sense for stuff like this. I knew she was something, from the moment she turned up in that plane." He sloshed whiskey in Maximillian's direction, to underline his assertion.

Franz struggled defiantly, but the invisible bonds that closed his mouth held him tight to his chair. His own muscles betrayed him, and he realised at last the true nature of Eva's ability. His body was no more than an extension of hers and he was a lost soul wearing a cage made of meat.

"There were whispers about your father, suggestions that he had a talent which helped with his work," Maximillian said softly, as Eva walked towards him. She held the spear by her side, dagger-like without the long wooden handle. A scrap of duct tape betrayed how she had carried it, and the section that was wrapped in gold gleamed with the light from guttering candles. "Did you inherit his power?" The Collector let his hand rest on Eva's left shoulder. The flames from the table candles streamed towards them, as if caught by a draught.

Franz focused all his willpower on his fingers. They lay lightly on the table but felt like they were made from the granite bones of the moor. He forced them forwards, millimetre by millimetre, towards the knife. The Spear of Destiny had driven the Fuhrer mad. Was this the artefact he had carried? Was this the curse that had brought down his plane?

Maximillian's eyes were unusually bright. There was no trace of the clouding that often came with age. Eva stared into them and felt the promise of sanctuary; soft and warm like the first pull of sleep. Her chest answered with a sharp pang of longing. She had stayed brave all this time. After the last vase had been smashed, and the final painting pulled from the walls, she had prised the gun from her father's hands and held him while he cried. When he woke in the night, begging for his wife and his son, she had brought him a cup of hot tea. But she was no match for his pain, and she never had been.

"Go on then, give us a show!" Blake demanded. Eva blinked, and the Collector's face was momentarily twisted in anger. But he rallied quickly, choosing to wear an indulgent smile.

"You are a precious thing, and so is what you hold in your hand," Maximillian said. Eva raised the spear hesitantly.

"My father told me that this would change our lives," she said, "that finding it would make everything alright." She fought back the tears. She pressed down the pain in her chest, forcing it deep into the darkness where she buried the memory of pulling the trigger.

"A wise man, your father. I don't have just anyone work for me. But, let me tell you, you are greater still! You

316

are the cure, Eva, the key to our new Eden." Maximillian's voice was quiet and coaxing. He held out one hand, as if it was an afterthought.

Eva placed the spear on his palm. But a sudden surge of jealousy closed her fingers round it like claws. Who was he to deserve it, when the spear had come to her? What of the curse, if she gave it away?

"I was only searching for it to give it to you," the Collector soothed, "the spear is your servant, and therefore so am I."

Eva's fingers loosened. It was such a burden. But the metal of the spear felt soft and smooth when she held it at night and dreamed of her vengeance. "The Huntmaster dies," she hissed through her teeth.

"As you wish," Maximillian said comfortingly, his fingers interlacing with hers, the spear held between them. Then he raised his hand, and she was compelled to follow, turning to face the table as she did. She had forgotten about the other people in the room. But they were there now, staring at her with open mouthed amazement. She was a myth come to life; the proof of everything Maximillian had said. Triumph and awe rose towards her like prayers, turning the air into fine wine and honey.

"May I present our new Eve," Maximillian proclaimed, "we are mere footsteps from Eden."

Blake banged his empty glass on the table. "Stop stalling and show us the goods!" The crystal decanter had been half full of whiskey and it now contained nothing. The other people sat around the table were nodding in agreement.

"Show us, and we'll believe it," said the woman with dark, calculating eyes.

Blake was on his feet, striding purposefully towards

a large dome in the corner of the room. It contained two pheasants, meticulously preserved, their glass eyes fixed in eternal surprise. "Nice and easy, hardly any brains, pheasants," he muttered, mostly to himself. Then he lifted the domed cover.

Eva felt Maximillian wince. Blake eased his fingers under the wooden base, making the perched cock pheasant sway, but he carried the taxidermy to the table with care. A space was cleared, and Blake slid the birds into it. Then he took a silk handkerchief from his pocket and dabbed at his brow. "Any more of the good stuff?" he asked Maximillian hopefully.

The Collector had no interest in Blake's question. Maximillian's bright eyes were flitting between Eva and the two dead pheasants. "They were the first birds I shot as a boy. That must have been fifty years ago. Do you think you can do it?" His voice was low, the tone almost offhand. But there was a challenge to it; Eva could sense it. And with the wide open eyes of the guests, and their syrup thick belief, there was no backing down.

"Of course," Eva replied. She fixed her eyes on the pheasants.

"That's my girl!" Maximillian patted her on the shoulder and slipped his hand, and the spear, out of hers.

Franz threw the full weight of his willpower into moving his fingers. It was torturously slow. His face shone with sweat, and salt stung his skin but, slow as old roots, he reached for the blade.

Eva closed her eyes. She had raised Franz and the plane, but since then her strange gift had failed her. Deep in the barrow mound, her father remained dead, surrounded by the bones of his minions. He had been able to raise an entire undead workforce, and she was doubting

318

herself over a dusty old pheasant. Franz had suggested she practiced, but she was always too tired.

Guilt prickled over her skin, sharp and icy cold. She could feel Franz struggling. His horror lapped against her like the incoming tide. *Are you really so caught up in this, when you have not been told the price?* She pushed his words to one side, forcing back the memories of the sun and the birdsong as they sat on the airfield and ate bacon rolls.

The pheasants felt like a hole in the pattern. The strands of life twisted and tangled around them, leaving two bird shaped gaps for Eva to fill. She smiled to herself. Having a visible target helped to focus her energy. This was actually easy! She stretched out her hands, feeling her blood flowing hot and the tingle of power on the tips of her fingers.

"Hurry up!" shouted Blake.

Her concentration was broken.

"Bugger!" Blake cursed, as the fresh whiskey in his hand boiled. The glass cracked, spewing out a cloud of blistering steam. There was a guttural screech.

Eva's eyes flew open and she glanced round to check the damage. Blake was shaking his hand like it stung, but no one else seemed to be injured. On the display branch, which was coated in places with dried moss, the male pheasant eyed her with a blank, glassy stare. But beneath him, on the plinth, there was an obvious gap.

"She's there," whispered the blonde woman, pointing towards the gramophone cabinet.

"The Lord bless us," said the priest, making the sign of the cross.

Perched on the gleaming wood, speckled dappled brown like the fields and the furrows, sat the frightened hen pheasant.

"Now call her," Maximillian murmured.

Eva hesitated. The bird was looking around the room; quick, darting movements that sought an escape. But the doors were all closed, and there was no going back now. For any of them. *Come*, commanded Eva. She spoke it in her mind, and it sang through the tangle of life until it wrapped round the pheasant. The bird flexed two strong wings, but her black and amber eyes rolled with terror.

"Come," whispered Eva, and she felt ashamed. The bird launched into awkward flight and landed with a thump back on the table. Her clawed feet made a sharp click, click sound on the polished wood.

Franz felt his fingertip meet the smooth metal of the knife. He pushed harder against the invisible bonds which held him.

Eva tentatively stretched one hand towards the pheasant. Her brown feathers lay sleek and smooth, mimicking the pattern of sunlight as it fell on the fields. Long ago, her father had raised pheasants. He always said that they loved nothing more than to die. But on cold nights, when frost mocked the spring, he would be up by the pens checking on the young birds. The pockets of his tweed overcoat were large enough to warm one pheasant poult in each.

"This is all well and good," drawled Blake, "but now for the real test." Eva watched him from the corner of her eye. He swaggered towards the head of the table, stopping to snatch the knife laying near Franz. One hand held a fresh glass and the other gripped the blade, which he tested with gleeful slices through the air. "Here," he said, pushing the handle into Eva's hand. "C'mon birdie," he cooed.

The hen pheasant came, as if in a daze. Her bright

320

eyes were now dull, focusing on nothing beyond Eva. Blake wrapped his fingers around Eva's and held the blade steady. The claws clicking on the table were the loudest noise in the room. The police chief narrowed his eyes and considered fascinating possibilities.

Franz cried. The tears fell silently and steadily. He cried for the pheasant, as she pressed the soft down of her breast against the tip of the knife. He cried for the people at the table, who were so desperate with fear that it had turned into madness. But he cried most for Eva, because he had seen it all done before, and there was nothing more monstrous than using love as a weapon.

Adrian opened his eyes. Clara screamed. Bones rained down around her, pattering onto the peat like strange precipitation.

"You're alive!" she cried, wiping her nose with her sleeve. Quiet sobs shook her shoulders, but she did her best to ignore them. "I thought, well-" her voice turned very quiet, "let's just say I was worried at one point."

Bright light scythed suddenly through the night. Fen growled, but the passing car was unmoved by his threat, trundling on down the road towards town. Adrian rolled to one side and rose stiffly to his knees. Everything ached. The cold water had seeped through his clothes and sunk into his bones.

"This is Gabriel," he managed, through chattering teeth.

Clara looked up at two men, who had appeared silently. Gabriel had pale hair which fell in soft waves to his shoulders. He wouldn't have looked out of place in the type of artwork that portrays angels posing in very minimalist robes. She had helped out on many a school trip to the museum and always took time to examine the marble statues, for educational purposes of course. It was a wonder of gravity how some of the cloth stayed up.

"I've heard a lot about you," said Clara. Pride told her that witches shouldn't bow down to the occult, but rather treat it as an equal. Plus, her charm had turned away Cabell.

"Is that so?" purred Gabriel. The way that he bared his teeth rather ruined the angelic look. Fian stood near the car, white fur raised in a display of defiance.

"I'm just curious, can you touch this?" Clara held out the clay pendant which had worked so well in the graveyard. Gabriel's eyes narrowed. He reached for the necklace and snapped it free in one sinuous movement. Holding his closed fist aloft, he watched as fine powder trickled out of it.

"It's no problem," Clara gulped, "I can make more."

"It would appear that I am not Huntmaster," Gabriel said darkly. He turned to Owain, who was trying to make himself as inobtrusive as possible. It wasn't working, because his face had turned nearly the same colour as his hair. The red hunt coat hung off his shoulders, oversized and threadbare without the assistance of glamour. It also clashed with the bright shade of his cheeks. "There will be an explanation," Gabriel predicted.

Owain nodded sullenly. Then his head jerked upwards with a sudden surge of memory. "Mike's still on the moor!"

Gabriel looked up at the cold stars. Orion glinted overhead, with Sirius keeping pace beside him, on a hunt that stretched through millennia. The air had stilled, and the clear sky promised frost. Out on the moor, small animals crept through the gorse, oblivious to the patterns that pierced the night sky. To them the stars only mattered when they blinked out, blocked by the spread of pale, silent wings. Somewhere nearby, a brief squeak signalled a meal had been caught. Then there was just the quiet trickle of water and Adrian's rattling teeth.

"Take him home," Gabriel said to the witch. She nodded, telling herself silently that taking an order was still being an equal when she equally agreed.

Gabriel extended a hand to the ground. Long seconds passed without anything happening.

"Oh," said Owain, summoning the skeletal horse with a flick of his wrist. Gabriel mounted, sighed, and pulled Owain up behind him.

"Let the hounds sleep," Gabriel instructed, gathering slick leather reins. Then he urged the horse forward, thunderous hoofbeats fading into the thick velvet night.

"A hot cup of tea," prescribed Clara, "and a blanket by the radiator. You better put on dry clothes too, those ones will need to go straight in the wash."

She drove carefully down the narrow country lanes, face pushed forward to inspect the darkness ahead. The headlights of her little car seemed to tease the shadows, rather than fully chase them away. But the air vents whistled and hissed, spitting out a stream of slightly stale warmth. Adrian held his hands right in front of them. His teeth had stopped chattering, but the thought of backing off from the heat was not to be entertained. His phone buzzed in his pocket as they drove closer to Princetown. He pulled it out from sheer habit and read the notification from Somerset Live.

"Apparently there's been a localised earthquake in the village of Wagg," he said.

"Hah," replied Clara, "nothing on what we have here."

"I think that might be a good thing," replied Adrian quietly. His phone was getting very hot, but he didn't want to move his hand away from the warmth.

"Did Owain say anything about Gemma?"

"I didn't get the chance to ask." Adrian looked down at his fingers. Both black ones were still black. The car filled up with a dense kind of quiet, only disturbed by the hard-working heater.

"I think," said Clara after a little while, "that he would have seen her."

"Humph?" asked Adrian.

"Well, if Gabriel was feeling sorry for himself, or whatever, in the Divide, then he would have seen Gemma if she came to cross over."

Adrian's eyes widened with slow comprehension. Of course! He would have seen her, and he would have had something to say about that. If the Huntmaster was so obsessed, then he'd never allow her to get beyond reach. *Ex-Huntmaster*, Adrian corrected himself mentally. "You're bloody right," he said, with renewed hope.

Clara turned Adrian's key in the door of Mike's cottage. Warm air seeped out from inside, accompanied by the smell of fresh coffee.

"Hello?" ventured Clara.

"Hello-oo," came the reply.

Adrian let go of Clara's arm. He loosened his grip on the cloak he'd made from her faded emergency blanket. Fian bounded through the door with a sharp bark of delight.

"Gemma?" he called incredulously.

There she was, pushing her chair back from the end of the kitchen table and kneeling to stroke an overexcited white hound. She was fine, and smiling in a way that suggested she hadn't fallen off a sheer fronted outcrop at all.

"What the hell happened?" Adrian asked, rushing into the room and reaching to lean on the table.

"He needs dry clothes and a hot drink," Clara called from behind him.

"Coming right now," said Gemma, dragging a wooden chair over to the radiator. "What the hell happened to you?"

Adrian laughed, and then shivered. He settled into the chair gratefully, pressing his legs against the heat of the radiator. "Good question," he said.

"Dry clothes!" ordered Clara.

Gemma ran up the stairs, taking two at a time. There was the tell-tale floorboard squeaking of a wardrobe being searched.

The witch refilled the kettle and rummaged out a dusty old teapot. It depicted a white mare carrying seven men on her back. They looked to be extremely cosy with each other, and far too heavy for the sorry old horse. Clara shook her head, evicted a spider, and left the teapot to warm. She was searching for a tea cosy when Gemma returned with the clothes.

"Just don't look," ordered Adrian, sticking close to the radiator while he peeled off wet garments.

"No one's looking," said Gemma, theatrically shielding her eyes as she crossed the room. She went back upstairs, more slowly this time, and pushed open the door to what had been Elaine's room. The ugly floral bed sheets

325

were folded neatly and a crochet blanket was laid over the foot of the bed. It looked warm and serviceable, and Adrian was too cold to be bothered by the slight clash of mustard and brown. But, somehow, her hand was already pulling the door shut. She grabbed the duvet from her own room and the patchwork quilt which lived in the cupboard.

Clara was stirring the teapot with a thoughtful expression. Two cups waited beside it.

"Are you staying for a bit?" Gemma asked her.

"Oh," said Clara, as if dragging herself back from somewhere distant, "I think you two have a lot to talk about. And I need to... tidy up."

Gemma helped Adrian with a speedy blanket swap and refolded the one belonging to Clara. It still smelt faintly of lavender, although the scent was now accompanied by half-dried muddy water.

"It'll wash up just fine," Clara said, holding out her hands. Part of her was itching to know how Gemma had escaped from Owain, but a slightly larger part was watching a plan ripen in her head. It was questionable, potentially illegal and carried the level of danger she had come to expect recently. In short, it was perfect. But she was running out of time. "After the tea, feed him something hot!" she added as a parting shot.

"Clara?" called Adrian.

The witch hovered by the door. Her face was smiling but one toe tapped the tiles. "Yes?"

"Thank you."

"Don't mention it. All part of the craft." She shrugged her shoulders, jangling the tangle of silver which hung round her neck. But her chin lifted just that little bit higher, and her eyes shone with pride. It was real. She was real. And she didn't need *Practical Spells for Teenage*

Witches anymore. "We'll talk more tomorrow!"

She swept out the door in a flourish of black and silver. Gemma smiled softly to herself. The woman had polished eccentricity into an almost unquestionable brilliance.

"Now," she said, rounding on Adrian, "start talking."

He looked up at her, snorted a laugh, and then gently began to cry. "I thought you were dead."

She strode over and gathered him up in a hug. She could feel the chill rolling off him, even through the thick blanket. "I have someone looking after me. I probably owe them now as well."

"That's not funny."

"I guess not. But look, you'll like this." She squeezed him extra hard for a moment, and then broke the embrace. Pulling open her laptop, she pointed expectantly at an image on the screen.

"It's a map," ventured Adrian.

"Yes, but look at the shapes on it."

"Someone's drawn animals on it. There's a dog next to Wagg!"

"Don't forget Earlake Moor and Walkies Farm." Gemma prodded the screen with enthusiasm. Fian twitched an ear from his comfortable spot at the base of the radiator.

"Wait," said Adrian, "Wagg was in the news. Apparently they had an earthquake."

"How interesting," replied Gemma innocently.

"Spill it. Immediately."

Gemma walked back to the kitchen and placed the laptop down with great care. She adjusted it until it made a perfect parallel line with the edge of the table. Seeing unbelievable things was Adrian's department. Her mind underlined the *was* with uncomfortable certainty.

"You saw the dog on the map?" she asked.

"Yes, miles of dog."

Gemma picked up a teacup and carried it over to Adrian. He accepted it and took a small sip. A few moments stretched out while Gemma waited for him to ask for more sugar. But he didn't ask. Perhaps he had met his match in Clara for obscenely sweet tea.

"And you know how Fen works?" she continued.

Adrian nodded. It was hard to forget how the hounds worked once you had seen them claw their way up from the earth. "Lots of blood and bones and glamour. No sign of any inclination for map reading."

Gemma laughed and felt her shoulders drop. There was no way to fully convey the terror and wonder of what she had seen, but Adrian wasn't going to judge her for trying. "I fell off the Dewerstone and landed on grass. The grass was covering a very large dog."

Adrian's eyes widened. He paused with the tea raised halfway to his mouth. "How large?"

"Miles of it," Gemma said. The dizzying vastness was hard to put into words. She had fallen, and then the earth rose to catch her. It could have been a wandering hill, or a moving mountain, except it had a turf green snout and split boulders for teeth.

Adrian carefully lowered the cup back down to his lap. He used both hands to stop it from spilling. "That must have been something," he managed. He wanted to ask how and why, but they were questions for later.

"I looked it up, and the dog is called Dormarth. He belongs to Gwyn ap Nudd who also, it would appear, leads the Wild Hunt." Gemma formed the last words hesitantly, while inspecting her teacup. "How did you get wet?"

"I lay down on the grass," said Adrian.

"Any particular reason?"

It was Adrian's turn to look awkward. "It was all part of the plan. We had no other choice."

Gemma raised an eyebrow. She took a swallow of tea which seemed to take an impossibly long time.

"I had to go and get Gabriel back from the Divide. I totally failed, but then Owain turned up, and he was in super Huntmaster mode, so Gabriel had no choice but to listen. Also, I think that I'm cursed, but that actually stopped me from dying." Adrian mumbled the last part very quickly.

"Could you just repeat that last bit?"

"Oh, Owain was really into being Huntmaster. It quite suits him, when he's not trying to kill you."

"Not that part," Gemma said.

Adrian looked down at his hands, and the two blackened fingers. He remembered how Cabell's hound had licked him. *One unholy thing to another.* He recalled the clinging branches, and the sudden recoil from the air between the two trees in the Divide. "I think it's just these two fingers. But I'm a tiny bit cursed, so the afterlife wouldn't have me."

"You mean, a tiny bit *more* cursed. You're already a piece of soul down," Gemma retorted.

"Alright, and that meant I didn't die *again*. I think I caught it off the fire on Squire Cabell's tomb."

Gemma pressed a hand to her forehead, but her lips curved with the threat of a smile. She attempted a sigh, and it spilled out as laughter. Then there was no going back, and Adrian was chuckling, because every part of this was insane. But it was also hilarious, even down to the awful parts, because it was just so wonderful that none of them were happening right now.

"Only you," said Gemma, between bouts of giggling, "could catch a *magically transmitted infection*."

Epilogue

The Plume of Feathers was busy. Drinkers sat round wooden tables and the content buzz of chatter hung thick on the air. Some people were eating, and the smell of hot beef mingled with years of spilt beer.

"The police said they were investigatin' it, and just to butt out," said a sullen voice, from a table tucked away in the corner.

"No appreciation for the extra ordinary!" his companion agreed, placating the stained skull of the Beast by raising his glass.

The pub door opened, and almost everyone stared. This wasn't unusual, as a local pub out of tourist season attracts very little excitement. There had been the incident with the hellhound a few months ago of course, but the landlord felt sure that a serving of his homebrew had dealt with all memory of that.

In the doorway stood a woman worth staring at. The pillar candles in the alcoves guttered, caught in the sudden draft, and the swell of talk turned quiet. She shut the door with a flourish of star covered silk.

"Good evening," said Clara. The barman nodded, mentally calculating the weight she must be carrying in silver. She jangled as she walked towards him. "Rosé for me please, and another round of whatever those gentlemen are drinking for them." She pointed a crystal encrusted finger in the direction of the corner table.

"Right you are, I'll have the girls bring them over." Nathaniel liked clean taps and a quiet life. He had managed to quiet down the amateur paranormalists once, but they were always just one over-excited suggestion away from flaming torches and pitchforks. Exactly what they'd do with these things, he didn't know, especially after the retirement of their ringleader. Also, he wasn't certain how they'd get their hands on the pitchforks. But the whole scenario was, all in all, worth avoiding. He hoped this *witc*-woman, he corrected himself, wasn't going to stir them up.

"Do I have the pleasure of joining the Wild Hunt Investigation Committee?" Clara asked the table of men. One took off his flat cap and began to fold it clumsily in his hands. There were far less of them than she remembered.

"We-ell, the thing is," he mumbled.

"Do you have information?" asked another. He wore a checked shirt and a few days worth of mud on his jacket.

"You may have been following my blog?" Clara suggested smoothly. The response was an uncomfortable silence, so she tried a different tactic. "The demon huntsman is dead," she whispered. That got their attention.

"How do you know?"

"I saw it happen," said Clara, producing a human thighbone from somewhere in her scarves. "He was killed by the Wild Hunt." She put her proof on the table with a confident *clonk*.

A barmaid arrived with the drinks. She placed them on the table very carefully, whilst glancing with interest at everything that wasn't a human thighbone.

"You best cover that trinket," said a gruff voice. The eldest of the committee leaned in towards his ale. He wore a green wax jacket, bleached by the sun. Around his neck hung a whistle on a loop of old baling twine. Clara felt she should have remembered him.

"I'm Rust," said the man in the checked shirt, "I remember you. This is Brian and Crazy Nige."

"I'm not actually crazy, they just call me that," Nigel

explained helpfully. Clara noticed he had put his flat cap on back to front.

"Who are you again?" asked Brian.

"Oh, I'm Clara. You know, the witch."

"I wouldn't have known," said Nigel.

"Well, Clara who knows she's a witch, what do you want from the Committee?" The man with the whistle fixed her with bright, calculating eyes.

Clara stared back at him. His white beard was stained yellow with tobacco and his face was wrinkled by a life in all weathers. "I wanted you to know that it wasn't the Wild Hunt who killed those people on the news. It was Squire Cabell, and he's different. So it's case closed, I'm sorry to say."

There was a pause. Brian whispered something to Nigel, who nodded solemnly.

"What do you think, Roger?" Rust asked. All faces turned to the older man expectantly. Roger picked up his glass and took a long, slow sip of ale. Then he placed the drink down and meticulously dabbed his beard with a sleeve.

"I've been thinking it's time for a change," he said steadily.

Gradually, nodding spread round the table.

Grey clouds raced across the night sky. The trees on the roadside bared the back of their leaves and Clara read it as the promise of rain. But it was warm in the car, and her cheeks glowed red as ripe apples. She would speak with the Committee again. But they had listened, and for now that was enough to fill her with triumph. The first flecks of drizzle fell as a fine mist on her windscreen, and she clicked on her wipers.

She shut her front door against the patter of rain. Turning the key in the lock, she reached down to pull off her boots. Then she paused, the rhythm of rainfall on the window reminding her of the weird rattle of bones. She unlocked the door again, just in case she had to leave quickly.

From the folds of her sleeve, she untangled the thigh bone. It felt warm from being next to her skin. Mostly it was white, but she noticed a dappling of black flecks where ash had been caught in the hollows.

She added it to the rest of the skeleton on her living room floor. The scene would have looked a lot more macabre without the pink sheepskin rug. But she didn't want ash on her carpet, and something soft felt somehow more respectful. Her hands were shaking as she made her slow trip to the fridge. Was this really wise? Would it even work? She checked the packet of the pork chop for the seventh time. It was definitely still in date.

Rearranging her bracelets for comfort, she took a steadying breath. The rain came down harder, rattling like ice on the glass. Her lighter flared to life on the second attempt. Strange shadows danced round the room, stirred up by the firelight, as she lit her circle of candles. Black wax dripped into the teacups that made do as holders. Solemnly, she lay the pork chop on a flower-patterned plate.

"Alright Cabell, let's see what you've got."

ACKNOWLEDGEMENTS

I am indebted to Karen Hamilton-Viall, Andrew Kleister, Val
Cartei and Rebecca Pollard
for their attentive proof reading.

Thanks are also due to Vera Nadine Boinn, Paula Wallwork and
Angela Muldoon for their encouragement and assistance.

facebook/heatofthehunt

The story continues in 'Truth of the Tale'.

BIBLIOGRAPHY

Bamberg, R.W. (1993) *Haunted Dartmoor A Ghost-Hunter's Guide.* Newton Abbot: Peninsula Press Ltd.

Bennie, Michael. (1995) *Walking the Stories and Legends of Dartmoor.* Newton Abbot: Peninsula Press Ltd.

Forest, Danu. (2018) *Gwyn ap Nudd Wild god of faerie and Guardian of Annwfn.* Winchester: Moon Books.

Gary, Gemma. (2017) *Silent as the Trees Devonshire Witchcraft, Folklore & Magic.* London: Troy Books.

Leitch, Yuri. (2007) *Gwyn Ancient god of Glastonbury and key to the Glastonbury Zodiac.* Wells: The Temple Publications.

Norman, Mark. (2016) *Black Dog Folklore.* London: Troy Books.

Wildwood, Rob. (2013) *Magical Places of Britain.* York: Wyldwood Publishing.